NEWBODIES

Rachelle Zalter

Moonshine Cove Publishing, LLC
Abbeville, South Carolina U.S.A.
First Moonshine Cove Edition SEP 2022

ISBN: 9781952439407

Library of Congress LCCN: 2022914771

Front cover image by Alan Dino Hebel, courtesy of the author; back cover and interior design by Moonshine Cove staff and Alan Dino Hebel

A SIXTEEN-YEAR-OLD DANCER IS SENT TO A PRISON "RESORT" FOR TRYING TO PROTECT HER MOTHER AND NOW TO ESCAPE, MUST TRUST A FORMER ENEMY.

Set in the future where a tightly controlled technology has been developed that allows rich old people to switch bodies with poor teens. The Government of Ameca captures sixteen-year-old Eliana after she illegally switches bodies with her mother in order to protect her from a painful death. Eliana is sent to a prison camp that capitalizes on beauty, where she can trust no one, but ultimately has to put her faith in a smug, authoritative enemy, Theo Jacobson. But the more time she spends with Theo, the more she wonders if he might not be that bad after all. He might even be the answer she's been looking for all this time.

Early Praise for Newbodies

"Rachelle Zalter presents a chilling dystopian future where people aren't even guaranteed the freedom to remain in their own bodies. Filled with mystery and romance, *Newbodies* will leave you never quite sure who to trust all the way to the final moments."—*Melanie Tays, author of the Wall of Fire Series*

"A dystopian Freaky Friday. Young teens are forced to swap bodies with rich Patrons, who can then do as they please. This book will definitely challenge your perception of what it means to be free."—*Eliza Green, author of the Breeder Files Series*

i

Mama is getting more exhausted by the day and weaker by the minute. Everything about her death is controlled. The government has mastered the Countdown; they have it down to an art. And they treat it like art, too. At some point, the government realized they couldn't have everyone live forever, so they created a "random" and "fair" system. The government vows everyone's number, or length of life, is assigned before birth, but no one in the low-status Groups believe that. We know better. We've seen the worst. They give you 100 days to prepare for your death in Ameca. Out of nowhere and at any given time, the number appears: "100." It's a digital inscription on your right wrist, like a tattoo. Every day from then on, the number decreases. The Countdown begins. My mother's number is seven today. She has one more week to live.

To my grandma, who taught me to write; to my savta, who taught me to fight; and to my parents, who gave me this story.

NEWBODIES

CHAPTER 1

When I get home, I smell Mama's moussaka roasting in the kitchen. I notice it immediately—the cinnamon, the garlic, the tomatoes. The casserole's smell has welcomed me home almost every day of my life. Mama loves to make moussaka. It reminds her of her childhood. I never complain; it's one of my favorite things to eat. I love the sharp flavors, the fresh vegetables, the way it warms me up. Mostly, I love how moussaka makes Mama happy. It reminds her of better days.

I can hear Mama's voice singing faintly. She's only as loud as her strength will allow. She's listening to a song she often danced to when I was young. I sing along with her when I enter the kitchen, knowing it will make her happy. When she notices me, she turns her head.

"Elloula," She uses my nickname. "When did you get home? Come, taste."

I want to tell her I'm not hungry yet, but I can't. I watch her serve me an extra-large serving and I try to give her a smile.

Something happened ninety-three days ago when I learned Mama was going to die. I think something happens to everyone—a switch in the way they act, the way they think—when they find out a loved one is dying. It's a feeling of guilt mixed with an instinct to protect. I haven't been able to say no to Mama's wishes since I found out; I regret every time that I did.

Mama sits down with me and watches me eat. "It's delicious," I tell her. And it is—just like every moussaka before. But this one feels special. I know it might be the last. I savor the flavors, noticing each of them like it's the first time I've tried it. Mama watches, satisfied.

"How is it?"

"It's perfect, Mama. Why don't you get a plate?"

"Not today," and I know what that means. Her stomach can't keep it down. She has barely been eating this week.

Mama watches me finish her carefully made meal. The meal she's made just for me. When I finish my last bite, I hug her. She pulls me in closer, kissing the top of my head.

She's not usually like this, Mama. She's not usually the first one to squeeze tighter or kiss me unannounced. My mother is warm, but not vulnerable. Even when she doesn't feel powerful, she wants you to believe that she is.

When the government took my brother, Loukas, two years ago, Mama did everything she could to find him. She protested on the streets, risked her life, and even called my father, who once told her that if she ever contacted him, he would *do whatever it takes to make her pay.* My father has a high-status job in the government. He has the power to help, but he also has the power to destroy. I try not to be angry at Mama for calling him, but I'm afraid my father kept his word. He's making Mama pay right now. Mama wasn't thinking of herself, though, when she called him; all she wanted to do was find her son. It's not her fault she imagined my father would want the same.

Mama is tough because she's been through a lot, but she's sensitive at heart, and I know that. If she was honest with me, she would tell me she's falling apart, completely, just like me.

When I try to imagine my life without Mama, I don't get far. She has always felt like more than a mother to me: she's been the only one I can turn to at hard times, a dance partner since I was very young, eventually a business partner at our dance studio, and a best friend to Loukas and me. A life without Mama feels impossible.

But, right now, I do my best to stay strong. It's the least I can do for Mama during her last days.

My mother falls asleep before dinner. She must have exhausted herself cooking all day. I put the moussaka in the fridge, not wanting to eat alone nor feeling overly hungry. Mama is getting more exhausted by the day and weaker by the minute. Everything about her death is controlled. The government has mastered the Countdown; they have it down to an art. And they treat it like art, too. It's disgusting how proud they are of their design. At some point, the government realized they couldn't have everyone live forever, so they created a "random" and "fair" system. I used to believe that was true, that it was random and fair, but I grew up with Loukas as my brother and Ethan as my best friend. Together, they opened my eyes to how the government really operates. How the people in Group6 and 7 have the shortest lives and the people in Group1 have the longest.

Most people have longer lives than my mother's no matter what Group they're in. Mama was twenty-one when she had Loukas and me, and she's only thirty-seven now. People in Group7, where we live, typically don't die until they're fifty. People in Group1 live to 150 on average, but the really important people can live much longer. President Ace has been alive for over 300 years. I'm not sure he'll ever die. But Mama, at thirty-seven, is an outlier. That's what Ethan keeps telling me. He's convinced that the government changed her number after she started protesting about Loukas. I'm convinced it was a specific person in the government, my dad. Either way, it's technically illegal. The government vows everyone's number, or length of life, is assigned before birth, but no one in the low-status Groups believes that. We know better.

Some people try to marry into a wealthier Group, or "Up-Group." so they can live longer and happier lives. It's not easy to do, because most people don't know or interact with non-Group members. I've spent my entire life around people from my Group. Our neighborhood is called 7N. I'll probably stay here my whole life; the man I will marry probably lives in 7N.

Even though Mama never admits it, I think she was trying to Up-Group when she married my father. My mother is proud to be from Group7. She fights for Group7 rights and always points out the beauty in our village, reminding me to be grateful for everything around us. But when you're given an opportunity to Up-Group, to receive better treatment, and to provide a better life for your children, it's hard to pass up. Mama says she wasn't thinking about that when she met my father. She loved him. He seemed good-hearted. But when it became clear he didn't actually want to make the changes he promised to make, Mama realized he was no better than any other privileged man in Group1. Over time, both of my parents hardened. They separated when Loukas and I were only three, and the three of us—Mama, Loukas, and me— were sent back to Group7. My father stopped caring about anyone other than himself and Mama stopped believing in the government or Group1's support.

If there was ever a time when Mama wanted to Up-Group, that is no longer the case. Now, she has no interest in moving—instead, she wants to put an end to Groups altogether. Since leaving my dad and Group1, Mama has spent over ten years trying to fight these injustices. Ethan's convinced the government has reached its breaking point. When Mama started protesting about Loukas's imprisonment, she gained a following. People gathered with her, people in other Groups held their own protests, and activism was increasingly being covered on the news. It was all too intimidating, too much, for the government to handle. So instead of changing their ways, or addressing my mother directly, they decided it was time for her to die.

They give you one hundred days to prepare for your death in Ameca. Out of nowhere and at any given time, the number appears: "100." It's a digital inscription on your right wrist, like a tattoo. Every day from then on, the number decreases. The Countdown begins. My mother's number is seven today. She has one more week to live.

CHAPTER 2

I walk over to the Cohens' house after carrying Mama to bed. She fell asleep on the loveseat again and I didn't want her neck to hurt in the morning. Mama danced her whole life. It wasn't only her job, as an entertainer, but her greatest passion. Her posture is perfect because of her background, but when she finally gets to sleep, her shoulders curl in and her neck becomes heavy. It's so odd, seeing her that way—so different from the upright and strong woman I know. Loukas used to joke about how Mama was too tough to die. "You're going to take their one hundred and shove it up President Ace's—" but Mama never let him finish. She was a hard-core fighter, but she doesn't like curse words.

I wish Loukas could be here now to help me take care of her. To get these last days with her. To say goodbye. At the same time, I'm happy he's not seeing Mama like this. He wouldn't believe how much she's changed—how much the Countdown has changed her.

The only person I can really count on now is Ethan Cohen. Since the moment my mom's one hundred showed up, Ethan's taken care of us. When I first met Ethan in kindergarten, I hated him because he was Loukas's best friend. Being twins, Loukas and I were always competitive with each other. Our interests were never the same because if he was good at one thing, I wanted to be equally good at another. Even when we got older, Loukas and I were still competitive. We loved each other but never could admit to being similar. It wasn't until Loukas was taken away that I realized how stupid that all was. All that matters now is getting Loukas back.

But winning over Ethan Cohen felt like a victory for me at the time. Everyone wanted to be Loukas's friend. He was kind and funny and charming. Me, on the other hand, well I was nothing like my twin brother. *You've got too much attitude for your own good,* Mama always

11

said, laughing, *stop asking for trouble.* I wasn't just tenacious, I was also stubborn and unfiltered. I had to learn how to keep things to myself, and I'm still not always good at that. Mama says she can read every emotion on my face—and they're not always kind. But for whatever reason, Ethan pushed through all of that. The more he came over to hang out with Loukas, the more the two of us talked. At some point, he started coming over to hang out with me. Loukas had so many friends he hardly noticed Ethan's departure, but I did.

When I go to the Cohens' house, I instantly feel at home. Although I love the life Mama created for Loukas and me, our family always felt small. There was nothing Mama could do about it, there were only three of us. But at the Cohens', the house feels different—it's bustling with life and love, it feels *full.*

Ethan's mother Molly used to live in Group4, but when she first became a teacher, she didn't accept some of the teachings the government mandated her to teach, and when the students' parents started complaining to the school, Molly was immediately fired and Down-Grouped. She was moved to Group5 at first, but then she married Ethan's mother, Leora, and Molly was moved down to Group7. Same-sex marriages are legal in Ameca, but they aren't rewarded. Instead of being Up-Grouped when you marry someone outside your Group, like all other couples, people who marry someone with a criminal background or of the same sex are forced to Down-Group. Molly and Leora never talk about it, but we know it's super messed up. Ethan and I have it on our list of things we plan on changing once we take the government down.

Leora and Molly have six adopted kids. Rich people don't want their babies to come from Group7 or 6 because they think they'll be defective. But some of the best people in the world live in the bottom Groups. Ethan especially. Ethan's the smartest, funniest, most loving person I know. And his sisters and brothers are wonderful too. Ethan's oldest brother, Raffi, was sent to prison five years ago, but I always knew him to be kind-hearted and hilarious. I remember when Raffi left, the Cohens seemed different for a while. They were so quiet and sad.

But eventually, over time, they found their way back. It's not easy—and I know that now with Loukas being gone—but we have no other choice.

Some people might find the Cohen home messy and cramped, given that it's small and houses eight people, but I think it's one of the best places on earth. Since I was seven years old, Molly and Leora have invited me to Friday night dinners at their house. Ever since Loukas was taken, Mama and I have been going there together. Even though the table is barely big enough for five, they find a way to fit ten.

I knock on Ethan's door and Leora lets me in.

"Oh no," she says when she realizes it's me. "You again! What are you two up to?"

I laugh. Leora loves having me around, but she's a very involved mother and has great intuition. Lately, I've been coming to see Ethan every night. Leora senses we're up to something. She isn't wrong, but we don't admit this. Ethan doesn't want her to worry even more than she already does.

"We're just hanging out."

Leora gives me a look but lets it go. "He's in his room."

I head upstairs, wondering what he's been able to accomplish while I've been with Mama. When I enter, I see he's busy with something, but the minute he notices me, all his attention is mine.

"You're back," he says.

"Yeah, sorry I'm late. How's it going?"

"It's been okay. I'm still trying to work on getting in, but they've changed their passwords."

"Did you check Loukas's book?"

Ethan nods, "I'm working through the possibilities now."

I get closer, taking the book from Ethan. When he hands it over, his fingers lightly trace my hand. I feel a jolt in my stomach and wish it would go away. We've been friends for so long. I know that's what we're supposed to be. But lately, with the extra time we've been spending together and the late nights working on our plan, I can't seem to get Ethan out of my mind. Our mothers always joke about the two of us getting married one day, but Ethan and I always thought they were crazy.

I try to focus on the combinations of passwords in Loukas's book. Even though Ethan was closer with me, Loukas and Ethan started to hang out more after Raffi was sent to prison. They spent all their time trying to figure out how to access government files and Hack. It was a passion the two of them shared.

Hacking is the process of taking your Essence, or soul, and moving it into another body. That's what we're trying to do now.

I skim through some of the possible passwords, disgusted by how so many of them have to do with President Ace's marketing. Words like "enhancement," "rejuvenation," and "longevity" are constantly repeated, which all seem like empty promises to me.

When President Ace's corporation, Ameca, discovered the Essence, which was formally known as the soul, they began to control people's lives in a much larger way. President Ace likes to say this discovery made all lives better, or "enhanced," but really that's only true for high-status Group members. The discovery of Essence allowed Ameca to begin tracking people, copying identities, and moving Essences from one body to another. The government could now control our souls.

The worst part of the Essence discovery is how it affects the Groups differently. People in high-status Groups can pay Ameca to transfer their Essence into another person's body, thereby switching bodies with someone else. The elites go on vacations, temporarily switching bodies with younger, healthier people, while people in low-status Groups are often forced to give up their bodies for the rich. The people who are forced into this are usually Group1's prisoners.

This is where Hacking comes in.

Very few people know how to do it, but there's a way for the Switch to occur without going through the government. Of course, it's illegal, but it's also free. And that's what Ethan and I are planning to do for Mama.

Every Essence has a matching Replica that is protected by Government Officials. The Replicas are used to transfer Essences into different bodies, and to allow for switches to occur. There's a place where the Replicas are stored, but Ethan doesn't need to physically see them to make the Hack happen. Ethan already knows how to Hack and he can access the government's computers via data servers, so he can do it from anywhere, at any time. He'll add the final pieces of code on the night of the Hack, which will switch my Essence with Mama's. My Essence, or soul, will inhabit Mama's body, and hers will inhabit mine.

Ethan and Loukas have worked on Hacking for years. They wanted to stop President Ace from exploiting Essences, or, at the very least, take away some of President Ace's power. *The knowledge could make things a little more equal.* That's what they would always tell me. And now that we're about to Hack Mama, I'm beginning to understand.

The only thing we have left to do is figure out how to keep from getting caught. When someone initiates a Hack, an alert is immediately sent to the government. Ethan thinks there's a way to get into the government's computers and temporarily turn off this alert for specific Replicas, but it will require breaking through passwords and firewalls.

We've got six days left to figure out how to safely Hack Mama. With Ethan's skills, I think we'll be able to do it, but the stakes are high. If we get caught, we could be sent to prison, and who knows what they'd do to us there.

Mama doesn't know what's going on, but we've had this plan since the beginning of her Countdown. She would never let us do this if she knew what we were planning. After Loukas was taken, Mama made me swear to never step out of line. Of course, Mama never listened to this rule herself; that's what got her into this trouble. But she expects obedience from me. And when I promised her that I'd be careful, I meant it. But everything changed after the Countdown. Now, this Hack is the only thing that's keeping me going. After everything Mama did for Loukas and me, I need to give her something in return. I want her to have one last dance in a strong body. I want her to dance in *mine.*

I try to focus on the different passwords in the book. We need to find a way to access the government's files so Ethan can turn off the alert. I type out the different combinations, hoping that one of them will be right. Nothing seems to work, but I keep at it. I'll do this all night if I have to.

Ethan seems to have stopped. He's looking at me, trying to get my attention. I finish typing and look up.

"Ellie," he says. I can tell he's trying to find the right words.

I nod.

"I know we're going to do this, and I want to, but I just think... we should talk about the risk."

"It's okay, Ethan. I know."

"It's just—especially if we can't get this password—"

"We *will*."

"I know," he says, "but if we don't, the Officials will be notified. They'll find us."

"So, we won't let that happen. We won't stop until we figure this out."

"But even if we do, that doesn't guarantee safety. Even without alerting them, they might still be tracking us—somebody might be watching and notify them."

"Why are you being like this? This isn't the first time—" I stop myself. He doesn't need the reminder. I know he still feels guilty about what happened with Loukas. Even though neither of them Hacked anyone, they were putting each other at risk. They were breaking into the government servers and unlocking restricted areas. Nobody deserved to be taken to prison, but that's probably where Loukas is right now. Ethan lives with that guilt every day. It's not his fault, of course, but I know Ethan blames himself. He hates that he's safe while Loukas is in danger. That's why we're having this conversation.

"I know I'm probably being paranoid. But this is different..."

"Why?"

"Because it's *you*."

I look at Ethan. The seriousness in his eyes. My heart stops, realizing how much he cares. For a second, I think Mama's theory about Ethan is right. Maybe he *does* like me. But I can't let myself get carried away. I'm his best friend. That's what I'll always be to him. Plus, I remind myself, there will always be the problem of my feet. My calloused feet. Ethan screams every time he sees my bare feet in flip-flops. They're completely wrecked from all my years of ballet. And if I weren't so used to them, they would probably scare me too. So, I'm sure Ethan would prefer to date someone with nice smooth feet, like Jessica Langley, his beautiful friend from work. Ethan's very attractive with his dirty-blond hair, warm hazel eyes, and soft freckles. He's tall too, and he keeps growing, but I like that because I'm tall, too, and I always feel embarrassed when I'm taller than the guys my age. I know I shouldn't and Mama always tells me I'm too smart to care about these things, but I can't help it. It's nice that I only reach Ethan's shoulders. When he hugs me, I feel completely protected, which is fitting because he's always been looking out for me.

"Did I say something wrong?" He asks. I realize I've been quiet for a while.

"No, just thinking."

"It's going to be okay. I'm not going to let anything happen." He changes his tune because he thinks I'm scared.

"I know."

He thinks about what to say for a moment. Then he adds, "I just wanted to say, even if we do everything right, there's no way to guarantee safety. If someone's under-cover or an Official's in the audience, there's no way to account for that."

"It's *Mama*, Ethan."

"I know."

"I need to make this happen."

He understands that and I know he does, but that's all I can focus on right now. I realize that I'm putting myself at risk. Hacking is extremely dangerous; it's seen as one of the worst crimes. If the government catches us, there's no knowing what they'll do. Some kind of imprisonment, but it depends. A person like me, who's young and fit from my years of dancing, will probably go somewhere where Group1s can use my body.

But it doesn't really matter where they take me. No matter where I go, it would be far from here. Far from home.

I can take the risk now because Mama is dying. If I get caught, I won't be leaving any family behind. I had to be more careful before when Loukas was taken and Mama only had me. But now it's starting to feel like I'm the only one left. I have Ethan, of course, and the Cohens. I can't imagine being taken somewhere, without Ethan by my side, but I also want to make sure he's safe. I know that if Ethan had a choice he'd go instead of me, but I can't let that happen. He has to live a long and happy life, and I'd like to be there with him. So, the two of us need to be very careful. Go over everything. Make sure we give Mama one last dance and then figure out our lives from there.

If anyone can make it happen, it's Ethan.

I grab his hand impulsively. He looks at me and I regret my boldness for a moment. But when I notice his expression, I feel relieved. He squeezes my hand, reassuring me.

"I won't mess this up," he says.

"Me neither."

CHAPTER 3

In the last few days of every Amecan's life, there is a meeting with a Government Official. This has been the protocol for as long as the Countdown has existed. Mama has to go to the Ace Building, talk to a Government Official, and thank them for their time. It's customary to bring a gift of thanks, but Mama will be going empty-handed.

I thought we might bring them some poisoned moussaka, but Mama talked me out of it. It isn't "worth the risk."

Mama is allowed to bring one family member with her, so I will be going as her guest. Some people are honored to be selected for this role. They're excited for their chance to see how Officials live—to see what it's like to be on top. But that's not the case for me. I'm happy to be Mama's guest because I don't want her to go alone. This isn't an adventure, it's a duty. At the beginning of Mama's Countdown, we started saving enough money for Mama to do one visit to the doctor. She got a small bottle of pain medication to help her with the aching. We could only afford five pills. She's using the last of the medication today, to ease this trip's strain on her body. I went to that doctor's appointment with Mama, dreading it, but happy to be by her side. That's what today feels like. Both of us would rather stay home, write a nasty letter, and get on with our day. But, of course, that's not an option. That would give us far too much freedom.

Maybe if Mama wasn't so young, if she'd lived ninety years, for example, we would be more enthusiastic. *Maybe.* More than anything, though, the two of us are angry today. My chest has been tight all morning. I see Mama's anger in the creases of her face. Her pierced eyes have been fixed on the door since she woke up. She is waiting for someone to pick us up. She is waiting to face the people who stole fifty years of her life.

They don't tell us when to expect the Official. We just know that at some point today someone in a suit will come pick us up. I try to distract Mama with other things, but nothing works. At some point, Mama tells me to change. "Wear something nice," she tells me. "I want them to see who we are." I fill in the rest of Mama's words: *who we are, despite what they have taken.*

I wanted to wear my worst t-shirt and pants. Something with stains and rips, to show how little I respect them. But Mama wants us to rise above. She wants to show them that people from Group7 can still show up looking like knockouts. We don't need hundred-dollar outfits to be beautiful.

I listen to Mama and put on my best dress. It's a warm yellow, with green flowers stitched into the bottom. I've always liked the way the dress makes me feel. Something about it makes me happy whenever I put it on. And most importantly, Mama loves the dress. I know she'll approve.

Mama smiles when I come out of my room.

"Beautiful, Elloula."

"Thanks, Mama. Not as beautiful as you."

Her face brightens. She's wearing a white dress. I did her makeup this morning. It's the first time she's worn it since the Countdown began. She looks beautiful.

I unclasp the necklace around my neck and hand it to Mama.

"For you," I tell her. "I think you should wear it today."

Mama takes the necklace from my hands and looks it over. The necklace belongs to Mama. Before the Countdown, she wore it every day. It's her favorite. But the day Mama found out she was dying, she gave the necklace to me. "I want you to have it." I was hesitant at first, but when she insisted I listened, and I've been wearing it ever since. I know Mama likes to see it on me. She wants to know it will still be appreciated when she's gone.

But today, the necklace should be worn by Mama. I know it will make her feel more powerful. I know it will make her feel more complete.

I help Mama with the necklace clasp. Once it's on her, she looks stronger, more radiant. I don't know how much of it is what she's wearing and how much of it is her will to impress the Officials.

Unlike me, this won't be the first time Mama has encountered Government Officials. She used to know some of them closely when she was still with my father. She used to know President Ace. She doesn't talk much about him, but I know she holds a lot of resentment. Back when she was dating my father and through the early years of their marriage, Mama had dinners with President Ace all the time. My father worked with him and they were close, so Mama became friends with him too. But it was a complicated friendship. Mama never kept her political views to herself and she always brought up things she expected the government to change. Her main talking point was that she wanted better treatment for the low-status Groups. President Ace would always listen to her politely and push back in a friendly way, but it was my father who hated it most. He wanted Mama to "stay in her lane." It didn't matter, though. Mama didn't listen.

Mama used to love recounting the many names she called President Ace when he said something hateful or ignorant. She called him names unapologetically and to his face, which she always says is "the only proper way to speak ill of someone." She's proud of her tenacity, but I think she's also proud that she knows President Ace personally. He's a celebrity in his own right and knowing him makes her feel important too. For someone like Mama, who doesn't get a lot of credit for her own talents, it's nice for her to feel special in some way. If Mama stayed in Group1 with my father, she could have been the most famous ballerina in Ameca. But Mama never put herself first. Not then and not now. So, really, what Mama's probably most proud of is that knowing President Ace didn't change her. She had the audacity to stand up to him. She had the strength to face all her wildest dreams, look them straight in the face, and say: *no, not on these terms.*

I'm proud of Mama too. Prouder than she knows. I'm proud of where she came from and the choices that she made. But I'm also proud of who she is now. Mama has difficulty with that. She doesn't recognize herself anymore—so weak and tired. I still see strength in her every day, in the way she gets up every day without complaint, despite the pain in her bones. It's that mindset that makes her a fighter. It's what's allowing her to get through today.

I know it's going to be hard for Mama to go to the Ace Building looking and feeling the way she does. The last time she was there, President Ace greeted her personally. She was young and on top of the world. She was seen as the powerful woman she's always been. But today, Officials will greet her with little care; they will think of her as one more dying person coming to say goodbye.

Mama's body can't represent the person she is inside anymore, so I see that as my role today. I need to embody her strength.

Around two in the afternoon, someone comes to our door. It's a man dressed in a navy and maroon suit, sporting the government's colors. He's here to pick us up. There is a car parked outside our house, which looks strange because we're not used to seeing cars in 7N.

The man introduces himself, but I don't pay much attention. He's a Government Official. That's all I need to know. I shake his hand absent-mindedly. I hope he gets the impression that I'd rather be anywhere else. I hope he knows I have no respect for him. The Official tries to reach for Mama's wheelchair, but I shove him off. "I'll take her," I say. There's no way this government Official is coming anywhere near Mama.

The Official walks us to the car and opens the door for us. After I help Mama in and enter after her, I pray that the Official will close the door and leave us alone. Of course, that doesn't happen. The Official follows us into the car and sits between Mama and me. There's a woman in the front seat, who will drive us. Neither of us pays the Official any attention. The car begins moving and we head out of our neighborhood. We reach an area I've never seen before. There's a sign that reads, "Ace Transit Center." I've never heard of this place. I wonder what it is.

The Official tells us to exit the car and follow him. I wheel Mama toward the sign, and I make out train tracks. There are other pairs of people waiting by the train tracks, and each pair has an Official beside them. I wonder if everyone here is going to the Ace Building. If every pair has a member who's about to die, like Mama. Minutes later, a train stops in front of us. The Official instructs us to get on.

When the door closes, the train starts moving immediately.

"Take a seat," the Official tells us. "The train moves fast."

He isn't wrong. I'm amazed by how fast we're accelerating. At the front of our railcar, there's a board that shows our speed. Once the train stops accelerating, we move at 250 miles per hour. That seems impossible to me.

The Official tells us the train ride will be long, so I make myself comfortable. I try not to look shocked by the ornate details of the train car's interior. They must have put more money into designing this than anyone in Group7 could ever dream of.

The windows are tinted on the inside so I can't see what's outside. I wonder why they've done this—what they're hiding. When I ask the Official, he stares back at me. It's a stern look that suggests I should keep these kinds of questions to myself.

The corners of Mama's lips curl slightly upward. "They like keeping secrets in Group1," she explains. "They'll let you in on a little—show you the Ace Building... only right before you die. But you can never know it all. Not even on the verge of death. Because you might get wild ideas..."

"Like what?" I ask, playing along.

"Like maybe they should share their wealth with you."

I laugh. The Official glares at Mama. She doesn't say anything more.

Mama doesn't seem phased by the elegance or speed of this train. I wonder if she once rode in trains like this with my dad. She never mentioned it, but then again, that wouldn't be the type of thing she'd brag about. I think about asking her, but I know a memory like that would only upset her now. I keep it to myself. We ride in silence. I hold on to Mama's hand, squeezing it ever so gently every once in a while, but let her get her rest. I know she wants to save all her energy for when we arrive.

There's a poster on the train with President Ace's face on it. Below his eerily white smile, it reads, "Yesterday, today, and tomorrow, we thank you. You saved us from our ruin. You made us one." A bitter laugh comes out of me, and I purposely don't make eye contact with the Official. I'm enraged by the poster. Do people really believe President Ace is their savior? Is that what they're told in Group 1 and 2?

Years before there were Essences, Groups, or even President Ace, there was a pandemic. It was devastating and billions of people died. The pandemic wiped out a huge percentage of the world's population, but President Ace didn't save them. He was only a kid at the time. The survivors of the pandemic were on their own. They retreated from their empty towns and cities and joined together with others, in safer areas. Bordering countries amalgamated. New Groups formed and small governments were made by natural leaders who volunteered to help keep things together.

It took a long time for the world to recover after the pandemic. But as it did, the economy began to recover as well. This is when things took a turn for the worse. Or, as President Ace likes to phrase it when he "*saved us* from our ruin."

One of the main industries that boomed after the pandemic was the healthcare industry. The pandemic created incredible fear for many, and people were desperate to avoid illness, death, or the pain that comes from dying. Corporations raced to create technology that could capitalize on this fear. New medicines and treatments were increasingly introduced into the economy, each one promising a longer and healthier life.

In the end, one corporation won the race by a landslide. One masterful CEO, who was willing to take down and conquer whomever necessary, rose to the top. Douglas Ace. CEO of Ameca. Ameca increased life expectancy, cured all natural diseases, and discovered Essence. Ameca was more than just a healthcare giant—it marketed itself as "God on earth." The corporation promised to eradicate death. Ameca gave people false hope.

But Douglas Ace was beloved by all Groups at the time. He claimed his efforts were motivated by the people. The name "Ameca" reflects this, as it contains parts of "America," "Mexico," and "Canada," the three lost countries, devastated by the pandemic, that formerly comprised a continent known as North America.

Ace was a master manipulator. He always has been. He proposed creating one nation for all Groups. He made big promises to do so, telling people that, through healthcare innovation, he would increase immortality by erasing the possibility of natural death. It took some convincing, but eventually Ace was successful. What he left out was that he was exceptionally afraid of sharing resources, so he would also be creating a system called the Countdown. When Groups were worried that the way they were accustomed to living would alter after electing Ace, he promised they wouldn't be; but what he really meant was that he wouldn't *allow* for the Groups to be altered. Everyone was stuck with what they were given. We are still forbidden to ask for more.

But nobody could know this at the time. The Groups were desperate for a "real" leader, and they put their trust in Douglas Ace. Just like that, the Groups became one nation: Ameca. And they were led by Douglas Ace, who would henceforth be known as President Ace.

And now President Ace controls everything. He is the reason Group7 is stuck with no money. He is the reason so many of my peers are already in prison. He is the reason Mama is dying. But somehow he *saved* us? From what?

Mama gives me a look of concern. I know what she's thinking. I need to calm down. She doesn't want me to get into trouble. I take a deep breath and close my eyes. I try to relax my mind.

Finally, the train slows down and the windows lose their tint as we arrive at our destination. I can finally see outside. I take in the view. The train stops at a massive building. It's like nothing I've ever seen before—so grand in scale and even taller than the mountains in 7N.

The building is made up of large glass windows and silver blocks forming geometric shapes. It's so sleek and modern, it doesn't compare to anything I'm accustomed to. "This is the Ace Building," the Official tells us nonchalantly. As if it's not a big deal. I've never seen anything this tall before, let alone anything so beautiful. My heart races. I try to stop myself, knowing I'm doing exactly what I shouldn't do. I have no reason to be excited, but I can't help feeling amazed by my surroundings.

I know the people who work here are terrible. I know the very fact that a building like this shocks me so much is directly related to why they're so terrible. And yet, I'm mystified. I'm in awe. And I hate myself for being so pathetic.

The Official leads us off the train and I wheel Mama toward the building.

When we enter, it turns out the Ace building is just as beautiful on the inside as it is on the outside. As soon as we walk in, we're surrounded by stone. The jagged, gray stone walls curl up into the ceiling, making it feel like we're surrounded by a cave. This natural look is juxtaposed with perfect lighting, glass-windowed rooms, and modern maroon and navy furniture. When we walk in a little further, we come to a large screen. On the screen, a video of swirling orbs of light is projected. The lights are all different colors and dancing around. I wonder if those are the Replicas, the copies of our Essences. I try to get a closer look to see if the orbs have tags or identifiers, but the Official demands my attention.

He directs us to a glass room with chairs. When I sit down and lock Mama's chair beside me, the Official finally leaves us alone. I squeeze Mama's hand once more. "This is it," I say, hardly believing we're here.

Mama's eyes focus on the room across the hall. "I can't wait to see him."

"Who?"

"Ace."

My heart drops. Mama thinks we're seeing President Ace? I'm not sure if the last days of her Countdown have made her brain foggier or if she's always believed that this would happen. I don't want to be the one to tell her that he's too important to join these meetings. He'll send one of his representatives if we're lucky. For people like us, in Group7, we'll probably have an intern sit us down. They'll give their condolences on behalf of President Ace and send us on our way. I don't have the heart to tell Mama. Not after she came all this way. I give Mama my encouragement instead. Tell her I can't wait to see her talk to the president.

"He's a tough guy," she says. "He might scare you."

"Me?" I let myself imagine what it would be like if we met President Ace. "Never."

Mama laughs. "Elloula. That's my girl."

A little while later, someone comes to get us. Mama signals for me to come help her. I know what she's asking because she made this plan weeks ago. She wants me to help her stand up. She wants Ace to know that the pain he's putting her through isn't going to keep her from fighting. As much as I believe in Mama's strength, I'm worried about this idea. I've seen how the Countdown has affected her. But I told Mama I would support her, so that's what I do. I grab Mama's hands and pull her to her feet. For the first time in weeks, Mama is standing.

She beams with pride. "I told you."

I laugh, both nervous and relieved. I help Mama turn and grab the handles at the back of her wheelchair. She uses the chair as a walker, and we follow the Official down the hall. I watch Mama walk slowly, amazed by her strength. Lately, Mama's barely been able to move her hands or straighten her knees. But not today. Not right now.

We finally make it to the room at the end of the hall. Mama takes a deep breath before the door opens. The two of us walk in and I hear myself gasp before I can stop it.

President Ace is sitting at the desk.

CHAPTER 4

President Ace stands up as we enter the room. Mama doesn't look surprised. She knew it would be him all along. I look from Mama to President Ace, trying to come back to reality.

"You didn't lie," Mama says. "How out of character for you."

President Ace chuckles, "I see you haven't changed, Selene." Mama nods. "I told you I would be here," he says, "and I saw no reason to change my mind."

"That was many years ago."

"Not too long ago." Back when the two of them spoke, President Ace must have told Mama he'd be the Official to bid her farewell. I'm sure at the time neither of them realized it would be so soon.

"It's all relative when you're over 300." Mama's voice is cold. "Not that I would know. You're killing me at thirty-seven."

President Ace's face grows serious. He takes a seat and gestures for us to follow. Mama stays standing. She wants to show him that she can.

"I must say," President Ace looks at my Mama. "I'm impressed you're not in a wheelchair. Usually by now... well, I shouldn't be surprised, should I?"

"It hasn't been easy, Ace. You've made this very tough. But I won't let you stop me. Not until you stop my heart from beating."

"It's not in my control, Selene. This isn't personal."

Mama gives a big laugh. "Bullshit." I've never heard her swear before. I'm shocked. "You and I both know that's not true. There's no need to use that line on me."

"Selene, I'm not going to get into this with you again."

"Just tell me, was he involved?"

Who is he? Is Mama talking about my father? There's something in President Ace's eyes. Like he's telling her something... something he's not allowed to say with his words. I'm shocked Mama asked this question. Every time I suggested my father might be involved she never seemed to believe me. But now, based on President Ace's reaction, I think Mama believes it's true.

"There's not much time before my next meeting," President Ace looks at the clock. "So let me say what needs to be said." He barely takes a breath before beginning, "On behalf of the government, we thank you, Selene Sagona, for everything you have done for Ameca. Your ballet and pure, raw talent have been inspiring. You have given our nation two beautiful children, Loukas and Eliana, whom I'm sure will pass on your legacy—"

"What the hell is this?" Mama interrupts him. "Is this what you say to everyone?"

"We thank you for your time and we're sorry it is ending—"

"Who wrote this?"

"Selene. I need you to be quiet."

"What for?"

President Ace takes a deep breath. "What would you like me to say, my dear?"

"Why are you killing me?"

"As I said, this isn't personal."

"Well, there's no point in talking then. If you're going to continue to lie."

"Selene. There is an order to things. Plans were made far before I met you."

"Just like old times," Mama scoffs, angrily. "You won't give me one straight answer. I'm dying in *days*, Ace. I'm no threat to you now. Can't you tell me anything?"

"It's never safe to be a martyr. You know that."

"So, I'm a martyr now? You're admitting it."

"I'm not admitting anything. But I will say this. In your years alive, you could have had a wonderful life here. You had *all* the luxuries of Group1, and then some. You had no reason to ruin your future."

"I was fighting for my *son*. You took away my *Loukas*."

"If you'd listened in the first place, Loukas would've been safe. People in Group1 rarely commit crimes."

"There's a reason for that."

"Your family would have been safe."

"And what about everyone else? What about the Group that I left behind?"

"It's not possible for everyone to live like this. For there to be a top there needs to be a bottom."

"Oh, please. Not that again."

"It's true, Selene. It's not so easy being a leader. I wish the ideal world you speak of could be possible, but it's not. I have to keep things in order."

"The divide doesn't have to be so exaggerated."

"We're never going to agree, are we?" President Ace frowns. "And so now, there's nothing I can do. There's nothing I can tell you that will satisfy you."

"You were scared of the riots and what they could accomplish. That's why you're killing me. Admit it."

"Selene..."

"Admit it!"

President Ace stares back at Mama silently. Neither of them speaks. There are years of memories in their silence. I can feel the tension.

Finally, President Ace speaks, "Well, as always, it's been lovely, Selene. But that will be all for today. I must prepare for my next meeting."

"That's it?"

President Ace doesn't respond. He looks hurt. He opens his mouth like he's considering what to say but eventually shuts it. "Goodbye, Selene." His voice cracks a bit before he says, "I *will* miss you, you know. In my 300 years, you've been a refreshing surprise. Out of everyone I've encountered, you certainly stand out."

Mama turns around faster than I've seen her move in weeks. She walks as quickly as she can, tightly clenching the handles of her wheelchair. "In my thirty-seven years," she turns her head and finally responds, "you have been the greatest disappointment."

I get up to follow Mama, feeling proud of her attempt. Before I go, President Ace stops me.

"Can I have a word with you, my dear?"

I look to Mama and she nods. I begrudgingly obey.

It's silent while we wait for Mama to exit. Once the door is shut and Mama's in the hallway, President Ace begins. "That's a nice outfit you have on," President Ace says. "Very colorful."

"Thanks?" It comes out as a question. I'm confused.

"Who bought you that dress?"

"It's a hand me down from someone in 6. I don't buy a lot of my own clothes. I have other priorities."

"Of course. Was it from a close friend? It's lovely."

"I can't remember." It was from Jocelyn, Mama's friend. We've known her for years, but I don't want him to know this. President Ace looks at me inquisitively. I wonder if he knows I'm lying. He doesn't say anything more.

"I've known your mother for many years. She's a good woman. I may not agree with much of what she stands for, but I like her. I'm very fond of her." President Ace stops. He seems to be waiting for me to respond.

"Thank you," I say, not knowing what else to add to such a strange proclamation.

"I like to keep an eye on people I'm fond of..." President Ace gives me a knowing look. "Do you understand?"

"Yes."

"And I do a lot of observing in this job, you know. Great leaders need to observe."

"I'm sure," I say, picking up on his threat.

"So be careful," he says. "You don't want to end up like Loukas."

I stare at President Ace, unable to say anything. I've always felt, to some degree, like my family was more in danger than others. The government taking Loukas seemed personal. But what did President

Ace mean by "keeping an eye" on us? How closely has he been scanning my whereabouts? What does he know about me? Ethan? Does he know what we're planning to do? I think about whether or not I should say something to Ethan about this. I know if I do that will be the end of Mama's surprise. Ethan will think the risk is too high. He'll tell me we have to shut it down. And then Mama won't have her dance. I can't let that happen. The only thing getting me through these one hundred days is knowing that Mama will have this one night of freedom. Something good. I still want to take the risk.

"You're not as talkative as your mother," President Ace says.

I look at President Ace sternly, feeling anger build inside me. "I'm a lot more like her than you think."

President Ace chuckles, "Well then. I hope you're a better listener."

I don't respond. I turn around to leave and join my mother outside. "Do take my words seriously, Miss Sagona." He calls out as I open the door to leave. "I don't usually warn people twice."

CHAPTER 5

When we get home, Ethan is there. I'm surprised to see him because it's Thursday evening and this is typically his longest shift. Ethan works in waste management and his schedule is usually inflexible. He must have worked overtime to clear his schedule for me. The thought makes me feel overwhelmingly grateful. I didn't know I needed him, but when I see Ethan I'm finally able to relax.

Mama lost her energy as soon as our train ride home began. She crashed immediately, falling asleep on my shoulder. It was a long day for her. She expended a week's worth of energy.

Ethan helps me wash off Mama's makeup and put her in bed.

"How are you doing?" He asks.

"I'm fine," I shrug, but when I talk to Ethan I realize I'm not as fine as I'd like to be.

I tuck Mama in under the covers and turn off her bedroom light. Ethan puts his hand on my back and guides me out of the room. "She's fine. I'm sure she's just exhausted."

"You should have seen her today. She walked."

"Really?" Ethan knows how impressive that is. Most people stop using their walkers in the first fifty days of the Countdown. *Nobody* stands in their last week. "That's incredible."

"Yeah, but I think it was too much. She wore herself out."

"She'll be okay."

Ethan leads us to the living room. "So... how are you feeling?" He asks. "My mom made a big dinner, and they're kind of hoping you'll come over." Ethan laughs, knowing I'd understand how his mom can be. When they're worried about someone, they tend to overdo things. "Anyway, I told them I'd see what you want. Because obviously, you might not be in the mood. So, I'm happy to stay here if you want. Whatever you're feeling. Or I can go and leave you alone."

"I don't want you to go."

But I have to think about this for a minute. Ethan waits. Mama's sleeping in her room. I know she'll be asleep all night. A part of me wants to stay with her and dwell in my sadness. I'm not sure if I have the energy to see people right now, even if it's only the Cohens. If I ask Ethan to stay here with me, I know he won't think of the dinner another moment. But we've got no food here and I'm starting to feel hungry. Plus, spending time with the Cohens is always the right decision in the end.

"I'm up for it," I say.

"You sure?" He asks, but he's already smiling.

I nod, letting myself smile too.

When we get to the Cohens', Molly and Leora greet me more warmly than they usually do. I know everyone in the house is thinking about me right now. It's the second last day of Mama's Countdown. Tomorrow's the recital and then that's it. I've been trying not to think about it, but I feel it in Molly and Leora's hugs. I try to let their warmth seep in. *It's going to be okay,* I tell myself. I won't have Mama next week, but I won't be on my own. I'll still have two loving moms to hug. They're not exactly family; mine can't be replaced. But they're the closest thing to family that I'm going to have, and it could be a lot worse. Ethan gives me a reassuring grin when Molly and Leora let me go. *It's going to be okay.*

Molly walks over to the kitchen, and we follow. "There's a ton of food," Molly says. "Leora even made her homemade fudge."

"Oh, wow," I say, knowing they did all this for me. "Thanks so much."

"It was nothing," Leora adds. "I've been craving it for weeks. I'm just happy to have an excuse to make it."

"You didn't have to do all of this, you know. Next time I'm good with just a bowl of soup."

"We know, honey. And I'm happy to eat all of the fudge myself."

"Well, I won't make you do that," I say.

"How kind."

Ethan and I set the table while Leora and Molly finish taking food out of the oven. Leora shouts for the others to come down, and Ethan's siblings barrel down the stairs. When Ethan's brother, Jonah, sees me folding a napkin, he pushes me away. "No way, missy," he says. "Go sit down."

"Come on. I practically live here."

"Yeah, and you're making me look bad. It's time for me to do a chore or two."

"Did you hear that, Moms?" Ethan says.

"Oh yeah," Leora says, "I'm just sorry I didn't record it."

"Ha ha," Jonah says dryly. "*Hi*larious."

I sit down on the couch, despite my best efforts, while the Cohens set up a beautiful meal. They've made so much food. Much more than they can afford. I feel guilty. Ethan didn't even tell me they were doing all of this. It's a good thing I agreed to come.

I can't help but feel emotional about the Cohens' love and the reason they're all supporting me. They want me to feel at home. They've invited me several times to come live with them once the Countdown is over, but I'm still not sure how I feel about it. There are so many memories in our little home. It's where I've lived my whole life. It's going to be hard to stay; I know that. Even now, the place doesn't feel the same. Loukas's not around and Mama's barely herself. But I get a sense of comfort being around all of our memories. It doesn't feel right to abandon them as soon as Mama's gone.

Plus, what would happen if I lived with Ethan? I can already barely handle being around him without making it stupidly clear that I have a major crush on him. And where would I sleep? In his room? That sounds like a recipe for disaster. Half of me wants to spend all of my time with Ethan, but the smarter half of me realizes I should probably distance myself. It's the first step to healing unrequited love. And the second step, which is essential to following through with the first, is refraining from *sleeping on his floor*. So, for the time being, I know I can't live with the Cohens. I have to make something else work.

Grandma Gerrie comes to sit beside me. She pats me on my knee. "Hey, little one, how are you doing?"

"I'm okay." We both know that's not true, but I say it anyway.

I've known Ethan's grandma most of my life. She's brilliant, like Ethan, but wiser from her many years. "You know, when Benji died, I didn't think I could live another day." I frown, remembering how hard it was for her when her husband died. "The whole Countdown, I dreaded that last day so much. But when it finally happened, there was a sense of relief. I mean, I was devastated, of course. And you will be too, with your Mama. But you'll also be relieved. The pain will be over for her. The waiting will be over. It's no good and it's no fair, but it will come with relief."

"I hope so."

Grandma Gerrie squeezes my hand. It's nice to look her in the eyes and get the sense that she really understands. It's the first time I've felt this since the Countdown began. I wish I could erase Grandma Gerrie's pain, the same way I'm sure she wishes the same for me. But at least we have this moment together. It's something I'll always hold on to.

Grandma Gerrie is the only real grandparent figure I have in my life, considering Mama's parents both live far away. They serve a family in Group2, living in their basement, taking care of their children, and cooking them meals. They were sent to work for Group2 families as soon as Mama turned fifteen, so Mama spent most of her life without them. I've met them a couple of times when they've been given days off work, but usually, they don't have enough time to make it back to 7N. I know Mama is sad about it, but she doesn't bring it up often. We sent Mama's parents a message at the beginning of the Countdown, and they told us they'd do everything they could to get off work and visit. But they were never given that opportunity.

Before I can think any more about this, the Cohens call me over to sit. The table is crammed with food, and I don't know where to begin. Ethan offers me green beans and I take them from him, lightly grazing his hand. We stare at each other for a moment and then I look away, feeling flushed and embarrassed. I don't want the Cohens to notice. I don't even know what it is they would see. Was Ethan looking at me the way I was looking at him? Is he secretly thinking I've lost my mind? Maybe I have. Maybe it's crazy to have a crush on Ethan, my best friend since freaking kindergarten.

I focus on the meal, overflowing my plate with delicious items like roast beef, corn bread, candied carrots, and mashed potatoes. I can't remember the last time I had this much to eat and this many options. Probably never. I listen to the chatter of the Cohens while taking in every delicious bite. I feel myself tearing up and try not to cry. Ethan notices me. He squeezes my hand under the table. "You okay?" He whispers.

I nod, whispering back. "This is so nice. I can't believe you all did this for me."

"We would do anything for you, Ellie."

I know that's true. And I would do anything for Ethan.

When we've finished eating dinner and dessert, I can barely fit into my jeans. I insist on helping with the dishes and after I pull the "I need a distraction" card, they finally let me. When we're done cleaning up and I've thanked the Cohens for the hundredth time, Ethan and I go to his room. There are still some finishing touches we need to attend to before the Hack.

Ethan closes the door and I plop down on his bed.

"What a meal," I say, "I'm stuffed."

Ethan laughs. "I'm glad you enjoyed it. My moms were so happy."

Ethan sits in his usual spot on his bean bag chair. He tells me that he was able to get into the government's server and he worked through everything while I was at Ace City. "Everything's ready now. They won't be alerted when the Hack happens. We're safe." But even when he says this, I can sense the nervousness in his voice.

"Ethan," I start. I know it's time to say what I need to say. "I want you to know that I can take it from here. I'll learn the last codes needed to make the Hack happen. I'll do it myself. I don't want you to risk your safety any more than you have already. There's no reason I can't do the rest."

Ethan shakes his head. "That's not happening."

I knew he would say that. "Listen. I'm breaking the law either way. I'm going to be in Mama's body. But you—you can stay out of it. You can be safe."

"I won't do that. I won't teach you the codes. I'm sorry. I won't."

"This isn't penance for Loukas," I say, as softly as I can. "Nobody blames you."

Ethan stares at me. I can see the sadness and sincerity in his eyes. "Ellie. I want to do this, okay? I'm nervous for *you,* but I'm not worried about myself. I want to be a part of this. I want to get back at them." He means the government. "And yeah, maybe it's about Loukas, but it's also about everyone. It's about Raffi. It's about my moms, my family, how unfair everything is, all of it. So, I want to be the one to Hack. I want to be a part of this."

"Even with the risk?"

"It's the only way I'll accept it."

I realize I have no choice. If Ethan won't give me the information, I won't be able to do it on my own.

After a moment of quiet, Ethan speaks again. He has questions about my visit to Ace City. We haven't had much of a chance to talk about it yet.

"We met with Ace," I tell him.

"*What?* How did that happen?"

"I guess his relationship with my mom still mattered to him. It was crazy."

"What happened? What was he like?"

"Just like he is in the videos. But then... kind of normal in some ways? Like when he talked to Mama... It kind of felt like they were old friends. It was weird."

"Well, I guess that makes sense."

"Yeah, but it's weird, you know? I always think of President Ace as this polished politician. But my mom kind of made him squirm."

"Well, if anyone can..."

I laugh with pride. "Exactly."

"That's basically unheard of, though," he says, still processing. And I know he's thinking about his grandpa, Benji. When Benji was doing his Countdown, Grandma Gerrie took him to the Ace Building. They waited hours to see someone and finally were given this short and insincere farewell speech from a fifteen-year-old intern. It was a horrible experience for Grandma Gerrie and Benji, reaffirming the government's view of their lives as meaningless. I was expecting this to be my experience with Mama, and I'm sure Ethan was too.

"Apparently President Ace promised Mama years ago that he'd be there to give the farewell, but I had no idea. And I'm shocked he stuck to his word. But in some ways, I'm glad we saw him. I think it made Mama happy. Being able to stand up to President Ace and show me that part of herself. She was spectacular, honestly. I wish you could have seen her."

"Me too," Ethan says.

"But then at the end, he asked to just speak to me. It was so weird. He kept asking about my dress."

"Your dress?"

"Yeah, he wanted to know who gave it to me."

"That doesn't make any sense."

"Right?"

Ethan thinks about this, and I wonder if I've already said too much. "So, he addressed you directly?"

"Yeah."

"Usually guests are just supposed to be observers."

I shrug, trying to calm Ethan down, but I can tell his mind is racing. I've already said too much. Now I know I definitely can't tell him about President Ace's warning. I can't risk the Hack not happening. "Anyway, I'm just glad it's over."

"Me too. I know you were dreading it."

"Thanks," I say, feeling guilty about lying to him. I promise myself I'll fess up as soon as the Hack is over.

Ethan senses something's up. "Are you okay?"

I nod, quickly thinking of something to explain myself. "Big day tomorrow."

"I know," Ethan gets up and comes over to the bed. He hugs me. His chest is warm against my heart. "It's going to be okay, Ellie. You're going to get through this. And when you feel like you can't, you just come over, okay? I'm not going anywhere."

"Thanks," I say weakly as I begin to cry. It's as though all the emotions I've been trying to avoid over the last few months are finally coming out. I can't keep the tears in anymore. Ethan lets me cry, rubbing my back, and reassuring me. "Thanks," I say again, and I hope he knows how much I mean it. "I don't know what I'd do without you."

"You'd be just fine." He wipes the tears off my cheek.

I laugh, a little embarrassed, "Sorry."

Ethan locks eyes with me. "Don't be."

We rarely both sit on his bed together. Usually, when I'm on the bed he's on the bean bag chair, or sometimes when he's on his bed I sit at his desk doing work. This feels different. I am suddenly very aware of my body and how close we are to each other.

"You okay?"

I nod, unable to find words. The sides of our knees are nearly touching. I wonder if he notices. And then, my question is answered. Ethan starts to lean in closer. His face is an inch from mine now. My heart starts beating at double its normal pace. The two of us stare at each other, our faces almost touching. I can feel Ethan's heart beating. I want him to kiss me, but I'm frozen. He seems to be frozen too. We're both in this together. Both freaking out.

It's Ethan, I tell myself, which is both reassuring and terrifying. I gain the nerve to move half an inch closer and Ethan closes the gap an instant later. And then, just like that, we're kissing. Ethan's lips are on mine and my heart is exploding. It's *Ethan*. I can't believe it. I'm kissing *Ethan*.

It feels like this couldn't possibly be my first kiss, like I've known these lips for years. Everything about it is natural and yet I'm swept away. I forget everything else around me. It's the first time in almost one hundred days that I'm at ease. I'm nothing but happy.

When Ethan pulls away, the two of us laugh. We can't help ourselves.

"Why did we wait so long to do that?" Ethan asks.

"I don't know. You tell me."

"What do you mean?" He says. "Don't be so old-fashioned, Ellie. You could have kissed me first."

We spend the rest of the evening finishing up the last few things we need to get done before the Hack. Ethan walks me home and we hold hands the whole way. When we get to my front door, I stop before going in. I'm sad to go inside because I know Mama will be sleeping and the quiet house will bring me back to reality. Ethan knows this, giving me an extra-long hug.

"It's going to be okay. Call me at any point if you can't get to bed."

"Thanks," I say, squeezing his hand. "You don't know how much these past months have meant to me."

"I haven't done much. You could have done all of this on your own."

I don't believe him, but I know he means it. "Well, thank you. For everything."

"Always. I'll see you tomorrow, okay?"

"Okay." I kiss him one last time. I let it calm me. When I'm about to go inside, I pull Ethan toward me. "Just another minute."

He laughs.

We kiss for a little longer until I'm ready to be on my own.

I say goodnight to Ethan and close the door.

From the window, I watch him walk away. He waves goodbye and then it's just Mama and me. I go to the kitchen and fill up a glass of water. I check on Mama sleeping and put the water by her nightstand. She'll need it when she wakes up.

I fall asleep trying to think about Ethan or anything I can muster to stay distracted, but I can only think of Mama. I wish Ethan was here to calm me down because I'm feeling more emotions than I usually do. My mind races with memories of Mama and Loukas. *I'm going to be the only one left*, I think, crying. *Soon it will only be me.*

I cry like I've never cried before, memories rushing through my mind. Eventually, the tears stop coming. I think I'm ready to fall asleep. But then I remember another moment, years ago, when Mama took us rock climbing. We climbed to the top of a mountain and Loukas almost fell. Mama grabbed his arm and pulled him up. *Don't be so reckless*, she yelled at him, *if you fall and die, I'll kill you!* Loukas laughed. *You won't be able to,* he said back, *I'll already be dead.* Mama whacked his arm, not appreciating his attitude. Mama was the only one who was allowed to have sass. We weren't allowed to give it back. It was a random moment in time, but it encapsulates so much. It was a beautiful day. We didn't often have outings like that. But Mama took the day off and surprised us with the trip. She loves us so much. When I think about how strong she was then, how she pulled Loukas up and climbed that mountain, it's almost hard to believe. Now she can barely walk... barely move. I feel the tears coming on again and I'm back where I was before, crying. I feel like I can't get a hold of myself. Eventually, I get up and move to Mama's bed. I cuddle up beside her and let her presence calm me. She's still here, I tell myself. She's right beside me. I feel my breathing settle. I focus on Mama's quiet breathing. I eventually fall asleep.

CHAPTER 6

On the day of the recital, Ethan is at my house. Mama's too weak to cook, so Ethan and I make moussaka. We're in the kitchen, listening to Mama's playlist. We're dancing along to the tunes while Mama bops her head to the beat, sitting on the windowsill. It's a happy moment despite our nerves. Both Ethan and I realize the risks we're taking this evening and what they could mean. At the same time, I can't stop the feeling of dread. This is my last full day with Mama. Tomorrow, at any time, she will go. The following day, I will wake up to a world that she no longer belongs to. I wish I could stop the time from ticking and the Countdown from ending. It's a feeling I haven't been able to escape since the "100" first appeared. And yet, we're dancing in the kitchen. Pretending it's any other day. *"It's the perfect day to dance and sing,"* as Mama always says, *"like every other."*

Ethan grabs my hand and twirls me. Mama laughs. She lifts her hand a bit and Ethan takes it, swaying Mama's hand while she sits.

I think back to when we were little, and Mama gave Ethan his first dance class. He was absolutely terrible. He had no flexibility, zero grace or balance, and the only thing he wanted to do was jump. Mama laughed at him—she told me there was no point. She didn't mind teaching a beginner, but between Ethan's excess energy and lack of talent, Mama assumed he had no real interest in learning. But she was wrong. Ethan loved his private lessons, which I usually joined. He was one of the most motivated learners Mama ever taught. When he puts his mind to something, when he really wants it, he always makes it happen. That's Ethan.

Watching him dance with Mama now, I let myself relax. I take in this moment. Mama always loved Ethan. I remember when Ethan had his Bar Mitzvah, the two of us slow danced to our favorite song. It was an innocent moment. I had barely even started to have crushes at that point, but Mama still had a smile on her face for the rest of the night. *Stop it, Mama,* I told her, embarrassed. *Elloula, you don't know.* I kept asking her, *What? What don't I know?* And finally, she said, *One day you're going to look at him and it won't be so simple.* I shook my head, feeling completely sure at the time that she was wrong.

And yet, only two years later, when Ethan and I danced to the same song at our friend's quinceañera everything felt different. I was vividly aware of Ethan's hands on my hips. I awkwardly placed my arms around his neck, but my elbows were stiff and rigid. I couldn't follow the basic steps. I was a professional dancer by then, but I was having trouble with a simple slow dance. For the first time in my life, I felt nervous around Ethan. I didn't exactly know what I was feeling, but I had a sinking suspicion that Mama was right. When the dance finished and I joined Mama at the table, I couldn't look her in the eyes. I didn't want to see the knowing look on her face. I hated that she knew me better than I knew myself.

But now, looking back, Mama's wisdom makes me overwhelmed with joy. Somehow, she was never wrong about these things. She knew intuitively.

When I was little, she told me and stories, which she always made up on the spot. The stories would take many twists and turns, always teaching me an important lesson. But the characters were always the same. It was about Mama, Loukas, and me. And whenever she made me the princess in the story, she always made Ethan the prince.

One time I asked her if she was sad that she was always alone in her stories. When I was a princess, she always gave me a prince. But when she was the queen, she never had a king. She laughed at me, saying, *There are so many ways to fill your life with love. I've got you and Loukas and ballet and that's more than enough.* But I still didn't understand. If she didn't need a king, why did I need a prince? She told me I didn't. *Don't be stupid, Elloula. You can be alone if you want but when you find a guy like Ethan, you've got a much better shot at the bullseye.* I asked her what that meant, what the bullseye was, and she said, *Everything you've ever wanted and not a single thing more.*

I will always remember that conversation. It makes me sad at times, knowing that Mama never hit the bullseye. But she never made us feel bad about it. She always celebrated what she had. And I know that's the best way to live.

I dance with Mama and Ethan. I look at the clock and feel my adrenaline rise with the beat of the music. There's not much time before I have to prepare for the recital. Get everything ready with Ethan. Surprise Mama and make her feel like, at least in that moment, she really hit the bullseye.

I'm all dressed up, in my black leotard, soft pink tights, and pressed-back bun. It's the same outfit I've worn for every show of my life, but this one feels different. This time I won't be on stage. This show, I share with Mama.

I examine myself, wondering how Mama will feel in my body. She's been weak for so long. Unable to dance in the living room on Sunday mornings, practice her routines, or, toward the end, even get out of bed without assistance. Aside from her children, Mama's whole life is dancing. Like me, she's been a ballerina since she was little, but unlike me she found her calling all on her own. Mama put Loukas and me in ballet shoes before we were able to say whether we wanted to dance or not. As we got older, I chose to keep with it and Loukas went on to pursue other passions. But Mama always proudly tells people how she danced before she even knew it was dancing. She is a ballerina at heart. She's filled with spirit, but her spirit soars when she's dancing on stage. I love ballet, but it doesn't compare to Mama's love. She's the greatest ballerina I've ever seen, including the videos of famous ballet dancers from the past. They all seem to pale in comparison to Mama. Anyone who sees her dance live is completely compelled by her. She's the main reason ballet has soared in popularity in the last two decades. People of all Groups, rich and poor, flocked to see Mama dance. She lifted people out of their seats. She made audience members cry with joy. It's how Mama first made a man from Group1 fall in love with her; it's how she met my father.

When Mama moved back to Group7 after my parents divorced, some of that popularity fizzled. People in Group1 and 2 felt personally offended. It was seen as completely radical, choosing to leave all the gifts Ameca had given her to go back to an impoverished life. The lower-status Groups idolized her for making this decision, but many didn't have the money to go to her shows. Mama's life changed when she left Group1. She lost all of the glamour tied to her success and a large portion of her fanbase, but she never lost her love of dance. That remained constant. She kept performing and people kept coming. It's rare to have any sort of fame or success in Group7. But Mama has always been an anomaly.

When I think of Mama's relationship with ballet, the first word that comes to mind is "life." Her performances make audience members feel on top of the world, but most importantly, Mama never feels more alive than when she is on stage.

The day Mama's Countdown began, she had to pack her things and say goodbye to her studio. That's the law. Once your Countdown begins, it's illegal to work. That meant the last time Mama danced in front of an audience or even taught her students ballet, she had no idea it was going to be the last time. She wasn't able to say goodbye to one of the things she loves most in life. She had no closure. That's why we're taking this risk. That's why Ethan was okay with it. Tonight, Mama will dance her final number. The audience will be amazed once more. I'll be able to return to Mama the greatest gift she ever gave to me—life.

It's not uncommon for people to switch bodies during their Countdown. People in Group5, 6, and 7 typically can't afford it, but the government has many different Explore options. One of the most popular ones is the Pre-Departure package, where people who are dying can live in any body, move from one to another, and experience any type of life they wish before they die. It's marketed to be the ultimate experience because it allows people to live their most exciting life right before they die. It also allows them to leave their body, escape the physical pain, and give it to someone else, namely, prisoners. The dying Group member can experience a pain-free Countdown right until their final breath. When the Group member finally dies, their physical body deteriorates along with their Essence. Even if the Group member is in another body at the time of their death, when a person's physical body dies, their Essence dies with it. The prisoner's Essence—which was inhabiting the high-status Group member's body—returns to its original body, and the cycle begins again. The prisoner waits for the next agonizing switch.

The Ameca government needs prisoners to keep the Explore programs running. The government terrifies its citizens into obeying the law by sending anyone who steps out of line to prison but relies on people misbehaving as well. In order for society to run smoothly, the government makes it difficult for people in low-status Groups to survive without breaking the law. When money is short and death rates are high, people become desperate. The government knows this. They created the problem. For as long as Ameca has profited from Essence, people like me fill their prisons, or Camps, as they're more typically called. It's a messed-up system, but it works without fail. Many Amecans who become prisoners end up spending their days in other people's bodies; they experience someone else's Countdown—someone else's agony. They live in one dying body and then move on to the next.

Camps are usually in remote areas. Once a person is sent to one, they are not seen for twenty-five years. No matter what the crime is the sentence remains the same. Many of them never return. Those who are lucky enough to come home aren't allowed to talk about their time away; it's against the law and nobody is less likely to break the law than an ex-prisoner. Because of this, everything that anyone thinks they know is based on stories and rumors.

The most common prisons are Work Camps, but some Camps are more specialized. Instead of factory work, prisoners are sent to Resort Camps. This is where rich people go on holidays to escape from real life and Explore in young, healthy bodies. It's unclear exactly what happens at these Resorts, but it's known to be unpleasant. All Camps are bad, really. We don't know much about what happens, but the only thing we know for sure is that their lives are demanding. And the likelihood of death is high.

The Pre-Departure package can last anywhere from one day to the entire one hundred days. People save up for their Countdown their whole lives, ideally saving up enough to experience the Explore program for all one hundred days. Ethan thinks that's why the Countdown is known to be so excruciating. People become so weak and tired of the pain, that they're desperate to pay for the best Pre-Departure package. Mama doesn't agree with Exploring. None of us do, really. Growing up in 7N, I've known many good people who were taken as prisoners. Loukas, my own brother, included. So, the idea of paying to pass the burden of your suffering onto someone else, who likely is innocent of any real crime, is immoral. It's not something my family could stomach. Even if there was a feasible option, even if we pooled our money together to afford one day of the Explore Program, Mama wouldn't take it. She'd rather endure one hundred days of this herself.

Hacking was the only option I had to give Mama one last opportunity to feel alive. It feels like the least I can do. I know she would be mad at me if she knew the risk I was taking, but that's because she's so selfless.

It will all be worth it in the end. I know it. I can feel it in my heart.

I remind myself of this as the lights turn off onstage. The dancers are in place and I'm center stage. I stand, strong, in my pose and lift my head high. I breathe deeply, trying to calm my racing heart. I know that at any moment, Ethan will Hack my body. Put Mama in my place. I'm filled with nerves but also exhilarated.

The next moment, I'm struck by pain. My body feels stiff and full of aches. I'm sitting down now; I'm in a chair. I look at my skin, my hands, and my legs. I'm in my favorite person's body. I am Mama.

CHAPTER 7

I can't believe I'm in Mama's body. I can't believe how much everything hurts. I've heard so many things about how agonizing the Countdown is, but never from Mama. She didn't complain once. It's hard for me to move my head and look up at the stage, but I know I must. I want to cry, unsure of whether it's from the agony I'm feeling or the knowledge that Mama felt this for the last ninety-nine days. I slowly lift my head, catching Mama's eyes in my body, on stage. Mama can't believe it. I can't quite make out the look on her face with the lights off, but I can sense it in the way she stands. She's elated. Terrified. In disbelief. The lights go on and the music begins. Mama knows the show from beginning to end, possibly better than me. She'd been preparing me for it all year. We spent hours together, choreographing the dances and perfecting the routines.

The show begins and Mama soars across the stage. She is fully alert, moving with power and grace. She commands the stage, as she always has, but she's in my body this time. I'm amazed by what she can do. She leaps higher than I've ever managed. Her spins are solid, firm, beautiful. She moves my body like she's always known it. Like it's hers. The dance numbers change, the story progresses, and Mama demands the audience's attention the whole time. I'm completely still the entire way through, utterly in awe of my mother. It might be her best performance ever. She hits every move with careful appreciation like she's writing a love letter to a body that does not ache. A body that obeys her desires. And her spirit envelops the room. Not a person moves in the audience. I can feel her passion from my seat. I know everyone in the room is amazed.

As the show comes to an end, Mama veers away from the practiced movements. She knows the music well and she's a brilliant choreographer, so everything feels right. Everything feels natural.

Mama's dancing is not the same as what we'd practiced, but it's not unfamiliar either. I know I've seen it somewhere. Somewhere with Mama. And then I realize it's from her clips. It was one of Mama's favorite dances. The first time she ever received a standing ovation. It was her first solo, and the first time she realized she could make this her career. She was only sixteen when that happened—the same age as me.

It's a little risky, changing the routine, but it makes me happy because I know this means Mama is in the moment. She's not thinking about the possible repercussions. She's finally free of worries, at least temporarily. She's completely present.

When the performance ends, the audience erupts. I know there are only seconds left before I will return to my body and Mama will return to hers. Jocelyn, one of Mama's friends, quickly unlocks the wheelchair and pushes me through the crowds as fast as she can. She brings me backstage, to Ethan and my mom. The moment we make eye contact, Mama cries.

"I can't believe you," Mama says. I can tell she wants to be angry, but she's too overjoyed. The rush of the show woke her up in a way I haven't seen in years. I know in that moment that despite the risk, despite any consequences, it was worth it. "Do you know what they can do to you?"

"It's okay, Mama," I wish I felt as confident as I try to seem. "I'm here with you. I'm fine."

This seems to relax her a bit. She lets out the smile that's been trying to escape.

"You were amazing," I tell her. "Did you see the crowd at the end? They exploded."

"Oh, Elloula. It was truly a gift."

Hearing her say this warms my heart. She bends down to reach me and the two of us hug, my body and hers connecting in a way we've never experienced. I am her and she is me. For the first time, I feel what Mama's felt when she's hugged me all these years. I can tell that both of us are thinking this. We hug a little longer and I try not to cry. I try not to think about how many hugs I have left. I don't want to let go of this one; I don't want my mom to go back into her slow, aching body. But before our hug ends, I'm on the other side. I'm strong and solid and familiar. This is the hug I've always known. I want to squeeze Mama a little tighter, let her know how sorry I am for the pain that I've now shared, but before I can do this I'm pulled away.

I am slammed against the floor and dragged by two hands that are cutting into my skin. I hear Mama shriek. Ethan's trying to fight the people off.

"Get off of her!" It's Mama. "Take me!"

But I know they won't do that. There's no use in taking Mama. She'll be dead tomorrow.

I use all my strength to try to get up from the floor, but the best I can do is lift my head an inch. I'm able to see Ethan pinned up against a wall. His hands and legs are being chained together. He's trying to break free but the force of two full-grown Officials is keeping him from me.

Mama is gone. I didn't know this would happen, but I prepared for the possibility. I told Jocelyn to wheel Mama away if anything bad happened. I didn't want her last memories to be of this. I know Jocelyn did what I told her to do. I've known Jocelyn for most of my life. Her daughter dances at our studio and she's Mama's closest friend. When I asked her to help me with something for Mama, she didn't question it.

The further I am dragged, the clearer it becomes that there's no getting out of this now. I'm going wherever these men take me. I have a flashback to them taking Loukas. I remember how terrifying it felt being on the other side. I hope Mama knows not to worry. Not on her last day. But I know she is, and the thought breaks my heart. All I want is a moment to say goodbye to Ethan—to give him a message for Mama. I fight for this moment, using all of my strength to kick down the man yanking me. I kick him in the shins, and he stumbles for a moment. The two men on Ethan run to contain me. Ethan's free and he moves toward me, still in chains. I scream to him, "Tell Mama I'm okay!"

He nods, promising that he will. Then he responds with words I'll repeat in my mind, over and over. "I love you, Ellie. Don't give up. I'm going to get you out."

Before I can respond, a man takes hold of my head. He smashes it to the ground, once, twice, and again, until everything fades.

CHAPTER 8

When I wake up, I feel a throbbing pain in my head. I am groggy and unsettled, but, slowly, the recital comes back to me. I remember being knocked down and dragged away. I remember Mama's scream. I think of Mama now. I'll never see her again. But how did the Officials know to come find us? How did they realize our crime? Ethan and I had been so careful. We did everything we could to keep the Officials away. And still, it wasn't enough.

All of the sudden, there's a thud and I jolt forward. My stomach presses against something hard. I realize my head's resting on a table, which now rattles violently against my cheek. The unpleasantness sends me upright, and I notice that I'm moving. I'm not being dragged and there's no one around me. This time, I'm moving in a vehicle. In a railcar of some kind, I think.

I look out the window and realize I'm on a train. It looks long; I can't see the end on either side. It's made of materials that are unknown to me. Everything is silver and sleek, nothing like what I'm familiar with from home. There's only one chair in my car, where I am sitting, and a bed across from me. The car is filled with silver cupboards and stainless-steel doors. I get up from my seat, curious about what's around me. I open the cupboards. They're filled with clothing, makeup, and hair products. I haven't seen any of these products before. They seem expensive. Based on the images and descriptions I kind of understand what they're for, but I'm not sure what I'm supposed to make of them. Am I supposed to get dressed up? Do my hair and makeup? For what? For whom? I'm too freaked out to think about it any longer, so I shut the cupboards. There are only two doors left that I haven't opened. One leads to a bathroom and the other is locked. There's no way to open it. I realize I'm stuck in this railcar. It's pretty small, almost like a cage, and for a terrible moment, I wonder if this is my prison.

I sit in the chair and look out the window. There's nothing to do but think.

When I was little, Mama prayed with Loukas and me when we were scared. I never really continued when I got older, but all I can think to do now is pray. I don't know how much time has passed. I don't know if Mama's still alive. But I pray that her departure was peaceful. I pray that, if she's still alive now, she's not in agony thinking about me or fearing the end of her life. I hope that Ethan was able to sleep at my house and spend Mama's last moments with her. But then I think that maybe Ethan's in trouble too. He broke the law with me. He was the one Hacking. He was caught and tied down by the police. But they were only dragging one of us. Why were they only dragging one of us? Did they get to Ethan after me? Is he somewhere else on this train?

I immediately dismiss the thought. It's too much. I need to believe that Ethan is safe. Maybe they were only coming after me. I tell myself that Ethan is home—that he's with Mama.

Ethan and Mama have always had a strong relationship. Plus, Ethan has a knack for calming people down. I know that Mama is being well taken care of if he's with her. But that thought, too, brings me to tears, and I can't cry right now. There's a possibility that someone will open the railcar door at any moment. I don't want them to see me cry. Not when they're about to determine my destiny. I try to think of something else, something happier.

My mind goes back to my last moments with Ethan. The way he said, "I love you." What did he mean? Could he already be in love with me, or did he just mean "I love you" the way he always used to mean it? We only kissed that one night. It's not like everything is different now. But then I think about the way I felt when he kissed me... it was definitely different. Was that *love*? I have no idea. And I'll probably never experience that feeling again. I try to ease my worries with Ethan's words, *don't give up. I'm going to get you out.* I need to believe them.

The train comes to a stop. I look out the window, but it's unclear where we are. It's nowhere I've ever been. The houses have yards here, but the roads are still covered in potholes. There aren't many cars, but it looks like some people own them. It's different from 7N, but it's not luxurious. I figure it's a neighborhood with mostly Group5s or 6s, but I'm not sure where. The landscape is greener than home. More hilly. Before I can make any more observations, somebody opens my door.

I'm startled, but I stop myself from jolting up. A woman with platinum blonde hair and gray eyes is looking at me. Her skin is radiant and her lips are bright red. Not a strand of her pinned-back hair is out of place. She's looking at me like I've already failed.

"Eliana Sagona," the woman says, and I try not to seem surprised that she knows my name. She's eyeing me up and down. I sit up straighter and cross my legs. "You haven't touched your possessions."

I'm not sure what she means by this, so I just stare at her blankly. Thankfully she explains, "Your clothing, makeup, and hair supplies. We saw that you looked through them, but you haven't put on anything." What does she mean they *saw*? Have they been spying on me?

"I didn't know what to do with them." I stop myself from saying more. I must seem like such an idiot. The truth is I couldn't care less about makeup and hair supplies. The only time I put on makeup is for performances. Any other time, the most I do is put my hair in a pony and quickly apply mascara. If I'm going out, I'll add some lip gloss and maybe blush, but I have no idea how to do anything else. I don't want to say any of this, because I know it will make the woman angrier. I don't know who she is, but I get the sense I need to impress her. I wait for her to speak.

The woman comes closer and puts her hands through my hair, brushing through my tangled bun. "Your hair is nice and thick." Then she makes a noise of disapproval. "When was the last time you brushed it?"

I want to tell her I'm not sure. It's still in the bun from the performance. I haven't done anything to it since I woke up on the train, but I have no idea how long I was knocked out for. "Not since yesterday," I say, hoping this is true.

"Yesterday?" You've been out cold for three days."

I'm shocked by this news. *Three days.* That means Mama must be gone... my heart drops as I realize this. I'm living in a world without Mama. At some point, while I was unconscious, Mama took her last breath. I pray that she wasn't alone. I pray that Ethan was with her, showing her love and compassion, the way I know he would. The woman is talking, but I can't make out her words. I do everything I can to hold back tears. The woman slams her hand on the window to get my attention. I snap back to reality.

"Stand up."

I listen. The woman looks me over, scowling. "They're right to say you're very beautiful. With some eye makeup, some contouring, highlighting... your face could be very striking." I have no idea what she's saying. "But you're lazy. You don't take care of yourself."

"I think I do. I just need to be conscious to brush my hair."

She gives me a look of warning. "And that attitude of yours." She sighs, already discouraged.

I fight the urge to respond. I want to tell her that there are more ways to take care of yourself than applying makeup and doing your hair. I want to tell her that when you're from Group7, when your brother has been kidnapped, and when your mother is dying, or now *dead*, taking care of yourself isn't a priority. But I stay silent. I know that's the best thing to do.

The woman is still examining me. She asks me to turn for her. I do a turn, but it's too fast. She asks me to do it again, moving slower this time so she can examine every inch of me.

She asks me to touch my toes. I bend down and touch them. It's a stretch I'm very familiar with. I do it before and after dance every day. But I've never had anyone behind me, assessing what I look like. I immediately wish I was wearing something less tight.

She asks me to release my hair from its bun, tuck it behind my ears, and smile. I obey every order. I try to make my smile seem real. After

I've done everything she asks of me, she says, "Very well." I feel completely violated, but I try to look unconcerned. She stops at the door and looks back at me. "I'll be back at the same time tomorrow. I expect you to be looking your best."

I nod, faking confidence. I have until tomorrow to figure out how to "contour" my face.

CHAPTER 9

The next day, the first thing I do is go through the drawers. I need help if I'm going to figure this out. Beyond the makeup and clothing options, there are also how-to books. I find a book that's called *Glow Up for Beginners* and I decide it's my best bet. Anything with the word beginner in it is a good place to start. The book tells me that if I want to "look like my most radiant self," the first thing I need to do is wash my face. Easy enough. I go through the basket of skin care products and realize there are more than twenty options. I almost laugh. I have no concept of how so many products can exist when they all seem to be achieving the same goal. Couldn't I just use soap? I sift through the options, trying to figure out the difference. I find something that looks simple and safe. I have no idea if my skin is oily or dry, but the one I pick works for all skin types. I rinse with water and then apply the wash. It burns my skin a little, but it feels kind of nice.

Once I'm done rinsing my face and gently "patting" it dry, I move on to the next step. I follow the book's instructions carefully. I apply foundation and tap concealer below my eyes until it looks "blemish-free." Contouring is a lot more difficult than I hoped it would be, but I try my best to follow the directions, giving myself defined cheek lines to "enhance the shape of my face." When I finish contouring, I get a good look at myself in the mirror. I am horrified. I look like an antelope.

The eye makeup is equally daunting. I need to make sure my hand stays steady to apply a clean stroke of eyeliner, but it's not something I'm used to doing. I fail the first three times, either making it too thick or too wobbly, so I remove the makeup and try again. Finally, I get a clean line I'm satisfied with and move on to the mascara. The last thing I do is my lips. I find a color that looks pretty in its case. It's a light, peachy pink with a glossy shine. I feel like the woman in the suit will like it. Or at least I hope she will.

After finally finishing my makeup, I go to the closet to pick out an outfit. There are so many options. I have no idea where to begin. There are fancy dresses, casual tops, and everything in between. There are accessories I have no idea how to handle, like scarves and hair ties, and then there are simpler items like black and blue jeans. But even the jeans are confusing. Half of them look identical to me. I decide to wear straight-leg black pants with a nice blue blouse. I have no idea if that's the right call, but it feels safe. And right now, with my knowledge, safe feels like the best option.

When I'm finally done, I'm too afraid to look in the mirror. I don't want to look at myself. I know I'll look ridiculous and foreign. Instead, I sit down in the train car's single seat and wait. I have no idea how long it will be until the woman returns, but at least I'm ready. And hopefully, my makeup will stay fresh. I'm horrified as soon as I have this thought. As if these are the things I'm worried about now. So, what if my makeup starts fading? Why should that even matter? Mama is dead.

My mind wanders until I hear someone coming toward my railcar. I stiffen in my seat. And then, just like the first time, the woman enters unannounced. She doesn't say hello or greet me; she simply starts to look me over. I stand up before she asks.

"Interesting outfit," she says. "The blue top doesn't suit the black bottom. The pants are a good fit. They suit you." I'm happy about the compliment. "But that top... I wouldn't wear that. Especially not without an accessory. You're too warm."

"Actually, I'm kind of cold," I say, confused as to why she mentions this. "Should I have paired it with a sweater?"

The woman snorts. I don't know what to do, so I just stare. "That's not what I meant," she says. "I was talking about your skin tone." She laughs again. I try not to feel humiliated. It's not my fault I'm learning about this for the first time. "The blue you've picked doesn't suit you. You need a warmer blue."

I nod even though I have no idea what that means.

"And speaking of tones," she continues, "your lip color is all wrong. You need a darker shade. A dark red—something with browns. Look for a book on shade and color selection. You need it."

"Okay," I say, making a mental note.

"And your eye makeup is sloppy. I can tell you made mistakes." The woman looks me over one last time and then folds her arms as if to say *that's all.* "I'd like you to try to look more formal tomorrow. And give more of an effort, will you?"

"Sure," I say, even though I feel like I already tried my best. The woman presses her finger against a small button on the wall, opening up a hidden door. It closes immediately after she exits. I quickly get up to examine the button. I put my finger over it, but nothing happens. I'm not surprised. It must use fingerprint authentication. There's no way for me to get out. I sit back down, defeated. I wash the makeup off and change into comfortable clothes. I know I should spend the rest of the day practicing my beauty routine, but I need to take a break. I close my eyes and rest. Somehow, I'll do better tomorrow.

The same thing happens every day for the next few weeks. Maybe it's been a month by now. I've lost track of time. I've learned that the woman's name is Lilith and she hates me. A lot. It took longer than she wanted for me to figure out how to look "adequate." She thinks I'm arrogant and that I feel like I'm better than her, which I guess is true. It's hard not to think I'm better than a cold-hearted authority figure with superficial demands.

We've been traveling in every direction on this stupid train; one moment the train's heading north and the next, we're headed south, going back to a point we'd been only two nights before. My days feel meaningless. I alternate from feeling incredibly sad to incredibly bored. At times, I'm convinced this train is my prison and that I won't be going anywhere else. But I know that's not true. I know they'll want to use my body somehow. Every night at the same time, a few hours after a tray of dinner is delivered to my car, the train stops. It stops for what feels like a night. Maybe this is when the driver sleeps and the Officials run into the darkness to find their new body... new prisoner... new victim to join me on the train.

I've used these late-night stops to track the days. By the twentieth day, though, I stopped counting. At some point, I realize, my birthday must have passed. I'm not sure which day it was, it doesn't really matter, but I wonder how I would have celebrated if circumstances were different. In a dream world, Loukas and I would have celebrated together. It was our sixteenth birthday. Maybe we would have spent the night with friends—Loukas would have been the life of the party and I would have been off in a corner, talking to Ethan. I would have left my own party early and walked home with my best friend. Maybe we would have watched a movie with Mama or played a game of cards. Either way, it would have been nice. Whatever we did, it would have been special, just to have everyone together. My heart sinks, realizing I'll never have another birthday like that. Mama is gone. I may never see Ethan again. Loukas is in prison and I'm about to be in prison, too. There's really no point in thinking about my birthday or trying to figure out how many days have passed since I turned sixteen. None of this really matters anymore. I'm stuck on this stupid train, and I won't be celebrating any time soon.

I spend most of my time thinking of home. I miss Mama and Ethan so much. It's hard to distract myself when I'm stuck in this small railcar with nothing to do but read or watch videos about makeup. Every time I remember Mama is gone, I can't help but cry. I go into the bathroom, curl up into a ball, and cry until there are no tears left. I hope there are no cameras in there. I don't want the Officials to see me that way. I wish I could be with Ethan or Loukas, to make the devastation I'm feeling a little easier to manage. I grow more numb to Mama's death with each day that passes, but it still isn't easy. I'm so lonely. I need to get off this train.

And yet, as much as I resent being on here, I know it's about to get worse. My railcar is small, but there's enough space for me. There's a bed for me to sleep in, a table for me to eat at, a bathroom, and even a painting on the wall. It's a small car, but I'm used to living in tight spaces. It's kind of surprising that everything is so well-kept because I don't see any reason why the government spends all this money on a train transporting prisoners. Loukas always said not to question the ways of the rich. They don't need a reason to spend money, he used to say, they just like wasting it.

Lilith visits my railcar every day. The only thing good about her visits is that they make me certain that I'm on this train for a reason. If I weren't getting off, there'd be no reason for me to learn how to look "beautiful." About a week ago, Lilith came in and investigated my body for "trouble spots."

"What are you looking for?" I asked her.

She glared. "Anything noticeably unattractive."

Lilith found a scar on my left elbow. I got the scar when I was little, falling out of a tree I was climbing with Ethan. It's a happy memory and I rarely noticed the scar, but Lilith told me it had to be removed. She gave me a cream to apply to the area, and after only two treatments, the scar was completely gone. I looked at my elbow in awe, wondering how a scar that I'd had since I was seven could disappear, just like that. I felt a sense of loss, feeling like I was leaving another piece of my old life behind, but Lilith seemed satisfied.

"That cleared up nicely," she said, examining my new elbow. And that was that.

I don't know if this is something to be proud of, but I'm starting to figure out my beauty routine. At the beginning, Lilith would always have something to critique. *Part your hair to the other side,* she'd say, or *That foundation's too light for your skin tone,* or *Please do something with your brows.* I found a digital book in one of the drawers that's filled with videos on how to look your best. It's much better than the first book. I've watched every makeup and hair tutorial in it. I learned how to apply eyeliner with precision, subtly cover any blemish on my skin, and pluck and shape my eyebrows to perfection. It's the only source of entertainment I have, but more importantly, I get the sense that my livelihood depends on my appearance now. I don't know specifics, but based on Lilith's interests, the government seems to be invested in making me look good. It's going to help me get off this train and hopefully lead me somewhere safe. Somewhere relatively safe at least. I hope.

Lilith rarely compliments me, but she no longer has many notes. The other day she came into the car holding a beautiful necklace. It was golden with a large yellow stone dangling from the center. It looked more expensive than anything I'd ever seen and from what I've learned in the tutorials, the color would have perfectly brought out the honey tones in my eyes. Lilith handed me the necklace and asked me to try it on.

I knew what she was doing—she was trying to get me to remove my mother's necklace—but it wouldn't work. Every day, she's asked me to take off my necklace, and every day I find a new way to say no. I ignore her, pretending to be unaware of her objective. I put the gold necklace on top of the one from my mother. It was as beautiful as I expected. My eyes glistened and I looked way more elegant than I ever believed I could look. "It's gorgeous," I told Lilith.

"Don't be daft," she said. "Take off your other necklace. You can't wear it like that."

I shook my head, but she already knew I'd resist. "Sorry, Lilith," I said, more for my own satisfaction than hers.

"Do you have any idea how much this necklace costs?"

"No," I told her, and I honestly had no idea. We have nothing extravagant like it in 7N. I could probably sell it in exchange for a different life. If I had the money to buy a necklace like that, I wouldn't be on this train. My mom would have never had a premature Countdown. I'd be home with Ethan and Loukas and a healthy mother if I owned that necklace. I didn't say any of this out loud, but Lilith could sense it on my face.

She looked at me, disgusted. "You're a waste of beauty. Do you have any idea how well you could do if you learned to be more grateful?"

I wondered what I was supposed to be grateful for. A necklace that I don't even want? Nice clothes I'm being forced to wear? Makeup and hairstyling tips that waste hours of my life every day? A body that's been objectified every moment since stepping on this train? I try to think of something else, realizing the scowl on my face is only angering Lilith more.

Lilith eventually gave up, grabbing the new necklace and putting it back in its case. I wonder if she would have let me keep it if I'd taken my other necklace off. I have a feeling she wouldn't. It was only a taunt. A new tactic to try to get her way.

Every day Lilith asks me to take off my mother's necklace, but I refuse. I've tried explaining to her that the necklace was Mama's. Being from Group7, it's the only piece of jewelry I ever saw before getting on the train. It was Mama's most prized possession. When her Countdown began, it was the first thing Mama gave me. I didn't want to take it at first. I'd never seen it off her neck. But I took it to make her happy. She wanted to know that after she went, the necklace would still be loved. And I wasn't about to let Lilith keep this from happening.

Today, Lilith tries a different tactic. She enters my car with something in her hands. It's a dress. It's on a hanger wrapped in plastic.

"Today's a big day," she tells me.

"What's going on?"

"Well, I'll let you know as soon as you take that necklace off."

"Lilith. I told you. I won't."

Lilith makes a noise. I don't say anything.

When I first said no to Lilith about the necklace, it was an instinct. I immediately panicked, thinking it would lead me to a much less pleasant imprisonment. But nothing happened. And every day she's asked me since Lilith's become more frustrated, but nothing has changed. I'm starting to think Lilith doesn't have the power I'd once assumed.

"You know, today can go two ways. You can listen to me and get off this train... or you can get comfortable because you won't be getting off any time soon."

I have a feeling it's an empty threat. If Lilith really had a say in things, I don't think I'd be getting off the train today in any case. She hates me too much. But there's a chance she really does have power. I think about the way she's probably been watching me on the camera feed, and the authority she has in her speech and movements. Maybe this really *is* my last chance.

"I'm willing to do anything else, Lilith." I start, not knowing what I'm going to say. "But this necklace is all I have of my mom. Don't you understand that? I can't take it off."

"You are completely ungrateful," she says, furious. "Do you have any idea what they could do to you? What kind of prisons are out there? It's in your best interest to behave. Don't you get that?"

"I do," I say. She's referring to the Work Camps. The prisoners who get sent there spend their days in dying bodies. I only know the rumors, but I've heard that Work Camps are the worst place to be. Only people who "really deserve it" get sent there; at least that's what the government says. Prisoners work long hours, usually in a factory, so that goods for Group1 can be manufactured cheaply. It sounds like the worst kind of torture. Thinking about the pain Mama experienced, it's hard to imagine prisoners having to work in that condition. Not everyone believes the rumors about Work Camps, but I think they're true. Lilith is certainly alluding to that now.

"I've worked my whole life," I tell Lilith.

"Not like that you haven't," she says, and of course I know she's right. "It's nothing like 7."

"What do you know about Group7?"

"I'd watch your mouth if I were you."

"I'm just asking," I say, but I try to cool down. She's right. I need to stay calm.

"You know," Lilith says, her bottom lip curling to a smirk, "I didn't know what you'd be like at first, but you're just like your brother. Loukas."

CHAPTER 10

I freeze. My brother? How does Lilith know my brother?

It's the first time Lilith has mentioned Loukas. I shouldn't be surprised, but I hadn't considered she might know him. Does Lilith know where he is? Was he on this train at some point? Did she know him personally? I have so many questions.

"That's right," Lilith continues, her grin growing wider now. "I know where he is right now."

"Where is he?" My voice comes out hoarse. I can't contain myself at this point. I need to know.

"Let's just say he got what he asked for."

I lose my ability to breathe. I've always been bothered by the horror stories about Work Camps, but I never thought that's where Loukas would go. He's too smart. I think back to Lilith's implications moments earlier, about how if I looked differently I'd be sent to a Work Camp. Did she mean that literally? Is that where Loukas is right now? "Is he alive?" I ask, pleading for her to tell me more. "Is he okay?"

"Don't be stupid." She looks away and finds the mirror, examining her reflection. She tends to a kink in her otherwise perfectly gelled hair. She is letting me know the conversation is over. But the conversation isn't over for me. I ask her again, "Is he still alive? What are you doing to him?"

"If you and your brother had obeyed the *law*, neither of you would be in this position." She states this as a matter of fact. When she finally makes eye contact, there's a warning in her eyes. "Now," she speaks slowly, "take that necklace off."

I wonder how much it matters whether this necklace stays on me or not. I think Lilith is just not accustomed to people saying no to her. At this point, I'm too angry about Loukas to think straight. If she's not going to comply with me, I won't comply with her.

"No. Take me wherever you need to take me. I don't care anymore. I'm not taking my necklace off."

Lilith's expression drops. Maybe she's finally realized she's lost this battle. She doesn't say anything, just angrily removes the dress from its plastic and hands it to me. "Put this on."

I look it over, wondering if I should even bother dressing. It's a deep blue dress. Perfect for my skin tone, or so I've learned. It's not as fancy as some of the other dresses in my closet, but it's nicer than anything I've ever worn. I feel the fabric and can hardly believe it. It's so soft. I didn't know clothing could be this soft.

Lilith clears her throat. She wants me to put it on now. I head to the bathroom, but she stops me. "No," she says. "Put it on here."

I don't like the idea of changing in front of her, but I also don't care that much at this point. Lilith, and whoever else, has been watching me on the camera feed for weeks. I have no privacy here. I slip my clothes off and put on the dress. I'm amazed by how it feels. The dress is tight and smooth on my skin. It feels soft and light, almost like I'm wearing nothing. When I look in the mirror, I can hardly recognize myself. The dress is luxurious. Between the outfit, makeup, and hair, I don't look anything like myself. I look like the Group1 girls I've seen in movies and magazines. I once thought they were so beautiful, but when I stare at my reflection, I feel disgusting. I wish I could take off the makeup and get into sweatpants. I wish I could never look in the mirror again. I feel like I've betrayed myself. Betrayed my Group.

"Smile," Lilith commands. My repulsed expression has angered her.

"I don't want to wear this. Can I take it off now?"

"You idiot. You think you can wear just anything to the Cube?"

"What's the Cube?"

Lilith looks aghast. I don't think she was supposed to say that. "You'll find out soon enough. Just keep your mouth *shut* or you'll be going somewhere else."

"I know that's not true," I tell her, still feeling angry about what she said about Loukas. "If you had any power, you would have sent me elsewhere already. But I'm still here, aren't I?"

Lilith doesn't speak for a moment. I know I've said too much. A creepy grin takes over her face when she finally looks up at me. "Oh, sweetheart, you think you're *so* special, but you're not lasting one second at the Cube. You're arrogant and disrespectful, and the only thing keeping you alive is your looks. But there are lots of pretty girls at the Cube. Don't you forget that. There's no way you're lasting one day."

"Well, I guess we're going to have to wait and see," I tell her, but I can't help but feel scared. Lilith might not have much power herself, but there are plenty of Government Officials who do. Maybe she's right. Maybe I need to start learning how to keep my mouth shut. If I want to get out alive and find Loukas and Ethan, I'm going to need to smarten up.

The next morning, I wake up to the sound of Lilith's scream. "What are you doing?" She's asking me. I look at her confused. Is this still a dream? Before I can respond, she yanks me out of bed. "Oh my god, Cordelia's going to be here any minute. Why aren't you ready?"

"Ready for what?"

"Did I not make myself clear last night? You're getting off the train."

"What?" I blink a few times to try to wake up. "Now?"

"Yes!" Lilith says. "Do you know how stupid I'm going to look if you're not ready?" She pushes me into the bathroom. "Go! Fast!"

I hurry, grabbing the makeup and hair supplies I need. As quickly as I can move, whilst also maintaining precision, I follow my morning routine. I skip as many steps as I can without interfering with the overall look. My hair is still smooth from washing it yesterday, so I don't have to do much to get it to where it needs to be. I apply a deep red lip gloss that Lilith approves of and put on the blue dress Lilith brought me yesterday. I choose a brown-red blush that complements this color and apply it very lightly. I'm pleased with how quickly I'm able to do my eyeliner, still managing to get the clean line I know they'll be looking for. When everything is as it needs to be, I look in the mirror of my well-lit bathroom and try to accept the reflection in front of me. I look the part, that's for sure, but I still don't like it. My lips seem too intense, my eyes too dramatic, and the natural glow I once had from the sun has now been replaced with blush and bronzer. The train comes to a complete stop. I get my things together and leave the bathroom.

When I meet Lilith's eyes, she stares at me.

"What?" I ask. If I've done something wrong, I need to know now. There's no time left.

But Lilith doesn't have anything bad to say. "Nothing," she says, almost annoyed. Then snaps back to her usual stern self. "Follow me. We need to go *now.*"

Lilith uses her fingerprint to slide open the railcar door. I've watched her do this every day I've been on the train, but this is the first time I'm permitted to follow her. The other side leads to an open area with tables and chairs. It's an adjoining car. I wonder how many times Lilith has sat there eating her lunch while I was right there, on the other side. We walk past and get to another set of doors. These doors face the other direction. They are larger and more intricately designed. I hold my breath and try not to show my eagerness, but I can't help myself. I've finally made it. These doors lead outside. My heart leaps as Lilith uses her fingerprint once more. When the door opens, I take a deep breath of the fresh, morning air. I feel free.

Outside, there are large entrance gates and a long black fence, where a small group of people is waiting. I briefly examine the people. They look young, roughly my age, and every one of them is beautiful. Across from the group, another woman stands, wearing the same burgundy blazer as Lilith. It's the first time I've breathed fresh air in a long time. I let out a sigh of relief.

I step outside the train with Lilith and give her one last look. I won't miss her, but it feels weird to be saying goodbye. She's the only human I've interacted with in so long. It seems Lilith couldn't care less because she barely looks at me. "Very well," she says. "Cordelia's waiting. Go on."

I walk away and head toward the other woman in a slightly more form-fitted burgundy vest, Cordelia. I can't help but feel elated by the fresh air and the sun's warmth on my skin. I don't know where I am and I try to remember that I'm a prisoner, but I can't help but feel free.

Cordelia looks at me, returning my happy expression. "It's beautiful here, isn't it?"

"Yes."

I feel safe for a moment, but then Cordelia makes an impatient sound through her aggressively cheerful smile. "All right," she says, "Would you mind getting in line with the others?" A group of people is standing in a line across from me. They're prisoners, I assume, each of them more beautiful than the next. I join them at the end of the line. Cordelia clears her throat. I stand up straight and listen.

"Now that we're all here," Cordelia says, "there's lots to discuss. The first thing I want to do is congratulate all of you for being here. The government is exceptionally generous with the Cube. We don't even call this place a 'prison.'" She whispers the word and puts air quotes around it. "It's more of a Resort. I'm sure you will all be amazed by the opulence of the Cube. It's quite extravagant, as you can see. We are the only Resort that's minutes away from Ace City, so we truly are the cream of the crop. It's quite an exciting place to be, especially for folks like you, who might not be accustomed to this luxury." Cordelia's disturbingly happy face magnifies. I can already tell she's intolerable. I'm struck with an unexpected feeling of missing Lilith. At least she wasn't so fake.

Cordelia's grin turns to a pout. "But before I can welcome *all* of you, I have the difficult task of letting you know that the gift of the Cube can only be extended to a select few." My heart drops when Cordelia says this. I've only just arrived at the Cube and I know nothing about this place, but I know I don't want to get back on the train.

"As you can imagine," Cordelia continues, "we set a very high standard here at the Cube. Our selection process is rigorous, and making it here is only the first step." Cordelia walks up and down the row, examining all of us carefully. "Throughout the day, you will all compete in a series of challenges. There will be three in total. Through these challenges, Officials will vigilantly examine your assets. How you perform will directly affect your future. And by the end of the day, only *two* of you will be lucky enough to stay. Two of you will unpack your belongings, meet the others, and begin your time here—the other six will go back on that train."

Cordelia stops speaking and nobody moves. "Any questions?"

I don't dare say anything and neither do the others. I have a feeling none of us want to get back on that train. I certainly don't. As long as I keep my mouth shut and pretend to be grateful, maybe I'll stand a chance. I think back to Lilith and her cruel laughter the other night. I finally understand what she meant when she said that there was no way I would stay here long. I didn't realize the significance of her words. Lilith knew that leaving the train didn't necessarily mean a ticket to the Cube. Looking a certain way isn't going to be enough.

But what Lilith doesn't know is that I've been fighting against the system and people like her my whole life. I know what it's like to be an underdog. I'm a lot more than a pretty face and I do my best work when I'm under pressure. Lilith may not believe in me, but she won't be the first person I've proven wrong.

My beauty might not set me apart from the rest of the group, but something else does.

I'm willing to do whatever it takes to win.

CHAPTER 11

We follow Cordelia down a path and toward a different area of the Cube. There is a beautiful array of cubed houses, all lit up identically across a smooth cement path. There is a tree between each house, each the same size and type, making everything look clean and orderly.

When Cordelia isn't watching, I get a good look at my competition. There are seven other prisoners—eight including me—and I can't help thinking that Lilith is right. Beauty is not remarkable here. Everyone is stunning, including Cordelia. Not a feature is out of place, yet something about all of these people stands out: wide-set eyes, piercing eyes, high cheekbones, round cheeks, long hair, shaved hair, thick hair, striking eyebrows, dark skin, pale skin, lips so plump it's hard to imagine they're real.

I feel completely out of place.

Even with the changes to my appearance since leaving home, I still don't feel like I fit in here. Back at home, I only put on makeup for recitals. And even then I waited until the last minute and ripped off my fake eyelashes as soon as I got off the stage. Ethan could never hold back his laughter when he waited for me at the stage door. Every time we went for juice after my shows—an affordable outing for Group7— Ethan would make at least one comment about how ridiculous I looked with my exaggerated lipstick and eye makeup. I am much more comfortable washing my face with water in the morning and giving my hair a quick brush. That's the way I've always been. That's who I am beneath this new façade. When I look at the others, with their hair perfectly crafted in styles that suit their features and makeup that equally complements them, I feel like even more of an imposter. These are not my people. I don't belong here. But then I wonder if they all feel this way too. They're all prisoners like me. There's no reason to believe they all looked like this at home. They probably didn't grow up wearing makeup either. They're probably just as uncomfortable as me.

And yet when I look around at the other seven prisoners in the group, it's hard to believe they're faking it. Between their natural beauty and poise, they *must* feel much more at home than me. They seem to be a lot more confident. One girl, for instance, is nearly bald. Only someone with incredible confidence could pull something like this off. It totally works, too. She has a shaved head, high cheekbones, and glowing dark brown skin. She manages to look gorgeous without much of a hairstyle helping her. I try to imagine myself bald. The idea scares me.

Another girl's eyes are a bright mint green, which looks striking with her long brown hair and dark skin. The girl beside her has short black hair, blue eyes, pale skin, and freckles. There's a guy with orange hair and orange eyes, unlike anything I've ever seen. Another guy has blue hair, brown eyes, freckles, and a striking jawline. The third guy has a dimple on his chin and intoxicating gray eyes. There's a girl at the front of the line with blonde hair, plump lips, and big blue eyes. She doesn't stand out from the crowd, at least to me, but her arrogance makes me notice her. She's had a smirk on her face since hearing the news that only two will be selected like she already knows she'll be chosen. It's hard to believe that she, or anyone, hasn't always felt beautiful and special. It's hard to imagine that these people are all prisoners like me. They all have stories and they're probably all coming from a bottom Group. Statistically speaking, nearly all prisoners are from Group 5, 6, or 7. None of us are as glamourous as we seem.

The last girl I notice has wide eyes and auburn hair. She's wearing a tight tan dress that's perfect for her skin tone but looks overly mature for her age. She's got a pin in her hair that I almost didn't notice. It's hidden behind her thick red hair. It's a green and yellow pin, with a sunflower in the middle. It doesn't quite go with her outfit, but I like it. It adds innocence to her look.

Everything about the auburn-haired girl is striking, but her quiet demeanor makes her hard to notice. She's biting down on her bottom lip and hiding behind the rest of us. She looks too young to be here, maybe twelve or thirteen. She reminds me of the girls I teach at the dance studio. She seems so out of place, but I know that's wishful thinking. I can't help but feel sorry for her. She's too innocent to understand her beauty—to recognize how dangerous it can be. It's hard to believe she could have gotten into trouble. Nothing about her looks threatening. It must have been bad, though, to have landed her here at such a young age. But that shows what people are willing to do when they have no other choice. I can't help but wonder what happened. I wonder if she'd known about the possible consequences. I know she is technically my competition, but I hope she stays here with me. Nobody her age should be subject to anything like this; she should be home with her family. But if she stays here, I can look out for her.

The girl may be too young to fully conceal her fear, but I imagine others are feeling the same way. I wonder who else is scared in the group. We were all taken from our homes. We are all seeing the Cube for the first time. Just because they seem confident about how they look doesn't mean they're confident about their place here. Behind their perfectly made-up faces, they must be just as afraid as the auburn-haired girl. Just as afraid as me.

I try not to let the fear build up inside me. I try to remember that all of this is out of my control. I need to focus on the task at hand. All I can do is stand out from my competition and prove my worth. If I can manage that, I have a chance at staying at the Cube. And the sooner I'm placed at a Camp—and off that train for good—the sooner I can escape.

Cordelia takes us to a boardwalk that runs parallel to the ocean. There are houses to our left, a community of beachside homes, and the beach to our right. The sand looks soft and creamy white. It's so clean, there's not a stone out of place or piece of litter in sight. It's nothing like 7N, where nothing is orderly or uniform. Even the ocean's waves are regular here. They have probably found a way to control the current and calm the waves. Loukas once told me they did that kind of thing in Group1 and 2, but I never believed him. Looking out at the ocean now, I think he's right. It looks too consistent to be real.

Cordelia pauses and we stop moving immediately, mimicking her actions. The houses have now ended and there's a densely forested pathway that begins ahead of us. Cordelia looks at us, waiting for the last person to stand still. It's the guy to my right. He's adjusting his jacket, completely oblivious to the pair of eyes glaring at him. When he realizes his mistake, he quickly apologizes. Cordelia shoots him a dramatic pout. Nobody dares to move. After a moment, she speaks, "The path ahead of us leads to Oparius. This is the area where you will live if you're chosen to stay. Take a good look behind you because you won't come back here often." Cordelia pauses. Some people look back, but I keep looking forward. It seems safer. Cordelia notices my lack of movement. "Not interested?" she asks me.

My heart stops. Have I already messed up? I try to figure out how to recover. "I got a good look while we were walking. It's beautiful."

Cordelia looks away from me and begins to walk again. I'm not sure if I've convinced her but it's the best I can do. The group follows. Cordelia continues talking as we head down the forested path. "If you're one of the lucky ones who stay, Oparius will be home to you. As you can see, we tend to the forests very carefully, despite the fact that Patrons don't come into this area. Here at the Cube, we pride ourselves on being kind to our Working Guests." Cordelia pauses, letting us take this in. "How many of you have been to another Camp before?"

Cordelia waits for a response. Three people raise their hands. The girl with the bald head, the guy with the orange hair, and the blonde girl at the front. I'm shocked. I hadn't considered that anyone had come from another Camp. I thought everyone was recently taken from their homes and families like me. I can't believe the blonde girl's been a prisoner somewhere else. She looks too elegant. Too comfortable in this setting. I can't imagine her in work clothes, being beaten and overworked. I wonder where she was before. I wonder how long she spent on the train—how much time she had to recover.

"Anyone care to share their story?" Cordelia asks.

The blonde girl raises her hand immediately. She begins, "Before I came here, I was at—"

Cordelia stops her. "Don't say the place, dear. That's none of our business." I almost laugh at the passive aggression. "How about you start by telling us your name?"

"Right. I'm Emma-Ray. I was working *somewhere* else for three months. It was different—it didn't look like this at all. We worked from five in the morning until ten at night. I usually got two or three hours of sleep. If I was lucky. I'd—well, I'd do my best to get all my work done, but it was challenging. Especially because the bodies we lived in were old, you know? Dying. Like, sometimes, they'd be in their last week or two. So, the pain—"

"Let's not get into that, dear." Cordelia swiftly cuts her off. "Anyone else?"

Neither of the other two raises their hand. They're probably too scared after Emma-Ray's failed attempt. Cordelia doesn't let that stop her though; she chooses the bald girl beside me. "Tearza," she calls out. "Why don't you tell us your story?"

"Thanks, Cordelia. As you mentioned, my name's Tearza. I don't have much to say except that I deserved everything that happened to me at my last Camp. I spent over a year there and it was a lot of hard work, but I think I learned a lot about discipline and obedience. I'm very honored to be here now and I pray that I can use this chance to prove I can do better. I feel very fortunate to be at the Cube."

Cordelia claps for her. "Lovely. Thank you, Tearza. That was beautifully said. I think the others can really learn from that."

I can feel the group's eyes on Tearza. The girl knew exactly what to say and, of course, it was complete nonsense. Cordelia ate it all up. It doesn't help that Tearza is gorgeous, too. Between her high cheekbones, full lips, arched eyebrows, and luminous skin, she's one of the most beautiful people I've ever seen. I notice Emma-Ray glare at Tearza. The competition is on. I'm not going to let it bother me, though. It's the beginning of the day and there's still a lot of time left for mistakes. Tearza might be at the top of the scoreboard now, but she won't be for long.

Cordelia keeps walking and I hang back so that I can walk alongside the young girl with the auburn hair. Something about her comforts me. Maybe if I walk beside her I can comfort her too. As we continue to walk through the forested path, we come to a clearing. The trees open up to a grass field and a large glass building. Cordelia leads us to it and once we've reached the entrance, she stops. The perimeter of the building is made of large windows and I can see that the inside is filled with gym equipment. I notice a tennis court and running track in the distance. I can't help but gawk at how big it is. And everything seems to be in pristine condition. It's not like any of the communal spaces in 7N. It looks brand new.

"This exquisite building," Cordelia says, "is where you will spend most of your time if you're chosen to be a Working Guest. It's a state-of-the-art gym, with everything you could possibly need to stay in tip-top shape." It's true. It's like nothing I've ever seen. "You were all invited here partially because of your level of fitness so of course, we expect you to maintain that while you're here. As Working Guests, that's really your main job. As soon as you're initiated, you'll be given a Chip that will track your calories and activity level. Based on your individual health exam, you'll need to meet a specific calorie intake every day in order to achieve your caloric equilibrium.

"Everything at the Cube is top of the line, especially when it comes to technology. Your Chip will be multifunctional, but one of its main purposes is to track your calories, as well as your Companion's calorie intake. This will ensure that you're able to keep track of how much food you can eat and how much exercise needs to be completed by the end of each day. Every time your Shell is re-inhabited by you, your Chip will update, displaying the number of calories your Companion consumed that day."

I try to make sense of Cordelia's words. My activity level depends on how much food my Companion eats. I can't imagine that people watch their calories when they're in a stranger's body. I start to think about what that might mean for me. How much exercise is required? Before I think more about this, I realize Cordelia is talking. I focus my attention back on her.

"As mentioned, the Chip also has many other functions. For instance, at the start and end of every day, your Companion will switch Shells with you. When your Companion is ready for the Switch, you will be notified by a buzz from your Chip. You will have five minutes from then to get yourself to the Switch-Pod, where the exchange of Shells will occur."

Five minutes. That hardly feels like enough time. I wonder why we have to go to a designated area for the Switch to occur. Switches can happen from anywhere. It must be to regulate things. If I've learned anything about the Cube, it's that they like to have control.

I listen to Cordelia. "The most important function of the Chip is to ensure the safety and peace of mind that everyone shares at the Cube. The Chip succeeds at this by, quite literally, tracking your whereabouts. If a Working Guest leaves the Cube or steps out of bounds, the Officials will immediately be notified. Of course, there is no reason to leave the Cube—we treat you very well here—but on occasion, at other Camps, duplicitous workers try to escape." Cordelia frowns for show, and then quickly returns to her cheery self. "Luckily, here at the Cube, your Chip can stop this from happening. Not that it *would* happen, I'm sure. As I said, there is every reason to find contentment at the Cube.

"Anyway," Cordelia returns to discussing the logistics, "because the Cube is a getaway for Patrons, your Companion will be accessing your Shell every day." She's using a lot of government words I'm not used to hearing. I try to translate. The Cube seems to be a prison where people come to leave their bodies. She said it's for Patrons—people who want to take a vacation in someone else's body for a little while. And so that's why we have to spend our days exercising. They need to keep us looking fit. I'm not sure what a Companion or a Shell is, but I'm too afraid to ask. Maybe a Companion is the person who we're paired with? I listen to Cordelia, hoping she'll further explain.

Cordelia continues, "It will be your responsibility to maintain your equilibrium once your Companion has returned to their own Shell for the night." So, a Shell must be a person's body. I try to make sense of what she's saying. I think she's telling us that whoever occupies our bodies for the day can eat whatever they want. Then, once they go to bed, it's our responsibility to burn off however many calories went in. It's our responsibility to maintain our physique. And all the while, we have to stay hidden. That's why we live in Oparius, away from the Patrons. We're not allowed to be seen. Cordelia keeps talking. I try to listen, but I'm too distracted, trying to absorb this information. It's not the exercise that bothers me—it's the idea that somebody else will be in my body every day. Somebody else will be nourishing it (or not) and moving in it. Somebody else will be *living* in my body. And it's my job to fix whatever problems they create. I will no longer have control.

I hear Cordelia call someone's name. Richard. I turn to see who that is and it's the guy with the orange eyes. He has a question. "So, if we enter our bodies—"

"We like to use the term Shells here."

"Sorry. Shells... If we enter them at night after the person using them goes to bed, wouldn't we be sleeping too?"

"That's a great question. But before I answer it, I want to remind you that we wouldn't say something like "the person using my Shell" here. That's negative language and we try to avoid that here at the Cube. The proper term for the person who shares your Shell is your Companion. Sometimes your Companion changes, but often you'll be paired with the same patron for a while. We want you to properly recognize your partnership with them, so it's important that you use this language. Your language controls your mindset and I truly believe that your mindset is *everything.*"

I want to tell Cordelia that her mindset is messed up. They're not "Companions," they're rich lowlifes stealing our bodies. I contort my face into a neutral expression. I nod along with the rest of the group.

"Now, to answer your question, typically our Working Guests adapt to a nocturnal schedule. That way they can spend their time awake in their original Shells, have ample time to work out, and do whatever they wish for the rest of the day. You'll find there's a lot of freedom at the Cube." Cordelia beams proudly. "Any other questions?"

The group is quiet. "Great. We'll be heading back out of Oparius then. I want to make it very clear that you should never leave Oparius unless you're escorted by an Official. Does everyone understand?"

We all nod. She seems satisfied.

When we get back to the beach area, we see Patrons walking around. I can tell they are in prisoners' bodies because of how beautiful they look. Two of them are heading toward the water, hand in hand, and I wonder if they are a couple. Did they come here together? Do the prisoners, whose bodies they are in, know each other? Everything about this interaction seems strange to me. I focus my attention on Cordelia again before she notices me staring.

We arrive at a building that looks similar to the gym, but more extravagant in design. Flowers are carved into the glass and the door is gold-plated. When we enter the building, I'm struck by how cold and dry the air feels. It reminds me of the train. I'm still not sure I like air-conditioning. It's not something we had in 7N, but I should have known it would be all over the Cube. People from the higher-status Groups seem to expect it on hot days, but I much prefer a fan. I try to get accustomed to the feeling on my body, or should I say "Shell."

The main lobby of the building has a massive chandelier and plush velvet chairs. Six people wearing matching government uniforms stand beside Cordelia. They must be other Officials working at the Cube, but I don't know why they're here. Or why *we're* here, for that matter. The Officials all look approximately Cordelia's age, somewhere in their thirties or forties, but one is distinctly younger. He looks about my age. The rest of them wear only burgundy, the government's color, but this guy is wearing a navy blue baseball cap. He's got large brown eyes, buzzed dark hair, and tanned skin. His shoulders are wide and he's noticeably tall. He's got a stern look on his face, but something about him is less threatening than the others. Maybe it's his youth. He's also extremely attractive, which helps. It's a weird thought to have about a

Government Official and a little unsettling. I'm sure once he opens his mouth he'll be just as unbearable as the rest of them.

After everyone is gathered in the lobby, Cordelia clears her throat in a distinctly annoying way. We all stand straight and pay attention.

"As I warned you before, only two of you will stay here at the Cube and join the other Working Guests. The other six will say goodbye. We want you to know that we take this process very seriously. You all might be a good fit in one way or another, but we're looking for a *perfect* fit here at the Cube. If you make one mistake, we will notice. If you try to fake compatibility, we will notice that too. The best advice I can give you is to be yourself. The rest is in our hands. Any questions?"

Nobody says anything. I don't take Cordelia's advice too seriously. It's hard to believe they actually want us to be ourselves. That sounds like a recipe for disaster.

"All right, then," Cordelia continues, "if you could all follow me to the runway. The first challenge will now begin."

CHAPTER 12

Before the first challenge is introduced, each Government Official is given introductions. I don't register most of their names. My mind is too busy mentally preparing for the competitions that lie ahead. Cordelia calls out each Official's name, reads some information about them, and then quickly moves on to the next. I know I should be paying attention, but by the time I refocus, she's more than halfway through the group. She's introducing the young Official now. Theo Jacobson. The guy with the navy baseball cap. His name must be short for Theodore, which I find shocking, considering where we are. Nicknames are highly frowned upon in the more affluent Groups. I'm sure everyone here will call me Eliana, even though I'm much more comfortable with Ellie. I wonder how Theo gets away with this.

I don't have time to think about this any longer, because Cordelia begins describing the first challenge. A "catwalk." I have no idea what this is. I look around for cats but don't see any nearby. Cordelia tells us we'll be walking down a runway, wearing various outfits. Do we have to walk like cats? Somebody else raises their hand. It's the blonde girl with the big blue eyes, Emma-Ray. I hope she asks for clarification. I don't want to be the one making a fool of myself.

"Will we get to choose our outfits?" Emma-Ray asks. It's not what I was hoping for, but it's still information I can use.

"The outfits have already been selected for you." I'm relieved. That's one less thing I have to worry about. Even by the end of my time on the train, Lilith still wasn't pleased with some of my outfit choices.

Cordelia directs us to the dressing room. There are clothing racks placed around the room, each with a different person's name on it. I read the first one. Tearza. She's got a beautiful white dress that I'm sure will contrast her dark skin gorgeously. There's another dress that's a deep purple, and on the far right of her rack, a mint green bikini hangs from the top. It looks impossibly small. I pray I don't have anything like that. Tearza notices me eyeing her rack and shoots me a glare. "Sorry," I say. She doesn't respond.

I quickly leave, looking for my rack. It's the last one on the left, right by the window. I examine each of the items. There are three outfits: a tight red dress, a yellow ball gown, and a small, gold bikini. Cordelia explains that we all must wear each outfit once and walk down the runway. She doesn't mention anything about how we walk. I listen closely for any references to a cat. Instead, Cordelia talks about how each item was carefully selected for us. She talks about how, before we arrived, Officials collected our sizes, skin tones, and style preferences. A dignified look is glued to her face. It's a little creepy, them having all this information ahead of time. I think about what this means. While I was on the train, anxiously waiting to find out where I was being taken, Cordelia and others were studying my body. They were examining pictures of me, perhaps watching me through cameras, and deciding if I looked better in navy or red. I wonder what they learned about my style preferences. I like wearing t-shirts and comfortable pants, but I don't see any of those choices here. I take a deep breath and relax. None of this criticism is going to help me today.

I wait in the dressing room. Richard is the first to go. He's wearing a tight navy suit. His pants look too short for him, but I remind myself they were "tailor-made." That must be intentional. He comes back after his first walk looking self-assured. I want to ask him what happened and find out more about what to do, but I know I can't. I decide to focus on something else until they call for me. Watching the others just makes me more nervous.

I put on my first outfit, the red cocktail dress. It's a deep red, which I've been told by Lilith is a good color for me. She always tells me to pair it with a dark red lip color. I don't see why I need to change from the dress I'm currently wearing. The styles are similar enough and they both look nice on me. But I do as I'm told and change from the blue dress I have on to the red dress on the rack. An Official comes over to fasten my zipper in the back. I don't recognize the Official, so I don't think she's one of the people judging me. I'm not sure if it's safe to talk to her, but I decide to risk it. When she's done zipping me up, I say, "Excuse me. Can you tell me what a catwalk is?" The Official doesn't respond so I keep talking, "I mean," I lower my voice to a whisper, "What does it have to do with cats?" The Official bursts out in laughter, repeating the word "cats" as if it's hilarious. Everyone looks over at us. The Official covers her mouth when she realizes the attention on her and contains her laughter. "Never mind," I say, realizing I must have made a fool of myself. At least I got my answer. The Official leaves, moving on to someone else.

I notice there's a mirror behind my clothing rack, so I go over to it. I get a good look at myself. The dress is tight in all the right places. It accentuates my shape, showing off my curves in a way that's new for me. I feel a little exposed, but I guess that's what they want. I quickly apply a lipstick I think Lilith would approve of, and head out of the room.

When it's almost my turn, an Official comes over to me and warns me that I have one minute before my walk. An Official is outside the door, waiting to escort me. He rushes down the hallway and I try to keep up. It's hard to walk in high heels. I've never done it before. There wasn't much room in my railcar to practice. The Official instructs me to follow the arrows. I follow them to a curtain, take a deep breath, and then enter the stage. The first thing I notice is the audience. There's a row of Officials judging me, but beyond them are Patrons of the Cube. The room is filled with Patrons, eagerly watching from their seats.

I've never walked down a runway before, so I'm not exactly sure what to do. My heart is pounding out of my chest, but I try to conceal it. I can't look nervous. I walk the length of the stage with confidence, trying to forget about the audience watching me. When I get to the end of the stage, a Patron in a flower bikini calls out, "Give us a pose!" I'm taken by surprise and don't know what to do. I go into arabesque, the first ballet pose I can think of, and hope that's what they're looking for. I'm too afraid to look at the Officials, who feel like judges, sitting in a row of chairs looking at me. I guess they are judges of some sort. I'm familiar with judges ranking my dance and giving me a score from my years of competitive ballet, but this is different. They never had my fate in their hands before. I turn around and walk the other way, looking back and smiling one more time before I exit.

When I get back to the change room, I let out a sigh of relief. I don't know who that Patron was, but I'm grateful for her help. That could have gone worse. I stare at the dangling gold bikini. I don't want to put it on; I'm not ready for my body to be scrutinized. But I know it's either now or I save it for last. I don't want to have the bikini be my final impression. I'd rather sandwich it in the middle and make it feel like the least important look. Before I can think too much longer about it, I quickly throw the bikini on and glance at myself in the mirror. Everything seems to be in place, so I don't linger any longer. I head toward the runway, following the arrows, and try to feel as confident as possible. I imagine myself in my black leotard and tights. That is when I feel at my most powerful. I take a deep breath before going on stage again. This time, my pose at the end of the runway is more relaxed. I look out to the audience and find the Patron in the flower bikini. She gives me a pose of her own and I follow it. I stand tall, with one hand on my hip, and pretend someone's taking my picture. I'm face to face with the judges and I decide to make eye contact this time. I need to seem brave. I get a glimpse of one of the Government Officials and see a hunger in his eyes. It's disturbing, considering how little I'm wearing. I quickly look away, noticing the rest of them now. They are all looking at me with satisfaction. They seem to be pleased with the look. Well, all but one. The Government Official with the navy hat and dark brown eyes. Theo. He's busy talking to the Official beside him. A beautiful woman with dark brown hair and blue eyes. The woman is looking at me as she listens, but Theo's eyes are turned to her. I spin around and walk back, trying not to feel insulted. The crowd of Patrons roars with applause as I walk away. I'm happy to get that reaction, but I'm still stuck on Theo's lack of interest. I don't know why it bothers me.

I give one last pose before exiting to the dressing room. The audience loves it. When I'm offstage, I wrap my arms around my stomach and rush back. I get out of the bikini as quickly as possible and focus on the next task: the ball gown. When I slip on the light-yellow dress and zip it up, I'm absolutely amazed. It's even more extravagant than it seemed on the hanger. It's grandiose and silky-smooth, and probably costs more than my childhood home. I put on a lighter lipstick and a pair of earrings that match my gold necklace. I tie my hair up. When I get to the runway, I feel less scared this time. I think of Mama and the way she used to call me her beautiful princess. I channel that as I walk down the stage, letting her love fuel my strides. I'm Mama's girl, I tell myself. I'm *Elloula*. When I look at the judges, Theo is looking at me now. We make eye contact and I hold it. I hope the judges find me bold.

When I get back to the change room, I feel relieved and proud. The first competition is over. It went relatively well, I think. Cordelia told us there are three challenges, so that means there are three left. I'm ready for whatever comes next.

CHAPTER 13

Cordelia explains the next challenge. It's a fitness challenge. We need to run a two-and-a-half-mile race, hang onto a pole for as long as we can, and swim laps. I'm confident in my running and endurance because I usually run before dance practice every day and I need to be strong for ballet, so the pole won't be too big of a challenge, hopefully. The only thing I'm worried about is swimming. I don't spend much time in the water because the lake in 7N has been contaminated for years. I know how to swim, but I wouldn't say I'm a strong swimmer. All I can do is my best.

For the run, we're split up into two groups. There are four different lanes on the track, so our races are timed and the best of the eight of us win. Each lap is a quarter of a mile—we have to run ten laps. I'm running against Tearza, Richard, and the young girl with auburn hair. I learn her name is Hanna when Cordelia calls each of our names.

I get to my place on the track. Once again, there's an audience watching us. I recognize some of the Patrons from the catwalk, but many of them are new. I find it weird that they're spending their vacation watching us compete, but I guess it's thrilling for them. The thought makes me sick. Our fate here is entertainment for them. They don't really care which one of us wins.

I try to clear the Patrons from my mind. I think about Hanna beside me. I hope that she can run. She's the only person I'm rooting for other than myself. I look at Cordelia and notice she is almost ready to get started. I stretch my legs quickly and look ahead. Cordelia fires the starting gun. The race begins.

I run fast but save some of my energy for the second half of the race. It's a two-and-a-half-mile run, which is not necessarily short, but definitely not long either. I'm used to spending my days dancing, so cardio has never been an issue for me. I often go for runs to warm up before dancing. Nevertheless, I begin to cramp and feel fatigued after the first lap. I realize my body isn't used to this. After spending so much time on the train, I'm not in the best shape. Richard is the first to take the lead. Tearza is behind him and I see no sign of Hanna. I realize she must be behind me and hope she can catch up. I try to focus on my own race, heading into the third lap. I push myself to go faster with each stride. The cramps intensify, but I fight through them. I need to win. By the fourth lap, the pain is substituted for adrenaline. I'm still behind Richard and Tearza, but I have time. I run as fast as I can, pushing through the next two laps. I reach Tearza in the sixth lap and pass her in the seventh. Richard is faster than I expected him to be; I hope he's running out of steam. I need to catch him before the race is over. I can't finish in any place but first because I know I don't have a chance of winning the swim. In the eighth lap, I finally get close to Richard. I run as fast as I can, trying to gain on him, but every time I try, he increases his speed to keep the distance between us. He's not making it easy. It's not until the tenth lap, when I'm giving it everything I have, that I finally pass him. The crowd reacts loudly. Some seem upset, but most of them cheer happily. I smile, feeling proud, but it doesn't last long. I sense him catch up to me. I don't know which one of us is in the lead. If I look sideways, I'll slow down. I focus on the finish line and keep running, faster and faster, until there's nothing left to give and I'm on the other side of the line. It's over. The race is over. The crowd roars with delight, but I don't know who they're cheering for.

While the other group races, I drink water and stretch my legs. I anxiously wait for the results, but Cordelia tells us we won't find out until the end. I try to clear my head before the next competition.

The endurance challenge seems to scare some of the other prisoners. There are long vertical poles stuck in the ground. Each pole is a different color and stands over ten feet high. The poles are bare, apart from very thin groove lines which wrap around the poles. Cordelia tells us we have to climb to the top of the pole and hold our position, using the tiny grooves as foot and hand holds, for as long as we can. There are mats below us, so when it becomes too difficult we can drop at any time. The last person standing, or hanging, on the pole wins the contest. Once again, there's an enthusiastic audience around us. The stakes seem higher because they get to watch us fall. Literally.

Officials come into the room with ladders and place one beside each pole. While we wait, I prepare myself for the challenge. It seems daunting, and I know it'll be tough, but I tell myself it's manageable. Although this is a test of strength, it is equally a test of willpower. Back at home, in the weeks leading up to competitions, Mama always would extend the number of hours her dancers were required to practice. I was often among the dancers, especially when I was younger, who Mama pushed extra hard. When we would get exhausted and beg for a break, Mama would say, *Mind over matter.* It's a sentiment she drilled in us. When things get tough, it's usually our minds that tell us to quit, not our bodies. I need this message to get through the challenge. It's the only way I might win.

Everyone gets in position. At Cordelia's command, we climb up the ladder and find a place to hold on at the top of the pole. As soon as we find a grip, the Officials take the ladders away. The grooves in the wood looked small when I first saw them, but they feel even smaller now. About a third of my hands and feet fit into the grooves so I have to use every muscle in my body to keep from falling. I squat, wrapping my legs around the pole as I dig my heels into both sides. I clasp my hands to the creases directly above my head. I expect someone to drop right away, but no one does. The competition is tough. We've all undergone fitness training in one way or another, so nobody here is weak. I have no idea how long we've lasted before the first person drops. A mix of disappointment and glee comes from the audience. I look down and see Emma-Ray. Her hands are shaking from the pain. The next one down is Hanna. I try not to feel disappointed as I listen to the crowd's delight. Hanna held on for a long time—longer than I probably could have at her age. The next few drop quickly. And once again, the last three left are Tearza, Richard, and me. The pain is increasing in my hands and feet, but I feel it in the rest of my body, too. The position

I'm in is beginning to feel stiff. I wish I could move my body around and find another position. It's too risky though. If I try to adjust, I might fall. I turn my head ever so slightly to glance at my competition. I can't get a good view. I wiggle my toes to gain sensation in my feet. The next thing I know, Richard drops. This shocks me—I expected him to challenge me right until the end. Tearza keeps going and I start to feel weak. Inside, I'm begging her to give up and drop down. But I know that's not an effective strategy, so I try to distract myself. I think of Ethan. I think of my family. I think of the hide and seek game we played as kids. I always loved hiding and Loukas always loved looking for me. He used to pretend he was a monster. Whenever he was coming to find us, he'd yell, "Ooh ga, ooh ga, Loukas ooh ga." It was a little ridiculous, but it always made us laugh. Especially Mama. She loved Loukas's silly moods. I think of Mama's laughter now, the way it could shake a room. The thought makes me miss her terribly. I wonder if she'd be proud of me right now. Before I think about this more, I hear someone shout "Eliana wins!" I notice Tearza on the floor below me and I am filled with relief. The crowd is on their feet now, roaring with approval. I collapse to the mat, exhausted. I wave my hands and feet around in pain.

As I walk off the mat, I notice some of the competitors glaring at me. Tearza scowls and she doesn't look away. Am I not supposed to try? I'm not going to apologize for winning and protecting myself. That's what we're all trying to do.

The swimming challenge is our last fitness test. We're only using one swimming lane, so each of us is called in one at a time. The rest of us wait in the change room beside the pool.

I sit on a bench against the wall and anxiously await my turn. Hanna is first and I watch her walk in with confidence. She hasn't had an easy time so far, so I'm happy to see that she hasn't given up. She's tough. I hope the Officials appreciate this. When she comes back from the pool, I give her a friendly grin. Hanna sits beside me on the bench.

Tearza is the next to swim.

Hanna and I are quiet, following the lead of the others. Eventually, a discreet chatter fills the room and I feel comfortable speaking.

I turn to Hanna. "How did your swim go?"

"Okay, I hope," she answers shyly.

"Good. I'm exhausted."

"You were amazing at the endurance test. I don't know how you stayed up there for so long."

"Me neither. Honestly, I tried focusing on my family and it made the time pass faster."

I'm surprised by how honest I'm being, but I feel like I can trust her.

"That's nice. Do you have a big family?"

"Not really..." the thought makes me sad. "Not anymore, anyway."

"I've got five siblings."

"Wow." I think about Ethan.

"I'm the youngest."

"That makes sense."

Hanna looks at me, curious. "Why?"

"You're young, but you seem old for your age. If you know what I mean."

"Yeah. You don't really get to be young in Group6."

"I'm from 7."

Hanna's face brightens. "Oh yeah?"

"Yeah, so I know what you mean." I don't know if I should ask, but I do anyway. "How old are you? If you don't mind me asking."

"Twelve."

"Wow," I try not to look too shocked. "I can't believe they sent you here. Not that you don't look the part—"

"No, it's okay. It surprised me too. I doubt I'll get picked, but I think they just want to see me fail. They're trying to punish me."

"What do you mean?"

Hanna shrugs. "I'm not like most prisoners. They've got their eyes on me."

"Who? The government?"

Hanna nods. "Sure. Anyone with power. They have it out for me."

"Me too," I say, but then again, I feel like any prisoner could say the same.

Hanna doesn't look convinced, but she doesn't say anything more. Before I can ask her to elaborate, Tearza cuts me off, having just returned from her swim.

"You two really shouldn't be whispering over there." She must have had a bad race, judging by the look on her face. I notice that the others have stopped talking. It's quiet in the waiting room again.

"Thanks," I try to sound nice, but she's beginning to annoy me.

"You're probably right," Hanna answers. "Sorry." She turns to me and shrugs apologetically. I roll my eyes and Hanna laughs inconspicuously.

I hope Hanna stays more than ever now. It's nice to have someone friendly around.

A long time passes, and we all sit in silence. One by one, prisoners are called and taken for their swims. Richard returns the fastest. I'm not surprised at all. He and Tearza are my biggest competitors. Finally, after everyone else is done, an Official enters the room and calls my name. It's my turn to swim.

I follow the Official out of the change room, through a hallway, and into a warm room that smells intensely of chemicals. The pool has one lane marked. There are bleachers on both sides of the pool, filled with people watching. The Officials have their own table at the front. I nod obediently at the Officials and wait for them to tell me to begin.

Cordelia sets her clock and motions for me to get in the water. I enter slowly, preparing myself for the cold. But the water isn't cold at all—it's the perfect temperature. I've never swam in heated water before. I'm amazed by how comfortable it feels. I get ready and wait for Cordelia to count me in. I need to do ten lengths to complete the race. Cordelia gives me the signal and I start moving. I can't remember the last time I swam, so it takes a moment for me to get comfortable. I swim as fast as I can, increasing my speed with each lap, but even still I feel sluggish. I try not to get discouraged. It's easy to relax underwater.

I'd forgotten how soothing it feels. Before I know it, Cordelia's shouting something.

I can't make out the sound underwater, but when I come up, she tells me I'm done. That was my last lap. I slow down and swim back to the other end. I get out of the water and immediately notice the sound of the crowd. It's a weak applause. I thank the judges, smiling at each of them as I leave. I hope it will leave a lasting impression, especially since my swim didn't. I'm not really the bubbly type, but I want them to think I am. Plus, if I don't force a smile I'm afraid my face will contort into something foul when I look the Officials in the eye. Theo's the last Official I make eye contact with. He looks disturbed when I smile at him, so I look away, embarrassed. I quickly exit the room.

When I arrive back at the change room, we all walk over to the showers and get cleaned up. We're told to meet back in the lobby once we're done. It's peculiar showering around strangers, but at least short stalls block us from seeing one another. Everyone here has a perfect body and I really don't need them comparing theirs to mine. What if someone looks over and notices me? What happens when people finish showering? Where will they stand?

Nobody else seems to be bothered by this. Everyone is talking freely and openly. It's the first time there aren't Officials around to keep us from acting like ourselves. I overhear several conversations, mostly of people talking about the swim challenge. They want to know where they stand in the competition.

When I finish showering, I dry myself off and put on the clothes laid out for me. I join the group of prisoners standing by the door. They're still talking about the swim. I find it strange, the way everyone is bragging about how well they think they did. It's not something I'm used to. Emma-Ray is talking now. She seems pleased with her swim, which isn't surprising. I can picture Mama laughing at her, saying something like *She's got too much confidence, Elloula. She's making herself look dumb.* But maybe confidence is a good thing here. It certainly seems to be intimidating to some of the others.

The only two people who stay as quiet as I do are Hanna and Richard. I expect this from Hanna, but I'm surprised Richard isn't chiming in with the others. Maybe I've read him wrong.

One of the chatty guys, William, finally says. "Yo, Richard, how'd you do?"

Richard seems to be pulled out of a trance. "Huh?"

"How was your swim?"

"Oh," Richard shrugs. "It was all right, I guess."

The others look at him for a moment, caught off guard by his discreetness. Tearza scrutinizes him. I think she sees him as a threat. An Official comes in before anyone can say anything else. I'm relieved. I was worried someone might start asking me questions.

"Cordelia is waiting in the lobby," the Official says.

We follow the Official out of the room. When we get to the lobby, Cordelia is at a podium. She waits for everyone to stand still before she announces our scores. I'm eager to know how I placed in each contest. I feel good about the run and I know I won the endurance challenge, but I'm worried about the swim. I try to relax, reminding myself that there's nothing I can do now.

Cordelia starts with the run. She begins by telling us who placed last. I hear her call out names. William. Hanna. Scottie. Sandy. Tearza comes in fourth. Emma-Ray comes in third. That leaves me and Richard and I have no idea who it will be. Cordelia calls out my name and my heart drops.

"In second place, Eliana Sagona."

That means Richard won. I look at him and we quickly make eye contact. I give him a supportive nod. It was a good race—I fought as hard as I could, but he was better. Richard nods back.

Next, Cordelia calls out the names for the endurance challenge. This one isn't as suspenseful because I know I placed first. Once again, Richard and Tearza are right behind me. Richard and I are tied for the lead, both claiming one second place and one first. It all comes down to the swim. I brace myself for last, or at least somewhere close to the bottom.

Cordelia begins calling out the names and the first name I hear is Richard's. I almost gasp. I notice the startled expressions of the others in the room. We all expected him to be a front-runner. I look over at Richard, but he gives nothing away. He looks ahead as if he didn't just hear his name. Cordelia continues to call out seventh place. I figure if Richard places eighth, I'm probably right behind him, but somehow it's not my name. It's Sandy. Sixth is Scottie. Fifth is Emma-Ray. I hold in my surprise. I somehow place fourth. There are three people left and they still haven't called Hanna. They say one more name, then another, and that's it. There's only one name left. Hanna places first for the swim. When I hear her name, I look over at her. She yelps with joy. "Good job!" I whisper. The two of us are beaming at each other. When I turn back, I notice Theo staring at me. He must have noticed my exchange with Hanna and I can tell he doesn't approve. I look away, hoping he'll let it slide. *You've got to be more careful,* I tell myself, moving forward. I don't know what I did to deserve it, but Theo's got his eyes on me.

Before we get to the third challenge, Cordelia leads us on a walk. We follow her through the many forested pathways of Oparius. I don't know my way around here yet, but I can tell it's a bit of a maze. There's so much forested area. So many trees. I try to focus on Cordelia's route and the turns she takes. If I'm going to stay here, I'll need to know my way around. The idea of asking an Official for instructions mortifies me.

The path we're on begins to clear and the trees become sparser. I look ahead and notice a pavilion in the distance with a Y-shaped column in each corner. As we walk toward the structure, Cordelia says, "I always like to announce this challenge somewhere enthralling." She says this to no one in particular, but everyone seems to hear it.

I look over to the others. Hanna whispers to me, "Did she just say *enthralling*?" Her face looks uncomfortable, which is exactly how I feel.

As we get closer to the pavilion, I hear William whisper to Richard. "Yo, what happened with your swim?"

"I don't know, man," Richard shrugs. "Tough luck."

William doesn't seem to believe this. "You don't know how to swim, do you?" I'm appalled by his audacity.

Richard is startled. He doesn't answer. He keeps walking silently.

"It's okay," William says, "My mom was from 7. She didn't grow up near water either."

Richard's quiet. He looks around to make sure no one else is listening. When he notices me paying attention, my gut reaction is to give him a look of understanding. I don't want to look away because he has no reason to be ashamed. Richard seems to appreciate this. "There wasn't much water where I lived."

"The water was contaminated in my community," I share, hoping it will make him feel less alone. "But I used to swim when I was little. Before we knew." Richard nods. "I'm sorry," I tell him, tentatively. We get closer to the pavilion now, so I know there's not much time to talk. "It's unfair to penalize you for something you couldn't control."

"None of this is fair," he says. And it's the first thing anyone has said that's honest. He sounds like Loukas, the way the words come out with such conviction. I'm too emotional to respond. Luckily, William chimes in. "At least you stood out in the other challenges," he says. "That'll help you." Richard doesn't seem convinced. "And who knows what's coming next?"

"Something enthralling," I say.

I hear a man clear his throat behind us. It's Theo. We turn around and Theo's looking directly at me. There's anger in his eyes. "Cordelia is waiting," he says. All three of us were talking, but I seem to be the only one in trouble. Cordelia has reached the pavilion. She's standing in the center.

We all gather around Cordelia. Instead of speaking immediately, she gazes around the area, basking in the silence for effect. Cordelia seems to be marveling at the pavilion: the gardens around the area, the careful placement and selection of the soft pastel flowers, and the blue sky overhead. We all pretend to be interested in the scenery as well.

When the moment is over, Cordelia begins. "I'm particularly excited to announce the last challenge of the day because this one is my favorite. Each of you will be paired with an Official. You'll be going on a date."

My heart sinks. A date? With who? There is movement from the prisoners beside me. I can sense that everyone's equally as uncomfortable as me.

Cordelia claps her hands together. "That's right. This will be the most important date of your life. You'll want to leave a lasting impression. Think of it as your final chance to convince us." Cordelia takes a dramatic pause. We all wait. She looks each of us straight in the eyes and says, "By the end of the evening, two of you will stay. Six of you will go."

Cordelia reads out our names and matches us up with a Government Official. Hanna is paired up with a guy named Patrick. He's probably three times her age. Richard is paired with an Official named Samantha. My name is called last and there's only one Official left. Theo.

I'm going on a date with Theo.

CHAPTER 14

I try not to get too nervous as I prepare for the last challenge. A date. I've only been on one date. It was with a guy named Robby Miller and it didn't go very well. I asked him to drop me off at Ethan's house at the end, so I didn't have to endure the post-date embarrassment on my own. Ethan laughed as I told him all about the stupid things I said and the way I pretended to sneeze when Robby tried to kiss me. The date was bad but sharing it with Ethan made everything better. By the end of the night, I was happy, wishing my next date would be with him.

But here I am now in a very different situation. My next date is not with Ethan; instead, it's with a complete stranger. And to make things worse, the stranger seems to hate me. I have no idea what I'm supposed to say to him or how I'm supposed to act. I don't even know what I'm supposed to wear. I assumed the clothes would be pre-selected, the way they were for the other challenges, but it seems this selection is part of the final test. On my date with Robby, I wore a black tank top and jean shorts. Something tells me that's not what they're looking for at the Cube.

The other girls put on cocktail dresses and high heels so I figure I should choose something similar. I put on a creamy white dress with a sweetheart neckline. It feels classy and safe. I clip half of my hair back and take off some makeup. I want to look like I've put in effort, but that I can be laid back and natural too.

When I'm finished getting ready, I wait with the others in the lobby. We're told this is where we'll return when our dates are over. I wish we could skip to that part now, standing in the lobby, waiting for Cordelia to read out the results.

Hanna walks in wearing a tight red dress and dramatic eyeliner. I try not to cringe, wondering how she learned to dress like that at such a young age. She sits down beside me.

"You look beautiful," Hanna whispers.

"You too," I say, wanting to make her feel confident.

"I look ridiculous," she says. "Emma-Ray helped me get ready... is it awful?"

"No," I say, trying to be positive. "I think the judges will like it. It's just what they want to see."

"Thanks," she says.

She leans in to tell me something else, but we're interrupted by a Government Official. It's Theo. Hanna and I both stop talking immediately. We look at him, nervously.

He shoots me the same look he's been giving me all day, like I've personally harmed him in some way. It's not my fault he's going on this date with me. I don't know why he's mad at *me* about it. "Did you dress her like this?" he asks. He's talking about Hanna.

I shake my head. "No way."

He doesn't say anything to this. "Come with me," he says. And then he walks away.

I mouth *sorry* to Hanna and she mouths back *good luck*. I give her a look as if to say *I'll need it* and she shakes her head, amused. I catch up to Theo.

I'm not sure where we're going but he's moving in such a hurry that I have trouble keeping up with him in my heels. I still haven't figured out how to walk like a normal person while wearing them.

"Pick up the pace, Eliana," he says.

"Where are we going?" I say, immediately regretting it. With any Official, it's probably safer to not ask questions, and with Theo it *definitely* is.

Theo doesn't respond. He turns down a path and stops at a large tree with a wooden ladder descending from it. There's a beautiful restaurant up in the trees. It reminds me of the treehouse Ethan's family built in their backyard, but this is obviously much fancier. String lights hang from the roof and around the trees. In cursive letters, a sign reads "La Spaghett." It's beautiful.

"What are we doing here? Am I making you dinner?" I'm nervous now because I've never made pasta before. The spaghetti I eat is usually made with ketchup.

"Have you ever been on a date?"

I don't respond. I'm definitely *not* going to tell him about Robby Miller. But I realize what Theo's implying... and it's ridiculous. The two of us are going to have a dinner date. An actual dinner date. I'm going to eat here. With him. And it's supposed to be romantic? It's hard for me to process this. He might be an attractive guy around my age, but he's an *Official*. We have nothing in common. Plus, the restaurant feels way too fancy for me.

"This is my favorite spot to eat," he says. "Their carbonara is delicious."

"Carbonara?" I have no idea what that is.

Theo's lips curl. Is that a smile? Is he laughing at me?

"I'll explain the menu inside."

He starts climbing the ladder. I follow after him, deciding to take off my heels first and hold them in one hand. Theo's in front of me so hopefully he won't notice. It seems less risky than trying to climb with my shoes on. Between the heels and the dress, there is no way I'd make it to the top without falling.

Theo looks back after he's made it to the top of the ladder. He reaches out his hand to help me up and notices my bare feet. He grabs my empty hand and gently pulls me.

"Couldn't make it up with those shoes on?"

"Sorry."

"It's fine. But probably wear something flatter next time."

"I didn't think running shoes would look good with the dress."

Theo turns before I can see his expression. Maybe I'm being too sassy. I make a mental note to tone it down. I'm supposed to be playing it safe.

We enter the restaurant and the inside is just as stunning as the treehouse's exterior. Everything is elegantly decorated in white and green. Large windows overlook the forest and ivy wraps around the walls. The light fixtures look like leaves themselves with candles hanging from every stem. The tables have candle holders that look like trees, too. The room is lit by warm candlelight.

"Wow," I say before I can stop myself. "This place is stunning."

"I know. And the food is even better."

Theo walks us over to our table. There's an empty one at the back of the room, which I think will be ours, but it's not. Theo walks past the table and toward a staircase. A wooden staircase takes us to the second floor. There's an area set up just for us. The upstairs is empty—no Patrons are here. It will only be Theo and me. I take a deep breath, realizing this, and follow Theo to our seats. Theo pulls out my chair and gestures for me to sit. I cross my legs to be lady-like. He tucks me in and walks to the other end of the table. When we're both seated, he looks at me. He doesn't say anything. He just waits.

This makes me very uncomfortable. I'm not used to silence, especially around people I don't know. "What now? What do we talk about?"

"Whatever you want. It's just supposed to be like a real date."

"This is so weird," I say before I can stop myself. I don't know why it's so hard to shut up around Theo. I keep trying to play it cool, and then promptly say something completely inappropriate.

"Why?"

"I don't know. Because it's not a date. Why is this even a challenge?"

"The G.O.s want to know what you're like in scenarios like this. If you end up being chosen, you'll need to charm the Patrons if you want to find a Companion. And without a Companion, you can't stay."

"How badly have I been doing?"

Theo just stares at me. He gives nothing away.

I've never heard anyone call a Government Official a G.O. It sounds so informal. But I guess that's how you speak when the government doesn't have a ton of power over you. When you get a say in your own existence. It's hard to imagine.

A server comes over with fresh bread. The man extends the breadbasket to me so I can pick for myself. I grab the white roll and put it on my plate. The server looks mortified, and I realize I must have done something wrong. I watch the way Theo graciously points to a piece of bread and waits for the server to use some sort of utensil to place the bread on his plate. When he finishes serving, the waiter leaves the basket on the table.

"Thank you, Sidney."

"Thanks," I say. "Sorry."

Theo looks back at me, once again with a look I can't decipher.

"Sorry. I've never seen that before. I promise I'll do better next time. I mean for the real people. Not that you're not *real*, but when it's not a trial. Like if I have to go on a real date here—"

"You're from Group7, right?" Theo interrupts my rambling. I'm grateful.

"Yeah. You?"

"You're not really supposed to ask that."

"Oh." I'm not sure what to say to that. "Can I guess?"

"What?"

"Can I guess your Group?"

Theo thinks about this. He doesn't seem to like the idea. "How are you going to do that?"

"From the way you walk and talk. And your name... Theo. At first I would think that name comes from a low-ranking Group because it's a short form. But you're an Official. So, my guess is Group1."

"Why?"

"Just a hunch." I don't want to say the reason, that only a Group1 would get away with a nickname at the Cube.

Theo shifts in his seat. He looks irritated. I instantly regret speaking. I'm completely blowing this date.

"Sorry," I say because he still hasn't responded. "I have a feeling I screwed up again."

He stays quiet for another long moment, and then he says, "I've never considered how a Working Guest would think of it. My

103

nickname, I mean." The way he says this sounds so honest. I feel like I've struck a nerve. I'm not sure how to move on from this, but I know I should if I want to salvage this date.

Thankfully, I'm saved by the presence of a server. This time it's someone new. A woman. I wonder if the other guy switched tables because he was too embarrassed by me, or if this is just how it works at fancy restaurants. Every step requires a different person to serve you. The woman asks for our orders, but I haven't even read the menu. Theo talks through the options with me, asking me what types of flavors I like. The woman doesn't seem to be in any hurry. It's a small restaurant and there seem to be plenty of servers, so I don't feel too bad about it. A little while later, we've placed our orders, and the server leaves. I'm grateful Theo didn't just order something for me. I was worried he might.

When it's just the two of us again, Theo starts the conversation back up. "So, Eliana," he says. "What do you think of the Cube?"

"It's nice." It's hard to think of anything positive to say about it. Everything here is so manicured and fake, from the people to the ocean waves. "I love the trees and greenery. Even in this restaurant. And it's nice to be by the water."

"I agree. Did you notice the waves?"

"Yeah, they're perfect," I say, which is true, but I don't actually mean it in a good way. I'll let him think what he wants, though. "What's your favorite thing about the Cube?"

"Um," he thinks about this, "there's this place I like to go beyond Oparius. It's a lookout that has a stunning view of the water and surrounding mountains."

"That sounds lovely."

"Yeah. Sorry, that's not a great answer because you can't exactly access it." Theo looks uncomfortable. He scrambles for something else to add, "There are a lot of great spots in Oparius too. I think you'll like it."

"Like where? The gym?"

Theo butters a piece of bread. He doesn't respond.

"Sorry. Sometimes I don't think before I talk."

"I've noticed."

"I didn't mean it. It's just an adjustment."

"I get it, but you've got a lot to be grateful for here. Trust me."

I try not to scoff. People from elite Groups always want people like me to be *grateful*. Especially their prisoners. They've created a system that is so unfair that it is almost impossible to get through life in a low-status Group without ever breaking the law. But once we do, the people who are part of the problem, who indirectly made us do it, look down on us like we are far below them. The truth is if Theo was in my shoes, if he had a sick mother who couldn't afford to leave her dying body, I bet he'd be here too.

After a long pause, I eventually say, "Thanks." I try to say it with a straight face. "I'm sure you're right."

"I'm just saying that I've visited some other Camps and they're a lot worse."

I try to calm myself down. I wonder why he's telling me this in the first place. It seems a little critical. Maybe he doesn't mean for it to be. I'm sure he doesn't. I push back, though.

"Are you admitting there are bad Camps out there?"

"Sure."

"But isn't that admitting a fault in your government? That they can be cruel, at least sometimes?"

"No," Theo doesn't like what I'm doing. "I think you broke the law and you can't expect things to be easy."

I sit back in my seat and glare.

"You should be grateful," he says again. "The Cube gives you many privileges—many things that most people in your situation wouldn't even dream of having."

I take a deep breath, trying to calm down. But I can't. I'm angry now. Theo has no idea what he's talking about. He doesn't know what it's like here, just like he doesn't know what it's really like at other Camps. Maybe he visited another Camp once with his private school to learn about the dangers of rebelling, but the likelihood of a person like

Theo going to prison is extremely rare. People like me think about prison all our lives. We know so many people who've been taken. Eventually, it starts to feel like our whole lives come down to two choices: playing it safe and accepting the little we're given or risking our freedom for something more.

I can hear Theo talking, but I'm not listening. My mind is racing. All I can think about is his previous comments. *You broke the law and you can't expect things to be easy.* Because I'm a "prisoner," a subhuman, a nobody? *Most people in your situation,* he said. What does that even mean? A poor person? An outlaw? A desperate girl from Group7?

Theo seems to be asking me something, but I don't respond. My mind is still racing.

Whatever he meant by that comment, it's clear where he stands. But even if Theo thinks I'm unworthy of the same treatment he receives, he should at least be able to admit that the Cube isn't some beautiful, wonderful place to be.

"Eliana?" He asks again.

"Hmm?" I say, half listening.

"Are you okay?"

"Yeah."

I'm about to say something more, to explain myself, but the waiter comes back to check on us. I let Theo do the talking. I can't help but notice how comfortable Theo looks in this role—talking to the waiter like he's his servant. This is what he's done his whole life. He has no idea what it's like to feel owned by the government—how it feels when somebody takes over your body. When Mama was in my body and I was in Mama's, it was unlike anything I've ever experienced. It was as if I was able to *be* Mama for a moment, feel what she feels, and experience all of this while knowing she was simultaneously undergoing the same experience. Since coming to the Cube, I keep thinking about that moment—how intimate it was—and try to imagine doing the same thing with a stranger. Does Theo assume it feels normal to have a stranger use my body against my will? Just because Cordelia calls it a

"Shell" doesn't make it feel any less personal. It's still our skin. Our flesh.

The server walks away graciously, and Theo returns his attention to me. "You seem to be elsewhere."

"I'm here," I say. "Just hungry."

"Well, if I were you, I'd probably engage."

He's right, but it still makes me mad. "I'm sorry."

"It's okay. Why don't you tell me more about yourself?"

It's the last thing I want to do, so I keep it vague. I tell him about the mountains of 7N and my years of dancing. Somehow, we get on the topic of Mama. I wonder if he knows what happened to her. Why I'm here. I change the subject.

"How long have you been working here?"

"Not long," Theo says.

"Do you like it?"

"Of course."

He's not giving me much.

"Have you ever been a Patron before?"

"No."

"Would you like to? Experience the Switch, I mean."

Theo doesn't respond right away. He seems to be eyeing me. "What are you doing?"

"What do you mean?" I don't feel like I'm *doing* anything. I'm just asking questions.

"Of course I'd like to be a Patron." Theo shifts in his seat. "Who wouldn't?"

"I imagine some people choose not to."

"Everyone has that choice," he says. "But it's a singular experience. It's a gift."

I let out a sound. "Sorry."

"We should talk about something else."

"I just think it's a deeply intimidating experience," I say, even though I know I shouldn't.

"I'm sure it is."

107

"But you have no idea."

I catch him off guard. His eyes seem to be warning me.

"It's like... it's like sharing your deepest secret."

"I get it," he says. He gestures for me to calm down, but that only makes me more upset.

"You don't, but I don't expect you to. Giving up your body—"

"Shell."

"Please," I say before I can think better of it. "Giving up *your body* is a feeling that's impossible to conceive. *Especially* when you're asked to do this with a complete stranger."

Theo's quiet, but my mind is still racing. "It might be the worst kind of torture," I say. "Despite what any of you think."

"Okay. We should go."

"What?"

"We are leaving."

"But we haven't even eaten."

"Eliana," he nearly raises his voice. My heart stops. The shock of it all snaps me back to reality. My anger's replaced with hopelessness. I've completely blown it.

I follow Theo down the stairs. We walk past the tables of Patrons eating on our way out and I can feel people's eyes on me. I want to glare at them, but I know I shouldn't. I keep my head down. I've done enough.

I take one last whiff of the delicious smells coming from the kitchen before I leave the restaurant. It's the closest I'll ever get to food like this. I don't like it at the Cube, but deep down I know there's truth to what Theo was saying. There are terrible Camps out there. Much worse than this. I try not to panic as I hurry after Theo. We're back in the woods now, walking through a forested path. If I thought Theo was walking fast on our way to dinner, I was wrong. He's practically running down the path now. I try to catch up with him, but I can't keep up in my shoes. He's too fast.

"Theo?" I call out. He ignores me.

I have no idea where he's going or what he's going to do, but I know it can't be good. I take off my shoes, hoping it will help me run faster, but by the time I look up, Theo is out of sight. I can't find him. I look for him down a few different paths, but he's gone. He's nowhere to be found. There's nothing left to do but go to the lobby, where Cordelia will be waiting for all her candidates to return. I walk back, preparing myself for the worst.

I can almost hear Mama saying it now: *You've got too much attitude for your own good. Stop asking for trouble.*

CHAPTER 15

An hour passes and I'm still waiting in the lobby. Cordelia isn't here, but most of the group is back from their dates. No Official has come to tackle me down or escort me from the premises yet. It feels like only a matter of time.

Everyone is talking about how well their mock dates went. Emma-Ray went stargazing. Richard said he had the best steak of his life. Tearza went dancing and came home with a massive grin on her face. Nobody seems to talk about how strange the whole thing felt. Nobody seems to be bothered by the power dynamic. The only person who seems quiet and reserved is Hanna. I can't imagine how hard the date was for her—I'm sure she imagined her first date going very differently. I wish I could talk to Hanna about it now and make sure she's doing okay. I tell myself that I'll check on her later, but even as I have this thought, I know I'm lying. There isn't going to be a "later." This is probably the end of the road for both of us.

The lights dim and a screen descends from the lobby ceiling. The Government Officials from each of our dates enter the room. Theo looks over at me. When I meet his eyes, he gives me a sharp, angry look, and then quickly averts his gaze. Cordelia is on screen, flashing us her haunting smile. My heart races. Is this how I'm going to be escorted? Over video? I look at the Government Officials. They all seem more relaxed and friendly after the creepy mock dates. I wonder if they'll look this pleased when they drag me to the train. Cordelia starts talking. "Congratulations everyone. Your challenges are complete. I always find it is most efficient to do this final step on camera, as it eliminates any awkwardness." I wonder if she can see our reactions through some sort of hidden camera. I try to hide my unimpressed look. If she's going to kick us out, she should at least do it in person.

"I've talked to all of the Government Officials at great length, and together we have come to a decision. It's worth pointing out that these votes are almost always unanimous, but this time it wasn't. Not at all."

I wonder why she's telling us this. There's some tension in her voice, maybe anger. "The two people that will be staying at the Cube will stay in this building for further clarification. The others will be escorted by two Government Officials. I trust that you'll make this process easy for everyone involved. Now, without further ado, the two fortunate people who will join the Cube as Working Guests are... Tearza Abebe and Eliana Sagona."

When Cordelia calls my name, I nearly gasp. This is the last thing I expected. I have no idea what happened or how I was chosen. I look at Theo to see if I can get anything from his reaction, but he's not looking at me. There's a blank expression on his face. I try not to show my shock. I know I should be happy. I don't know where the others are headed but I'm pretty sure this is the best Camp I can expect. I think of Hanna. When I look at her, I see fear written all over her face. She knows she's headed for trouble. My heart sinks, realizing there's no chance a young girl like her will last more than a couple of months in a Work Camp. She'll be dead by next year.

Hanna catches my gaze. She's teary-eyed, but she smiles at me. "You did it!" she says, and there's no bitterness in her voice.

I know we don't have long before someone notices us talking. I can tell from Hanna's face that she's worried. "You're going to be okay. They know you're talented. Maybe they'll take you somewhere that's not too bad."

"Every prison is bad," she says.

I know she's right. I try to think of something encouraging to say to Hanna when an Official comes over and grabs her. "It's time to go," the Government Official says.

"Can I hug her?" I ask.

The Official glares at me. She pulls Hanna away without answering. "Goodbye!" I yell out. "Good luck!"

Hanna looks back at me. She mouths the words *thank you* but doesn't say anything out loud. I don't blame her. She needs to keep safe.

I notice the rest of the Officials staring at me. They're angry, but I'm not going to apologize for saying goodbye to Hanna. If they weren't so entitled and selfish, maybe they would understand. Theo is the only one not looking at me. His eyes are on Hanna. He watches her attentively as she leaves the room. I detect concern on his face, but I'm probably imagining it.

The Officials escort the rest of the prisoners out of the room. Only Tearza and I are left in the lobby. Cordelia shuts off her camera and promptly joins us in person. We wait for her to speak.

"Well," she finally says. "I have to say this certainly was an interesting group." Cordelia seems to give me a look of warning as she continues. "I want to remind you that just because you've made it into the Cube doesn't mean you'll stay. The Cube's reputation depends on respect, mutual understanding, and," Cordelia stares straight at me, "obedience."

I return Cordelia's gaze.

"Tomorrow, orientation will begin, and I will explain what is expected from you both. For now, you will wait here for the Officials to return. Theo will take you to get your Chips before you go to the Cottage."

Cordelia exits the room before we can ask follow-up questions. We do as instructed and wait. I decide to take a seat in one of the comfortable chairs in the lobby, but Tearza remains standing. She stands for over thirty minutes until Theo finally returns. As soon as he enters the room, he beckons us to join him. When we reach him, I try to read Theo's expression again. I want to know why I'm here. What could have possibly happened? He doesn't give me anything. He starts walking, with the same quick pace. Tearza and I hurry behind him.

Theo takes us to a building by the entrance of the Cube. We have to leave Oparius to get here, but because we are with an Official it's permitted. The building looks similar to the houses that Patrons stay in, but the sign on the front distinguishes it. It says, "Welcome Center," so I figure this must be where we get our Chips. I wonder why this place is in such a public area. I would have figured the Chips would be given to us in Oparius.

"Do Patrons get Chips too?" I ask Theo. This seems like the only logical explanation.

"Officials, Patrons, and Working Guests all do."

He doesn't elaborate. At the front desk, a woman in a navy lab coat waits. Theo introduces us and the woman promptly leaves to prepare something in a back room.

The fact that Patrons and Officials also have Chips seems strange to me. I know I shouldn't ask any more questions, but I can't help myself.

I look at Theo, and he already seems to be looking at me. "Why do Officials and Patrons need Chips?" He doesn't immediately answer, so I continue, carefully. "I just thought they wouldn't... because the Cube can probably trust them."

"It's not a matter of trust. It's a matter of order. It's in everyone's best interest for the Cube to account for our whereabouts and actions. There are certain rules that Patrons and Officials have to abide by, too. Chips help with that."

I don't know what these rules are yet, but I nod.

To me, this sounds like too much control and surveillance, but I'm not surprised. That's how things work with the government. High-status Group members probably don't bat an eye about the Chips. They are accustomed to working with and living nearby the government.

The woman enters from the back room with a black and white apparatus. It's shaped like a hollow cylinder with a hole in the center large enough for a person's arm to poke through. Tearza is instructed to put her arm through the hole. The woman enters a code on the top of the cylinder, which leads to a quiet buzzing. There must be a circuit board inside the plastic casing. It's creating Tearza's Chip, measuring her wrist to find a perfect fit. When the process is complete, a green light flashes from the corner of the apparatus, and Tearza is told she can release her hand. There is a metal bracelet, about half an inch thick, securely wrapped around her wrist. Theo has a similar one. Tearza officially belongs to the Cube.

It's my turn to receive my Chip. I can't help but feel angry as I put my arm into the cylinder and am instructed to keep still. I look over at Theo and notice him peering out the window. He's not even paying attention. The process of losing one's freedom doesn't faze him. When the green light flashes and I pull my hand out of the apparatus, my wrist feels lighter than I expected it to. The bracelet looks bulky, but it's surprisingly light. I could almost forget about it, if only it weren't tracking my every move.

The woman briefly explains how the Chips work. She tells us that the Chips will provide Officials with our whereabouts, but they will also severely shock us if we ever go out of bounds.

"A fence borders the perimeter of the Cube." The woman tells us. "It is there to keep others from coming in, but it's also there to keep people from leaving before they are expected to. Be careful of this fence. If at any time, you touch the fence, your Chip will cause an intense shock to your system, which can leave you debilitated for hours. It's very important that you keep your distance."

So, this is how they keep us from escaping. I imagine myself trying to run away and being shocked by the fence. The force of it might throw me to the ground. I wouldn't be able to move, supposedly for hours. That would give the Officials ample time to find me and punish me however they wished. The Chip seems impossible to take off, too. The metal is thick, and the woman explains that it's indestructible. I'm caged in, I realize. There is no way to escape.

Theo thanks the woman for her help and we exit the building. He tells us he's going to take us to the Cottage now.

"What's the Cottage?"

"It's where the Working Guests sleep."

"In a cottage?" I can't help myself. The term is so swanky, that it's hard to believe that's where the prisoners stay.

"We want to make you feel comfortable at the Cube. You're not going to find any of our facilities to be a disappointment."

I don't say anything to that. He's probably aware of the face I'm making behind him.

"I can't wait to see it," Tearza says.

I roll my eyes and keep walking.

When we get to the Cottage, I'm struck by how substantial it is—it's far too big to be a house. Where I grew up, homes weren't even a tenth of the size. Our community center in 7N is smaller than the Cottage.

When we first walk in, there's a living room with leather couches, love seats, and fancy chairs. There's an enormous wooden bookcase on the wall, filled with more books than I knew existed. Everything is oversized and glamorous, but there's something cozy about the Cottage, too. The walls are made of wood and there's a fireplace in the center of the living room. It looks like the country homes I once looked at in magazines. I can't deny it's beautiful, but that doesn't make me like it any more. It's hard to imagine I'll actually be living in a place like this.

Theo leads us to a room beside the common room and quickly shows us the bathroom. Everything is lavishly designed, including the showers, stalls, and toilets. When I notice the gold trim of the toilets, I hold back laughter. It's absurd. I had no idea toilets could look so expensive.

The bathroom leads to another room, which Theo calls "the wardrobe." It's filled with so many different pieces of clothing, and each one looks more expensive than the last. I notice that there are nametags on each of the pieces. I wonder where my clothes are. Theo explains that Patrons will usually dress themselves and these clothes are just for "emergencies."

When I ask him what that means, he merely stares. He doesn't like the question. I wonder if it's because he can't think of a reasonable answer.

The next room is our makeup room. The room is mostly empty, except for a massive table in the center. There are chairs around the table and each chair has its own mirror and drawer filled with makeup.

"A chair has been added with each of your names. The makeup in the corresponding drawer has been specifically chosen for you."

Tearza and I nod as if this is completely normal behavior.

We follow Theo out of the makeup room and head back to the living room. There's one last room to see. To the right of the living room is a massive bedroom. The room is dark, and there seem to be no windows, so Theo shines his flashlight.

The room is filled with people, each of them fast asleep. I've never seen so many people sleeping in the same room. There are too many bunk beds to count. It's overwhelming. Theo explains that the people sleeping are the other Working Guests. He tells us to find an empty bed. When I get a closer look at the people sleeping I realize they can't be in their own bodies. They must be in the bodies of the rich people visiting the Cube. The Patrons.

Most of them look older and not very attractive. Asleep, they seem normal and almost kind, but I know that must not be the case. Everyone looks innocent when they're sleeping. But these people are to blame for this Camp's existence. Without their business, the Cube wouldn't be able to operate. I wish I could wake them up and tell them exactly how I feel. I wouldn't be talking to them, though. These are just their bodies. Inside them, other prisoners are sleeping. Prisoners just like me. And soon, I'll be in their position, sleeping in another person's body, counting down the minutes until I return to myself.

"Eliana," Tearza's voice snaps me out of my thoughts. "Theo is talking to us."

"Huh?"

Theo is looking at me. "I was just saying that there are other places you may want to tour on your own. But the most important thing is that you stay within Oparius." Theo pauses for emphasis. "Is there anything else I can help you with?"

"No, I think we're good."

"Okay," Theo says. "People will start getting up in an hour or two. Have a good night."

I look at the clock. It's nearly 7:30 p.m. "Why are people getting up?" I ask.

He doesn't really give me an answer. I remember Cordelia saying something about nocturnal schedules. "You'll get the hang of things soon," Theo tells me. "Get some sleep."

Tearza thanks him for the tour. He gives me one last look before exiting the house. I'm not sure what to make of all this. Theo doesn't seem pleased with me, but he also didn't kick me out of this place when he had the chance. I don't understand what happened after our "date." He disappeared, completely furious with how I behaved, and somehow I'm still here? Cordelia did mention that the vote wasn't unanimous, though. Maybe Theo wanted to get rid of me. But then who wanted me to stay?

I look around the room for an empty bed. There are some top bunks still available. One is five rows up and the other six. "Any preference?" I ask Tearza, gesturing at the empty beds.

She shakes her head. "I hate heights."

"Sorry."

"It's not your problem. I guess I'll take the lower one. Good night."

I leave it at that and climb up one of the ladders to an empty bed. It's clear Tearza doesn't like me very much, and I don't blame her. We're so different. She is polished and put together and everything I've been trying to be since arriving here. But despite my best efforts, the Cube has seen right through me. I'm too angry and opinionated to be here. I totally don't fit in. I look at the other prisoners before going to bed. I can only hope not everyone's as perfectly mannered as Tearza. Maybe one of them will get along with me. Maybe I'll stop feeling so alone.

I try to fall asleep, but I'm wired. I still can't believe I'll be staying here. At the Cube. I think about Ethan and wonder what he'd think if he could see me now. I wonder what he'd say if he knew I went on a date with someone else tonight. I'm sure that's the last thing he thinks

I'm doing. I wish I could talk to him and let him know that I'm safe. That I'm alive. I hope he's doing okay too, wherever he is. I hope he's home with his family, and not at a Camp. I wish it was Ethan who took me on a date. I miss him so much. I miss the comfort he gave me, the happiness, and the warmth. I miss home and I miss Mama. I keep forgetting that she's gone.

When I'm far from home, I can almost pretend Mama's still alive. I picture her in our little house, dancing in the hallways and sipping on a glass of cheap wine. I wonder what she'd say to me now if I was with her. *You're going to get through this. Everything's going to be just fine.* I'm not sure I believe that right now. Everything I love feels so far away and Mama isn't here. She's gone forever. All I want to do is lie in bed and cry until there's nothing left inside me, but I know I've got to suck it up. It's just the beginning. I can't give up already. I promised Ethan that I'd find a way out. I know that wherever he is, he's trying to find me too. We're in this together and it's not the end.

One way or another, I'm going home. I'm escaping from this place. It's only a matter of time.

CHAPTER 16

When I wake up, I'm completely disoriented. There are no windows in the bedroom because everyone sleeps through the day. But it makes determining the time quite a challenge. I find a clock on the wall and realize it's 2:30 a.m. Could it really be 2:30? Have I slept for six hours? I look around the room and see that everyone's still asleep.

"Psst," I hear someone say. Maybe not everyone. Tearza is sitting up in her bed, gazing eagerly at me. She gestures for me to join her outside.

I quietly get down from my bunk bed and meet her in the living room.

I sit beside Tearza on one of the many couches. I'm amazed by how comfortable it is.

Tearza tells me that she couldn't fall asleep, that she was up most of the night, and that Theo was right. Most of the prisoners woke up around 10:00, others around midnight, and they all headed out. They didn't come back until 6:00 or 7:00 in the morning—some of them came even later. Apparently, some prisoners came in and out of the Cottage during the middle of the night, looking beautiful and young, but when they finally returned to sleep, they were in their Companions' bodies again. Tearza says they kept her awake, talking loudly, so I'm shocked I slept through all of it. As Tearza explains this, I realize I must have slept much longer than I realized. It's 2:30 p.m. now. I must have slept for eighteen hours.

When I process everything Tearza tells me, I ask, "Where do you think they go during the night?"

"I don't know. I guess they go to the gym. Get their work done."

"Right."

"Their Companions are in their Shells all day. And then whenever their Companions sleep, the Working Guests get their Shells back. We're lucky that happens here."

"Not always. Not when we go to bed."

"Sure, but it could be a lot worse. We're lucky we get our Shells while we're awake. At least they give us that."

"I guess." I notice that Tearza uses the Cube's terminology even when we're alone. I try not to be annoyed by this. "But they kind of *need to* give us our 'Shells' back." I use air quotes. "That's the only way we can keep our bodies looking the way they want."

"You can look at it that way if you choose," Tearza says.

Hours pass before the other prisoners begin to wake up. At 9:00 p.m. I hear Cordelia's voice echo through the Cottage. I walk to the living room, where there's a projector screen hanging from the roof, and Cordelia's face is looking straight at me. Tearza's already in the room, staring attentively at Cordelia.

"Tomorrow's the big day!" Cordelia says. "For those of you waiting to be matched with a Companion, tomorrow we will host our Mingle. Get ready for an afternoon BBQ where you'll meet the new Patrons of the Cube. At the end of the day, most Patrons will pick someone to pair with. If they pick you, they'll become your Companion. It's as simple as that. Now, this can be a nerve-wracking day, but there's not much to be worried about. The Government Officials selected you specifically because we think you'll have no trouble finding a Companion. Of course, we can't always be correct and it can be a challenge, especially when we don't come to a unanimous decision... but, nevertheless, we have every hope that you will succeed." Cordelia gives one of her fake smiles. It's just as annoying as it was yesterday.

"Of course, if you're not able to find a Companion at the Mingle, you won't be able to stay here. If the other Working Guests see you without a Companion, the Cube becomes imbalanced and unequal. That simply won't do. The only way for the Cube to function is if all sides are exactly equal. Just like the shape." Cordelia pauses for dramatic effect. "Take this time to get ready for the Mingle and make sure to look your best. A Government Official will pick you up at noon tomorrow. Make sure you're ready."

Tearza looks at me, nervous. "You don't think I'm the one who wasn't unanimously voted for, do you?"

"I doubt it."

"You're probably right. You're much more divisive."

"Thanks."

"Sorry, I'm feeling a little nervous."

"It's all right. I'm sure you've got nothing to worry about."

That doesn't seem to settle her. "I should probably start getting ready." We have lots of time before the event, but I don't stop her.

At 11:30 a.m. the following day, other prisoners start getting ready for the Mingle. One guy with bright, narrow eyes and light brown skin comes over to Tearza and me. He's got tattoos along his right arm and one on his calf. He's way too attractive to be in a Companion's body. I know he must be in his own skin.

"You guys Newbodies?" He asks.

"What?" I say, confused.

"Newbodies. That's what we call ourselves here. You're a prisoner, right?"

"Yeah."

He explains to us that he and some of the others have just finished their time with a Companion and will be reassigned. They're coming with us to the Mingle to find someone new. I'm not too thrilled by this idea because that means more people to take away a spot from me. But at the same time, it's nice to have an expert around. He introduces himself as Dylan and I tell him to call me Ellie. He explains how things work around here, telling us that people usually wake up whenever their Companions notify them that they're ready for the Switch, and spend the nights going to the gym or doing whatever else they have time to do. In the daytime, when their bodies are being used by their Companions, they sleep. Dylan explains that sometimes people have the same Companion for months at a time, but other times it only lasts for a week or less.

Another Newbody joins us. She's got blue hair with a silver streak and soft freckles on her cheeks.

"Yeah, it's pretty much doom and gloom for people like us."

"People like who?"

The girl flashes a shrewd grin. "You know... the hair, the tattoos, and it doesn't help that neither of us is white. Sometimes people come for a 'cultural experience.' That's what they say at least. But really they just want to steal the body of a skinny girl who looks 'exotic,'" she points to herself, "and then go drink margaritas on the beach."

I laugh a little because I know the girl is trying to add humor to the situation, but the reality behind what she says is frightening.

She continues, "When you don't look or act 'traditional,' or whatever you want to call it, you usually end up with the fun ones. Or, you know, relatively fun. Nobody who comes here is *fun*, per se, but these people are special. They come for a week or two just 'to see what it's like' or whatever. Then they leave. But they're the ones who choose people like Dyl and me."

"What does that mean?" Tearza asks.

"I just mean if you smile nicely and say 'please' and 'thank you' maybe you'll get some boring dude who goes to bed at nine, eats three meals a day, doesn't snack, and stays for a few months. Those are the best bodies. But they usually go to the friendly blondes or, you know, whatever, the type of prisoners boring people like. I've tried fooling them but it doesn't work."

I nod, understanding. It's refreshing to meet someone like this girl here. I don't know who she is but I already like her.

"It's not always good having a long Companionship," Dylan says. "Remember that time with Efia?"

"Oh yeah," the girl says. "An old friend of ours got stuck with this horrible man for so long. Like seven months or something. And he ate so much. He'd eat like 10,000 calories a day. And Efia's equilibrium was set at 2000, so she had to burn off 8000 calories every day. She worked her butt off, but she barely had time for anything else. She completely exhausted herself... anyway, she ended up getting kicked out. She couldn't keep up."

"Geeze," I say. "That's horrible."

"Yeah," Dylan says. "They're ruthless here. But overall, Minji is right." I register the blue-haired girl's name. Minji. "Generally, the longer your Companionship the better. That way you get to figure out what works. How long they sleep. How much they eat in your body. It's just easier."

"Any tips for how to make that happen?" Tearza asks.

"Talk to the older people," Minji says. "Usually the older they are, the more boring they are. Or, you know, try to get a sense of them and figure out if they're the type to play it safe or be a jerk. Don't waste your time on a jerk. I personally try to talk to women because I find they're nicer. But sometimes that can backfire, especially if they're skinny because they've spent their whole lives being told to look a certain way. So, the second they get in your body, they'll eat the whole world. You know what I mean?" I nod. Minji continues, "Basically, there is no safe bet. Just try to be careful, and hope that you're lucky. But try to find someone that looks nice and safe. Then once you choose, work your magic, say the right things, and hope for the best. But always talk to a few others just in case. And then if you're lucky, the one you like will pick you."

"That doesn't sound difficult at all," I say.

"When in doubt just remember," Minji says, "either way you're screwed."

I laugh bitterly, knowing she's right.

"Anyway, you'll be fine," Minji assures me. "You're hot as *hell.*"

It's a bright and sunny day, perfect for a barbeque. About fifteen prisoners are here, including Minji, Dylan, Tearza, and myself. We all gather under a large white tent that's tastefully decorated with white and silver ribbons. Rows of picnic tables, placed together to make long lines, are carefully laid out and covered with food. There is so much food. I can't imagine that even half of it will be eaten. I think about the amount that will inevitably be wasted but push the thought away. I turn my attention to the enormous bouquets between the large platters of food. The flowers are bright and colorful, just like the outfits of the Patrons attending. I try to count the number of Patrons under the tent. There are almost as many of them as there are of us. I scan the area, taking in how happy the Patrons seem to be. They're on vacation. They don't have a care in the world. The concept of the Mingle doesn't seem to disturb them at all. They seem to be completely at ease with the idea—excited, even.

There are others at the Mingle, too. Officials guard the area and several men and women dressed in burgundy dresses and suits walk around, tending to things. They clean up spills and refill the food trays. I wonder who they are. They can't work for the government. Maybe they're maintenance staff.

Dylan notices me observing.

"Quit staring and go talk to someone," he says.

Minji joins him, shaking her head as she stands beside Dylan. She sighs. "Rookies,"

"Who are those people setting everything up?"

"They're the Keepers. But don't bother with them, because they're so *uptight.* I've been trying to make friends with them since coming here, because, you know, this job can't be easy for them. They live here, away from their families. You'd think they'd want a friend. But it's technically prohibited for them to talk to prisoners, and they seem to be afraid of me."

Minji laughs as if this is amusing.

"Are they from our Groups?" I ask.

"They're mostly from 7."

I nod. In Group7, we are essentially the servants for Group1 and 2. We work wherever and however we're told. I think about how hard that must be for them, working at this Resort, never getting to see friends or family. I think about my grandparents, whom I've only met once or twice because they've spent their lives in the shadow of a Group2 family.

"That's awful," I say.

Minji shrugs. "A job's a job." But I can tell she's upset. None of us say anything for a moment. We're thinking of our own experiences.

"Anyway," Dylan says. "We should *really* start mingling."

"True," Minji says, making a face at Dylan. "*You* do, especially. With those looks, let's hope you have a good personality."

I laugh. Minji squeezes my hand and whispers, "Good luck."

Minji and Dylan walk away. I watch Minji head toward an elderly woman who's talking to another prisoner. She cuts in, politely joining the conversation.

I look around the tent and try to follow Minji's advice: target kind-looking people. I take advantage of the fact that people are eating. I look for reasonably full plates. Normal portions. Hopefully if they have healthy eating habits in their own bodies, they will in mine as well. It might be wishful thinking but it's all I've got.

Before I finish surveying the crowd, a man interrupts me. "Well, hello there beautiful."

I try not to gag. "Hi." I give my best smile. The man is older, in his mid-fifties, with a potbelly and a terrible sense of style. He's wearing skinny jeans and a leather cowboy hat.

"Can I get you something to eat?"

"That's okay," I try to sound as polite as possible. "I was just about to get something for myself."

"No kidding! Let me get it for you. You look like you could eat a burger or two." The man plops a bun on my plate and loads it with two patties, cheese, and some sort of fancy doughnut. "My specialty," he winks. "I hope you're not one of those vegetarians." He snorts. He doesn't put a single vegetable on my burger, loads the other half of my plate with fries, and hands it to me.

"Thanks. Looks delicious."

"No problem, pretty lady." He picks up his burger and takes a massive bite. He keeps talking, not waiting to chew. "You know, this is my first time talking to a girl like you—you know, the reckless type." He winks again. "I had no idea you'd be so charming."

I don't know what to say to this. I want to kick him in the groin and tell him he has no idea what he's talking about. If I weren't from Group7, he wouldn't think of me as "reckless," whatever that means. If I had his money, I'd do a whole lot more with my privilege than he's doing. I take a deep breath. "We come in all different shapes and sizes."

"That's for sure." He grins. "I'm certainly a fan of your shape."

I nearly choke on a fry.

My shock makes the man laugh. "Damn, you're adorable. I'd love to live in your body. But how am I supposed to get a lady if I'm in your body, huh?" He seems to find this hilarious. "What's a man supposed to do?"

"Are you allowed to do that here?" I ask before I can stop myself. It's the first time I consider that people might come here to hook up with others. Can Companions just use our bodies to meet people and do things without our consent? The thought horrifies me.

"Of course!" He continues to laugh. "Why else would I be here?" The man seems to spot someone in the distance. "Oh, now that's a good-looking dude. I'm sure a girl like you would like a piece of that, eh?"

I don't reply.

"I'll see you later, pumpkin."

The man goes to talk to Dylan and I'm relieved to be alone. I try to signal for Dylan to run, but he doesn't notice me. I silently wish him good luck.

Once I'm alone again, I try to process the idea that my body will not be solely mine tomorrow. It will be mine, but also someone else's. They'll get to do whatever they want to me, and however they want. They'll probably do extremely damaging things—things they wouldn't dream of doing in their own bodies where they have to live with the consequences. Even if I tried to find a Companion who seems tamer, there is no guarantee I'd be right. I could try to find a married person to reduce the possibility of them having sex, but would that actually lower the chances?

"You know, being a sad sack alone over here isn't going to score you a Companion." Minji cuts me off from my thoughts. I'm glad it's her and not that grotesque man.

"You're probably right. It's just—how do you *do* this?"

"Do what?"

"I don't know, get used to this place. And the idea that anyone can use your body however they want to."

"You just kind of... do it. It takes some time, but you'll get numb to it all soon. It'll just become normal. And it helps that there are some regulations. People can't do *whatever* they want."

"They can't?"

"No, they sign a contract before coming. Like they can't murder someone or commit suicide in your body. Because even though it's their Essence in there, it's your body that dies. Their Essence can just go back to their body after. You're the one who's screwed."

"Right," I say, a little frightened by the idea.

Minji senses my discomfort and reassures me. "The contract's thorough, don't worry. It protects you. And it's not just to keep you from dying. It helps with other stuff too. Like they're required to have protected sex if that's what you're worried about. The Cube doesn't want to deal with the complications of pregnancy just as much as you don't."

"How would that even work? Whose baby would it be?"

Minji shrugs. "Just don't think about all that. It's not going to help you."

I know she's right. Minji takes a look at my plate of overflowing food.

She laughs. "What the hell are you eating? Is there a doughnut in your burger?"

I point to the man I was talking to. "He served me."

"Yikes." She watches the man talk to Dylan. "They're definitely going to match. Poor Dyl..."

"Yeah, he was kind of the worst."

"It's okay. Dylan is tough. He can handle pretty much anything."

I watch the way Minji looks at him. I wonder about their history. Could they be dating? Are prisoners allowed to date? Something tells me it's not allowed, but something tells me neither of them cares much about rules.

"Anyway," Minji continues, "you'll get used to things, don't worry. But you've got to start meeting people. Why don't you try that old lady in the blue dress? I just talked to her and she's surprisingly sweet."

I follow Minji's advice and go over to the lady. She's standing by herself at the salad bar. She must be in her nineties. I watch her carefully pick at the salad on her plate and decide she seems like a worthwhile prospect. I put down my ridiculous plate of food and get some veggies instead. I need to create a certain image and the doughnut burger isn't going to help. I take a deep breath and walk over to the elderly woman.

When I reach her, the woman beams at me. "Hello," I say, "I'm Eliana."

"I know who you are."

I'm shocked by this, but then I remember the crowds from the competitions. "Were you at the challenges yesterday?"

"Oh, no, dear. I just arrived."

"Of course." I'm embarrassed for asking.

"I watched your videos on my way here, though. You're actually one of the girls I wanted to talk to."

"Videos?"

"Yes, sweetheart. The Cube gives us access to your challenge videos before we choose who we want to meet. I was amazed by your running. And the way you spoke so naturally with that man on your date... It was wonderful to watch."

My heart races. My date with Theo was filmed? This lady watched it? I wonder if she's playing with me. Or just trying to be polite.

I try to stay calm. The Cube probably edited the film. I remember Minji and Dylan's advice. I need to stay likable and sweet. "Aw," I put a hand on my heart. "Thanks so much. It was a tough day, but I'm so honored to have made it here."

"I'm sure. It looked tough to me. But then again, you're a lot younger than me!" She laughs. "So how does it work? If I access your body will I be able to move like you?"

I have no idea how that works, but I tell her yes. I keep the conversation going, saying whatever I need to in order to make her like me. I ask her about herself and tell her pleasant things about my life. I learn that her name is Mary, she's ninety-five years old, and she has two bunnies and a bird back home. Her Countdown recently started and she has ninety-two days to live. The Cube is the first stop on her Explore Program. I wonder if I should tell her about Mama and that I know a little about the Countdown too. I decide not to, keeping the conversation light. I make her laugh and I pretend to laugh in return when she makes corny jokes. When the conversation is over, I thank her for talking to me.

Shortly after, Cordelia wraps things up and we all go back to our respective homes. Cordelia explains that our Chips will buzz in about an hour and tell us who our Companions are. Once we are matched, we'll have the opportunity to learn more about our Companions by looking through their profiles on our Chips. Cordelia says the profile is made to help us feel more comfortable and "empowered" throughout the process. Minji and Dylan say that the profile is complete nonsense and not worth any of my time.

We talk openly about everything once we're back at the Cottage. At first, I'm nervous to say anything too critical, but Minji reassures me.

"The Officials are watching our locations through the Chips, but they don't listen to us. As long as we're not around them, we can say whatever we want. Trust me."

I look skeptical.

"I'm serious." Minji continues, "We bad-mouth this place all the time and nothing happens." Then Minji proceeds to scream very loudly, "EMMANUELLA IS THE DEVIL WRAPPED IN

RAINBOW CONFETTI UNICORN CRAP," and smiles, satisfied when nothing happens. "See? Nobody's listening."

I can't help but laugh at Minji's outburst. "You're crazy."

"Listen," she pats my knee. "You stay here long enough, and you'll be screaming out weirder things. Cordelia has that effect on everyone."

"I'm sure," I say, getting more comfortable. "And it's not going to take me long. Cordelia already makes me want to scream."

We talk more about the Mingle. Dylan tells us that the man in the cowboy hat goes to Resorts like this twice a year. Apparently, the man couldn't stop boasting to Dylan about all the women he's picked up throughout the years. We all laugh at the absurdity of this, considering he's probably never been successful in his own body. Whatever has allegedly worked for him in these environments has nothing to do with *him*. It is all about the bodies he uses.

Minji tells horror stories about the different people she met. At one point, Tearza joins us. She talks kindly of a red-headed woman she got to know with a family of four at home. Tearza says the woman seemed very kind and she liked that the woman was married. Minji chimes in saying, "I talked to that lady too. She is one hundred percent here to cheat on her man and escape her spoiled-rotten kids." This makes me laugh, but Tearza doesn't say anything. Eventually, the conversation becomes a bit too critical for Tearza, so she gets up and leaves.

Minji makes a face when it's just the three of us. "That girl is something else."

"Be nice," Dylan says. "Everyone's got different ways of handling this."

"Yeah, but she doesn't have to be so supportive. I mean, did you hear the way she talked about Cordelia? It was like they'd been friends for life. Doesn't she know that she's Cordelia's prisoner?"

"No, she's her *Working Guest*." Minji and Dylan laugh. It makes me feel more comfortable. "She's been like this since we got here," I explain. "I thought she was sucking up at first, but now I think she is genuinely like this. She sees the good in every one or something."

"What good?" Minji asks. "What's *good* about arresting a girl for stealing food for her sick grandma?"

Dylan puts an arm around her. That's why Minji must be here. She was trying to feed her grandma. "I agree," I tell her. "If I could punch Cordelia and not face any consequences, she'd probably be in rough shape right now."

Minji lets out a weak laugh. "I just hate it when people come in here supporting the government. Our government is the reason we're in this mess, you know?"

"Yeah. I'm with you. Trust me."

There's a buzz coming from one of our Chips. I look at the others. Dylan reads something off his screen.

"Thank god," he says. "I didn't get the Cowboy. I got this guy, Bernard. He seemed pretty chill."

The next Chip to buzz is Minji's. She matches with Mary Ames, the old woman I spent most of my time talking to. When Minji realizes this, she squeezes my hand and apologizes. I try to reassure her, telling Minji it's not her fault. I'm happy for her, but I can't help but feel disappointed. Mary was the one person I felt good about. Now that she is matched with Minji I know I'm going home. I didn't really talk to anyone else at the Mingle. I can't blame Mary for picking Minji, though.

Minji reads my mind. "Stop planning your departure." She whacks me on the arm. "I rarely get matched with the person I expect. That's just the way it goes."

"I didn't really talk to anyone else."

"Sure you did," she says. "You'll be fine."

A few minutes later, Tearza comes into the room and tells us she didn't match with the red-headed lady she had been expecting. Minji looks at me when Tearza tells us, thinking it'll give me some reassurance. Tearza got some other man she talked to named Anthony, but seems happy with the result. I doubt she'd admit to being unhappy though, so this doesn't mean much. It does seem weird that she got a man though. I wonder how often that happens. I don't know how much of a difference it makes, but I hope a woman chooses me.

I'm the only one left who is unmatched.

Minji and Dylan continue to reassure me, but they can't be certain I'll be matched. In the middle of their pep talk, my Chip finally buzzes. I expect it to tell me that my time here is finished and that I didn't match with anyone. But instead, it shows a picture of a man with his arms around two blonde women. He's wearing a cowboy hat.

"Oh god," my heart sinks. "I got the Cowboy."

CHAPTER 17

Minji and Dylan convince me to stay up all night with them so I can adjust to my new sleep schedule before tomorrow's Switch. It's normal for me to run on little sleep so I'm happy to do it. If I'm going to be successful here, I should get used to the nocturnal schedule as soon as possible. Plus, it's fun staying up with Minji and Dylan. It's easy to hang out with them and forget how messed up this place is. At some point in the night, I learn that my suspicions were correct. Minji and Dylan are a couple and that's not technically allowed. But as long as they keep their relationship to themselves, the Cube doesn't really care. At least that's what they tell me. Minji says all the Cube Officials care about is how things affect their reputation or their Patrons. So, if the Patrons don't find out about Minji and Dylan's relationship, there is nothing to worry about. It sounds risky to me, and I'm not sure I completely believe that they're safe, but it's worked for them so far. It makes me think about Ethan. I wonder if I'd risk getting kicked out if he'd come to the Cube with me. The answer is easy. Of course I would.

Around 7:00 in the morning, Minji and Dylan go for a walk. They invite me to join, but I'm too anxious. I stay in my bed and wait for my Chip to buzz. I tap its screen. I know Minji and Dylan are right; the Patron's profiles won't be accurate. But I still want to feel as prepared as possible. Tomorrow's a big day.

A message pops up on the screen to tell me that my caloric equilibrium has been calculated and my Chip has been updated. I look down at my Chip and a number flashes at the top: 2000. I'm allowed to retain 2000 calories every day. I have to burn off the rest.

I don't like the sound of that—I'm pretty sure the Cowboy will be eating well over 2000 calories. When I go to the Cowboy's profile, my suspicions are confirmed. The first thing I notice is his favorite quote: "Eat good food, explore good women." I want to puke. Is that even a quote? Or did he just write down his objective for his time here? I read through a couple more pieces of information, like his favorite food ("beer") and his main objective ("a good time") but it's not long until I stop. Maybe I was wrong about needing to feel prepared. The less I know about the Cowboy the better.

Before I leave the screen, I notice there's one more section I can search through. At the top corner of the page, there's an option to view more information. There's a brief description of the Cube, written in flowery language. It glosses over everything problematic about the Resort and only focuses on the "state-of-the-art amenities." But below the description, there are pictures of the Officials, with their names and ages listed below. I look through the pictures, trying to learn as many names as I can. When I get to a familiar face, I pause. Theo Jacobson. I read his age: seventeen. He's only one year older than me. I stare at his picture, noticing how different he looks with a smile on his face. He has a great smile—it lifts his cheekbones and brightens his eyes—but unfortunately, he rarely shows it. Especially around someone like me, whom he clearly sees as his inferior. I roll my eyes, not wanting to think of Theo Jacobson a moment longer. I turn off my Chip's screen.

Around 7:45, my Chip buzzes. As anxious as I am for the Switch, I was hoping it would happen later because this means the Cowboy likes to have an early start to the day. Minji says that the best-case scenario is having a Companion who sleeps in late and goes to bed early. The longer they're asleep and in their body, the longer we have in ours. But I have a feeling the Cowboy will be the worst-case scenario. If my alarm is going off at 7:45 that means he wakes up relatively early—and based on what he was saying at the Mingle, he's probably going to party late into the night. I hope I'm wrong because the Cowboy has requested my body for the next two months.

I quickly rush out of the Cottage and find an Official waiting by the door. There isn't much time before I have to meet the Cowboy for the Switch. They only give us five minutes.

I recognize the Official. She's the one who Theo was talking to during the competitions. The one who went on Peter's mock date. I remember reading her name last night. Samantha.

"Eliana Sagona," Samantha says.

"Yes?" Am I already in trouble?

"The Cube was notified that Wyatt Montgomery," a.k.a. the Cowboy, "is ready for the Switch."

I nod. "I'm going to find my way there right now." I hope I can figure it out from Cordelia's walk around the premises.

"I'm here to escort you," Samantha says. "Follow me."

Once we begin walking, I realize things look different in the light. I'm not sure where I am and I'm grateful to have Samantha guiding me. I don't know what would have happened if I got lost and arrived late. I imagine it would have been bad.

I make sure to note the route we're taking so that next time I'm able to do it on my own. When we get to a Cube structure with metal sliding doors, Samantha tells me to press the open button to the right of the doors. The doors swiftly slide open and I walk inside. Samantha follows.

"This is the entrance to the Switch-Pod," Samantha explains.

The doors close and we immediately drop. We move fast and I can feel my stomach sink as we head deeper underground. A moment later, we stop. I can feel something shifting under us, and then we change directions. We move forward like we're on an underground train. And then, thankfully, we stop. The doors open. I follow Samantha out, and into an empty room with nothing but a white, egg-shaped chair in the center.

Samantha gestures for me to sit in the chair. "This is your Switch-Pod," she says. "You see that red light?"

There's a red light on the wall in front of the chair and a circular mirror below. I nod.

"When the light turns green, that means your Companion has reached his Pod and is ready." I sit down in the Switch-Pod and listen. "Once that happens, the Switch will occur, and your Essence will transfer. An Official will be waiting for you on the other side to assist you with the rest."

"Where will you be?" I ask.

Before Samantha can respond, the light turns green. My heart beats faster and I begin to panic. I wish I could get out of here, but there's nowhere to go. I look at Samantha, hoping for reassurance. Did she respond to my question?

Before I can ask her again, I'm somewhere else. I'm in a similar Pod to the one I was just sitting in. But now I'm in someone else's body. My body is not mine anymore. I am the Cowboy.

There's a rectangular mirror on the wall in front of me and I get a good look at myself, or not myself, really, but the body I'm inhabiting. I stand up from the chair and stare at my reflection as I move around in the Cowboy's body. It's disorienting. The Cowboy has a large belly and disproportionately small legs. He's about the same height as me, but his proportions are nothing like mine. I try walking, but I feel heavy and stiff.

There's an Official watching me. I do a doubletake and realize I recognize him. It's Theo. He must have been the one to escort the Cowboy to his Pod.

"This is so weird," I say. "I can barely walk."

"You'll get used to it."

I nod, but I'm not sure I will. At least I don't have to do much living in the Cowboy's body. Mostly, I'll just sleep.

Theo guides me out of the room and back into a similar metal contraption I arrived in. We move underground, then up. The doors open and I'm back in the place I first entered. I'm happy to be out from underground.

I look down as I walk, trying to come to terms with my new reality. Right now, the Cowboy is in my skin and he can do basically whatever he wants. And at the same time, I'm in the Cowboy's body, without any desire to be here. There's a foreign smell to him, too, which doesn't help. It's not exactly pleasant, but the worst part is its constancy. I can't escape it. And every time I get a whiff, I'm reminded that I'm someone else.

Theo escorts me back to the Cottage. When we arrive, Theo pauses before leaving. "Are you okay?" he asks. He must have noticed how quiet I was on the walk back.

"I'm fine," I say.

"It will get easier."

"Thanks." I hate that he's seeing me this way.

Theo looks at me for a moment longer and I think he has more to say. But then he gives a curt wave and turns to leave.

I'm left alone with this new body. I go inside the Cottage before I can think about my circumstances any longer. There's no use dwelling on the situation. What I need to do is sleep. I climb the ladder to my bed, finding it more difficult as the Cowboy. When I get to the top, I try to find a comfortable position. I usually lie on my belly, but this doesn't feel right anymore. I roll to my right side, trying to settle there. I bend my knees and realize the Cowboy has joint pain that I'm not used to. I flip to the other side. I can't tell if his body temperature runs warmer than mine or if I'm overheating because of how worked up I feel.

I know I'm tired and need rest. I feel exhausted but wired at the same time. I close my eyes, but my mind races with a million different thoughts. Eventually, I get up and decide to unpack my things.

I spend the day trying to sleep, reading magazines, and staring at my new body in the mirror. At some point, I actually manage to doze off. It doesn't last long. I wake up to the sound of my Chip buzzing. It's time to head back to the Switch-Pod and switch back. This time, when I hear the buzzing, I'm excited. I'm eager to get my body back.

I go to the Pod by myself this time. I find my way and arrive with time to spare. The Cowboy isn't here yet; I wait for him eagerly.

Finally, over ten minutes later, he arrives. The Switch happens almost instantaneously and the moment I'm back in my body I feel like crying. I'm so relieved. I touch my arms, my legs, my toes, my head. I've never appreciated my body more than in this moment. I look at myself in the mirror in front of me. When I lift my arms, it's my own arms that follow. When I kick my legs, I see my legs in the reflection. When I point my toes, my beautiful, callused ballerina feet mimic me. I take one last look at myself and leave the room.

Once I'm above ground again, I realize I'm starving. I look at the clock on my Chip. It's 1:00 in the morning. People will be at the gym by now, or maybe back at the Cottage, but I know what my first stop needs to be. Food.

I head to the Oparius cafeteria. It's not as enormous as the gym, but it's not small either. There are rows of picnic tables and many different food stations to choose from. I take some time to look over the options. I decide to get pasta with cream sauce and all kinds of vegetables because it looks delicious. Plus, I never ended up eating the pasta I ordered on my mock date.

It's weird to order food and not need to worry about the cost. That may be the one perk of being a prisoner. I don't have to worry about money anymore.

There aren't many people in the cafeteria. I notice someone sitting at a table alone. When I get closer, I realize it's Theo. We make eye contact and I wonder what to do. I decide to take the seat across from him. I've been meaning to apologize after our "date," so I figure now is a good time.

"Hey," I say, taking a seat. "Mind if I sit with you?"

Theo doesn't say anything back. He gives me a subtle nod and keeps eating his food.

"What's that you're eating?" I ask.

"It's falafel."

"It smells delicious."

Theo's quiet. Eventually, he says, "How are you feeling about your match?"

"With the Cowboy?" I say, dryly. "I'm delighted."

"Who?"

"That's what we call him. Because of the hat."

Theo doesn't say anything to this. I decide to change the subject.

"So, at the Mingle, someone mentioned they watched my videos from the competitions... is that true? Were people able to watch our date?"

Theo doesn't respond. I decide to keep talking. "I mean, if it's true, I just wanted to say I'm sorry... I had no idea we were being recorded. And either way, it was stupid for me to act that way. On the date, I mean. I know I shouldn't have said those things."

"Mock date."

"Right. That's what I meant."

"You know, Lana, you could have gotten yourself into a lot of trouble."

"I know," I say, but I'm shocked that he called me Lana. That's my stage name. Nobody calls me that outside of ballet. "It won't happen again." I'm not sure if I should say anything more, but I can't help myself. "I also... I just wanted to say thanks."

"For what?"

"I don't know. I'm sure you could have kicked me out of the Cube after our mock date. But you didn't." The way Theo's looking at me makes me think I can continue. He doesn't look angry. He's listening. "And, I mean, of course I have no idea what happened with the vote... for who got to stay. Cordelia said it wasn't unanimous... so if you had anything to do with me staying, I just wanted to say thank you. I appreciate it."

Theo's quiet for a moment. When he finally speaks, his voice is cold. "What makes you think I had anything to do with it?"

My heart stops. I can feel myself blushing and I try to stop it. "I don't know. I thought..." I have no idea what I thought. "I just don't understand how I wasn't kicked out after my outburst. I thought maybe—"

"Listen, you're here because you're here. Don't start overthinking things. All right?"

"Okay."

"Just focus on staying out of trouble." Theo takes the last bite of his sandwich. He looks at my plate of pasta. "And should you even be eating all that?" He asks. "What's your Chip at?"

"My what?"

"Your equilibrium."

"Oh my god." In my hungry-exhausted state, I'd completely forgotten about tracking my calories. Theo gets up and leaves without saying goodbye. I finish my bowl of pasta because there are only a couple of bites left. Then I check my Chip. While I was asleep the Cowboy ate 6700 calories. My meal was 900. I'm at 7600 and I need to get to 2000. That means I've got to burn 5600 calories before the night is through.

I head to the gym, trying to think of anything other than how much of a jerk Theo Jacobson is.

CHAPTER 18

Over the next few days, I adjust to life at the Cube. Minji and Dylan introduce me to many of the other Newbodies. There are roughly one hundred of us, so I don't meet everyone. I follow along with their schedules, getting accustomed to waking up at 10:00 at night and going to bed around 8:00 in the morning. I usually don't switch with the Cowboy until the Cube's curfew at 2:00 a.m. so I only have about six hours in my body. I have to do a lot of exercise during that time to meet my equilibrium. It's frustrating because my day is wasted until then. For the first four hours, I'm stuck in the Cowboy's body with nothing to do. That's one of the hardest parts.

But there are some good moments, too. Minji's friend, Keya, usually leads a Pilates lesson every day around 3:00 a.m. Many of the movements remind me of ballet. It's nice to practice with everyone and it helps me get to know the Newbodies.

Tonight, Keya, Minji, and I go to the gym together after Pilates. Minji tells us about the dream she had last night. She says Cordelia was in it, giving her a foot massage. Keya and I laugh.

"That's horrifying," Keya says.

"Honestly, I remember being like 'this feels really good.' Is that weird?" Minji asks. "I'm kind of ashamed."

I say, "Maybe it's a good thing. Maybe your subconscious sees Cordelia as your worker. Like she's *your* 'Working Guest'. Tending to your aching feet."

"That's a nice thought," Minji says. "Thanks, Ellie. I knew I liked you."

I smile. We get to the gym and Minji tells me that she's going to the rowing machines. Keya is going to play tennis. I go in a different direction, finding an empty room where I can dance. When I find a room, I roll out a mat and begin stretching. I play some music from the stereo and let my mind wander.

I think of Keya's Pilates class. I was one of the first people to join today. When Minji came, she took the spot beside me. During the difficult movements, Minji and I made faces at each other, exaggerating the pain. Joking around with Minji felt good. I've been having a really hard time adjusting to the Cube—living in the Cowboy's body, not being able to eat, and realizing that home is a place I may never return—so it's nice to have a friend like Minji. We clicked instantly, and it makes things a little easier. I can't imagine how lonely I would feel without Minji and Dylan, who instantly welcomed me into their group. Even with them, I find myself missing home a lot. When I'm not busy exercising or distracted by the people around me, my mind is constantly wandering back to Mama, Ethan, and Loukas. It's been hard to stay strong around these new people. None of the other Newbodies know about what happened before I came here, or why I'm in this position. I thought about telling Minji and Dylan about Mama, but it just hasn't come up. Or maybe I've avoided it. In some ways, it feels easier when nobody knows. That way I can pretend my grief doesn't exist. If nobody else knows that Mama is dead, I can tell myself she's not. At least sometimes.

When I was on the train, I spent most nights crying myself to sleep. Now that I'm surrounded by so many people when I go to bed, I try to keep the tears to a minimum. I still think of Mama, but I find myself crying less. It's hardest when others bring up their parents. There was a night when Tearza mentioned that she didn't have parents back home. I thought about telling her I didn't either, but I decided not to. It would have felt insincere, sharing a moment like that with her. She hasn't liked me since we first met.

But I find myself thinking about Tearza sometimes. It is easier in some way, knowing that I'm not alone in this grief. When people bring up their parents, I know that Tearza must be feeling the way I do. Maybe I should tell Tearza so that she can have that comfort too. I tell myself that I will—and Minji and Dylan too—when the timing is right.

But I don't only think of Mama when I think of home. I think of Loukas. I wonder how he is doing. When I was on the train, Lilith alluded to the fact that he was at a Work Camp. Ever since then I have been even more worried about him. Loukas is tough, but that doesn't matter. Even the tough prisoners can be unlucky. I can't let myself believe that Loukas is dead, though. I need to believe that we'll find our way back to each other.

The only thing that helps me in these moments is thinking about Ethan. When I feel alone and scared, I remember that there's still someone out there who is a constant. Someone I love who loves me too. I miss Ethan so much. I miss spending every day at his house. I miss laughing at his jokes, listening to his voice, and feeling completely understood. Although it's been nice spending time with Minji and Dylan, nobody compares. It sometimes doesn't even feel like I'm hanging out with someone when I spend time with Ethan—it feels like he's a part of me. It's hard to explain, but I know I'm lucky. Or at least I was.

I finish stretching and play my dance music. I practice an old routine, one I performed years ago. It's a fast-paced dance that always makes me happy. Ethan was my dance partner for this one. It feels nostalgic, but happy, and that's what I need right now. I practice the routine over and over again, trying to remember the dance moves in each section. I change things around to make it more challenging and add to sections where I can't remember exactly what the original moves were. Hours pass without me realizing it. I'm so engrossed in the music. Engrossed in the dance. Before I know it, I've burned 3500 calories. I have about 1000 more to go. I turn off the music and decide to burn the rest on the bike. I head over to the bikes and push through as fast as I can. My legs are sore from the many days before, but I push through the pain. When I finally finish, my legs feel like noodles.

I meet the others back at the Cottage. Minji and Dylan are sitting on the living room couches with some friends: Keya, Rayan, Matt, and Lex. Matt seems to be giving some sort of performance. He's got his head tilted forward and his chest sticking out. "Get back to your workout, Matt*hew*! Stop following me!" The others laugh. I join them.

"What was that?" I ask.

Matt looks a little embarrassed. "We're doing impressions," he explains.

"Matt was being Thomas, the Official that's always hanging around Cordelia. You know him?"

I nod. I remember seeing his picture and name. I sit beside Rayan and notice Tearza across the room. She's glaring at us. I wonder if she got the invitation to join, but I know she wouldn't even if she was invited. She would find this kind of thing disrespectful.

"You should hear Minji do Cordelia." Keya says, "She's amazing."

I laugh, as I watch Tearza get up from her bed and angrily leave the Cottage. The door shuts and I mentally rejoin the group. "Really?"

Minji adjusts her posture and facial expression to emulate Cordelia. Her lips form a massive smile and she looks at me. "Eliana, *dear,* don't you look radiant today."

"Thanks," I go along with it, playing my part.

"Now, now," Minji continues in Cordelia's high-pitched voice. "Don't interrupt me, dear. I did call you in here for something important. There's something I wish I didn't have to say." Minji frowns.

"Oh my god," I say. "I feel like I'm actually in trouble."

"You are." Minji talks like herself again. "Just kidding. Okay, Dyl. Your turn."

Dylan does his best impression of my Companion, the Cowboy. Dylan puts on a southern accent and talks about all the men and women who have suddenly started paying attention to him now that he's walking around in a nice-looking body. "Of course, I'm only interested in the women," Dylan says in the Cowboy's thick accent. "I'm very, very much a heterosexual." We all laugh. When he finishes, Dylan calls on me. "Okay, Ellie. Your turn."

I'm caught off-guard so I think quickly. The first person that comes to mind is Theo. I stand up and give a stern face. "Hi, I'm Theo," I say in my deepest voice. Everyone laughs, so I'm encouraged to keep going. "I have no emotions and I like to stare at people for a very long time. I don't stop until they're uncomfortable." Everyone stops laughing, so I think of something else to say. "Hey Lana," I say in Theo's voice. "Is it okay if I call you by your stage name? I thought it might be sexy—" Minji clears her throat and I look at her. I notice that she's signaling me to stop. My stomach drops, realizing there is someone behind me. I turn around and there he is. Theo. Staring into my soul.

"Oh my god," I blurt out.

"Nice show," he says.

"Sorry, I didn't mean it."

Theo looks away from me and turns to everyone else. "Someone just informed me that you all have been acting quite inappropriately. I take it that there was a lot more of this?"

"It wasn't them," I quickly say, not wanting to get anyone else in trouble. "It was only me."

"That's not true," I hear Tearza say. I didn't realize she was behind Theo. She must have come back quietly. I see Minji glare at her.

"It doesn't matter who it was," Theo says, "but it better not happen again." He looks at all of us. I feel his gaze linger when he gets to me. "Because if it does, I'll have no choice but to inform Cordelia."

"It won't happen again," Minji says for all of us. "Sorry."

Theo doesn't say anything. He simply gives us one more glare and walks out the door. When he's gone, Minji glares at Tearza. "What the hell is wrong with you? Did you really have to get an Official involved?"

"It was inappropriate," Tearza says. "If the Officials came in here unexpectedly, they might have thought I had something to do with it. I didn't want to get in trouble for your childish actions."

"If you had a problem with it, you could have just said something yourself," I say.

"What good would that do? You never listen to me."

"If you want our respect, you have to give us respect," Minji tells her.

Tearza walks away, uninterested.

Minji rolls her eyes and then looks back at me. "Oh my god," she whispers. "I *can't believe* Theo saw you do all that. That was kind of hilarious."

"Hilarious for *you*," I say. "He's going to kill me."

"I think he likes you."

"Yeah right."

"You called him sexy."

"No, I said he *thought* he was *being* sexy."

"Sure," Minji smirks. Nobody on the couch looks convinced.

"Whatever." I try to laugh it off, but the thought unsettles me. "I'm going to shower," I say, leaving the group so I can think on my own. *Obviously* I think Theo is attractive. Everyone must. But that doesn't mean I'm attracted *to* him. He's insensitive, rude, and has an enormous, government-sized ego. If anything, I hate him. I decide to stay away from Theo altogether. All the trouble I have gotten myself into since coming to the Cube seems to be linked to him.

I take a shower and relax, allowing the hot water to settle me. I stop thinking about Theo. About Ethan. About Mama. I close my eyes, feel the water run down my back, and find a quiet mind.

CHAPTER 19

The longer I stay at the Cube, the easier it is to avoid Theo completely. I've figured out his schedule, more or less. He is quite the recluse. He doesn't like spending time with most of the Officials, but occasionally I find him talking to Samantha. They seem to be friends. She's older than Theo, but not by much. She's got a youthful appearance with her hazel eyes, light blond hair, and round cheeks. I remember reading that she's twenty-one when I scrolled through the Officials.

Still, Theo is often by himself. He usually goes to the cafeteria during off hours and when he's on duty, he hides in corners and makes it hard for him to be seen. He usually watches over the forest and the pathway exiting Oparius so it's not too difficult to stay away. I've accidentally run into him a few times over the past month, but I've managed to avoid eye contact.

When I tried complaining about Theo to Minji once, she shrugged it off. "He has always been a bit quiet, but he's never rude to me. I actually find him much nicer than the others. Plus..." Minji smirks. "I think he just bugs you because he knows you think he's so sexy."

"I *don't.*"

"Uh huh, There's nothing wrong with it. I think he's pretty damn dreamy myself."

I don't know why it's so hard for me to agree with Minji. To just admit that he's attractive and move on. But I can't. Not out loud. So I vow to not bring up Theo in front of Minji.

Aside from the Theo issue, though, Minji and I have gotten along perfectly. I spent most of my time with Ethan and Loukas at home and never had a close female friend. Unless you include Mama, but as nice as it was to have her, there's a difference between sixteen-year-olds and thirty-seven-year-olds. Dylan is great to have around too, but Minji and I experience things in a way he probably doesn't. Giving your body or

"Shell" to a stranger isn't easy for anyone, but it is especially hard for girls. Even before coming to the Cube, I experienced a number of different scenarios where guys felt like they could control or dictate what happened to me. I don't know Minji's past, but I'm sure she has had similar experiences.

Back home, after performances as a dancer, men would always come up to me. Sometimes, the "polite" ones would merely flirt, but other men would put their hands on me when it was clear I was not interested. The men could never do much, but the feeling always lingered, like I can never really be safe in my own body. And having these memories changes the way I react to the Cube. Knowing a man is living in my body is difficult. And there's nothing I can do about it.

Minji once explained why prisoners call themselves "Newbodies" here.

"We're picked for our young and fresh bodies," Minji said, "but we're treated like nothing. Like nobodies."

Tearza purses her lips every time she hears someone use the term. She seems to especially hate when she hears Minji or me use it. For a while, Tearza would correct us, reminding us that we're *"Working Guests,"* but she seems to have finally dropped it. She knows we're not going to stop.

Tearza hasn't loosened up a bit since arriving. Every night, she wakes up, switches bodies, and immediately goes to the gym. Her Companion eats a lot of food, about the same amount as the Cowboy, so she diligently exercises for hours, never complaining. Most of the Newbodies have one or two light snacks throughout the night, but Tearza doesn't eat anything. We're in a similar situation, the two of us. One time I thought it would be a good idea to bring this up.

"How are you doing?" I asked her.

Tearza seemed startled by my question. "I'm fine, thanks."

"It seems like your Companion makes you do a lot of work." Tearza still looked uncomfortable, so I tried a joke, "He almost seems as bad as the Cowboy."

"I don't mind it," Tearza told me and walked away. That was it. There is clearly no way for me to bond with Tearza. I've stopped trying.

I've become accustomed to my routine at the Cube, but I'm also completely exhausted by it. I'm usually called for the Switch around curfew, which is 2:00 a.m. It's the cut-off time for Companions to be in our bodies. The Cube only enforces a curfew to ensure that prisoners have enough time to work off the necessary calories. And because the Cowboy likes to party as long as he can, he typically waits until right before curfew to return my body. This means I don't start exercising until much later than most of my friends. Luckily, Keya usually leads her Pilates after this. I skip breakfast. The Cowboy typically puts about 6000 to 8000 calories in my body, so I have my work cut out for me. There's no room for me to add any calories and no time for me to delay my exercise. I spend most of the night at the gym, alternating from dancing to rowing to biking. When I need a change of scenery, I go for runs. I find that they help me relax.

It's not easy getting through the days here. Most of the time, I'm completely drained. I've spent most of my life exercising, but I've never had to exert myself like this. Plus, since my body always alternates from the Cowboy to me, it never physically gets put to sleep. Our scientifically altered bodies are adjusted to survive this, but that doesn't mean it's easy. My body feels fatigued from the lack of rest, in addition to the aches and pain I've developed from exercising. Apparently, the Patrons are given pain relievers to counteract this, but the Cube doesn't also extend the favor to Newbodies.

Some days, I'm so tired I can barely walk straight by the time I go to bed. The Cowboy is making the most of his vacation, with no regard for how it makes me feel. I want to give up almost every day, but that's not really an option. I can't escape. I can't just ask for another Companion. They say that Working Guests are treated with the same respect as Patrons, but of course that's not true. The Cube has no problem letting me suffer while the Cowboy happily enjoys my body. I'm trapped in a helpless situation, and the only thing that gets me through is knowing that it's temporary. Eventually, the Cowboy will leave the Cube. I'll be free of him. And hopefully, my next Companion will be a little kinder.

There are some good moments at the Cube though, like right now, sitting in the cafeteria with Minji and Dylan. I really shouldn't be here. I should be at the gym, but sometimes when the Cowboy returns my aching body to me, I desperately need a break. I tell myself I'll go for a long run after this. Maybe do sprints. I'll make up for this indulgence. I have to.

Minji and Dylan are sharing a bowl of granola and I wistfully watch them eat. Dylan is currently complaining about his Companion, Bernard. "I don't know what the old man did last night. He didn't give my body back until right before curfew. I woke up with a scraped-up knee and a bloody toe."

"He must have been partying with the Cowboy," I say, pretending it's all a funny joke.

"I don't know how you do it, Ellie." Dylan says, "And now I've got to burn 2500 calories today, with a hangover and a scraped-up body. So that'll be nice."

"Sorry, babe," Minji pats his back. I feel bad for Dylan, but it's hard not to feel envious too. This is the first time Bernard has partied until curfew. The Cowboy does that every night.

When the Cowboy returned my body tonight, I had a hangover too. The feeling isn't new to me. I feel hungover after almost every Switch. Some nights, when I'm back in my body, I am drunk instead. That can make exercising extra difficult. Most of the time, though, my head is throbbing and I'm nauseated beyond belief. I've been surprised by injuries a few times and then have to deal with exercising through the pain. Complete disregard for consequences is one of the perks for the Patrons. If they time their drinking correctly, they can experience all the benefits without any consequences. They leave us to endure their hangovers and fresh injuries. Some people are much luckier than others, but my situation is hell. The Cowboy drinks like no one else.

Tearza joins us at the table. She's eating a bowl of celery. Zero calories. "Hey," she says. I'm shocked she's here. We all seem to be. "Can I ask you all a question?"

"Oh no," Minji says. "What now?"

"I was just wondering... do you know the rules about leaving Oparius? I remember Cordelia saying that we can only go if we're invited by an Official or Patron. Isn't that right?"

"Something like that." Dylan sounds suspicious. "Why?"

"No reason," Tearza says. "I was only wondering because I heard Sandra talk about leaving. I wanted to make sure she was safe."

"You wanted to see if you could rat on her."

Tearza looks hurt. "No, Minji, I only like to rat on you." Tearza walks away in a huff and Minji comically gasps at her animosity. Dylan and I laugh at the exchange.

I begin my run at the Cottage and decide to take the path around the perimeter of Oparius. I've done this run before and I like it because it leads me to the water, where I can listen to the ocean's waves as I run. Lights run along each of Oparius' paths, but the lights by the water are my favorite. I love the way they make the ripples shine. Most of this route could be considered boring because it's a bare path with an electric fence on one side and trees on the other. But I like it. Even though I know I'm trapped inside, I like to be reminded that there's a world outside the Cube.

My body feels stiff at the start of my run. I usually run after the gym, but tonight it's the first thing I do. Every part of my body is sore from the endless days of exercise and I think about stopping to stretch. I don't have time, though. After the Switch, I started the night too slowly and if I don't push myself now I risk running out of time before meeting my equilibrium. I've heard horror stories about Newbodies who don't meet their goals and the punishment that they face. I don't want to risk that happening to me. I run faster because I have no other choice. I feel like crying because in this moment it feels like the pain will never end. If I'm not thinking about Mama or Loukas or Ethan then I'm exhausting myself at the gym, or worrying about what the Cowboy is doing. I miss the ease and relative happiness of my life in Group7. I didn't know how good I had it. Of course, there were challenges, but life was simple back then. I didn't have this pain running down my legs, swelling around my knees, and tenderness at the balls of my feet. I try to take a deep breath to ease the cramping in my chest. It doesn't work. My breath is shallow.

When I get to the part of the run where the path borders the water, I try to relax by listening to the ocean's waves. This usually works, but I find it hard to calm my brain tonight. I think of the Cowboy, dancing at a pool-side bar in my body and sipping on drinks. I feel angrier by the moment and quicken my pace to compensate for the rage building inside me. When I get to the end of the beach, I stop. I don't have much time to spare, but I give myself a couple of minutes. I pull off my running shoes and I run across the sand and into the ocean. I splash my face with cold water and instantly feel more awake. I lie in the water for a moment, looking up at the stars. It doesn't solve everything, but it gives me the energy I need to keep going. I get up, put on my shoes, and start running.

I turn away from the beach and keep going. I tell myself I won't think of the Cowboy for the rest of the run. I try to think of something outside of the Cube, but I'm distracted by movement ahead of me. There are two shadows in the distance, in front of me on the path. I realize they must be people. There are no animals in the Cube. The Patrons wouldn't like that. The people are not quite on the path, they're off to the side, in a gathering of shrubs and trees that separate us from the fence. I'm not sure what they're doing, but it seems bizarre. As I get a little closer, I realize they're in Official uniforms. They're standing beside the fence. One of them is keeping watch, flashing a light into the forest, while the other one seems to be stepping closer to the fence.

I stop running. The Officials haven't noticed me yet—I'm too far away—and something tells me I don't want to be detected. One Official seems to step through the fence and then the next one follows. Just like that, they're gone. They're on the other side.

My heart beats faster, trying to figure out what's going on. Did they just go through the fence? But how? Do they not have Chips? My mind races with questions. I wonder if what they did was illegal. What would happen if they saw me? Would I somehow get in trouble for witnessing this? But what do I have to be guilty for? I decide that it's possible to pretend I never noticed them. I start running slowly, pretending to be going for a light jog. When I get to the spot where I saw the Officials, I can hear their deep voices muffled from beyond the fence. One of them laughs. I'm still not sure how they managed this, but they're definitely outside of the Cube. I know I can't investigate any further right now, so I keep running along the path. Once I've given them some distance, I stop. This is too big of a mystery to leave unsolved.

I step off the path and into the forested area to my right. I do jumping jacks and burpees, trying to burn calories as I wait. About twenty minutes pass until I hear the chatter of the two Officials. I hear them coming my way so I quietly move deeper into the trees. I watch the Officials walk by me, completely unaware of my existence. I recognize them from around the Cube. One Official hangs around Samantha a lot and the other I often see with Cordelia. I think his name is Thomas. One of the men squeezes the other's hand for a moment and then they let go, as if nothing happened. I wait a minute until they're out of sight.

I imagine that one of them is supposed to be watching over this area, so there is no one at the nearby Official's post right now. I look around to make sure I'm right. I don't see anyone. I carefully walk to the fence and try to retrace their steps. I need to figure out exactly where they were. I step beyond the shrubs and trees to get a closer look. The fence looks exactly like it does in other areas, where there aren't shrubs obstructing the view. I keep searching along the fence, but I'm not sure what I'm looking for. Nothing seems out of the ordinary. I walk along the fence for about fifty feet and then turn around, tracing my steps in case I missed something the first time. Nothing stands out. I think about leaving. There's a good chance the Officials have certain tricks and secret knowledge about how to turn off their Chips. If that's the case, they could have touched the fence and remained unharmed.

I'm about to give up when my foot brushes against a large rock resting beside the fence. There are many of these around the fence as a part of the Cube's landscaping, but this one feels different than the others. It's strangely light. I realize it's a fake rock. It doesn't take much strength to kick it away. And once I do, I notice a significant hole in the fence.

My heart races with excitement, realizing what I've found. A way out. A chance at freedom. After all my time here and all the pain, I stopped believing I'd ever escape. But here it is, an actual chance. I don't think twice about it. I drop to the ground and slowly, carefully, begin crawling through the hole.

The hole is big enough for me to get through, but it's small enough to require precision. If I touch any piece of the fence, the Cube will be notified. I'll be severely shocked, possibly injured, and will lose this opportunity. I can't imagine what the consequences might be and I don't want to find out.

I move my head through the hole first, slowly bring my arms through, shimmy my upper body, and then carefully step my legs through one at a time. When I'm finally on the other side, I'm filled with relief. I run. I run fast.

Beyond the fence is more forest. There are rocks and branches on the ground so I'm careful where I step. Although I don't know where I'm going, I see lights in the distance. The forest must lead to Ace City. I don't know if it's safe there, but I'll need to find somewhere to take off my Chip. The longer my Chip is on, the more time the Cube has to track me. I didn't touch the fence when I escaped, so the Cube wasn't immediately notified, but if any of the Officials look up my whereabouts, they will see I'm no longer in the Cube. I need to get my Chip off me fast. By morning, when the Cowboy tries to call me for the Switch, the Officials will definitely be surveying my whereabouts.

I don't know where to go, but Ace City seems like the best bet. I run as quickly as I can and the cramps I felt before are gone. I'm filled with adrenaline. I don't know what I'll find in Ace City, but I know I'm heading in the right direction.

Eventually, the lights become brighter. The trees start to decrease in number and I can make out skyscrapers in the distance. I reach a road and start jogging on the sidewalk. It's nighttime, but I'm still wary of passersby. I need to look like I'm from the city, or at least try.

A van pulls up beside me as I run. My heart beats faster, but I don't look over. I don't want them to know I'm concerned. It doesn't take long for the van to stop. Someone emerges and before I can think, the person knocks me down.

"What do you think you're doing?" The person asks angrily. I know that voice. It's Theo.

He pins me down and looks me square in the face. "You're going to get yourself killed!"

I'm so shocked I don't know what to say. "Why are you here?"

Theo grabs my wrist and pulls me into the back of the van.

"Wait! Please!"

He glares at me as he slams the door of the van closed. He locks me in and gets in the front. I try my best not to cry as we drive away.

CHAPTER 20

When the van finally stops, I'm not sure where we are, but I know we're not at the Cube. Theo carries me out and I try to make out my surroundings. I think we're still in Ace City. I try to squirm out of his arms and escape, but he's too strong. I don't stand a chance of getting away and he knows it.

Theo takes me to an office building. The door of the building is locked, but Theo breaks through like it's nothing. There are no people inside because it's after hours. He carries me into a room, ties me to a chair, and sits across from me.

"Now," he says, "are you going to tell me what the hell you were thinking?"

I had time to think about what I'd say while he drove me here, but I couldn't come up with anything plausible. My best idea was to tell him that I was drunk. If I blamed it on the Cowboy's irresponsibility, maybe I wouldn't get in as much trouble. But there is probably a way for Theo to check and see if that's true. The Cowboy was hungover at the time. Not drunk. Plus, even if my Companion got my body drunk, I would still probably be the one to face the consequences.

The only thing I can think to do is skirt around the topic and buy time. Eventually, I'll find a solution.

"Why were you following me?" I ask.

"I wasn't."

"You knew I left the Cube somehow..."

"I'm a Government Official. It's my responsibility to notice suspicious behavior and report it."

"But you didn't report it. You dealt with me on your own."

Theo looks uncomfortable. "It's my job to protect the Cube and the people inside it. You could have gotten yourself killed."

"Yeah, you said that. But I still don't know what you mean. Who would kill me? Someone at the Cube? And if that's the case, why don't you?"

Theo stares. We lock eyes for a long moment. "Don't test me," he finally says.

I smile. An idea comes to me that Theo might believe. "You know, I can relate to you more than you might think."

"What do you mean?"

"About protecting me—"

"I wasn't—"

"Or the Cube. Whatever. I was also trying to protect someone tonight."

"What are you talking about?"

"I was on a run tonight, minding my own business when I heard a scream in the distance. It was coming from outside of the Cube. I did the only thing I could think of doing. I ran toward it. I wanted to help. It sounded like a young girl."

Theo thinks about this. He doesn't say anything for a moment. "Why didn't you get an Official?"

"I tried to. There was nobody around. That's how I knew about the hole in the first place."

"What do you mean?"

"There's a hole in the fence. I saw two Officials crawl through it. They seemed to be sneaking away."

At least this part is true. I feel bad for bringing the Officials into this, but I don't see another way. Plus, they're Officials. Why should I protect them?

"When was this?"

"Earlier tonight. Before the scream."

"So, there's a hole in the fence? That's how you got through without notifying us?"

I nod, feeling relief. He seems to believe me.

"And are you willing to show me the hole when we get back?"

There's nothing I'd rather do less, but I say yes. Theo is silent, thinking about his options.

I wait for him, and reality sinks back in. I was so close to freeing myself. If Theo hadn't been keeping tabs on me, I might have actually had a chance. My heart sinks at the thought of returning to the Cube. I was lucky to find a way out once, but twice? There's no way.

Theo finally speaks. "You know, even if what you're saying is true, this sort of thing can't happen again. *Ever.*"

"I thought it was the right thing to do."

"If you ever hear or see something, you find an Official next time."

"Okay, I will."

Theo nods. "All right, I'm going to take you back to the Cube, but don't say anything about this to anyone."

"I won't."

We walk back to the van and this time Theo lets me walk by myself. He holds my arm just in case, but at least he's not carrying me. I think about making a run for it, but I know I won't get far. He has a van. Right before he's about to put me in the back again, he stops. He squeezes my arm and turns me to face him. He puts his other arm over something on his shirt. It looks like it could be a microphone. "I know you're lying, Lana," he whispers. "We're off the Cube's premises so Cordelia is watching. We're being recorded. Don't make any sudden moves.

I freeze. I have no idea what's going on. I try not to show any fear.

Theo continues to whisper. "I think they'll believe you after I talk to them, so you're okay. But I swear to god stop being so reckless. You're going to get us both killed."

Before I can respond, Theo grabs me by the waist and throws me into the back of the van. He glares at me and shouts for me to stay still, as if his last words to me were never said. My heart races as he shuts the door and starts to drive.

When we arrive back at the Cube, it's like nothing ever happened. We pass the entrance gates without any issues. Theo tells the guards that he's driving me on Cordelia's orders, and the guards don't question him. I quickly show Theo the hole in the fence and then he drops me off at Oparius. He reminds me once more to inform the authorities next time someone needs help, then walks away. I head to the Cottage to digest everything that just happened and get ready for bed.

Minji looks worried when I get inside. "Where have you *been*?" she asks. "I've been looking for you everywhere."

"I was just... I went for a run around Oparius."

"So, you weren't with Tearza?"

"Tearza? Why would I be with Tearza?"

"I don't know. Sandra said she's been missing all night."

I tell Minji I have no idea where she is. I wish I could tell her where I really was and what happened with Theo. I keep running through it in my head. *Stop being so reckless; you're going to get us both killed.* It's still too fresh to fully process. Why would he be willing to get us both killed? He knew I was lying. Why wouldn't he just report me to his authorities? It doesn't make any sense. I feel like Minji would have some ideas, but I know I can't talk to her. Especially not after Theo's request to keep this to myself.

Minji is taking off her makeup in the mirror beside me. She looks so different without the thick eyeliner she wears. She looks so much younger. "My back is killing me," she says. "Do you ever have days where you're just like 'no, I'm not going to the gym today.'"

"I have that thought pretty much every day."

"I'm sorry."

"It's fine. I'm just complaining."

But the truth is I can't stop thinking about how close I was to getting out. Before either of us can say anything else, the door of the Cottage swings open. Minji looks over.

"Tearza!" She screams.

Tearza is being carried in by one of the Cube's Keepers. The Keeper is barely big enough to carry her. Tearza's body is limp, her eyes are closed, and her mouth is wide open.

"What happened?" I say as I move toward her. When I get closer to the two of them, I notice the Keeper. Even with her auburn hair pulled up and her body covered by the long uniform dress I recognize her. "Hanna?" She looks at me. "What's going on?"

"There's something wrong with Tearza," she says. "I found her like this in the bushes. She wasn't in Oparius. She was—she was on the other side."

"Oh my god," Minji takes Tearza from Hanna and lays her down on a chair. "Is she dead?"

I bend over and put my hand on Tearza's wrist, checking for her pulse. "She's breathing," I tell them. I already know what's wrong before I smell her breath. "She's drunk."

"Drunk?" Minji's shocked. Tearza's Companion hasn't had access to her body for hours. Tearza would have had to do the drinking herself.

"Minji, can you go get water and bread? I'm going to try to wake her."

"Bread?"

I look at Tearza's Chip. She's way past her limit for the day. She might as well eat something.

I nod. "It will help her."

Minji doesn't argue. She leaves to find some food. There won't be bread in the Cottage because nobody eats that kind of thing. Too many calories.

Hanna watches me turn Tearza on her side and cover her with a blanket. I pinch Tearza's ear hard and she opens her eyes. I'm relieved.

"Eliana?" She looks scared. "What's going on?"

"You're okay," I speak softly. "You're safe."

Tearza stares at me confused. Hanna brings a glass of water from the kitchen and I slowly force Tearza to take sips. She doesn't want to, but she listens.

Hanna watches me. "You're good at this," she says.

I shrug, "I've never done it before. But I've seen it."

"Oh, sorry."

"It's okay. It was my best friend's brother, but he's better now." That's not exactly true, but I don't tell her the whole story. There's no need to upset her. The truth is that Ethan's oldest brother, Raffi, has spent most of his life battling an alcohol addiction. Raffi was adopted like the rest of Ethan's siblings, but he always had the most trouble dealing with his past. Five years ago, when Raffi was only sixteen, his drinking got him sent to prison. It's illegal to drink alcohol before turning seventeen, and Raffi was caught by Officials. He wasn't drunk, but that didn't matter. They sent him away anyway.

When Ethan and I were younger, I watched Leora and Molly take care of Raffi. They never wanted us to get involved, but we both knew what was happening. I learned some things along the way. Plus, when Mama started getting sick, I was the one who took care of her. It's not the same, of course. But she needed someone to watch over her—to make sure she was the right temperature, in a comfortable position, and safe.

Tearza tries to roll on her back, but I gently move her back to her side. It's weird to see her so stubborn, resisting the water and being forced to lie down.

When I get Tearza settled again, I look back at Hanna.

"So, can you explain to me how you ended up here?"

Hanna whispers. "I'm not really supposed to be. In Oparius, I mean."

"What happened?" I've seen other Keepers around. They spend most of their time cleaning up after the Patrons, but they also work at our gym and cafeteria. They're supposed to be workers from Group7, though. Not prisoners.

"After I didn't get picked, I didn't leave on the train. When the rest of the prisoners got on, everyone was sent to a different location. They put me in a railcar and I waited for the train to start. But it never did, not for me. A few minutes later, someone came and pulled me out. They said to follow them, they put me in a Keeper's outfit, and told me not to get noticed by anyone. I didn't ask any questions. This is obviously a lot better than whatever was waiting for me at a Camp."

"This whole time, you've been right here? At the Cube?"

"I know. I'm sorry I didn't try to contact you. I didn't want either of us to get in trouble."

"I get it," I tell her. Of course I do.

"Hanna, can you tell me who did this? Who got you off the train?"

She thinks for a moment before she answers. She checks to make sure Tearza isn't listening, but she's fallen asleep. Hanna whispers in my ear. But I already know who she's going to say:

"Theo."

CHAPTER 21

We take turns watching over Tearza throughout the morning and early afternoon. Minji and I have switched bodies now, but Tearza missed her switch. We thought about taking her, but she wasn't in the position to go. Every time I wake up, Tearza is still fast asleep. I turn her on her side and check to make sure she's breathing. Around 3:00 p.m. I look over at Tearza and see her sitting upright in her bed. I climb up her ladder to check on her.

"How are you doing?" I ask. I realize I don't look like myself. "It's Ellie."

She's shocked to see me. "I'm okay. What happened last night?"

"I don't know. You tell me."

"The last thing I remember... Oh, god. How much trouble am I in?"

"Tearza," I try to reach my hand out, but she jerks away.

"Why are you being nice to me, anyway?"

"You were passed out drunk all night. We *helped* you."

"Did Cordelia see me?"

"I don't know," I say, annoyed. That's all she cares about. "I don't think so. But can you tell us what happened?"

"Why should I?"

"Tearza... I've barely slept trying to take care of you. I don't want you to get into trouble, okay? I'm on your side."

Tearza considers this. I keep going. "Just tell me what happened," I plead. "I want to help."

She hesitates, pausing to think before she speaks. Finally, Tearza says, "An Official sent me a note yesterday... It was from my Companion, asking me to meet him. He said he'd gotten to know my Shell so well he wanted to know the person inside it. I didn't know what to do. I thought I should say yes... I thought that since an Official gave me the note it would be okay... but then when I got there my

Companion, Anthony—he had a bottle of vodka and shot glasses." My stomach drops as she speaks. "He told me to have a drink, and I tried to say no. I didn't think it was allowed... I didn't want to. But then he kept asking and I didn't know—" Tearza breaks into tears. "Oh god, Eliana. I'm going to get into so much trouble."

I rub Tearza's back. My heart breaks for her. I think about asking her what she did, but she's too hysterical. "I can't go back," she cries, but I don't know where "back" is. "I can't go back."

When Tearza finally catches her breath, she looks at me angrily. "I'm sure you and Minji are thrilled to see me like this."

"Like what?"

"Finally in trouble. The roles reversed."

"It's not like that."

"Do you know what they do at the other Camps? Do you have any idea?"

Tearza is silent for a moment. She bends forward, bringing her head to her knees, and lifts her shirt in the back. "Do you see any marks?"

I look at Tearza's back. It looks as smooth and perfect as the rest of her skin.

"No, nothing."

"They must be fully gone now," she says. "But when I got here, my body was covered in scars. I've been putting on this cream every day—something they gave me on the train. I guess it worked."

I remember the cream Lilith gave me. It completely erased the scar on my left elbow. I think about how amazed I was watching the mark, which I thought would be permanent, disappear. Tearza's scars must have been much more intense if she was still using the cream. She pulls her shirt down and sits back up.

"Anyway, I got my scars from the previous Camp. I would wake up at 5:00 in the morning and work until midnight every day. They waited until the body I was in expired, or died, and I was back in my body. That's when they'd hit me, for any tiny mistake I made in the previous days. And the bodies they put me in... they were always days from dying. I was in *so much pain*." I think of Mama. Of being in her body. I could barely move my head. I can't imagine working for hours in that kind of pain.

"I thought I was going to die," Tearza says. "So many times I thought I'd die. I mean I almost did. I collapsed at the end... they sent me to a hospital. They barely treated me because I was a prisoner. And then... Cordelia came to see me. The nurse must have told her about me or someone did. And she was so *nice*. Cordelia was the first nice person I interacted with since leaving home. Even if it was fake, it still felt good to be cared for. She told me I was beautiful. And that was crazy to me because, you know, before I was taken to the Camp I had hair down to my bum. It was long and thick and it had always been like that, ever since I was a kid. But the first thing they made me do when I got to the Camp was shave my hair. They didn't want it falling into the products we were making. I couldn't look at myself for months. I thought I was so ugly, so strange, without my hair. Cordelia changed everything."

Tearza looks up at me, maybe to see if I'm still listening. She continues. "When I got here, I was like, there's no way I can screw this up. I wasn't really supposed to be here. I was supposed to get the fluids I needed at the hospital and go back to the other Camp. They probably wouldn't have even taken me to the hospital if I wasn't one of their best workers. But I was getting weaker over there. I'd probably be dead by now if I hadn't gone to the hospital, and eventually, they would have stopped taking me for fluids. So when Cordelia found me, she saved my life. This *place* did. I know I'm still a prisoner, or a Newbody, or whatever. I know Cordelia doesn't really care. But if I'm good, if I do everything right, I can stay. You don't get it. This is the only Camp you've known."

"But don't you get how wrong this place is? They take our bodies and use them however they want. I'd rather work my butt off every day than give somebody my body."

"Maybe, but they take our bodies at other Camps too."

"You're right."

"I see what you mean more now, though. About them owning our bodies... last night I... well I really felt that."

"It's bad any way you slice it. It doesn't matter where we go."

"Yeah, but at least at the Cube I can live," Tearza starts crying again. "Anyway, it's over. The second they find out what I did, it'll be over. They'll send me back to the other Camp. I'm sure they're waiting over there for me to screw things up."

"That's not going to happen. You've been so loyal and so respectful this whole time."

"It doesn't matter. This was *bad*."

I still don't know exactly what happened, but I say, "It wasn't your fault." I know that's true.

"Do you really think they're going to blame a Patron? Or the Official who delivered the note?"

I don't know what to say to that. She's right. Even though she was pressured into saying yes to her Companion, and the only reason she went was to be obedient, she will still be the one they blame. It doesn't help that her equilibrium was completely neglected. Our only chance is Theo.

Maybe he can help.

We spend the rest of the day waiting. I drift in and out of sleep, wondering what will happen. Every time I wake up, I notice Tearza is wide awake. I can't imagine how scared she must be.

Nothing happens until right when I get back from my Switch. It's 2:00 in the morning. Curfew. An alarm goes off and all prisoners are ordered to report to the lobby of the main building, the same place we gathered after every challenge. Most people are confused, but my friends and I know what's happening. Tearza walks between Minji and me. Minji has her arm around Tearza. Tearza squeezes my hand tightly.

When we get to the lobby, Cordelia and the other Officials stand along the front wall. The alarms stop ringing after everyone arrives. It's quiet. Cordelia gets confirmation that every Chip is accounted for.

We wait for her to speak.

"Hello, my beautiful Working Guests," she finally says, "Thank you for coming." She begins with such fake kindness, it's almost like we weren't all ordered here by loud sirens and a Government Official's voice blaring over a speakerphone. "I wish I could be bringing everyone together under happier circumstances," she sighs, "but unfortunately, there has been a terrible incident. One of our Working Guests broke an essential Cube regulation. She trespassed into a Patron's sleeping quarters and brutally attacked one of our guests." Gasps and whispers travel throughout the room. Cordelia hushes everyone and continues, "The other Officials and I have been visiting the hospital all day to ensure that the injured Patron, Anthony Taylor, will be all right. He suffered a severe head injury and had to get stitches on both arms. Luckily, he will survive. But can anyone tell us why this happened to Anthony Taylor?"

I look over at Tearza. She is horrified.

"Would the person who did this like to speak up?" She is looking straight at Tearza. Everyone in the room turns to her. Tearza is in shock. She doesn't say anything. I take her hand and squeeze it. She looks at me, and then finally looks at Cordelia.

"I was defending myself," Tearza finally says.

"Excuse me?" Cordelia's voice raises an octave.

"It was an accident. I only meant to push him off me. I was defending myself."

Cordelia's angry. I've never seen her like this. "I'm sure you all know that exiting Oparius without permission is *illegal*. We talked about this in your orientation sessions. Raise your hand if you didn't know this rule." Nobody dares to raise their hand. "That's right. Everyone knows. And we have this rule to protect *you*."

I suppress a scoff. The only reason the rule exists is so that Patrons can come to the Cube, use our bodies, and never have to worry about actually engaging with prisoners.

"I know," Tearza's voice is louder now. She's fuelled by anger too. "I'm aware of this rule too, Cordelia. But I *was* invited to exit Oparius.

I was invited by my Companion, Anthony Taylor. And an *Official* delivered Anthony's note, requesting this of me. You can ask the Official yourself."

"We've done a careful investigation of the matter," Cordelia says. "I expect you know that neither Anthony nor any of the Cube's workers have made any claims about inviting you to leave Oparius. Lying about this issue will only make matters worse."

"But I'm not—"

"That's enough," Cordelia stops her. She looks sternly at Tearza. "I expected more from you, Tearza. You were the good one." Cordelia seems to glance at me now. She addresses the crowd, "I wanted everyone to be here to ensure we all have a clear understanding of what happens when Working Guests disobey the rules. We are kind here at the Cube, but don't mistake our kindness for weakness. If you disobey the rules, you *will* be punished." Cordelia nods at the Government Officials. "Tearza Abebe, you can follow Nathaniel and Douglas to your train. You are to leave the Cube immediately."

Two Government Officials walk over to Tearza. When they reach her, Tearza is frozen. The Officials yank her off her feet and pull her toward the door. When Tearza finally starts moving, she looks back at Minji and me. Neither of us knows what to do or how to help her. Tearza screams at the Government Officials, "Get off me! I'm not going anywhere! This isn't fair!" When she passes Cordelia, Tearza shouts, "You're evil! You don't care about any of us!" I try not to show my shock. Tearza continues screaming at Cordelia and the other Officials until she finally gets pulled out the door. The door shuts behind her.

When Tearza is gone, I look at Theo. His face is pale. Theo notices me looking at him and he subtly shakes his head. I wonder what this means. Does he want me to stop looking? Is he showing that he disagrees with what Cordelia did? I shake my head in response. I'm not happy either.

Cordelia tells us to leave, and everyone begins to exit. Minji and I look at each other, neither of us knowing what to say.

"That was insane," Dylan finally says. "I mean I didn't like the girl, but that was brutal."

"She was okay in the end," I tell him, feeling like I understand her more. She tried so hard not to step out of line. And still.

"What do you think happened? Do you think she just snapped?"

I shrug. I'm about to tell him I don't really know, but that I believe Tearza. Before I can start, a Government Official grabs my arm. It's Samantha. "Eliana," she says. "Cordelia wants to speak with you. It's urgent." Samantha pulls me away from my friends. She seems angry.

"Is everything okay?" I ask nervously. "Did I do something wrong?"

CHAPTER 22

When I arrive at Cordelia's office, she promptly escorts me to another room. It's empty, with only a table and two chairs. She sits across from me and waits for me to talk. I'm uncomfortable in the silence. I don't know what to say.

"Did you want to talk to me about something?" I say. I hate that my voice quivers.

"Do you know why you're here?"

She always brings the conversation back to me. I have no idea why I'm here. I've done many things that could possibly get me in trouble. I'm not sure which she could be referring to. "Is this about Tearza?"

"Of course not. Unless you know something about that."

I don't say anything. I only shake my head.

"I talked to Theo. And do you know what he told me?"

I shake my head again.

"He said you've been going out of your way to help others. You've been helping your friends. Helping other Working Guests... Even protecting *Officials*. And you know we really appreciate that here." What does she mean *protecting Officials?* I know not to ask. I try to smile. "But you know, we have a system here. Our staff takes care of everything and everyone."

I nod.

"So the next time you hear a noise that you think *needs* tending to, trust that someone will tend to it. There are boundaries for a reason. And the next time you cross those lines... even if you're trying to help someone... well, you don't want to end up like your friend Tearza, do you?"

I shake my head.

"Good." She grins again and takes my hand. "You know, Theo spent a long time trying to convince me you were innocent."

"Really?" I ask. I try to keep my voice from shaking.

"Yes," she says, but she doesn't give me any more information. She looks at me for another moment. After she gets the effect she's looking for, making me noticeably uncomfortable, she relinquishes. "I'm *so* glad we had this chat."

"Me too," I say with as much fakeness as I can muster.

I get up to leave because I think, and hope, the conversation is over. Cordelia stops me. "I'm not finished, dear."

I sit back down, afraid of what's coming next.

"Tomorrow morning, you'll be given a new Companion. Naomi Adams. She's just arrived."

A new Companion? Is this my punishment?

"What happened to the Cowboy?"

"We're trying something new out at the Cube. Male Patrons will only be paired with male Working Guests from now on."

This must be because of Tearza. Cordelia knows that what happened to Tearza was Anthony's fault. And yet, she's happy to let Tearza take the blame. I hold back my disgust.

"There won't be a Mingle?"

"There will be for some people, but not for you. Naomi has specifically requested your Companionship."

Once again, this doesn't seem right.

"Will that be all?"

Cordelia doesn't respond. I wait for her to say something, but she seems to be finished. I take this as my cue to leave.

This time when I get up, Cordelia doesn't stop me. When I reach the door, I hear Cordelia say, "You really are so beautiful." The door shuts behind me before I can think of a response.

At 8:30 in the morning, my Chip buzzes to let me know Naomi is ready for the Switch. It's later than I expected it to be, so I'm pleased I was able to spend this extra time in my body. There were many mornings when the Cowboy would request a switch at 6:00 a.m. after only leaving

171

my body at 2:00 a.m. That barely gave me any time to myself, so I'm happy to have this additional time.

I leave the Cottage as quickly as possible and head to the Switch-Pod. I enter the elevator and anxiously wait for the drop. By the time I get to the Pod, I'm nervous. A green light is lit in my Pod room, indicating that Naomi is already sitting in hers. Once I sit down, we'll switch. I will be in Naomi's body. I know nothing about my new Companion. I tried to find her profile, but it hasn't been uploaded yet. Naomi could be anyone. I wonder how old she will be. I wonder if she'll be strong or weak. What I'm most afraid of is the state of her health. I'm worried she might be in the midst of her Countdown. I take a deep breath and enter the Switch-Pod. The moment I do, I'm instantly transferred into Naomi's skin.

I stand up and look down at the body I'm inhabiting. Naomi is much bigger than I am. She's got wide shoulders, sturdy legs, and a tight and firm belly. I feel further from the ground than usual and realize she's noticeably tall. Most importantly, I feel no pain. I look at Naomi's body in the mirror. She's strikingly beautiful. And *young.* She has straight, black hair; gray eyes; and a long, elegant nose. She doesn't make sense as a Patron—she's gorgeous, maybe in her early twenties, and appears to be in good health. Why is she here?

When I get back to the Cottage, everyone seems to be asleep. I'm not used to being one of the last to bed. I don't feel tired at all because my mind is racing. Between Hanna showing up, Tearza leaving, and my new Companion, nothing feels right. I close my eyes and take deep breaths. I try to clear my mind, but it's difficult. Every time I start to doze off, I wake up in fear, reliving everything.

I don't know how long it takes, but eventually, I get some sleep. Around 5:00 p.m. I wake up. Someone's snoring in the bed beside me. I decide to give up on sleep.

I sit up in my bed and see if Naomi's profile has been added. When I turn on my Chip's screen, I see it there. I read through the information. It says that Naomi is 24 years old, she's a fan of gardening and water sports, she has a turtle named Claire, and she believes in justice for all living beings. I laugh at that last part, wondering how a person who believes in something like that could be at this Resort. She already seems like a phony. I keep reading through her profile. Apparently, Naomi has never been to a place like this before.

Last night Dylan said that might be why she didn't want to go to the Mingle. He said she might do things differently if she's new. I thought that was wishful thinking, but now I hope he's right. I can't think of a better alternative. I wish there was a way to get some clue from Naomi's body. It's so strange to be so intimately attached to someone else while still not really knowing anything about them. Why didn't she go to the Mingle? Why did she choose me?

I scroll through her photos. She looks peculiarly happy for a Patron, and it seems like she has a nice life. I don't think she's come here to escape, or at least it doesn't appear that way in the photos. Minji says the photos can be deceiving. "They always want to make it seem like their lives are perfect, but *obviously* they wouldn't be at the Cube if that were true." I know Minji is right, but I can't help thinking how different she is from the Cowboy. The way she smiles and her eyes glisten when she looks at the camera, she seems like someone with pride. In her last photo, Naomi wears a green and yellow tie-dye shirt. There's a woman beside her in matching colors. They seem young and weirdly *normal.* I still don't like Naomi, of course, but something about the photo is compelling. I remind myself that the woman I see in these pictures signed herself up for a stay at the Cube. Right now, Naomi is going about her day in my body. She chose that. Miss "justice for all" *chose that.* It doesn't matter how enticing she might seem in her profile—she's a complete hypocrite.

No one else will be up for a while, but I can't start working out until Naomi returns my body. I feel strangely hungry, but I know I can't eat in her body. I *definitely* don't want to be breaking rules right now.

I eagerly wait for the notification when Naomi's ready to sleep. I know it likely won't be for hours, but I don't know what else to do. I could try to go back to bed, but there's no use. I don't want to read through Naomi's profile anymore either. I decide to go to the Cottage's living room and read through one of the books. I've never had time like this before. I cherished every minute of sleep the Cowboy gave me.

I pick a book that's called *The Merits of Grouping* and bring it with me to the couch. It's a ridiculous book, and I know that before opening it. But it reminds me of home. When I used to hang out with Loukas and Ethan, the three of us loved finding books like this. It was sometimes sad or shocking, reading the propaganda defending Groups, but other times it was so absurd we couldn't help but laugh. I imagine Ethan snickering at certain phrases or the sarcastic tone Loukas would use reading the passages aloud. My heart aches for them. I wish they could be here with me now.

It happens around 9:00 p.m. I hear my Chip buzz, but I'm confused. It doesn't make sense for my Chip to be buzzing already. It's too early. I look at my Chip, expecting it to be something else, but sure enough, it's Naomi's call. She's ready for the Switch.

I hurry to the Switch-Pod. Once again, Naomi's green light is already on when I arrive. I'm not used to having such a punctual Companion. The Cowboy always kept me waiting. I sit in my Pod, relieved to be getting my body back. It happens quickly, and all of the sudden I am me again. I can't help but smile, realizing it's only 9:00 and I have the whole night ahead of me. It almost feels surreal. I'm accustomed to starting my day at 2:00 a.m. so this is a huge improvement. I look down at my Chip and see that Naomi ate 3900 calories. I have 1900 calories to burn and much more time to do so. I don't know what Naomi's deal is, but so far things are working out for me.

As soon as I complete the Switch, I go for a run around Oparius. I'm hungry, but I decide that if I run to the cafeteria instead of walk, and do an extra loop around the main building, I might burn enough calories for a small bowl of oatmeal. It's all I can think about while I run.

When I get to the cafeteria it's fairly empty. It's still early for Newbodies to be awake. "Sagona," Theo calls out my last name. He's sitting in the corner. "A word, please."

I go over to him, wondering what this could be about. Maybe he wants to talk about Tearza. Maybe I can ask him to help. "What's going on?" I try to seem casual, attentive.

"You completed your first Switch with Naomi Adams, didn't you?"

"Yes." That's not what I was expecting. "So far, she seems like a great Companion."

"She had a stain on her shirt all day. It was disgusting."

"What?"

"When she was in your Shell. She didn't get out of the white t-shirt I assume you dressed her in. There was tomato sauce everywhere."

I was wearing a plain top before the Switch. I figured she would change. "I don't think the stain was mine." *Why* is he even telling me this?

"Well, be more careful next time."

Sure, I'll be more careful of the stain that wasn't *mine.* "Of course."

"It was repulsive."

"As I said, it wasn't me. I haven't had tomato sauce since arriving."

"Then maybe don't wear a white shirt next time."

"Sure." I'm about to walk away when Theo says my name.

"Sagona." He wavers. I'm not sure he even knows what he wants to say.

"Yeah?" I ask impatiently.

"Never mind."

I take about two steps before Theo clears his throat. What on earth is wrong with this guy? I turn around.

"Can you come sit for a moment?" he asks.

"Sure." I obey.

I sit across the table from Theo, waiting for him to say something. He doesn't. He just looks at me. We both stare at each other awkwardly while I imagine a million different places I'd rather be.

Finally, Theo says, "I'm sorry about that."

"It's fine."

"I do have emotions, you know."

I think back to the night I was mimicking Theo and he walked into the room. I said *Hi, I'm Theo and I have no emotions.* Does he still remember that?

"Sorry for implying you don't. I mean, doing that impression of you. It was uncalled for."

"You know, we're supposed to be aloof here. We're not really allowed to have friendships with the Working Guests."

"I understand."

"But that doesn't mean I need to be rude." I agree, but I don't say anything. "Honestly, you get on my nerves sometimes."

I don't know what he expects me to say to that. I want to tell him that he gets on my nerves too. Often.

"Is this a terrible apology?" he asks.

"Is this *supposed* to be an apology?"

"I'm just tired of you hating me."

"I don't hate you." Although that doesn't *not* describe the feelings I have for him. "I just hate what you stand for."

Theo looks down at the floor. He seems to be studying a crack in the tile. "We're not all the same, you know."

Maybe that's true. I think about what Cordelia said to me when she called me into her room. Theo's been helping me. When he covered his microphone and warned me to be more careful, he was protecting me. And he did the same for Hanna, too. He risked his position at the Cube, and maybe even his life, taking her off that train.

"You're right," I say. But Mama fell in love with a Group1 man who pretended to be more than who he was at the beginning. I'm not falling for that, too. "Why are you still talking to me if I get on your nerves?" I ask.

"I could ask you the same thing," he says. I hold Theo's gaze almost as if it's a challenge. Theo continues after a breath, "I'll try to stop being so 'emotionless' if you stop trying to avoid me."

I didn't realize he noticed. I feel my heart beating faster, despite myself. "Deal," I say.

After a moment, Theo asks, "Are you hungry?"

"Hmm?"

"You came to the cafeteria."

"Oh. Right." I forgot I was hungry. "Yeah, I'll be right back."

I head to the serving area and get myself a bowl of oatmeal. I try to wrap my mind around the conversation I'm having with Theo. When I head back to the table, I put my tray of oatmeal down in front of Theo.

"Lana," He looks down at my bowl. I notice he's calling me Lana again. "What on earth are you eating?"

"Oatmeal."

"But it's plain." He looks around to see if anyone else is watching. When he sees that they're not, he takes a sniff of my bowl. "Yeah, that's gross. It has no smell."

"What were you expecting?" I'm caught off guard by Theo's behavior. "It's not like I can load it with maple syrup." I raise my Chip at him.

"There must be a better option."

"I like this option. I can't believe you just *sniffed* my bowl."

"When you say it like that," he shakes his head. "Sorry. I haven't slept in three days. I'm a little loopy."

"Me neither. Not since Tearza."

We're both quiet for a moment.

I know I'm taking a chance, but I decide to risk it. "Do you know what happened to her?"

Theo stiffens. I immediately regret asking.

Before I can apologize, Theo looks around and whispers. "When you finish eating your oatmeal, come find me. I'll be at the back of the building."

I finish eating as fast as I can and leave the cafeteria. Theo is waiting for me. I walk toward him, both eager and confused. As soon as he notices me, Theo looks away and begins walking. I follow him, keeping the distance I realize he's intending to create. Theo takes me into the forest. We eventually leave the Cube's paved paths and walk into an area I don't recognize. I haven't stepped on dirt since arriving. We're technically in Oparius, but this feels off-limits.

Once we are completely submerged in the forest, Theo stops. He stands beneath a tree and waits for me to reach him. When I do, he looks nervous. "Sorry," he looks around to make sure no one followed us. "They don't necessarily record our conversations on the premises, but it's still safer to talk over here."

I nod, understanding. Theo is off duty, but he still shouldn't be seen having a long conversation with a Newbody.

"I've been wanting to talk to you about Tearza. I don't know everything, but I saw part of the footage. It was terrible."

I wonder what footage he's talking about. Why didn't he watch the whole thing? I decide not to ask. He might be sharing this information with me, but I don't want to press my luck.

I say, "I talked to Tearza about it a bit, but she didn't really tell me what happened... I know Anthony asked her to meet him. He gave her a lot of drinks."

"Yeah," Theo looks disturbed. I can tell he's upset. "I didn't see that part, but I saw what she did. She looked drunk. And angry."

"What was he doing to her? Before she got angry?"

Theo shakes his head. I know what he's implying with his silence. I can see it in the way his eyes crease. The man was assaulting her.

"It's not fair," I say before I can stop myself. "Tearza shouldn't have gotten in trouble. She was defending herself."

Theo looks pained.

"And what about the Official who sent her the note? Aren't they going to be punished?"

"Nobody's fessing up to it."

I roll my eyes in disbelief. Of course they aren't.

"So, what can we do about it?" I ask Theo, hoping he has some ideas.

Theo looks discouraged. "I tried talking to Cordelia..."

"And?"

"I don't think there's anything else I can do."

I think of Tearza and how scared she must have been when she was alone with Anthony. It's unforgivable that she's being punished. Her life's in jeopardy because of some privileged man's indecency.

"Aren't you mad?" I ask Theo. I want him to do more.

"*Of course* I am, but I can't help *everyone.*"

"What's that supposed to mean?"

"How do you think Cordelia responded after you tried to escape? I had to convince her that you were being honest. She barely believed me."

"I *was* being honest—"

"Lana, I know what you were doing. I probably sounded like an idiot when I told Cordelia I believed you. You're lucky she trusts me."

"I didn't ask you to save me," I mumble, but it sounds stupid as soon as I say it. "Why did you?"

Theo doesn't respond.

Instead of asking again, I say, "I saw Hanna, you know. She's the one who brought Tearza back to the Cottage. She carried her."

Theo stiffens, looking down at his fidgeting thumbs.

"Why did you save her?"

"I don't know. Because I'm an idiot."

"What do you mean?" I wasn't expecting that. "Do you regret it?"

"No, that's not what I mean."

I wait for him to continue.

Theo lets out a long sigh. "Look, I'm risking my job, risking my *life*, doing these things. I'm not sure what I'm doing half the time, but I'm trying, okay? I'm trying to be a good person."

I take this in. Theo's not the person I'm mad at, but at the end of the day, he's an Official. If he has any power to make things better—to help Tearza—I want him to use it. And yet I understand that there's only so much he can do. And he's already doing a lot. I risked my life for Mama because I love her, but Theo is risking his life for people who are practically strangers.

"There's nothing else you can do for Tearza, then?"

Theo barely looks at me. His voice is weak, "She's already gone."

I have to put it to rest. I know that.

"I'm sorry if it feels like I'm asking a lot of you... it's the right thing to do, *obviously*," I have to get that in there, "but I really do appreciate what you've done. It takes a lot to risk your life for someone."

Theo looks uncomfortable. He doesn't like being complimented.

I continue, "I guess I'm just confused. I mean, what are you doing with this government job if you agree with what I'm saying? Why are you helping me?"

Theo seems to be deciding what to say. Eventually, he says, "I took this job because it's a great opportunity. Working for the government... there are a lot of perks." By perks, he means money and status. "I'm really lucky to be an Official at the Cube... at least that's what I've always been told. They don't usually hire people my age. But I guess I've been seeing things a little differently lately."

"What changed?"

Theo's face becomes emotionless, something that happens to him a lot, and I can tell he won't say anything else. "We shouldn't be talking about this."

I'm frustrated. We were so close. "Sometimes I think you hate me," I say.

Theo shrugs. "I kind of do." He says it like I shouldn't be offended. But as soon as he sees the look on my face, I can tell he regrets it. "It's just... I really need to stay in line. Especially this year." He must be doing his placement year. I've heard about this before. When you turn seventeen, high-ranking Group members who want to work as Government Officials have to complete a placement first. They get placed somewhere "random"—but of course, there's lots of favoritism and nepotism—and if they finish with a good recommendation, they can choose to work in any area of the government they want. It's not something anyone from Group7 would ever dream of doing. We're not seen as competent enough for these jobs, not that I'd ever want to work for the government anyway.

Theo notices that I'm silent, so he continues. "It's just that you being here kind of throws everything in jeopardy. And I can't afford to be reckless. At least not now."

"I'm not asking you to do anything for me."

"I know," he says, and then he doesn't say more. I don't push him. We're quiet for a bit, both looking at each other. I look away.

"Anyway, thanks for following me here," Theo says.

"No problem."

"You know, next time you're hungry, I can get you something better to eat. Something better than oatmeal."

"For 200 calories or less?"

"Come on, Lana. Forget about that. I know how to pause your Chip. It won't even register the food."

I stare at him in disbelief. Didn't he *just* say he can't afford to be reckless? I don't point this out. I've spent the last few months starving myself. I haven't been able to enjoy the taste of food, except for the occasional reduced-calorie treat. The idea of eating anything I want seems surreal to me. Theo laughs at my disbelief.

"You have no idea how amazing that would be."

He smiles a nice broad smile. "Good. Let's do it sometime soon."

"Okay."

I leave Theo and walk to the gym, refreshed and hopeful. It's a weird sensation, feeling energized after a conversation with Theo. I still don't know what it means or what he wants from me. Are we friends now? But he also said he "kind of" hates me. And a part of me kind of hates him too. It's not like I keep asking him to rescue me. If he doesn't want to help, then he shouldn't. I'm not going to apologize. I didn't make things the way that they are. The government did. And he's still working for them. He's still planning a career with them. So, if all of the sudden he's socially conscious, I'm not going to feel guilty.

I try to shake off my feelings of frustration. Excitement. Confusion. Whatever is happening, I tell myself I'll be fine. With, or without, Theo as an ally.

CHAPTER 23

A week passes. I become more accustomed to my routine with Naomi as a Companion. I usually wake up around 10:00 at night. Most nights, I have my body back before many of the other Newbodies. I start my day off with a run, then go to the cafeteria for an underwhelming snack. I usually go to the gym after that and then finish my workout with Keya's Pilates. Naomi typically puts about 3000 to 4000 calories in my body, so I need to burn off quite a bit, but not nearly as much as I needed to with the Cowboy. I've gotten used to having more time in my night—it allows me to slow things down and gain energy. It's still not easy being a prisoner, but I'm fortunate to be rid of the Cowboy. The bad news is that when the Cowboy had to match with a new Companion, he ended up pairing with Dylan. For the last week, Dylan's been experiencing what I went through. He's already more cranky and exhausted. I feel bad for him, especially because I know exactly what he's going through. I know he'll be okay, but it's still not going to be easy. The Cowboy doesn't make anything easy.

I've noticed Theo around more often this week. I notice every time he stops to talk to Samantha. I try not to get annoyed, and really why should I be? But he also seems to go out of his way to spend time near me. When I go to the gym to dance, I catch him monitoring the area. He watches over everyone, but he seems to linger when he comes to check on me. He doesn't say much. He usually just watches me for a while. I smile at him and he'll nod, and then he'll leave to monitor the others. It's kind of exhilarating, knowing he's there. It's part of his job as an Official, to watch over prisoners and make sure everything is running smoothly. It's what he does with the rest of the Newbodies too. But when he comes over to my area, I imagine that he's an audience member. I imagine I'm performing and back on the stage. I pretend that he actually cares about what I have to say. I like to believe that it might be true.

When I come out of the gym one night, Theo catches up to me.

"We never got that food together," he says. Theo looks down at my Chip and I know what he means. The calorie-free food. Or, at least, the untrackable food. I can eat whatever I want and the Cube will have no idea.

I'm ecstatic about the idea. I'm starving after my dance and would love to finally eat something substantial. At home, whenever I finished dancing for the day I would eat Mama's food. Mama never let me eat just a little, and honestly, I never wanted to. After a day of work and dance, I would sometimes eat too much. Food was always our biggest expense and the only reason I would ever ration food at home was to keep down costs. But tonight, with Theo's Chip trick, I can eat whatever I want. And I am planning on it.

Theo can tell from my expression that I want to take him up on the offer. "Come on," he says. "I'll take you somewhere."

I follow Theo down a path and into the forest. It's the same area that we went to the other night. Theo finds the tree and we sit in the same spot again. There are no other Officials in sight. Theo pulls out something from his bag; it's a long, gray cylinder. I can't quite make out what it is, but he puts it down beside him. Theo asks for my Chip. I bring my arm to him and rest my wrist on his hand. When our skin touches, my heart beats faster. I wonder if he feels it too.

Theo drops my hand to his lap and picks up the hollow cylinder. I get a better look at it. It seems like a smaller version of the plastic apparatus that was used to first activate my Chip. I follow Theo's instructions and put my wrist into the cylinder. Theo presses a couple of buttons, waits for a light to turn off, and tells me I'm all set. My Chip will be turned off for the rest of the night, which will allow me to eat whatever I want. The Cube won't be notified.

"How do you know how to do that?"

Theo shrugs. "Officials aren't forced to eat a certain amount of calories but eating healthy is *encouraged* here. That's the sort of lifestyle they're promoting." I think about the Officials at the Cube and realize everyone is in good shape. I hadn't thought much about it, but it makes sense. Beauty is what they're selling. Theo continues, "Cordelia says our Chips count our calories 'to keep us honest,' or motivate us to look our best," Theo uses air quotes, and it almost seems like he's mocking the Cube. I'm surprised by his honesty. "Anyway, I like eating a lot and it's never been a problem for me. But the other Officials could see how much I was eating. I used to get a lot of comments about my calorie intake, and well, I didn't love it. So, now I find it easier to keep things private."

"So, this cylinder..." I start, hoping for Theo to fill in the blanks. I still don't know what it is or where it came from.

"I did some investigating and on my days off and I started making this. Now I can turn off my Chip whenever I want."

"You *made* this?" I ask, in disbelief.

"Yeah. I like projects like this. It's what I hope to do one day."

"Wow."

Theo shrugs. He looks at me for a moment, registering my expression. "What?"

"What?" I say back.

"You're looking at me funny."

"I'm impressed. And I guess I'm shocked you're telling me about it. You seem different than... I don't know."

"You know, most of the times we've talked we were being watched or recorded by someone." I think back to our awful mock date. "It's not like I could show my true self."

"Your *true* self? Tell me more."

"Don't get too excited. I'm basically the jerk you think I am. But I have a nice side too."

I grin, already knowing this is true.

"So, if your Chip's turned off, does that mean they're not tracking you right now?"

"Sort of. The tracking is paused."

"So, they don't know where you are right now?"

Theo gives me a look that confirms the answer. Theo's location is hidden. They don't know that he's here with me.

"The pause only lasts for an hour though. So, we better get you food. What do you want? Any requests?"

I'm happy to eat anything right now. "Just bring back as much as you can," I joke.

Theo nods. He stands up to leave for the cafeteria.

I lie back against the tree and eagerly wait for Theo to return. It's pitch-black outside, so I can't help myself from feeling a bit scared all alone. But I know there are Government Officials nearby and nothing "dangerous" happens in Oparius. It might be ironic, but it is not unsurprising that the prisoners here are harmless. The only people we need to worry about are the Patrons and Officials on the other side. I wonder how far Theo's home is from here. I wonder what Theo would think of my life in Group7. Theo still hasn't told me what Group he's from, but I know he must be from Group1 or 2. All Government Officials are. I wonder what life was like for him growing up. It would have been completely different from the life I knew, of course. Theo could have had whatever he wanted. He never had to worry about money. And everyone around him probably worked for the government, or was a part of the government, ruling over the rest of us.

It's hard for me to imagine Theo coming from that world. He doesn't seem like the kind of guy who had everything in life go his way. He seems sad, I think, but then I dismiss the thought. He's probably just bored, trying to find ways to pretend his life is complicated.

When Theo comes back, he's carrying a large basket, a blanket, and a lantern. It smells amazing. He sets the basket down and lays out the blanket on the ground. He lights the lantern and opens up the basket of food. "A picnic. Thank you."

"You deserve it. It's crazy how little you guys eat here. I don't know how you do it. I'd be so cranky."

"Wow, I wonder what *that* would be like."

Theo laughs. He takes out the food and sets it on the blanket. There's everything I could have ever imagined. Croissants and danishes, a fruit and nut salad, chocolate chip cookies, curries, French fries, pizza, and falafel. I try all of the different options and can't believe how delicious everything tastes. I insist that Theo eats with me. As hungry as I am, there is no way I can eat everything on my own.

Theo shows me that he even brought a cooler with a bowl of ice cream so I could have some with the cookies for dessert. It's the kindest thing anyone has done for me in such a long time. This reminds me of the last big meal I had at the Cohens. When I was on the train, I would constantly think about that dinner. I wondered if I'd ever experience anything like that again. I quickly remove the thought from my mind before I get too emotional. Instead, I focus on the food in front of me. I take a bite of the pizza and melt away.

I eat quickly and ferociously, as if I've never eaten before. I sense that Theo is watching me and I can picture a smirk on his face. Once I start feeling full, I sit back and realize I haven't said anything but "thank you" since I began gorging down food. I give Theo my thanks again to make sure he really understands how grateful I am. He tells me to stop thanking him, so I finally shut up about it. "It's just, I've never eaten anything like this. All these different flavors. And the amount of food..."

"I know what you mean," Theo says, but of course, he doesn't. Money has never been an issue for him. "I never really ate anything like this at home either. My parents aren't really the type."

"What do you mean?"

"Oh, you know. We just usually eat the same meals every week. Roast beef on Mondays, pasta on Tuesdays, that kind of thing."

I somewhat understand this. Mama loved cooking her favorite foods and didn't often venture outside of her comfort zone. It's weird to compare Mama to Theo's parents. It's hard to believe they have anything in common.

I look at Theo, trying to imagine his family eating dinner with mine. It's a funny thought. Theo notices me looking at him and asks, "What's that face about?"

"Nothing." But when I explain what I was thinking, he's not impressed.

"Just because a family has money doesn't mean they're perfect, you know."

"Maybe," I say, caught a little off guard. I was only trying to joke around. "But money certainly makes things easier."

Theo doesn't say anything more. I know we are never going to see eye to eye on this. We continue making small talk and the mood lightens. Theo tells me about what it's like to be a guard and I tell him about the things that make being at the Cube not miserable. I tell him about the friends I've made, like Minji and Dylan, and Theo tells me what he really thinks of Cordelia.

"She's the happiest and cruelest person you'll ever meet. It's quite the combination."

"But do you actually think she's that cheerful?"

Theo shakes his head. "Oh, absolutely not."

We laugh. Theo asks me how I'm liking my new Companion.

"She's okay, I guess," I tell him. "She's much better than my previous one. I actually have time in my body now. Or, sorry, I mean Shell."

"That's okay. It's interesting... I know Naomi's never visited the Cube before, but something about her seems so familiar."

"Oh yeah?"

"I probably met her at some event with my family. This happens with the Patrons sometimes."

"It must be hard being *so* important."

Theo rolls his eyes.

When we finish eating, Theo walks me back to the Cottage. We say goodnight quickly, knowing there might be others around. He waits for me to go inside and close the door before he leaves. I wipe the smile off my face, but I can still taste the chocolate ice cream and cookies. I look at my Chip, in disbelief that none of the calories were counted. My stomach is full for the first time in ages. I'm happy. I can't remember the last time I've been happy. I know I'll get a good sleep tonight.

CHAPTER 24

I'm at a party in a grand hall. I've never been in this room before, but it's beautiful. It's a part of the Cube that's usually reserved for Officials and Patrons only. Not tonight. I'm wearing the white dress I wore on my first date with Theo. Or mock date, I guess. The hall is alive with music and dancing. Minji and Dylan are twirling beside me, smiling from ear to ear. Even Cordelia and Tearza have joined in. I'm watching everyone dance around me, and then Theo is there. He's looking at me from a distance, the way he always does when he's on guard. But now he's coming toward me. He is walking with purpose, a look of joy comes over him. When he reaches me, he puts his arm out. "Dance with me?" I'm giddy with excitement. I take his hand. Theo places one hand on mine, and the other on my waist. I feel my heart beat faster. We move across the floor. Theo naturally leads. He spins me around, again and again, and I feel myself becoming dizzy. I look away to get my bearings and when I look back, Ethan is looking at me.

"Ethan?" I say, shocked.

Ethan is beaming. He looks so confident that I'm sure it's been him this whole time.

"I've missed you," I tell him. I know he's missed me too.

I feel the warmth I always feel when Ethan is beside me. He holds me tight and I never want him to let me go. I feel him squeeze me tighter like he has read my mind. This kind of thing always happens with Ethan. We've known each other for so long.

"What are you doing here?" I ask him.

But when he answers the question, it's Theo again. "I can't stay away from you," he says.

Before I can respond, something grabs at my ankles. I panic for a moment until I realize it's Minji. She is talking to me. I'm in bed.

"Are you okay?" she asks.

I remember coming back from my run tired. I must have napped. "Yeah, sorry, I just had a weird dream."

"No worries," Minji says. "We're starting Pilates. Just thought you'd want to know."

"Thanks," I tell her. "I'll be there in a few."

I slowly get out of bed, muddled after the dream. It doesn't help that my waking thoughts aren't any clearer. I'm starting to have feelings for Theo. I know he's an Official, and can sometimes be unnecessarily rude, but I can't seem to keep him out of my thoughts.

But whenever I think of Theo, I also start thinking of Ethan. I don't know where I stand with him. I kissed Ethan before I left, but I don't know if I'll ever see him again. If I'm being completely honest, there's a good chance I'll never see anyone from 7N again. The thought petrifies me, but I have to acknowledge it. I still hope that I'll find a way to escape, but there's obviously no guarantee. And even if I do, how do I know Ethan will be waiting for me? By the time I eventually make my way back to 7N, how will I know where either of us stands?

My thoughts always come back to Theo. Now that I've seen a different side of him, I can't help myself from wanting to learn more. But even that seems like a bad idea. Minji and Dylan might be able to date each other without worrying too much, but I'm sure the Cube keeps a close eye on relationships between prisoners and Government Officials. What would happen if Cordelia caught us sharing food? Laughing together? Kissing? I know I'm getting ahead of myself, but it's hard not to think about it.

For now, I'm willing to take the risk. But that doesn't make things any easier.

I get out of bed and throw on a clean pair of workout clothes. *It's just another day at the Cube,* I tell myself. I will join my friends for a workout and ignore the sinking feeling in my stomach. Nothing's happened... and yet I already feel like I'm in trouble.

After I finish working out, I head back to the Cottage. While I'm walking, I hear someone behind me. I'm afraid to turn around, so I walk a little faster, hoping the person will leave me alone. But they quicken their pace and the next thing I know they are tapping my shoulder. "Lana." It's Theo. I turn to face him.

"What's going on? You *freaked* me out."

"Sorry, I didn't want anyone to see us."

I'm relieved to see him. The smile on Theo's face makes me happy. I can't help but return it.

"You hungry?" He asks, gesturing to a bag in his hand.

"Always." And at the Cube that is very true.

The two of us head toward our usual spot. We sit in silence as I wolf down a delicious sandwich with fresh vegetables. I'm enjoying it too much to pause for conversation. Theo doesn't seem to mind; he watches, amused.

Finally, after I finish the sandwich, I thank him. Theo laughs and I ask him why.

"You eat like nobody I've ever met."

"Thank you," I say, although I don't think it's supposed to be a compliment. "I'm a big fan of food."

"I can tell."

We talk about our favorite types of food, and I tell him about the meals Mama made for us growing up. I talk about the Cohens and Friday night dinners, but I'm careful in how I explain my relationship with them. I refer to them as my family friends, but nothing more. It's hard to explain my relationship with Ethan to Theo.

I'm not sure if it's what I said or the tone I used, but something about Ethan piques Theo's interest. I answer Theo's questions, explaining how long I've known Ethan and the kinds of things we liked to do together, but I can sense Theo becoming more guarded.

I try to change the subject. "Anyway, we don't have to talk about all that anymore."

"That's okay. I can tell you two were close."

"He's my best friend."

"You must miss him."

"Yeah," I say, and then I add. "I feel terrible."

191

"Why?"

I look at Theo, wondering what I should say. "How much do you know about my family?"

"What do you mean?"

"I mean, you're an Official..."

"Yeah, we're debriefed about every Working Guest before they arrive. We get the highlights, you know, the things the government's most concerned about. But we're not told everything."

"Did my highlights include information about Loukas?"

"That's your brother, right?" Theo nods. "I know about him."

"Do you know about his friendship with Ethan?"

"No, we wouldn't be told those kinds of things."

I stay quiet for a moment. I'm not sure what information I should share. I still don't know if I can fully trust Theo, but I want to. I have reasons to believe I can.

I look at Theo and he's staring back at me. I decide to take the risk. Plus, telling Theo might lead to him giving me more information.

"Ethan helped me Hack my mom. He was the one who knew how to do everything. And before that, when Loukas got in trouble, Ethan helped him too. So, I know Ethan is a complete mess right now. He must be feeling so guilty. He never wanted me to be in this situation. If he could, he'd be here instead of me."

Theo doesn't say anything for a moment. His face is blank, almost annoyingly so. "What makes you think he's still at home?"

I don't know what to say. Of course, I've considered Ethan might not be safe, but the way Theo says it seems callous.

"Maybe he's in trouble," I say, "but maybe he's not. It's easier for me to imagine him in 7N. He's the only piece of home I have left."

"That seems like wishful thinking."

"There's only so much sadness I can handle," I say.

"I know, but it sounds to me like Ethan was involved... so most likely he's at a Camp."

"Yeah, I understand that." I shove a piece of broccoli into my mouth. I really don't want to have this conversation anymore.

"I'm just saying... you should prepare yourself."

"But you don't know anything about where he is, so maybe you're wrong."

"Maybe. I doubt it."

"Why are you being like this?"

Theo doesn't respond, so I continue. "Of course, I've considered every possibility. Of *course,* I've imagined the worst-case scenario. But Ethan is someone I really care about and I want to believe he's okay. I thought you'd be more..."

"More what?"

"I don't know," my voice raises, "compassionate."

"You're getting mad."

"Well, I don't like the way you're acting."

"How am I acting?"

"I don't know. Jealous."

Theo lets out a sound. "That's *not* what this is."

"Then what is it?"

"I'm just trying to prepare you—to help."

"But *why?* Why are you helping me?"

Theo doesn't answer. I hate how aloof he's being. I feel my blood rushing and I can't stop myself from saying more. "If you're going to close yourself off like this and pretend you don't care, then I'm going to go, I think."

I wait for him to say something, but he doesn't. I get up and run to the Cottage, feeling my adrenaline building with every stride. I'm angry and hurt. But most of all, I'm scared for Ethan. I hope that if he's at a Camp, he's not in too much pain. I hope that he stays safe. I pray that I'll one day see him again and that he'll stay alive until then. I wish there was a way that I could help him. But I've known Ethan for a very long time and I know that if he's in trouble, he doesn't need my help. He'll be okay.

A few hours pass and I prepare for my Switch. It's 8:50 a.m. and I know Naomi will call on me soon. Most people are already asleep and it's quiet in the Cottage. I hear a knock on the door. Nobody else seems to be awake or hear it, so I go to answer.

When I open it, Theo is on the doorstep. I think about closing the door on him, but I decide against it. I've calmed down a bit. I look around to make sure no one is watching me and then I join him outside.

"What are you doing here?"

"I want to apologize."

"You couldn't wait?"

"I feel awful," Theo says, and I can tell from his eyes that he means it. "I know I'm not easy to deal with sometimes. But I'm trying. I'm really trying."

"What do you mean?"

"I just..." Theo thinks about what to say. "I know what kind of person I *don't* want to be. And whenever I start being that person..." He seems to be holding back tears. "I'm sorry."

"It's okay," I tell him instinctively. I don't like seeing him this way.

"I'm working on opening up more, I promise. I know I can be a complete jerk."

"That's for sure," I say, half joking. Theo doesn't return my smile. He's being sincere.

"This isn't an excuse, but I don't want you to take it personally. I'm not being cold because I'm mad at you, okay? It's just because... I don't know, it's in my DNA or something."

"I don't believe that. People aren't born that way."

"Aren't they?"

"I think being a good person is a choice."

"Well, I'm trying to choose it. It's just not always easy for me."

I know what he's trying to say. Theo doesn't find it easy to be vulnerable. I'm happy he's able to acknowledge it. "I get it," I say, but I know I have to protect myself, too. "I can be patient with you if—" I think about what to say, not wanting to be presumptuous, "if you want to be friends. But I need you to respect me. I don't want to hang around somebody that makes me feel like an idiot."

"I know. I'll do better."

I nod, unsure of what else to say.

"And you were right before. I was jealous."

This shouldn't make me happy, but it does. "You were?"

"Ethan sounds like a great guy. You're lucky to have him."

"He's just a friend," I say before I can stop myself. "You know, like Samantha."

"Samantha's *barely* a friend," he says.

"Sure." I roll my eyes.

"I mean it. She's super full of herself and kind of annoying, but she was the best company I had for a while... before you."

I freeze. I don't know what to say to that.

"Okay, Lana, I guess I should be leaving. Have a good sleep."

"You too," I say.

I watch Theo walk away in a remarkably better mood.

CHAPTER 25

Over the next few weeks, I spend a lot of my free time meeting up with Theo in secret. On some days, Theo comes in a great mood, and on other days he is more closed off. There are still conversations we can't have without his guard going up. I try my best to navigate them, and he tries to let me in. Some nights I feel so exhausted and worn out from exercise, I consider not meeting up with Theo. But I always do. I can't pass up the food and the chance to eat whatever I want. Of course, I don't always overdo it the way I did at the beginning. But an extra sandwich here and there hasn't done any harm. With all the exercise I do, my metabolism can certainly handle the extra food, whether the Cube believes it or not.

Even without the food, I wouldn't pass up on the time with Theo. With every interaction, I feel a little closer to him. I can sense his trust building. He's slowly letting me in.

Certain moments feel so magical that I'm shocked by how happy I can be here. Theo and I spend most of our time at the same tree, talking and eating together. But sometimes we go on adventures. Theo takes me to different spots around Oparius. The other night we walked along the ocean and stopped to sit on a dock. The water was peaceful and nobody else was around. There was a moment I thought Theo might kiss me. We had just been laughing about something Cordelia did and our faces were nearly touching. We looked at each other, our eyes locked in an electric moment, but it left as quickly as it came. I looked away, too scared to make it happen. But even still, just sitting with Theo on the dock was special. I didn't want it to end. In moments like that, I think of Ethan. I can't help but feel guilty. But I also think of Ethan when things don't go well. When Theo is closed off and doesn't want to talk, that's when I miss Ethan the most. Ethan's never like that with me, or anyone, really. He always tells me how he's feeling. It's never an uphill battle.

The more time I spend with Theo, though, the less I compare him to Ethan. I start to know Theo for who he is on his own. That doesn't mean I've forgotten about Ethan, but honestly, Ethan feels further away from me with every passing day. So much has changed since coming to the Cube. It doesn't help that the idea of getting out of here and seeing Ethan again seems far-fetched at this point. It's hard for me to imagine that he's still at home. I was naïve to think he might be safe.

Ethan's somewhere out there, far from me, and there's nothing either of us can do about it. When I think about that for too long, my heart breaks, but talking to Theo makes it easier. Spending time with Theo gives me hope. He might not give me the comfort of home, but he gives me something else. He makes me forget. And since I've become a prisoner, lost Mama, and been taken from my brother and best friend, there's a lot I want to forget.

Tonight, sitting under the tree with Theo, I sense his relaxed energy. He's sipping on a beer that he won't let me try, because of my age, telling me about his mom. I know it's a memory I will hold on to almost as soon as he begins talking. Theo tells me about a time his mom brought the wrong flowers to a visit with President Ace. French Hydrangeas. Apparently, Group1s believed French hydrangeas were exclusively to be given to widows. Ace never married. When Theo's mom gave them to him, Ace thought he was being mocked. When Theo's mom left the visit, she found the bouquet scattered on the sidewalk. The president must have tossed them out his window. Theo's father was mortified by the ordeal, but his mom couldn't have cared less.

It's an entertaining story, but mostly I like the way Theo tells it. I can tell how fondly he thinks of his mom. "That's hilarious," I say. "I wish our moms could have met."

Theo looks at me, smiling. "Me too."

After I finish eating, Theo asks me to get up. "Where are we going?"

"Come on. I want to show you something."

I follow Theo through trees and hidden paths. We walk on an uphill slope, climbing higher and higher as we go. Eventually, I see a lookout spot in the distance. I remember Theo telling me about this place on our mock date. It's his favorite part of the Cube. I realize he's taken me outside Oparius. We are technically breaking the rules. When we get to the lookout, I'm overwhelmed by the view. It's gorgeous, like nothing I've ever seen. There are mountains so big that I can't see the top of them. The ocean is clear and bright, sparkling in the moonlight. There are beautiful parts of 7N, but nothing compares to this.

"This is your favorite spot," I say.

"Yeah. I thought you might like it."

"I love it." It's hard to believe how special Theo makes me feel sometimes. I wish I could put it into words, but all I can manage is "thank you."

I remind Theo of how he mentioned this place on the mock date.

"I remember," he says.

"You do?"

"I don't think you realize the effect you had on me."

I can't believe he's saying this. "Why?"

Theo looks down, twirling his thumbs around each other. He pauses for a moment, then says, "I saw you dance once, you know? Before the Cube. I grew up in Group1."

It's the first time Theo tells me what Group he's from. He says it so casually. Group1.

"My dad was born there and my mom married up. My mom loves doing Group1 activities because they're still so exciting for her, but my dad never goes. He's above all that, you know? Plus, he's always working and my mom much preferred hanging out with us." Theo brushes this off, but I can tell there's more to the story. I wonder who Theo's dad is. "My mom used to drag me and my sister to different events and parties all the time. Sometimes she'd take us to shows. I didn't really like any of it, really. I'm not that kind of guy. But I remember one show I went to... my sister was with friends so I just went with my mom. It was a ballet. And I came out thinking *holy moly*. I didn't know people could move like that."

I laugh. "Did you just say *holy moly*?"

"I mean it. It made me feel so... alive. And I remember you. I remember this other woman, too—she was the star of the show... you danced just like her." He's talking about Mama. Theo finally looks up from his hands. He stares at me. "Anyway, I never forgot it. And when you first arrived at the Cube, I instantly recognized you. So, I guess that's why I said you bothered me. You scared the hell out of me."

I nod, understanding things a bit more. "So, that's why you call me Lana. I was wondering how you knew my stage name."

"I hate the full name thing here. I know you think I'm 'entitled' because I ask to go by Theo and not Theodore, and maybe I am..."

I laugh. He's referring to when I guessed he was from Group1 on our mock date. "I'm sorry about that."

"It's okay," Theo says. "But I really think it's more than that. I've always hated how bourgeois the forced full names sound in high-ranking Groups. We never did it in my house. My mom never calls me Theodore."

This makes me smile. It's nice to know we have this in common. Before meeting Theo, I didn't think anyone from a high-ranking Group felt this way.

"Why do I scare you?"

"Because..." he looks down again. "The way you care about things... I don't know. It scares me."

I don't know what to say. "That lady," I tell him, "the one you saw dancing... that was my mom. She died right before I came here." I know he already knows this, but I say it anyway. It's the first time I'm able to voice the words. "She's why I'm here."

"I'm so sorry." Theo's already been debriefed all about this, but this feels different. These aren't bullet points from the government; these are real experiences, real emotions, expressed by me. "You were really brave, the way you switched bodies with her."

Before getting to know Theo, I never would have thought an Official would consider my actions brave. It's nice to hear him say it like that, too: "switched bodies." If he had used the word "Hack" it would have sounded aggressive coming from an Official. And he also didn't use the word "Shell." Maybe deep down he understands the distinction.

"It was our final show of the season. I wanted to give my mom one last dance."

Theo smiles. I think of a younger version of him coming to watch me dance. I like the idea of Theo knowing me before all this, before the Cube. When both of us were free.

The night is almost ending. I feel myself wishing I could stay here a little longer. I think we both feel it. But I know the sun will rise soon, Naomi will take over my body, and I'll be expected to sleep. We take in this moment for one last minute. I feel grateful for Theo. There's something magical about long walks in the dark, or sitting on a porch on a hot summer night, talking about everything and nothing. It feels effortless. It's so comfortable and pleasant that I almost forget how bad things can be at the Cube.

Of course, something always happens, whether it's a conversation with Cordelia or a bad story about a Companion from my friends, that reminds me I'm a prisoner. This can't be permanent.

But leaving here would mean leaving Theo, and the longer I stay, the more I find it hard to imagine a life without him. It's hard not to feel something in my shared moments with him. Sitting beside him, listening to him talk, it's hard not to feel my crush growing. It doesn't hurt that he's so nice to look at. His warm brown eyes and broad shoulders make me feel protected, like if we were caught by Cordelia everything would be okay.

Theo walks me back to the Cottage. He stops before we get too close, just to be safe. I think about kissing him before we say goodbye. I wonder if he feels the same way. Theo hugs me and then turns to leave. I watch him walk away before I enter the Cottage and reality sets back in.

CHAPTER 26

When I wake up the following night, I'm eager to see Theo again. As soon as my Chip buzzes and I return to my body, I go straight to the gym.

I look for Theo while I run the track and again before I start my dancing. He doesn't seem to be anywhere. He must have tonight off. When I finish exercising and reach my goal for the day, I take a quick shower and head to our tree. Since I can't find Theo anywhere, I expect that's where he'll be.

Theo always brings the same blanket and lantern to the tree. I can always see the light in the distance as I walk toward our spot. While I head there tonight, Minji finds me. She calls my name as she runs to meet me. "Hey, I haven't seen you all night."

I try to sound casual. "I know. What's up?"

"Not much. Just going to go for a run with Dyl. Want to come?"

"Maybe next time," I say. "I think a walk's more my speed tonight."

"Okay." Her tone seems suspicious, but I hope I'm just reading into things. "See you later, then."

I wave goodbye to Minji as she runs off. I make a left and head into the forest. As I walk toward the tree, I don't see any light. I wonder if Theo is late. Maybe something is keeping him or there's a line in the cafeteria. When I get to our tree, I wait around for about an hour doing jumping jacks and various exercises so that when the food eventually shows up, I will legally be able to eat some. But Theo never comes. Eventually I give up and head to the cafeteria. I might as well get a muffin with the extra calories I have to spare.

The same thing happens the next few nights. Every time I go to our spot, Theo isn't there. I wait for him less and less, not wanting to feel pathetic.

Finally, on the fourth night of this new routine, I find Theo under the tree when I arrive. He has a basket of food for us and the place is set up like nothing happened. I sit down beside him.

"Theo..." I say, but he doesn't look up. Something's wrong. "Where have you been? What's going on?"

Theo still doesn't respond. He takes out a sandwich from the basket and starts eating.

"Theo, what's going on?"

"I brought some food. Do you want a burrito?"

"What happened?"

"There's also a salad. And some soda—"

"Theo—"

"Can you stop, please?" I look at him, disappointed. I want to know what's wrong so I can help. He knows that. When he looks up, it's clear he feels guilty. He takes a deep breath. "Sorry, it's been a hard few days."

"That's okay."

I wait for Theo to gather his thoughts. He looks at me sympathetically. When he's ready, he begins. "They found Hanna the other day. She was cleaning the main building and they recognized her."

"Oh my god," my heart sinks. "What happened?"

"They took her into questioning. They weren't happy. She's not... she's hurt. They beat her."

"No..."

"Yeah. They are blaming her. They have no idea I was involved."

"Of course," I say bitterly. I can't help myself.

"I don't know what to do," Theo looks devastated. His eyes are swollen and large bags have formed under them. I wonder when he last slept. "I'm scared."

"Why didn't you come to me?"

"What were you going to do about it?"

I look down.

"Sorry," he says. "I just mean..."

"I know. I get it. I just want to help however I can."

"I've been thinking about it for a while, and I think I'll tell them. It's the right thing to do. Hanna shouldn't be the only one who's blamed for this. I'm the one who got her the Keeper uniform and told her what to do. She wouldn't be in this situation if it wasn't for me."

"You were trying to help her." Theo shakes his head. He's blaming himself for something the government is responsible for. If they hadn't put Hanna in this vulnerable position in the first place, Theo never would have done this. Same with Hanna. The two of them didn't do anything wrong. The system did. "Don't say anything," I say, surprising myself. "All you'll do if you admit your involvement is get yourself in trouble, too. You won't save Hanna. They'll still blame her."

"But maybe I deserve to be punished."

"For what? Trying to keep a young girl from dying in a Work Camp?"

Theo looks at me for the first time since sitting down. There are tears in his eyes. "I can't believe they caught her, Lana... I should have known this would happen."

"You took a risk. You did the right thing."

"What are they going to do to her?" He asks desperately. I wish I had an answer. I shake my head. It's quiet for a moment. I inch closer to Theo and lean my head on his shoulder. He moves closer to me, letting me in. I rub his back, trying my best to reassure him. After a while, he says. "My sister, Izzie, almost died a few years ago. She..." Theo stops for a moment, thinking about what to say. "She got into a bad car accident. She was in a coma for weeks."

"I'm so sorry." I think of Loukas. I know how hard it can be to see a sibling in danger.

"I don't know what I would have done if she'd died. But ever since, I don't know, I've been kind of numb. And then when I saw you and the way you were taking care of Hanna... that's not normal here, you know? Usually the new Working Guests, or, sorry, prisoners..." Theo knows I hate that term. "Usually they don't help each other or even have conversations. It's so competitive, trying to get a place at the

203

Cube." I nod, making the connection. Hanna reminded him of his sister, Izzie. Me protecting her reminded him that he could protect her too.

"You did a brave thing helping Hanna. I'm sure she's still very grateful."

"It wasn't enough, though."

"That's not your fault. Izzie ended up being okay, right? So will Hanna." I say these words without really believing them. Theo shakes his head, doubting it too. I wish I could give him more reassurance. I try to think of another plan. A way to protect Hanna. "Is there any way you could convince Cordelia to keep her on the staff?"

"Prisoners don't get that kind of job," he explains what I already know. Cleaning jobs are too easy. They keep them for law-abiding citizens in the bottom Groups.

"What if you recommend her?"

Theo shakes his head. But then he says, "They have her detained right now, but they haven't removed her yet. I don't know what she's been saying to them but whatever it is, it seems to be working. I expected her to be gone by now."

"That's good at least," I say, without really knowing what that means or where it will lead.

Theo shrugs. We sit together in silence for a while. It's comfortable with him, neither of us feeling like we need to put on a show for the other. Our shoulders brush against each other, the sides of our bodies touching. I wish I could hug him, let him know that everything is going to be okay, but right now, right here, this is enough.

As if he reads my mind, Theo whispers, "Thank you."

I give him a soft smile. He squeezes my hand. "Does it surprise you? That a guy like me could have a hard time?"

He's mocking me a little and I can sense it. "Don't say it like that."

"I'm honestly curious."

"Look, maybe you've had hard times, but that doesn't mean you're not privileged."

"That's not what I'm saying."

I look at him, but I don't say anything more. If it were another night, I might have continued, but not tonight. I might have said that, yes, his sister got into a bad car accident and almost died. But Izzie also probably survived partly due to the medical care she was able to receive in Group1. Plus, now that Izzie is okay again, she will probably live a long life. Pretty much the only way you can die young in Group1 is due to an accident. Health problems don't affect young people in high-ranking Groups. I might have said all of this to Theo, but I know he's too upset.

"My mom was like you, you know?" Theo says. "I mean, she wasn't from Group7, but she was from Group5. And when she first met my dad she thought he was such a jerk, just because he was from Group1. Well, it turns out that my dad *is* a massive jerk... but maybe he wasn't back then. Anyway. We're not all bad. You'd love Izzie if you met her."

"But I won't."

"You could."

"No, don't say that," I say. "You only have to stay here for a year. After that, you're free. But me? I've got another twenty-four. And even when I'm free, I'll never be allowed to come to Group1. I'm a prisoner. So, I'll never meet her."

"You can't be sure."

"Why not? It's true."

"Well, maybe things can change.".

"How?"

"I don't know. But if anyone can figure something out, it's you."

I look at him, wondering if he means it. He looks serious. We stare at each other for a while, neither of us saying anything. Maybe Theo will help me out. Maybe we can escape together. I try not to get carried away. I don't say anything more about it. Not now, at least. I don't want to push it.

"I wish you would tell me more about your family," I say, changing the subject back.

"What do you want to know?"

"I don't know. Tonight's really the first time you've said anything. It's nice to hear you talk about them."

"I'll tell you anything if you ask."

I laugh at that.

"What?" he asks.

"I don't know if that's quite true. You're so secretive."

"I'm not," he says, but he's not fooling anyone. "There's nothing else to tell you about my family. We're just as messed up as the rest of them. It's not interesting."

"What does that mean? Messed up? I wouldn't say all families are messed up..."

Theo doesn't respond. I can tell he's thinking about his family; maybe he's wondering about mine. I think about Mama and Loukas. Maybe I was lucky. Other than my dad, nothing really seemed "messed up." At least not things in our control. The fact that my brother was taken and my mom was sentenced to an early death might be "messed up" but neither of those things were their faults. Before that, everything was good. We were happy.

"You don't have to tell me anything you're not ready to share." I can tell Theo's thinking about what to say.

"No, it's okay." He shakes his head. His voice is tentative. "I guess things with my parents have always been weird. At least for as long as I can remember. I don't really know my dad well. He lives with us and everything, but we don't really talk. We've never really clicked, you know. He's an angry guy." Theo's voice is soft. He doesn't usually look at me when he's uncomfortable, but tonight he does. "My dad's temper used to be terrible, but it's gotten better. I think it helped that I grew up. Having a third man in the house, I mean. Not that my mom and sister need me, but that's how my dad saw it."

"What do you mean 'a third man in the house?'"

Theo stiffens. "Oh. My brother." Theo's mentioned his sister and parents a few times now, but I never knew anything about a brother. "He works here," Theo says, a little too nonchalantly. "That's why they positioned me at the Cube. Well, that and my dad."

"Your dad?"

"The government loves him. Cordelia loves him. So, I suppose that makes me lucky. I'm sure Cordelia would have kicked me out of here by now if it wasn't for my dad and brother."

It's a lot to take in. "How does your dad know Cordelia?"

Theo shrugs. "They run in the same circles. He comes to the Cube sometimes."

"Do you ever see him here?"

"Not really. He usually visits Jamie."

"Jamie?"

"My brother."

"Well, I'd love to meet him. Your brother," I say.

Theo hesitates. I pick up on the silence. "I'm not really close with him." I nod. "Jamie was always a lot more like my dad than Izzie and me. He's six years older than me, so he spent a lot of time with my dad when he was young. We don't really get along." There's a long pause before Theo finishes. I can tell he feels bad saying no to me. "I'm sorry." I know he means it.

"That's okay. Don't worry."

"He does computer programming for the Cube, anyway. He doesn't really spend time in Oparius."

"Is it weird being here together?"

"I think we're used to it, being near each other, but not *really*. You know?" Theo's mind seems to wander to a memory. He says, "Whenever my dad was in one of his moods, Jamie was on his side. It kind of felt like three against two growing up. Izzie, my mom, and I were on one side and the 'men' were on the other. It took me some time to catch up to Jamie, size-wise, because of the age difference. I used to pray to God every night that I could get bigger. I was so desperate. I don't even know if I believed in God, but I just wanted to be strong. I wanted to be big enough to scare them, you know? So that if things got bad, everyone would be safe." I nod, understanding. The idea of a young Theo pleading with God so he could protect his mom and sister breaks my heart. "And eventually, when I did start catching up to them, it felt good. They listened to me more." He pauses again before continuing. "These days, it's not bad all the time, though. Usually, my dad's not around. And when he is we all just kind of avoid each other. So, I'm used to it."

"I'm so sorry," I tell him. I know there's nothing more I can say.

"I would never hurt you, Lana. I want you to know that."

"I know," I tell him because I know it's true. "I'd never hurt you either."

We lock eyes for a moment before Theo continues. "Sometimes it bothers me, being here, though. Because I can't check on my mom as much. But I know Izzie's there. And she's really grown up. She always gets mad at me when I worry about not being around to protect her. She doesn't need me."

"You're lucky to have a sister you love so much."

"I'm sure I could say the same thing about Loukas."

It's nice to hear Theo say my brother's name. It makes me happy to imagine the two of them knowing each other. We sit in silence for a moment, absorbing our conversation. Theo and I are still touching, his shoulder leaning slightly against mine. I feel him move slowly, his torso curling toward me. We're inches apart now. I touch my fingers to his chest. Theo's hand comes behind my neck. He gently guides me closer and the next thing I know we're kissing.

It's our first kiss, but somehow, I know just what to do. It feels as effortless as our private conversations and walks in the dark, but it's so much more intense. I feel like I'm exploding and floating at the same time. It's a mix of fire and water. After a while, Theo pulls away and smiles. It's a big smile, like at the end of a good laugh, and it reassures me all over again. I know this is as special for him as it is for me.

He kisses me again and the world disappears. We're not at the Cube. I'm not a prisoner. He's not an Official. We're just two people kissing under a tree.

CHAPTER 27

The next night, as soon as I complete my Switch, I'm eager to find Theo. I head to the Cottage first, needing to pick up a few things. Before I leave, I find a note resting on my pillow. My heart races, thinking it's from Theo. But as soon as I open it, I know it's not. It says, *Meet me at your tree when the sun comes up. I'm working with Hanna. I'm on your side. -Naomi.* I read it over, again and again, unsure of what to make of it. How does my Companion know about the tree? What does she mean she's working with Hanna? I think about showing it to Theo, but I don't know if I should. Did he tell Naomi about our spot? What if he has been tricking me this whole time? I can't imagine that right now. Not after last night and our perfect kiss. It's impossible to imagine that Theo would hurt me like that.

I shake off the thought and focus on Naomi. I try to think of why she might want to see me. I assume she found out about Theo and me. Who else has she told? Maybe Cordelia will be there, waiting to take me away on a train. But why would Cordelia send a message through Naomi? Why wouldn't she just come here and punish me herself? And what does any of this have to do with Hanna? Could Naomi be the reason why Hanna hasn't been sent away from the Cube yet? Why would Naomi be helping her?

I spend the next hour worrying about what this could mean and what I should do. I go for a long run, thinking over every possibility and trying to figure out my best and safest option. When I can't think or run any longer, I look for Minji. I need someone else's opinion.

I find Minji in the gym. She's on the rowing machines beside Dylan and Keya. When Minji sees me, she stops.

"Hey, girl!" She says. "It's about *time* you woke up."

As soon as Minji registers the worry on my face, her amused expression drops. "Are you okay?"

I try to mask my concern. "I'm good. Sorry to barge in like this." I don't want to worry the others. "Minji, do you want to go for a run?"

Minji gets up immediately and says goodbye to Dylan and Keya. She doesn't need me to ask twice. My heart swells with appreciation. Minji and I jog away from the gym, and I prepare for my second run of the night. My legs are heavy, but I know I have to persevere. I need to talk to Minji. Before I get any further, though, Minji stops running.

"How many calories do you need to burn? Any chance we can take a break?"

I'm relieved she says this because I don't feel like running at all. "Definitely." We head into the woods and find a quiet spot. I look around and make sure nobody else is near. It's safe. I take a deep breath and explain the situation. Minji listens carefully. I tell her about Naomi and the note, but I leave out the parts about Theo and Hanna. I don't tell her about the tree, or the connection Naomi might have to Hanna.

The first thing Minji says after I explain is, "Don't do it. Tearza *just* went through this, and nothing good came from it. Remember?"

"I know, but Tearza's Companion was a man." I'm not sure why I'm saying this. "Tearza's Companion was aggressive and tough on her from the beginning. Naomi's different... I don't know. She's been easier on me. Compared to the Cowboy, it feels like she's being nice."

Minji scoffs. "*Nice?*"

"That's not what I mean."

"She's a Patron. She's here to use you and abuse you just like everybody else."

"I know," and I know it's true. Minji is right. But the more Minji tells me not to go, the more I try to find excuses for why I should.

Talking to Minji makes me realize I've already made up my mind. I need to know what Naomi wants from me. I need to know what she's doing with Hanna. If Hanna's in danger, I can't leave her behind. And what did Naomi mean when she wrote she's *on my side*? I don't believe that for a second, but I want answers. Plus, she mentioned the tree. What if Theo and I are in trouble? I have to stop whatever's happening before it gets any worse.

"You're thinking about going," Minji says, reading my expression. "Aren't you?"

I don't answer her. I'm scared to admit it.

Minji sighs. "Listen, I really don't think you should go. Only bad things can come from this." She stares me down for several seconds before she looks up. "But *if* you choose to, you need to be careful. You need to have a backup. I'll come with you."

"No way. I'm not going to involve you in this."

"You already *have,* and I'm happy you did. I don't want you getting hurt on your own."

"I'll tell you when I'm going," I say, compromising, "but you're not coming. I won't jeopardize your safety like that."

"You'll tell me when you're going *and* where you're going. I won't come to check on you unless you're gone for a long time. I promise."

I think about this and after a moment I accept her terms. I don't plan on talking to Naomi for long. All I need is a quick explanation. "Okay."

"Okay," she answers.

We head back to the gym together, completely lost in our thoughts. Neither of us has ever been this quiet around each other. I know I've worried Minji now too, and I hate that I have. This better be worth it.

For the rest of the night, I try to preoccupy myself with working out. When I meet Theo at our tree, he senses something is wrong. I tell him I'm not feeling well. I've already told Minji about the meetup, and I know telling Theo will only make it worse. He'll insist on coming with me. I don't want to put anyone else in danger.

I feel terrible keeping this from Theo, especially because I know he's still on a high from our last night together. I kiss him before leaving and I almost crack. I wish I could forget about Naomi and stay here beside him all night. But I know if I stay, Theo will me feel too comfortable. And then I'll accidentally tell him what's happened and possibly threaten his safety. I can't risk that happening, so I tell him that I have to go. Theo's sad to see me leave and seems a bit confused, but he doesn't ask too many questions. He can sense my urgency. I spend the rest of the night waiting around in the Cottage, looking at the clock, looking out the window, anxiously holding on until sunrise.

Finally, when the sun comes up and everyone's gone to bed, I sneak away. I tell Minji where I'll be, but I make sure she promises not to follow.

I've usually switched bodies with Naomi by now, but today I'm still in mine. There aren't rules about staying awake throughout the day, but most people avoid it. There's no point in wasting time awake when you are in a stranger's "Shell." Even though what I'm doing is technically not illegal, it feels dangerous. I can't help but think about Tearza. Is this how she felt when she went to meet her Companion? I think about turning around and forgetting this whole thing, but I can't. I'm too close. I need to know what Naomi wants from me.

When I make it to the tree—a spot I once thought was secret—I see Naomi standing below it. I stand across from her but keep a distance to stay safe. Naomi is beautiful in her body, and it makes me hate her even more. It's weird to see someone else in the body I've slept in for the last few months. I wonder how she feels seeing me. It's empowering in a way, owning my body and showing her that it belongs to me.

Naomi and I exchange hellos. She asks me how I'm doing, and I try to be quick. I don't have time for pleasantries. Minji is waiting for me to come back and if I take too long, I'll risk her safety.

"Don't be afraid," she says, irritatingly relaxed. "You've done nothing wrong. I know this must be strange for you, but I'm so glad to finally meet you. I've been waiting for this moment for so long."

I force my lips into a smile even though I'm completely creeped out. I look around the area. There's no sign of Cordelia or anyone else, so that's something, at least. I kind of wish I had told Theo about this now. What if Naomi hurts me?

"You're probably very confused," she says, answering my thoughts. "I wasn't supposed to meet you for a while, but I'm afraid everything has changed quite rapidly. Let me explain. You're friends with Hanna, right?"

I don't know how to respond. I'm still not sure how Naomi knows Hanna, but I'm afraid to ask. Hanna's been in questioning for the last few days, and I don't want to make things worse for her. Eventually, I decide the safest thing to do is shake my head. "Not really."

"You don't have to lie," she says. "I'm on your side."

Again, with that comment. I wonder why she asked me the question if she already knew the answer. "What can I do for you?" I ask as kindly as I can.

"I'm planning to go on a series of trips, and I'd like you to join me."

"Trips?" I have no idea what she's talking about. Does this mean I would leave the Cube?

Naomi explains. "I need some time away. Hanna's in trouble—I don't know if you know that. She's been working for me for a while. I mean, she's been cleaning my cabin at the Cube, but I've known her for much longer."

Naomi and Hanna know each other? In what capacity? I try to read Naomi's facial expression. It's just as vague as her words.

"I want to help Hanna and I want to help you," Naomi continues, "but I can't explain much more." She meets my gaze and holds it. "I'm going to take my first trip this weekend. I'll be going to a beautiful, quiet island where I can clear my head. I have a beach house there, and I want you to come with me. It's just for the weekend. If you don't like it, you'll never have to come on another trip with me again. I've already talked to Cordelia and she says it's fine for you to go as long as we bring an Official. Theo said yes."

My stomach drops. Theo said *yes?* When?

"Of course, you're allowed to say no if you want. I would never want to force anyone to do anything."

Except for stealing my body, I think. I don't remember her asking for my permission then.

"But I want you to know the circumstances. I'm going to be bringing Hanna with me. She's still in isolation at this Resort and they haven't sent her away because of me. I'm adamant that she continues to work for me. I won't have anyone else clean my place. The Cube has been reviewing whether this is something they can offer, because, of course, Hanna's seen as a prisoner. But I think if they know she will be in the hands of a high-ranking Group member like me, they'll let her come. She can, for all intents and purposes, become my prisoner." Naomi pauses for a moment, and I take this in. I'm shocked that the Cube would allow something like this. Naomi must be extremely important.

"I know it sounds awful, but this is what I'm telling the Cube. Hanna knows that." Naomi looks sincere, but I don't know if I believe her. I wish I could talk to Hanna or Theo. Why did Theo accept this job? When did this happen?

"If you come with me on this trip I can explain more. Theo and Hanna have already said yes, so the rest depends on you. What do you think?"

I try to weigh my options, but it doesn't feel like I can say no. Saying no could potentially jeopardize Hanna's safety. I'm sure that's why Theo agreed to it, too. I wonder why he didn't say anything to me. Maybe Naomi told him not to. But what does Naomi want from us? I think back to Naomi's profile. She seems as confident and radiant in real life as she did in her photos. Maybe I can trust her. And if I can't, at least Theo and Hanna will be there with me. We'll figure something out together. Maybe we can find a way to escape. I make up my mind. If I don't take a risk, I'll never get out of here.

I tell Naomi I'm in and she hugs me. "You won't regret it!" Then she whispers in my ear, "Sorry about this whole Companion thing. I hope I've been good to you. Relatively, anyway."

I look at her, confused. I don't know what to say. She's apologizing? Does she mean it, or does she just want to make me feel better? Before I can say anything else, she releases me from the hug and sighs. "All right, well you're probably exhausted. I'll have the Officials get the rest of the information to you, okay? And then we'll be off this weekend!"

"Okay." I'm still in shock as she walks away. I have no idea what I've just signed up for.

The following night, I wake up and go to the tree immediately. I know Theo will be there. When I arrive, Theo's standing up and looking at me. I expect to get my answers from him but he's just as confused as I am.

The second I reach him Theo wraps his arms around me. We only stay there for a moment because both of our minds are racing. I can feel his heart beating against my cheek.

"Why did you say yes?" We pull away. I know he's talking about Naomi.

"Because you did. I figured you knew what was happening."

Theo shakes his head. "I only said yes after you. When she came to me, she said you had already agreed to go."

"What?" I'm shocked by this, but maybe I shouldn't be. There was no reason to trust Naomi. Theo looks just as dejected as I do. He shakes his head.

"Why didn't you tell me you were planning to meet her?" Theo asks.

"I could ask you the same thing."

Theo looks at me knowingly. We were both trying to protect each other.

"So, what do we do now? We don't have to go."

"The Officials already signed off on it. We have to." Theo pauses, "Plus, she saved Hanna. If the weekend goes well, Naomi is convinced that they'll let Hanna stay with her. Work for her."

"Really?"

Theo nods.

I have no idea what to make of any of this. Is Naomi on our side or not? Is she working with Hanna? Maybe we shouldn't be trusting Hanna after all. Theo and I talk it through, trying to understand everything as best as we can. We come to the conclusion that going on the trip might bring some advantages.

"I think we go," Theo says, "and we assess the situation. We see what Naomi's up to..."

"And then maybe," I say tentatively, afraid to say it aloud, "maybe we can escape."

"Escape? You mean both of us?"

"Well, yeah." My heart beats faster as I keep talking, "I mean I was thinking this trip could be a good opportunity. We'll be away from the Cube. You'll be the only Official guarding me..."

"But you'll still have your Chip. And even without the Chip, there are Replicas. You'll still be tethered to the government. They can find you. They can find both of us."

"But maybe we can turn off our Chips like we do when we eat? That way they won't be able to track us from the Cube at least. And I think there's a way we can turn off Replicas too... Ethan and Loukas used to say that was possible."

"Well, I'm not Ethan or Loukas."

"I'm not saying you are," I say, but I don't like the comment.

"You never talked to me about any of this."

"It was just an idea."

"You know this year is important for me."

I can't believe he says this. "Why? So, you can spend your life working for the government? Is that really still what you want?"

"I don't know."

"Wow."

"What?"

"Nothing. I should have seen this coming."

"What's that supposed to mean?"

"Of course you don't want to escape. You've got your whole life ahead of you here. You'll finish your time at the Cube and then you can go anywhere you want. Your dad will help you get your dream job, you'll become a high-ranking Official, and then what? You'll exploit prisoners like me. Sounds awesome."

"I don't think that's fair."

"It's true, Theo."

"I'm trying to do better. I've been helping you, haven't I? And Hanna."

"Yes, but if you actually want to be a good person, you have to leave this world eventually. You're still a Government Official. You're a part of the problem."

"So, what do you expect me to do? Give up everything? Escape with you and most likely get caught? Then what? I would become a prisoner and we'd achieve nothing. There'll just be one more prisoner in the world."

"Yeah, maybe, or maybe we don't get caught. Maybe we escape and join with others to destroy the Group system. The prison system. I don't know!" I'm getting carried away. "But anything we do is better than nothing."

"It's easy for you to say. I want to help, Lana, I do. But maybe I'm better off helping from the inside. At least I'll have some power. Maybe I can go into government policy and change things..."

"When was the last time anyone changed anything from the inside? President Ace does what he wants and listens to nobody."

"I disagree. I think there's a way to accomplish things. It just takes time."

I roll my eyes. "I hate when people say that. Do you realize how long we've been waiting? You have no idea what it's like to be me. You don't know what it's like in Group7. If we keep 'waiting' for things to change slowly and orderly, we'll waste away generations of people's happiness and freedom. And that's *if* things ever change."

"Well, I think they will."

"How? When the people in power have everything they want and more, what's their incentive to make changes?"

Theo is quiet. He doesn't have an answer.

I continue, "Theo, in Group7, my life expectancy is less than half of yours. Most of us end up in prisons. The ones who don't have zero opportunities. We're hungry and exhausted *every day*, and there's little room for hope. Do you have any idea what it's like to spend all your life wishing you were born somewhere else?

"When I was little, I used to resent my mom because she took us away from Group1. I used to imagine a world where I had all the money in the world and everything I could possibly want. But as I got older I realized it's not the money I crave. It's the freedom. And there's no real freedom for *any* of us in these Groups. We shouldn't be stuck in the Group we're born into. We should be able to choose our jobs based on our passions and abilities, not where we come from."

"I agree, of course, but it's not that simple. This system has been in place for years."

"And it'll continue to be until we stop it. It might not be simple, but we have to do *something*. Theo, the government targeted my mom because she was protesting Groups and prisons. That was the reason for her premature Countdown. And when she got sick and had to deal with the excessive pain without *any* help from the government, I always wondered if she regretted the protests. She would still be alive right now if she decided to play it safe. She could be living in Group1 with my dad, and decades from now, when my mom finally died, she could have spent all one hundred days at a place like the Cube. But when my mom went to the Ace building to meet with President Ace, I'd never seen her look prouder. I knew in that moment that she didn't regret anything. She spent her life doing something meaningful. She risked her life protesting, but it was worth it. And for me, that's always going to be the way I choose to live."

Theo doesn't speak for a while. He seems to be thinking about this. Finally, and slowly, he speaks. "I want you to know that I care. I really do. But this is a lot for me to absorb. You have to understand that for my whole life, I've... well I've seen things differently. I don't know if I can be who you want me to be."

"So, what does that mean? You won't help me escape?"

"I think there's another way."

"What way? I'm stuck in here for like the next twenty-five years, Theo..."

"I just have to think about everything. Don't you get that?"

"Yeah," I say, coldly. "I think I do." And then, before Theo can say anything else, I walk away. I can't be in this conversation any longer. I hear him call my name in the distance, but I don't respond. This is what happens when you let yourself have feelings for an Official, I tell myself. I'm so stupid. I should have seen this coming.

When I get back to the Cottage, I don't talk to anyone. I wait for Naomi to call for the Switch. I lie in my bed with the covers draped over me. Minji comes over, but I pretend to be asleep. I don't have the energy to explain things right now. My stomach twists in knots and I feel sick. I don't know how I'm going to go on this trip.

CHAPTER 28

The next night, I do my best to avoid Theo. I'm too angry to speak with him right now. I know that I'm not going to be able to avoid him once we leave for the trip, but until then, there's nothing left to say. He doesn't want to help me. He doesn't understand how important this is for me.

But as hard as I try to stay away, Theo seems to be following me. Everywhere I go, Theo doesn't seem far behind. He joins me in every room, trying to make eye contact. He follows me into the gym, the cafeteria, everywhere. He clearly wants to talk.

I'm sitting with Dylan in the cafeteria now, watching him sip on an orange juice. I'd love to have some myself, but I decide to stick with water. When I look away from Dylan's drink, Theo meets my eyes. I decide to hold his gaze, giving him the signal to meet me at the tree. There's no point in continuing cat and mouse. Theo clearly won't leave me alone and he's an Official from Group1. He doesn't know how to not get his way.

I excuse myself from the table and walk out of the cafeteria. I head straight to our tree, but without the feeling of excitement I usually have. I know Theo won't be far behind.

When Theo joins me at the tree, I don't wait for him to start.

"I don't really have anything to say, other than please stop following me."

"I don't want you to be mad, Lana."

This makes me laugh. "How do you want me to feel? I'm a prisoner from Group7—don't you get that? I have no hope unless I somehow manage to escape. And you don't want to help me."

"I didn't say that. I just said it was a lot to think about."

"It seemed like you were saying no."

"Well, maybe I was, and I'm sorry for that. I'm not perfect. I'm still figuring things out."

I look at Theo, wondering what he's implying. I wait for him to say more.

"I thought about what you said. About your mom's decision to leave Group1 and live a life worth living. And I thought about you... how you must be feeling. How scary and hopeless this all must be for you." I nod. "I don't want to be like my dad, Lana. I want to be better. But I'm scared."

I don't know what to say to this. I'm still mad. "Where was all of this yesterday?"

"I just had to think—"

"I know, I get it. But that's the problem, isn't it? We're too different, the two of us. I can't imagine *not* being angry at the government. I can't imagine *not* wanting to help free someone I love. These thoughts have been with me my whole life. And you... your instincts are so controlled and measured. You have no anger. You have no reason to be angry."

"*Of course* I'm angry. I'm angry every day. I'm angry you're in here. I'm angry I can't have a normal life with you. I... I want that. I want you to be my actual girlfriend. I want you to meet my mom. I don't want to hide with you. And, mostly, I want you to be happy."

My heart leaps. I want to tell Theo that I want these things too. Of course, I do. But before I can dream about all of that, I need to be free. "I can't be happy here. Not fully."

"I know. And I wish my instincts were more like yours. Maybe I'm selfish."

"You're not selfish," I tell him, and as I say this, I can feel myself forgiving him. "You've saved me more than once already. And you saved Hanna. You're just scared to take this next step." I speak honestly, "And I get that."

Theo's quiet for a moment. He knows I'm right. "Were you scared when you Hacked your mom before she died?"

"Yeah, of course. I was scared the whole time. But the thought of her dying scared me more."

"You're really brave." He says, "I mean, I know this might sound corny or whatever, but I'm really trying to be more like you."

I know he's telling the truth. I reach for Theo's hand. "Thank you. For thinking about all of this. I know I'm asking a lot."

"You're not. You're asking me to be a decent person," he says, and my heart lifts, relieved. "We just have to do it strategically. If we're going to escape, we have to be very careful."

"Of course," I say, and I squeeze Theo's hand, wanting him to know how much this means to me.

"There has to be a chance we can actually avoid prison and *do* something with our freedom. Or else there's no point."

"Yes, but I think with your knowledge and influence, we have a shot at this. I think it can happen."

"I'll start thinking about our options. But for now, I don't think we should do anything on this trip. It's too soon. Naomi mentioned other trips she wanted to go on. We should make sure everything runs smoothly on this one and then, once she trusts us, we can start thinking about making an escape on a future trip. I promise."

I trust Theo's word. "Okay, but I don't want to wait too long."

Theo agrees.

We talk more about this. Theo and I both realize that our best chance at escaping is on a trip with Naomi. When we leave the Cube with her there will be so many more opportunities. There won't be any guards around us. Theo will technically be the guard. There is the problem of this trip being on an island, but we're not going to try this time anyway. Theo and I decide to request a different location next time. We'll try to get her to take us somewhere less remote.

Theo grows more animated, dreaming about our possibilities. I tell him about 7N and all the things I could show him if we get out of here. He talks about his mom and sister and how happy they would be to meet me. Of course, if Theo and I actually escaped, there would be people looking for us. We would probably have to hide. But I let myself believe this could all happen.

"Maybe we'll leave the prisoner part out when your mom asks about me."

"I don't think she'd care, especially when she finds out you're her favorite ballerina."

Eventually, after hours of talking, the sun begins to rise. Theo and I have been so enraptured by the idea of leaving the Cube together, we completely lost track of the time. He walks me back to the Cottage and we discreetly say goodnight.

I lie awake in bed, going over everything again and again. I think about Mama and wonder what she'd think of my speech to Theo. I wonder what she'd think about my plan to take down the government. I hope that she'd be proud. I picture my life with Theo, outside of the Cube. I worry for a moment, wondering what Ethan would think if they met. I try not to think about that, though. So many things need to fall into place for that to happen.

I focus on Theo instead. He is who I have right now, and he is more than enough. I close my eyes and picture him: Theo's warm brown eyes looking down at me and his big arms wrapped around my body. Nothing feels more exhilarating than spending time with Theo. Tonight felt like a breakthrough. I know we come from two different worlds, but Theo's beginning to understand mine more. I think about what he said tonight about me inspiring him, and all the ways he's changed. I'm proud to be with Theo. I might even love him. And if I didn't know better, I would say Theo loves me too. I hope he does.

I speak with Naomi one more time before the trip. She tells me to meet her at 5:00 p.m. on Friday by the entrance of the Cube. Theo will escort me out of Oparius to make sure it's safe for me to leave. We will spend the weekend on an island, as Naomi mentioned before, but that's all the information she gave.

She says, "It's going to be *fun*. Don't worry."

But it's hard not to worry. Theo and I can't figure out what Naomi could possibly have to gain by taking us on a trip with her. We're happy to enjoy a weekend away from the Cube, but that doesn't mean we're not skeptical. The whole thing feels bizarre.

When the time finally comes, I wait in the Cottage living room for Theo to pick me up. I've packed a weekend bag with different pieces of clothing from the wardrobe. I usually wear a basic t-shirt and pants every day at the Cube, but something tells me I should make an effort for Naomi. I need this trip to go well so she brings Theo and me on her next one.

Minji comes over to the couch and sits beside me. "I can't believe you get to go on a vacation. You're so lucky."

"It's not *exactly* a vacation. I'm going as Naomi's prisoner."

"Yeah, yeah," Minji says. "I saw the dresses and bikinis you put in that bag," she gestures to my luggage. "Call it what you want, but you and Theo are honeymooning."

Minji winks, and I don't know what to make of it. I try to look disgusted, as if the idea of me and Theo grosses me out, but Minji laughs. She looks up and says, "Speak of the devil."

Theo's here to pick me up.

"Sagona," Theo says. "You ready to go?"

"Mmhmm," I say. I'm excited to see him but I try to seem nonchalant. I turn to Minji and say goodbye.

"I'll miss you," I hug her.

"No, you won't!" Minji says. "But I'll be thinking of you the whole time. Eat some good food for me, will you?"

I laugh. "I'll be back on Monday. You won't even know I'm gone."

"It's okay. I'll have the Cowboy to keep me entertained."

"Never a dull moment with that guy."

I hug Minji one more time and then Theo and Minji exchange an awkward goodbye.

Theo and I walk away from the Cottage and down a path that takes us out of Oparius. As we're about to leave, Theo tells me to stay by his side at all times. If an Official sees me outside of Oparius without a chaperone, I can get into a lot of trouble. I already know this, but it's nice to see Theo so concerned.

We keep walking, side by side, like any other Government Official and Newbody who barely know each other. Finally, I see the Cube's front gates from a distance. Naomi is already waiting there. She's wearing a yellow sun dress. It reminds me of one of my dresses from home. Mama's favorite dress. The one I wore when we met with President Ace.

I think about telling Naomi I have a similar dress, but think better of it. I'm not here to make friends. When we reach Naomi, she welcomes us. Her face lights up with excitement. "I'm *so* glad you're here. This is going to be a very special weekend."

"Thank you for inviting us," Theo says, courteously. I echo his sentiment, trying my best to sound sincere.

Naomi claps her hands together. "All right you two, follow me. We have a big weekend ahead of us. Hanna's waiting with my bags in the limo."

Naomi starts walking and Theo and I trail behind her. When Naomi gets a bit ahead, I whisper to Theo, "What's a limo?"

"A limousine," Theo says. "It's like a stretched-out car."

I think I remember learning about them. Loukas once read about limos in a book. He said they're just another way that the government likes to show off their money.

When we get to the limo, I'm amazed at how big it feels inside. It feels like a room in a house. The floors are hardwood, and the seats are spacious. There's plenty of room for the four of us. There's a table with drinks in the center. I try to imagine what I'd think of this car if I hadn't spent so much time at the Cube. It's definitely extravagant, but I've become accustomed to the government's overindulgence. For someone like Naomi, this limousine must merely be seen as a means of transportation. I get the sense that Naomi's spent her whole life surrounded by nothing but the very best. Even for a Group1 member, she seems important. I don't know what she does in her regular life, but she must be closely linked to the government. That's the only way I can explain the Cube's behavior. They seem to be scared of Naomi. She makes Cordelia seem like chopped liver.

Hanna is staring at me. I realize I haven't said hi to her yet, so I wave. "This is crazy."

"I know." She looks younger now that she's out of her maid's outfit. She's wearing a light blue T-shirt dress and rainbow socks. Her hair is loose, aside from some layers she's tucked away. I notice the same clip on the side of her head she wore on the day I first met her. This time I realize the clip is not just a random shape. It's an X.

The limousine starts moving and we leave the Cube. Naomi offers us all a drink: orange juice mixed with vodka. I find it weird that she's asking me because I'm too young to drink alcohol. I wonder if it's a test. I accept a glass of orange juice, but nothing else. Theo and Hanna do the same. Naomi is the only one to add vodka, and she looks at all of us and says, "Relax a little. It's a vacation."

The four of us bring our glasses together after Naomi demands a toast.

"Here's to a memorable weekend together," Theo finally answers. Naomi likes this one.

"Cheers!" She says.

We don't drive for long. Almost immediately after we finish our drinks, the limousine stops. I look out the window and take in our surroundings. We're on a slab of cement. It looks like an empty parking lot.

We exit the car and take our bags. it's not until I'm outside that I notice the vehicle waiting for us. At least I think it's a vehicle. I'm not really sure what it is.

"What is that?" I ask, quietly. I hope only Theo can hear me, but that's not the case.

"That, darling," Naomi answers, "is a helicopter. I hope you're not afraid of heights."

I'm not sure what that means, but I follow everyone to the helicopter. When we get inside, Naomi hands me a headset with a microphone attached. I follow everyone else's lead and place it over my ears. We get into our seats and Theo sits beside me.

"You're going to wish you had a drink right about now," Theo says.

"Why?"

But before he answers, the helicopter starts making a loud noise. Even with the headset on, I hear the abrasive sound of the motor. The propellers above us must be spinning. I can make out the movement from the shadows on the ground. A moment later, we start to move. The helicopter slowly lifts from the ground.

"Oh my god," I scream. Theo laughs. "Oh my god!"

We start to lift higher, and it doesn't take long for us to be a good distance from the ground. We're about one hundred feet off the ground and we keep moving higher. I look out the window as the helicopter climbs into the sky. We're flying. I can't believe we're flying. I've never done anything like this before. Not even close. I can hear my heavy breathing through the microphone. I squeeze Theo's hand before I think better of it.

"Are you okay?" Theo asks. His voice sounds different through the headset.

"This is wild."

Again Theo laughs.

Naomi joins in the conversation. "What do you think, Lana?" She asks, using Theo's nickname for me. I try not to cringe. "A bit excessive, maybe, but not too bad."

I hate the way she says this. It's so condescending.

"It's awesome," I tell her, hating myself for actually meaning it. I can't help but be amazed. We're *flying*. "Thanks for taking us."

"Of course."

Naomi tells us that the flight will be over in an hour. It's hard to imagine we'll be up in the sky for that long. What if the engine stops working? Would we just drop to the ground? I try not to overthink it. These things must be very safe if people like Naomi use them.

I spend most of the flight looking out the window. The view is breathtaking. We fly over the ocean, which looks enormous and bright from a distance. I watch the water ripple like a beautiful blue parachute. It's incredible. Something about being up in the sky makes me think of Mama. When I was little, Mama used to tell me that no matter what

227

happened to her, she'd always be around. During her Countdown, she'd echo this. I think Mama truly believed in heaven, and maybe a part of me does too. It's a nice thing to believe in. I hope Mama is still around, watching over me. And when I'm up in the sky, I feel closer to her. The thought makes me tear up. I imagine Mama next to me, somewhere in these clouds, shaking her head at me. *You're the only prisoner who's ever taken a helicopter ride!* I can hear her say. The thought makes me smile. Theo looks over at me. As if he knows what I'm thinking, he squeezes my hand.

After a while, I start to make out an island in the distance. It's shaped like a banana. I wonder if this is where we're landing. We begin to fly over parts of the island and slowly begin to descend. The closer we get to the ground, the safer I feel. We land on the beach in a large, empty area. I let out a sigh of relief when we touch the sand. As much as I liked the experience, I'm pleased to be back on safe, steady ground.

Naomi is the first to exit the helicopter and the rest of us follow. We take our bags and make our way toward the large beach house ahead of us.

"That's where we'll be staying," Naomi says, as she drags her bag through the sand. I'm surprised she's lugging it herself. "This is what happens when you ask the Cube to organize a holiday for you. I know it's quite extravagant. Believe me, this is *not* my taste."

The beach house is massive. It's bigger than any house I've ever seen.

I'm not sure why Naomi is telling us this. Is she apologizing for the Cube's willingness to spend money? Does she think I believe her act? She's a Patron from Group1 who received a limousine, helicopter, and beach house from the Cube. I don't know what her "taste" is, but I imagine it's nothing like mine.

The house is extravagant. It seems the entire exterior is covered in windows. It's only three stories high but feels even bigger. From my viewpoint, I can see terraces on each of the upper levels, wrapping around the house. There's a rooftop patio as well. The house is surrounded by palm trees, which makes it feel private and hidden, despite its size.

Naomi takes us inside and I'm overwhelmed by how oversized everything is. We enter a massive foyer. The ceiling is unbelievably tall and a palm tree grows in each corner of the room. Two matching chandeliers hang from the ceiling and a winding staircase leads to the second floor. Naomi gives us a tour of the rest of the place. Upstairs, there are five bedrooms, more than enough for each of us to have our own space. Theo takes the room beside mine. I've never slept this close to him before.

"Please make yourself at home," Naomi says. "You're welcome to use any room, any appliance, anything you'd like. The kitchen is stocked with food as well. Help yourself."

There's an indoor swimming pool, a games room, a movie theatre, and a bowling alley. It's hard to believe this place could be someone's home. While the Cohens are crammed into an apartment smaller than this place's master bedroom, people in Group 1 live in houses like this.

Naomi must notice the look on my face because she says, "I know it's a lot to take in. I'd much prefer a shack on the beach, personally. But let's make the most of it, shall we?"

I try not to roll my eyes. "It's very nice," I tell her. "Thank you for inviting us."

"Of course. Thank *you* for accepting."

Theo saves me from the conversation. He pats me gently on the back and whispers quietly in my ear, "Want to take a stroll on the beach?"

I smile, relieved to have Theo here. "I'd love to."

CHAPTER 29

The next morning, I find Naomi in the kitchen. She's drinking coffee at the table while looking over a pile of notes. When she notices me, she quickly turns over the notes and looks up.

"Good morning, Lana. How was your sleep?"

"It was fine," I say awkwardly, wondering what I should be doing with myself. "Can I help with anything? How can I be of assistance?"

Naomi laughs as if what I've just said is hilarious. "You're on vacation! Enjoy yourself. There's nothing to be done."

This confuses me. Didn't we come here to protect Hanna? Shouldn't I be doing something to help?

"You seem to be reading something," I gesture to her notes. "Can I help with that?"

Naomi shakes her head. "Sorry, love. Top secret business." Naomi winks playfully. "Why don't you find Theo? I promise we'll have more of a chat later. I'll explain things then."

I don't like the thought of this. I want answers now. But there doesn't seem to be another option. I grab a muffin from the pantry and go find Theo.

As soon as I spot him, I tell Theo what happened with Naomi. He reassures me that we'll get our answers soon. "We shouldn't push Naomi, though. We need her to trust us."

I agree with Theo and try to let it go.

Theo suggests we go snorkeling. I've never heard of the activity before, but Theo finds the equipment in one of the closets and convinces me to go. We get ready on the beach, and I feel giddy as Theo puts on his swimsuit and flippers. He looks ridiculous, and I'm sure I look the same. I've got goggles pressing against my forehead and I waddle like a penguin with these flippers on.

We head into the ocean and Theo takes a picture of me with the waterproof camera he found. I smile wide and kick up one of my legs.

"I have a feeling I don't want to see that picture."

Theo laughs. "You look great."

We swim out into the water and Theo explains how to use the snorkel to breathe. I follow Theo's lead, looking out at the clear, vast ocean. It's been a long time since I've swam in natural water. I'm scared to take my first breath. It's hard to believe this snorkel will work underwater, but when I inhale, I breathe clearly without any water entering my lungs. It's incredible. A few fish swim by, each a different color, and then all at once, hundreds of fish surround us. It's nothing like I've ever seen. It's breathtaking. There's a pack of fish with green and blue stripes and then, behind them, smaller orange fish. The fish swim together in a line. Theo looks over at me and I wonder if he can sense my excitement underwater. He grabs my hand, and I squeeze it. I'm so happy I get to share this moment with him. It's something I never would have dreamed of doing growing up. Most of the fish are dead in 7N's water. The thought makes me sad, realizing that even this natural phenomenon is regulated by the government. I'm able to swim safely here because it's Group1 water. It's only accessible by plane or helicopter, so very few people get to experience this. *I* shouldn't be experiencing this. I doubt many other prisoners have spent time on this beautiful island. It's hard not to question my purpose here. Why did Naomi invite me and Theo? What does she want from us?

I tell myself to revisit this thought later. Theo swims further along and I follow him. We reach an area with various string-like colorful structures. Fish surround each structure everywhere, entering and exiting the grooves in them. It looks like an underwater garden. I remember reading about these before. It's a coral reef—an underwater ecosystem.

I look over at Theo and he's looking back at me. He lifts his head above the water and I follow him. We lift off our goggles and snorkels.

"What do you think?" he says.

"It's incredible. Everything is so colorful."

Theo swims closer to me.

"You keep looking over at me. Every time I look at you, you're looking at me," I say.

"I can't help it."

"But the fish—"

"Fish are fish. You're far more interesting." Theo swims a little closer and pulls me into his arms. We are far away from the beach house now and no one is around. I've never felt so connected to Theo—it's like we're the only two people in the world. He rubs his hands along my back and kisses me. His lips taste like salt water. When we pull away, I take in his dark, wet curls in the water. He's always attractive, but the sun-kissed, beachy look suits him.

"You are so good-looking."

Theo laughs. "Have you seen yourself?"

"Yeah. The Cowboy and Naomi seem to think I'm quite the catch."

Theo frowns. "I'm happy you're getting some time away from that."

"Me too, but I haven't been able to stop thinking about all this. What does Naomi *want?*"

"I don't know. I'm trying to figure it out too. Something about her seems... off. It's almost like she's critical of the government. I've never heard a Patron talk like her."

"Do you think it's an act?

Theo shrugs. "I can't decide. If it's an act, where does that leave Hanna? Why did Naomi save her? Why do they seem so close?"

"That's the most confusing part. Do we trust Naomi because of Hanna? Or do we stop trusting Hanna because of Naomi?"

Theo thinks about this. "I'm hoping we'll find out more tonight. She brought us here for a reason. She must have something to tell us."

"Yeah, but we shouldn't just give her information, you know? At least not yet."

"Of course."

"Should we make a plan?"

"It'll be hard to without any context." That's true. "How about I follow your lead?" He says.

"I don't know if that's a good idea."

"Why not?" Theo holds my hands underwater. "I trust you."

In the evening, Naomi gathers us all for dinner. The table is set on the rooftop patio, featuring a stunning view of the sea. The sound of the waves and the smell of gourmet food overwhelms me. Once again, I'm struck with a longing for home. Everything about this dinner looks lovely, but it's almost *too* lovely. It's a Group1 dinner, and I don't fit in here. I don't think I ever could.

Naomi has made sirloin steak, roasted potatoes, and barbequed vegetables. Hanna made an apple pie for dessert, but, surprisingly, Naomi cooked the rest. She seems to be very proud of this accomplishment. *I sent the chefs home early,* she told us earlier in the day, pleased with herself. *I'm going to cook tonight!*

We sit around the table and fill our plates with food. There are wine glasses in front of everyone but Hanna, and three bottles of wine. Does she expect me to drink a whole bottle to myself?

When I asked Theo about the drinking last night, he told me not to worry. "When you're at home with your family, drinking wine underage isn't illegal. The government views it as safe."

"That's not true. At least not in Group7."

"The rules are different in high-ranking Groups." This shouldn't have been surprising, but it still made me mad. Ethan's brother, Raffi, went to prison for getting caught with a drink. All he was drinking was a can of beer.

We also talked a little more about how to handle Naomi, and we decided the best thing to do moving forward is accept a glass of wine. If it appears like we're all drinking, Naomi will be more comfortable. We might not want to be open with her, but we want her to be open with us. Plus, we want her to enjoy our company enough to ask us on another trip. That's the only way we'll be able to escape.

I hand my empty glass over to Naomi and she pours me a hefty amount of wine. She does the same for Theo and herself. Hanna pours herself some iced tea.

Hanna gives a toast this time. "To the four of us. May we become great friends and even greater troublemakers."

Theo and I look at each other. We don't know what to make of the toast, but we clink our glasses together and smile expectedly.

Naomi is the first to dig into her food. She's excited for everyone to try what she's made. "I'm not a great cook, but I love to barbecue. Let me know what you think of the potatoes. I tried a new recipe."

I taste a little bit of everything and tell Naomi it's delicious. She's delighted.

"So," Naomi continues, "I'm so *overjoyed* to have you both here. I saw you two swimming in the ocean earlier and it warmed my heart."

"It was lovely," I say, "and such a nice treat for me. Is this your regular vacation spot?"

"Not really. I like to go all over the place."

"Which is your favorite? Anywhere closer to the Cube?"

Naomi thinks. "There's a spot I like to go below the mountains. It's a beautiful valley, not too far from Ace City. I've always liked it there. It's so quiet and serene."

"That sounds wonderful."

"Well, I hope I can take you some time. Maybe for our next trip."

I'm satisfied and let my face show it.

Naomi continues, "Did you know this was my first time at a Resort like the Cube? I'd never, you know, used someone's Shell before. You were my first."

Naomi laughs a little at this. She takes a large sip of her wine. I try not to look disgusted.

"Anyway, I feel awful about it and I just want you to know that. But you *have* to trust that this is all justifiable. There's a reason behind all of this."

I look at Theo, wondering if I should pry. He doesn't seem to stop me. "A reason?" I ask.

"Oh, you know, we all have our reasons." Naomi takes another sip of her wine. "Let's call it research for now."

I don't know what to make of this. I wonder if Naomi is a reporter. Maybe she's one of those investigative journalists. Maybe she's writing a novel about the injustices of Group1. It would be quite ironic, coming from the woman currently drinking expensive wine and staying in a beachside mansion. But perhaps it might be better than the other books I've seen about the government. I certainly hope it would be less laughable than *The Merits of Grouping*. I push the thought aside and focus back on the current conversation.

Naomi is asking Theo a question. "So, what's Cordelia really like?"

"She's fine," Theo says, nonchalantly. "I don't know her very well."

"I find that hard to believe," Naomi says, testing him. "I hear she and your father are quite close."

Theo seems thrown off by this. He pauses. "I see you've done your research."

"Not much research needed there," Naomi says lightheartedly, but there seems to be some depth beyond her airy tone. "It's not exactly a well-kept secret, is it?"

"My father and I are very different." The sound of his voice makes it sound like some sort of warning. Naomi seems to receive the message. She leaves that topic alone.

"What else do you know about Cordelia? Does she ever take days off?"

"Days off?" It's an odd question to ask. Theo waits for clarification.

"Oh, you know, does she ever leave the Cube in the hands of others? Or is she always there, looking over your shoulder?"

Once again, Naomi tries to pose the question as a joke, but she seems to be digging for something. Theo doesn't budge.

"Well, actually she's just as much of a mystery to me as she is to you. It's hard to know what she's truly thinking, let alone where she spends most of her time."

Naomi frowns at Theo's answer. It's clear she was hoping for more.

"So, you don't have anything critical to say of her? I mean, I know you saved Hanna. You *must* have something to say about that."

Theo looks at me, hoping to get some guidance on what to do. I shake my head slightly as if to say your guess is as good as mine. Is it better for Theo to speak honestly or keep this information to himself? What is Naomi planning on doing with what he says?

"I can't take credit for what happened to Hanna."

"You can't?" Naomi looks annoyed now.

Theo shakes his head.

"So, you're saying you didn't put her in a maid's costume and hide her from Cordelia? You're saying what Hanna told me isn't true?"

Theo looks at Hanna and then back to Naomi. "I *did* do that, but I can't take credit."

"Then who deserves the credit?"

"I can't say."

Naomi sighs. She's frustrated. Instead of continuing her interrogation, she refills her wine glass and takes another long sip. When she's finished, she changes the subject. "And what about your home life, Theo? Do you have any siblings?"

"A brother and a sister."

"Three children." It's clear from her tone that she's evaluating this. Theo doesn't say anything more. He lets her think what she wants.

The number of children in a Group1 or 2 family is a common way to boast status. Having three children is considered to be few, compared to the elite families with five to ten kids. I remember reading about this phenomenon with Loukas and Ethan and thinking it was absurd. Apparently, the more children you have, the richer your family appears to others. Coming from a family of eight, Ethan always found this to be amusing. Ethan's parents adopted six children because they wanted a big family and loved nothing more than being moms. But most Group1 parents barely raise their children. The reason they have large families is to display their prosperity. For each child, an extra houseworker and nanny are hired. The cost of living increases, and they are seen as wealthier by others. At least that's what I've read in books. Not every family chooses to do this. There are also many smaller families in Group1 and 2. But the "big family phenomenon" isn't uncommon.

"Did both of your parents grow up in Group1?" Naomi asks Theo.

Theo shakes his head. "Only my dad," he says, but once again, he doesn't elaborate.

Naomi nods. "That makes sense."

"It does?"

"You don't seem like a Group1 kid. That's all." Theo stiffens in his seat. Naomi laughs a little. "Relax, I'm trying to give you a compliment."

I reach for Theo's hand under the table and squeeze it. I don't want him to let Naomi get to him. Theo squeezes my hand back as if to reassure me that he's okay.

"My parents had seven kids," Naomi says. "We were one of *those* families. So, I know what it's like to be the typical Group1 kid. And let me just say... there were a lot of problems. There's a lot of things I'd like to change." Naomi looks at me when she says this. Does she think the two of us have anything in common?

"What about you?" Naomi directs the questions to me now. "What's your family like?"

"I've got a brother. It was just him, my mom, and me growing up."

"That's nice."

"I guess, but I like big families too. My... best friend from home has one. He's lucky. There's a lot of love in that family."

"That's the key ingredient, isn't it? It doesn't really matter the number as long as there's love."

It's a nice thought. Of course, the number *does* matter when you can barely afford to feed the small number of children you have, but I don't say this to Naomi.

Surprisingly, she corrects herself. "Well, love and money." She says bitterly. "Without a fair shot at living, you don't have the same options, do you?"

Naomi's looking at me again, but I don't know what to say.

Hanna chimes in, "Exactly. It's not the same for Eliana and me."

"You can still have big families in Group7," I say.

"Right, but it's not easy. Some days, you wouldn't have enough food for everyone. That's just a fact."

"While the rich," I start before I realize what I'm saying, "the rich have ten kids and hire a nanny for each one of them. They dangle their children like fancy cars as if their existence is somehow impressive—as if they've somehow earned it. Even though they were born in Group1 and didn't earn anything." When I stop talking, I immediately regret speaking. "Sorry, I shouldn't have said that."

"No, it's okay," Naomi seems elated by my response. "I completely agree."

I doubt that's true, but I nod along anyway.

"So, tell me more about your family," Naomi keeps talking to me. "What's your mother's story? What's your brother like?"

"My mom was a dancer," I start, careful not to say too much. "But she died recently."

"I'm so sorry." She looks sad, which feels strange because she doesn't even know my mom.

"That's all right." But as I say this, I feel myself starting to cry. I don't know what's come over me—I never cry in front of people. I'm so embarrassed. I look down, trying to cover my face, but it's too late. Naomi's noticed.

"Oh, honey, it's okay," Naomi leans over and pats my back. "It's okay."

"Sorry, I don't know why I'm crying."

"Don't apologize." Naomi pauses for a moment, and then she asks. "Was it sudden?"

I nod before I can think about it, but then I shake my head. "It wasn't an accident or anything. It was the Countdown."

"But she must've been so young."

"Yeah." I think about telling her my suspicions about why she was scheduled to die—about how the government was threatened by her—but I keep it to myself. I've already said too much. I try to pull myself together and stop crying.

I take in a deep breath and hear Naomi whisper to Hanna. It sounds like she says, "Poor Loukas."

Loukas?

"What did you just say?" I ask.

"Nothing," Naomi seems startled. "It's just so sad."

"But you said my brother's name. How do you know Loukas?"

"Loukas?" Naomi looks so confused I almost believe her. "I don't."

"But you said his name to Hanna."

"I don't think so," Hanna says. "Are you sure that's what you heard?"

I feel positive now, but I don't push it. I look over to Theo and he gives me a look of warning, reminding me to stay on my best behavior. I shake my head, "Sorry." I wipe the last tears away and give my best performance, "I'm so overwhelmed, I must have been hearing things."

Hanna and Naomi look at me sympathetically.

"Anyone want more wine?" Naomi asks as she pours herself another glass.

The rest of the night fades away with fake laughter and pleasant conversation. Naomi continues to ask personal questions and vaguely critique the government, but no real information is disclosed. Theo and I are on our best behavior. When the dinner party is over, Naomi insists on clearing our plates herself. "Please," she says. "It's the least I can do after living in your body. Go enjoy the night. You're free."

It's hard to argue with Naomi's logic. She *does* owe me. And I don't mind making a Group1 Patron clean up after me. It's quite satisfying. But I try one more time for answers before we leave.

"Naomi..." I think about how to say this. "I was hoping you might explain our roles here a little more. I'm wondering how we can help."

"Don't worry about all that. You're here so we can get to know each other. That's all."

"What about Hanna? How does she fit into all of this?"

"Hanna is a dear friend of mine. And I know you like her too. So, I think we're on the same page, at least I hope. Now, go!" Naomi laughs. "I've freed you!"

I look at Theo for help, but he just shrugs. Naomi doesn't want to give us any answers. She seems to be feeling us out for something, but I'm not sure what. If I keep asking questions, though, she's going to know we don't trust her. So instead, I thank Naomi for the dinner and leave.

Theo and I head down the windy rooftop stairs, but we don't get far before Hanna stops us.

"Can I talk to you both for a minute?"

She sounds more like the Hanna I remember when Naomi isn't around. Maybe it's all in my head.

"Sure," I say. "What's up?"

"I wanted to thank you for everything. I mean, Theo, I know you're denying that you helped me, but that's not true. I know what you did. And I just want to say *thank you.* You keeping me off that train... letting me stay at the Cube. You have no idea what that means. You saved my life."

"It was nothing." Theo looks uncomfortable, not knowing how to react.

Hanna moves on, looking over at me. "And Eliana. I just want to thank you for being my friend. And I want you to know how much I appreciate our friendship. I know this all must seem very weird to you. To both of you. But I hope that you can trust me. Naomi is a good person—she's a really good person—and I hope you come to see that for yourselves. We want to work with you both." She looks over at Theo now, "But Naomi has to trust you for that to work. It's in everyone's best interests, *believe me.*"

Hanna pauses for effect. It's strange hearing her talk this way. Is she threatening us?

"Anyway," Hanna continues, "I'll let Naomi explain everything else when she's ready, but I just wanted to say something when I had the chance."

Hanna stops talking and looks up at us longingly. I'm not sure what to make of this, but I know I have to say something in return. "I appreciate our friendship, too," I say, but truthfully, I'm a little skeptical. Was this ever a friendship, or was Hanna always using me for some other means? It's hard to reconcile who Hanna *was* with whom she appears to be now.

"I'll think about what you've said, but it might take some time before I can really trust Naomi." Another trip, ideally, I think.

"I understand, but I don't know how much time is left."

"Until what?"

But Hanna doesn't answer. "We should get to bed," she says.

I look at Theo, but he seems just as confused as me. What is Hanna talking about?

We walk to our bedrooms and say goodnight to Hanna. When Hanna shuts her bedroom door, Theo comes over to me. We go into my bedroom for the night and close the door.

I sit on my bed and Theo follows me. We both sit there looking at each other, our minds racing with what we just heard.

"That was super weird," I finally say.

We talk about everything. We try to figure out what Hanna could have meant when she said there wasn't a lot of time left. The only thing we know is that we don't trust the two of them, at least not fully. It's still safer to try to escape on our own.

At the end of our conversation, I feel exhausted. Theo laughs as I stumble over my words.

"You should get some sleep," he says.

I don't disagree. I lie down almost immediately and get comfortable under the covers. Theo leans back in the bed and lies beside me. He runs his fingers through my hair, gently tracing the strands behind my ears. Tomorrow, we will head back to the Cube. This weekend will come to an end. But not yet; not tonight. I listen to Theo's soft breathing and feel his warmth beside me until I'm somewhere far away.

CHAPTER 30

Almost two weeks pass before we hear news of the next trip. Naomi doesn't give us much notice, and I wonder if she does this on purpose. It's not until Wednesday night, two days before the planned departure, that I get a message from Naomi.

Ready for a fun weekend in the valley? Meet in the same spot, same time. See you then. Xo.

When I show Theo the note, he tells me he received a similar one. We're both thrilled. Although Naomi didn't give us much notice, we've been thinking about our escape since coming back to the Cube after the first trip. We didn't know when we'd get the chance to go away again, but we were hoping it would be soon.

Everything is ready for the escape, or at least as ready as it can be. If we want to leave the Cube unnoticed, we need to untether ourselves from the government. That way we won't be trackable once we remove our Chips. Theo and I need to destroy our Replicas; it's the only way to remove ourselves from the government's database. It will be like we don't exist. Untethering ourselves won't be easy, but it's the best way for us to get as far away as possible unnoticed. It requires going on a secret mission, back into Ace City. It's not far from the Cube, but leaving will be risky. We will need to break into the Ace Building and use codes that Theo knows from when he worked for the government in another role. It will require some luck, but it's our best shot.

After getting the note from Naomi, we plan to go to the Ace Building the following night. That way we'll be untethered by Friday morning, and ready to leave on the trip. Theo and I thought about escaping from Ace City instead of waiting until the trip but decided it would be too high risk. So many Government Officials live in Ace City, we would be surrounded by people who might come after us. On the trip, however, Theo will be the only Official in the area.

Minji wakes me up after a restless day of trying to sleep. I'm too jittery for sleeping. She invites me to go to the cafeteria with her and Dylan. I jump at the opportunity, needing the distraction. There is still some time before Theo finishes his shift. He will know to look for me in the cafeteria.

Minji, Dylan, and I share a bowl of cherries. Minji complains about how the Cowboy, or Dylan, always snores beside her when the two of them fall asleep together. Apparently last night Minji pushed the Cowboy off her bed and Dylan woke up from the fall. I laugh at the idea. "It's not the Cowboy who feels pain!" Dylan says. "It's me!"

"I know, but I always forget that. All I know is when I go to sleep, I'm cuddling *Dylan*. And then by the time you switch I'm fast asleep and there's a fat snoring jerk in my bed."

Dylan rolls his eyes and playfully pushes Minji. "Hey!" She pushes him back. "At least wait until I look like Mary to bruise me."

"I don't think that's allowed."

We're all laughing when Minji nudges me. "Your lover boy is here," she whispers. I look up at her, alarmed. Theo's just entered the cafeteria with Samantha. He's early.

"What?" Minji says. "You thought we didn't *know?*"

I don't know what to say. Theo and I have been keeping it a secret from everyone.

"Don't worry, no one else does. I only suspected it because I'm half psychic. But come on, you disappear for half the night, and do you have any idea how he looks at you when we're all in the gym?" I can't help myself from smiling. "So, when were you planning on telling us?"

I feel myself blushing, and wish I knew what to say. I notice Theo saying goodbye to Samantha and start walking over to us.

"Oh my god, look at her, Dyl! You're, like, in love with him," she says. "I hate you for not telling me, but just so you know I completely support this. He's smoking hot."

"Thanks," I say. "I've been dying to talk to you about it."

"Mmhmm," Minji pretends she doesn't believe me.

Theo reaches our table.

"Sagona," Theo talks with authority, "there's an important matter I need to speak with you about. Come with me."

Minji and Dylan burst out laughing and I whack them. "Stop," I say. "Stop it!"

Theo looks at them, concerned.

"We know the deal, Jacobson," Minji says back, mimicking his voice. "You can cut the act."

Theo stares at me. I shrug. "I didn't say anything. They guessed."

He tenses up.

"They're not going to say anything, don't worry. You can trust them."

"Your secret's safe with us, Jacobson," Minji says. "But whatever favoritism she's getting, I expect to receive some too."

Theo's embarrassed, but he seems to relax.

Some other Officials enter the cafeteria and Theo stands up straight. We say goodbye to Minji and Dylan and I walk out with Theo, doing my best impersonation of a person in trouble. Theo's got a stern look on his face as we leave the cafeteria. The other guards nod to him. When we make it back and no one else is around anymore, Theo grabs my hand and squeezes it. We head to his van, the same van he once captured me in. I open its back door and hide under a blanket we placed below the seat. Theo starts the engine and calls out to me. "You ready?"

"I hope so," I say, nervous.

Theo begins to drive, and I stay very still in a crouched position. When we get to the front gates, Theo slows the car down to a stop.

I hear him speak to another Official. "I'm going to meet my father for dinner in the city," Theo explains. "My shift's over for the night."

I can't hear the Official's response from under the blanket. My heart beats fast and I pray the Official doesn't find anything suspicious. Thankfully, a moment later, we're moving again. I stay frozen under the blanket, just in case. But shortly after, Theo tells me we're clear. We're on the road now and there's nobody around but us. I lift the blanket off and climb into the front seat. I open the windows, feeling the fresh air. It's nice to be out in the world, sitting beside Theo. With every second, we drive further away from the Cube.

Ace City is quiet at night. Theo explains that most of the people who live here don't go out late on weekdays. If anyone is out, they are by the bars and restaurants, but the street we're on is reserved for government buildings. Ahead of us, I start to make out a tall building, reaching more than one hundred stories high. Theo points it out, "That's the Ace building." I recognize it from when I came here with Mama. It's still beautiful, but I'm not as shocked after spending so much time at the Cube. Realizing this makes me a little sad. I'm not the same person I was when I last saw Mama. I wonder how 7N would look to me now.

We drive toward the entrance of the Ace Building. There's a guard at the front gates, so Theo prepares me. "Act confident, like you're with me and this is any other night."

Theo flashes his badge at the guard. The guard looks from Theo to me, skeptical. I try to look as self-assured as I can, but it doesn't seem to be working.

"Let me see that," the guard says, gesturing to Theo's badge. Theo hands it over. My heart beats faster, hoping they don't notice the expiration date. Theo's badge is from when he interned at the Ace Building. It's not valid anymore.

"You're an intern?" The guard asks Theo. He doesn't look at the date.

"I work with Samuel Jacobson. He's my father."

The guard straightens up and doesn't ask any more questions.

"Of course, sir." The guard quickly hands Theo his badge back and opens the gates for us. "Sorry for the trouble."

Theo continues to drive down a long driveway toward the front doors. I still feel wrought with nerves. When I finally calm down, I look at Theo.

" *Who* exactly is your father?"

Theo just shrugs this off. "We were lucky they let us through."

I nod, realizing that's all Theo's going to say.

When we get to the building, Theo parks the van. We walk to the front doors, and I realize they're already open. The guards at the gates have unlocked them for us. We walk into the Ace Building and head straight for the elevator. Theo presses a few buttons to program the elevator to take us to the top floor. He's comfortable here, and I try to imagine what it must have been like for him to work at a place like this. Was it intimidating for him at all? Or is a building like this commonplace when you're the son of Samuel Jacobson?

The elevator door doesn't open. Theo enters a code on the keypad and there's a loud beep as if he's entered the wrong code. He tries entering the code again, but the same thing happens.

"What's going on?" I ask.

"They must have changed the codes."

I can hear the panic in Theo's voice. I try to stay calm—think of something. "Are there any other codes you remember? Maybe they rotate through them?"

"I'm trying to remember." He closes his eyes to concentrate. He tries a different code, and then another. He keeps trying different variations, but every time the same thing happens. There's a beep and the doors don't open. Theo tries another code, but this time we don't hear the noise. For a second, I think it might have worked. I expect the elevator door to open. But instead, an alarm goes off. It's loud and intrusive and I know there's no way out of this now.

About a minute later, there's an Official running toward us. She's glaring at Theo and me.

"What are you doing in here?" She asks. "Who are you?"

CHAPTER 31

The Official is staring at us, waiting for an answer. I try to think of an excuse, but I've got nothing.

"We didn't mean to set off that alarm," Theo says, and I'm relieved to hear him speak. "I'm just an intern and I still don't know the codes that well. I must've forgotten."

"What are you doing here so late?"

"I left something here, something important."

The Official stares at Theo, looking for an explanation. "Government files I need to go over for tomorrow. I couldn't wait until morning to pick them up."

The Official looks skeptical. "And what about the girl?"

Both of them look at me now. My heart's beating out of my chest. I don't know how to answer.

"She's with me. I was out with her when I remembered the files. She's just here as a friend."

The Official stares at the two of us. She brings her attention back to Theo.

"What did you say your name was?"

"Theo," he says, his voice gaining confidence back. "Theo Jacobson."

The Official pulls out a device and speaks into it. I don't know who she's talking to. "I've got a Theo Jacobson claiming he works here. Can anyone confirm? I'm at the entrance."

"Samuel Jacobson is my father," Theo tells the Official.

That doesn't seem to faze her. "Can I see your badge?"

Theo puts his hand in his pocket. He moves slowly, pretending he doesn't know where his badge is. The Official becomes impatient. I hear some footsteps behind us but I'm too scared to turn around.

"Do you have a badge or not?" the woman asks.

"I do. Sorry."

Theo pulls it out, but only moments before someone taps Theo on the shoulder from behind. It's another Official, but this man seems friendlier.

"Theo! My man!"

The female Official looks at the two of them. "Bradley," she acknowledges the Official and returns Theo's badge before she looks it over. "You two know each other?"

"Yeah, of course. He's Jacobson's son."

"So I hear," the Official says. "Theo works here then? You can confirm this?"

The male Official, Bradley, looks confused. He looks at Theo, whose eyes are now filled with urgency, and then back at the other Official. My heart's beating out of my chest, waiting for Bradley to answer. "Yeah, of course he does. I work with him."

"Okay then," the Official still looks skeptical. "I'll leave you with these two, then?"

Bradley nods.

The Official gives us all one more look before she walks away. It's just us and Bradley now. When the Official is out of earshot, Theo starts talking again.

"Wow. Thanks." Theo says. "Sorry I got you into that."

"What's going on, man? Why are you here?"

"It's secret business for the Cube. I wasn't supposed to say anything but clearly the plan didn't go so well."

Bradley laughs. "Cordelia sent you?"

"You know how it is. Still at the bottom over there, trying to make the boss happy."

Bradley seems to believe the lie. "It'll get better, man. With a name like yours... no doubt."

Theo gives Bradley a smile. I don't know who this Bradley guy is, but I don't think I like him very much. At least he's helping us. He seems to be a fan of Theo's.

"And who's the lady?" Bradley looks at me approvingly.

"I'm Eliana."

"*Eliana,*" he repeats, exaggerating the sounds. "Cool name."

I try not to roll my eyes.

"So, anyway," Theo says. "We really need to get upstairs. Like I said, Cordelia's kind of relying on me. I can't mess this one up."

"Right," Bradley returns his attention to Theo. "Okay, no problem. I'll help."

"Thanks, man." Theo says, imitating Bradley for my entertainment. Bradley doesn't seem to notice.

He keys in a code and, just like that, the elevator door opens. I think back to the last time I was in this building. I remember looking at the glass elevator with fascination. I still can't help but feel a little excited that I get to use it. On the way up, I look through the glass floor and watch as the bottom floor moves further and further away from us. I watch the fountain and plants in the lobby grow smaller. It feels like we're blasting away from the ground and into the sky. It reminds me of the helicopter.

When we get to the top floor, we exit into the hallway. There are several offices, all separated by glass windows so we can see into all the rooms. Theo leads us down a long hallway, and I look at the rooms on either side. They all look identical, with long wooden tables, navy chairs, and red accents.

The final door we stop at will lead us to our destination. The Replica room. It's the only one that has no windows; the only room that hides itself. It's not surprising that it would be so hidden, even for the people working on the top floor. Everyone who works in this building has something to hide, but the people working in the Replica room are doing things that other Officials can't know about. It's the room where Officials change life expectancies, order low-status Group members to die, or follow innocent, but threatening people until they make one minor slip up. It's the room that leads to deaths like Mama's, prison sentences like Loukas's, and experiences like Tearza's at her first Work Camp. It's the room where they first discovered me and Ethan.

Somebody probably made a call from this room that led to me being knocked out, captured, and sent to the Cube.

We pause at the entrance of the room.

"You want to go in *here?*" Concern is all over Bradley's face.

"Like I said, it's pretty important business."

Bradley falls silent, thinking about it. Is he turning against us? "Why did they send you? I mean, no offense. Usually, when Cordelia needs access to this room, she comes herself."

"I know, but I've been working alongside her for a while now. She's starting to trust me more. This is a pretty big step for me."

"Right..." Bradley says, but he doesn't seem convinced. He looks at me now. "And she's coming with you?"

"She's part of the mission. Cordelia needs her to be here."

This is just vague enough to convince Bradley. "All right, but I'm trusting you, my man." He looks Theo in the eyes as if to say *don't let me down.*

"It's all good, I promise."

Bradley agrees and enters the last code for us. Theo quickly opens the door, and we walk in. He turns to Bradley. "I wish you could come in, but like I said, it's top-secret business."

"I'll wait outside."

"That's all right, we should be good now. Thanks again for all your help."

Bradley looks at Theo, concern still in his eyes. As he turns to leave he tells Theo to be careful.

Theo nods and closes the door. "We will."

It's just Theo and me in the Replica room now. It's hard for me to believe.

"You okay?" Theo asks.

"That was crazy. This whole *thing* is crazy."

"I know, but it's worth it, right? We're so close." Theo is filled with hope and it's nice to see him like this. I know he's right.

The Replica room looks like nothing I've ever seen. It might be a room where terrible people come to do terrible things, but when it's just Theo and me, the room feels almost magical. Little orbs of light surround us, swirling and moving through the air. It feels like we're immersed in the stars, but the orbs move around us slowly, each one dancing to its own rhythm. I remember the video that played at the entrance of the Ace Building when I first came with Mama. It was a video of these lights. I get a closer look, trying to figure out if they're actually what I think they are.

Before we got here, Theo explained that the Replica room was where we would untether our Essences from government surveillance. If this is the place to do that... I finish my thought aloud, "Theo... are these lights Replicas?"

Theo nods. "It's beautiful, isn't it? A little eerie, but..."

"It's amazing."

Since the government creates Replicas by making a copy of each person's Essence when they're born, there are millions of Replicas in this room. The orbs are copies of every Essence living in Ameca right now. They move around us, each in their own pattern, just like the people they represent. I can feel the life around us. An orb floats right in front of me. On the top of the light is a tag with a long number written on it. This must be the DNA tag.

"Before we untether, I have an idea..."

"Oh yeah?" I ask, my curiosity piqued.

A slight grin is on Theo's face. "Yeah, there's something cool that you can do with Replicas. I've never actually done it before because it's kind of illegal for someone like me. But, basically, you get to feel what it's like to be someone else. If you hold onto someone's Replica, you can explore their Essence. It's the opposite of swapping bodies. Instead of feeling what it's like to be someone externally, you get to feel what it's like inside. It's like peeking into another person's soul and experiencing their most intimate memories. You can control where it goes, or just let it happen. The government does this to understand a person's motives about something."

"I've heard about them using it in court," I say, thinking back to a conversation I had with Loukas and Ethan. They were debating the ethics behind it. You're still yourself when you hold onto someone's replica, but at the same time, you're seeing into somebody else's soul. The government doesn't ask for your permission.

This is probably how they found my brother. Maybe even me. I'm confused now, trying to understand why Theo is telling me this. I don't want anything to do with government tracking.

"The way we could use it, though, would be different. If we both agreed to it, we could experience each other's Essence. I could see you and you could see me. You know, learn more about what the other person thinks and feels. I know it sounds a little strange, and if it's too intrusive, I completely understand. But I thought it might be... I don't know. I'm not always good at telling you about me, so maybe you can experience it?" Theo pauses, looking up at me. "What do you think?"

I think about it, feeling my heart race. I wonder how much time we have before Bradley comes looking for us. But Theo did say we were on top-secret business—who knows what Bradley is expecting? I don't think Bradley would come inside, and it's late, so I doubt anyone else will be using this room either.

It does sound romantic, the idea of sharing that kind of experience with Theo. But it's also scary. What will he see? I don't feel like I have hidden much from Theo, but maybe I have. There are things about my past, about Mama, about Ethan, that I haven't really shared. What if he sees my kiss with Ethan? I'm afraid to know what he'll think of me after he learns all of that. But then I think of Theo and how much he holds back. It's a huge gesture, him wanting to share all his thoughts and feelings with me. He'd literally be sharing everything. Nothing could be held back. And for someone like Theo, who finds it so hard to open up, I know this means a lot to him. And so I can't say no to the offer. I can't let my own fears stop us. "Okay, let's do it."

Theo beams. He searches our names in the system. The instant he enters his request, two shining orbs come down toward us and begin to glow different colors. One of them glows a warm, deep green and the other glows a bright, shimmering yellow. Without looking at the tag, I already know which one is mine. I can feel it. I confirm by reading the number on the tag—it's the same number I was given at birth when they placed me in Group7. My Replica dances with beautiful grace and glows like the sun.

I follow Theo's lead, cupping my hands around his glowing green light. It expands into my palms, fitting perfectly inside. It feels warm and comforting in an almost overwhelming way. And then, suddenly and all at once, I feel Theo. I can't explain it, but it's like I am him.

His thoughts are in this room with me. He's firmly in this moment, but I have the power to take him anywhere I want. I think about his family, and I'm instantly struck by a powerful sense of love and pain. I see a woman who looks just like Theo, his mother, dressed in a gorgeous ball gown. She's stunning. She's in Theo's childhood room, brushing back Theo's gelled dark hair. He can't be any older than six or seven years old. Theo is wearing a black tuxedo. His mom is humming a song as she tames his hair. I experience this moment as if it were my own. I feel happy and comforted. I realize how much Theo loves his mom.

And then there's a flash of something violent. Theo's mom is thrown against the kitchen cabinet. She drops to the ground in pain. Theo runs to help her up; he's boiling with rage. And then he's small again. Theo is swimming in a pool with his brother. He's young. He's hopeful. He idolizes his brother, Jamie, and he wants that love to be returned. His brother is much older than him and hardly pays Theo any attention.

And then we're back in Theo's childhood room, with his hair being combed by his mother. Theo's younger sister, Izzie, comes storming in. She's yelling about something and Theo's mom laughs. Theo feels safe in this moment. He is happy and grateful. He looks forward to a night out with his mom and sister, away from his father and brother, where everyone will be safe.

And now he's at school. He's walking through the halls with his friends. He's older now, maybe fifteen or sixteen. Izzie is sitting on the floor of the hallway crying. Theo watches Izzie, feeling angry and embarrassed. His friends laugh at Izzie and Theo watches as they walk past his sister. He wants them to stop laughing at her, but he also wishes Izzie would stop asking for trouble. Why is she crying on the floor? Izzie looks up at her brother, but Theo looks away. This is the first time the moment doesn't quickly fade. I'm still here, and now I start to hear a conversation.

"What's wrong with your sister, Jacobson?" one of Theo's friends says. "Did she forget one of her dollies at home?" Theo laughs along with them, but I feel that he's disturbed.

"Hey, her dollies are important," another one says, "they're her only friends."

Everyone laughs but Theo.

"Jacobson," one of the guys notices Theo's stiff demeanor. "Chill. We're just joking."

"I know," Theo says, hating himself. "It's all good."

The next thing I know, Theo and Izzie are in the car. Theo's driving. They're arguing about something. A shirt Izzie wore to school. Theo thought it was embarrassing.

She says, "I don't really care what you think about it. Has that ever occurred to you?"

"Don't be angry with me. I'm just trying to protect you."

"If you actually cared, you'd be happy knowing I *am* happy. I like my shirt. I don't want to change."

"I don't believe you." He hears Izzie crying herself to sleep almost every night. She's being bullied. She desperately wants to fit in. But for some reason, Theo thinks, she just won't admit it. "If you stopped trying to be so *radical* and *different* people would love you, Iz. It's like you're trying to scare them away. Just be yourself, you know? Why can't you just do that?"

Theo turns to his sister, but before Izzie can say anything else there is a car coming toward them. Theo slams on his brakes but it's too late.

Theo's a bit banged up, but Izzie's in bad shape. She seems to be unconscious and she's covered in blood. Theo screams her name, crying for help. He calls for an ambulance. My heart stops for a moment, taking in this moment. I can't believe Theo caused the accident. The guilt he carries is enormous. I feel it now.

And then the memories move to the hospital. Izzie's in bed. Theo and his mom are watching over her. I feel Theo's pain as if it were my own. He feels so guilty. Hopeless. He wishes he could take Izzie's place. Nothing distracts him from his misery. And then it's another day, in the same hospital, and Izzie wakes up. Theo cries in relief. He vows to himself that he'll never do anything to hurt his sister again.

And then Theo's younger, maybe thirteen years old. He's in his room, listening to his parents fight through the wall. It's loud, but this isn't anything new. He listens. He's vowed to himself that the next time his father hits his mother, he's going to protect her. He feels big enough now. He can handle it. And then it happens. Theo runs downstairs in anger. But before he gets to his dad, Theo is tackled to the ground. It's Jamie. "What the hell do you think you're doing?" Jamie asks. I do a double take in this moment. I instantly know the man holding Theo down is his brother because Theo's mind tells me so, but he also looks *just* like Theo. He's much older than Theo in this moment, and much bigger. Jamie is pinning Theo to the floor. There's no way Theo can get out.

"Get off of me!" Theo yells.

"You think you're such a big guy now, huh? You're pathetic. What do you think you're going to do?"

Theo bites Jamie's hand unexpectedly. Jamie jumps up, as alarmed as I am. Jamie screams out, but Theo runs away. He is heading for his dad when his mom sees him. Theo's mom yells at Theo to go back to his room. But it's too late. Theo's dad grabs Theo and pins him to the ground.

"Stay the hell out of this!" He threatens to hurt Theo more next time. And I can feel Theo's shame.

He won't let himself fail like that again.

I see more memories flash by quickly. Theo's getting stronger. He's working out. He's feeling more distant from his friends and family after the car accident. He's feeling isolated and alone. I see Theo much older, about a year or two ago, punching his dad in the kitchen. His mom is beside him. And then I see Theo and his mom in the audience, watching Mama and me dance. I see Theo meeting me for the first time. I feel his heart racing. I feel his attraction. He looks at me until we lock eyes. Then he looks away. I remember this moment, the first time we met, but from my perspective, it seemed like he hated me. Theo didn't want me to know he was interested. He didn't want to get in trouble. He was afraid of how he was feeling.

And then on our mock date, I realize he runs away to protect me. He goes to the footage of our date and erases the second half. He lets Cordelia believe that there was a problem with the video and that the rest of their date must have been erased. I can feel how Theo doesn't trust himself around me at the beginning. And then I feel him getting to know me more and more. His feelings grow with every visit. The feelings are powerful. They feel a lot like my own.

The memories begin to fade, and soon I'm back in the present, looking at Theo. He's right there with me. We release our Replicas and they float away. We look at each other. We've both learned about the other. We've learned everything there is to know. I think we're both afraid to say anything. I feel exposed but in the best way possible. There's nothing to hold back anymore. And then we're kissing. His hands are on my back, and he lifts me onto a table. I feel warm and full of happiness. I want to tell Theo I love him, but I'm too afraid. He knows it anyway. He knows exactly how I feel.

When we stop kissing, Theo remembers what we have to do, rushes to the computer, and searches our names in the system again. Our Replicas dance. He keeps typing, explaining that he needs to enter a code that permits the Replicas to be deleted. Once Theo finishes, we take our Replicas to an incinerator, in the corner of the room to permanently destroy them. It's huge, ugly, and black, with a pipe that leads up the wall and through the ceiling. I follow Theo's lead, opening a hidden door to a shoot and dropping our Replicas inside. As soon as the door shuts, I hear an explosion. Our Replicas are on fire. The remnants are traveling up the pipe and vanishing into thin air. There is no way to track Theo or me anymore. We are free.

"That's it?" I ask, feeling relieved.

Theo gives me a look of intense relief and I know that the answer is yes.

"How did you know how to do that?"

"The government sometimes does that when they need to hide evidence. I've seen it a few times."

"Oh," I say, in disbelief. "Can you do that with Loukas and Ethan too?"

"I thought we could do exactly that, but we should look inside their Replicas. We might be able to find out where they are."

I can't believe I hadn't thought of that. If we can look inside them, we might be able to track them down and help them escape. We go to search their names in the system. I see Loukas's name: Loukas Sagona, Group7.

Theo's about to click on it when noise comes from the hallway. People are coming toward us. Theo whispers for me to hide. I don't want to leave Theo alone, exposed by himself, but I listen. I know he's right. Theo's an Official. I'm a prisoner. I run to a closet and shut the door. I try to catch my breath, stay quiet, and pray that whoever's at the door doesn't have plans to kill us.

A moment later, the door opens. It's quiet for a moment and I pray it's a custodian—someone on our side. But before my next breath, a voice startles me.

"Care to explain what you're doing here?"

It's Cordelia.

CHAPTER 32

I can hear quite clearly through the closet door. Cordelia's here with others, probably Officials from the Cube. Theo sounds casual and nonchalant. If I didn't know better, I'd think he wasn't doing anything suspicious.

"I was just looking up something for Charles." I'm not sure who Charles is, but I figure he was Theo's boss during his time working in the Ace Building. "He asked me to come."

"In the middle of the night?" Cordelia doesn't sound like she's going to buy that one.

"Yeah, it's my night off. It's urgent."

"I would ask you what it's for, but you'll say it's top-secret. Is that right?"

Theo sounds a bit scared now. "Exactly. I'd tell you if I could."

"It's a little peculiar though, isn't it, that he'd ask you for help? You were his intern last year? You'd think there was someone else who could come in for him."

"I wondered that too but didn't ask questions. I just obeyed orders."

Cordelia laughs at that. "*Obeyed orders.* That's interesting... So how, exactly, did bringing Eliana along help you to 'obey orders?'" I don't hear anything for a moment. Then Cordelia continues. "We saw the footage, Jacobson. We know she's here."

"I can explain," Theo starts, but no one listens. I hear footsteps coming closer. Cordelia orders the other Officials to look for me. I don't know what to do. I'm trapped in the closet. If I come out now, I'll give myself away, but if I stay in here, they'll find me in a second. Before I can make a decision, I hear someone by the door. Theo's pleading with Cordelia, telling her it's not my fault, and that he forced me to come with him.

"I thought you were better than this, Jacobson. I trusted you."

"I'm so sorry. It was just a slip-up. I don't know what made me bring her here. It was a mistake."

Someone opens the door while Theo is speaking. Theo turns to me. I can see the panic in his eyes. Before I know it, two Officials pull me out. I don't know where they are taking me, but the Officials are strong. I struggle to free myself, but I can't.

"You'd better follow her," Cordelia tells Theo, "if you want her to stay alive."

The Officials drag me down the hall to the elevator. Theo runs after me, and I try to look brave for him. I don't want him to know that I'm scared. I don't want him to blame himself for this. We both decided to come here. He didn't force me. I want him to know this because I can already feel him taking responsibility for everything.

When we get to the elevator, I make eye contact with Cordelia. "What about my trip with Naomi?" I ask, thinking this might be my only way back to safety.

Cordelia just looks at me and laughs. She laughs manically, as if it's the funniest thing she's ever heard. "Your *trip*," she says. "That's fresh." I swallow, trying not to feel humiliated.

I let the news sink in. I'm not going on that trip with Naomi. At least I'm still with Theo, though. And our Replicas are destroyed. We'll figure something else out.

The elevator stops at the bottom floor. One of the Officials picks me up and carries me outside into the darkness. Theo and I are thrown into the back of a truck. The door closes and we're driven away. It's just the two of us for a moment. I don't know what to say.

Theo's the first to speak. "I'm so sorry."

I shake my head. "It's not your fault." The truck is too dark for Theo to see me. "We couldn't have stopped it."

"How did she know to look for us? They must have needed me for something... then realized I was gone."

"We knew it was a huge risk. Where do you think they're taking us?"

"I have no clue."

It's a short drive before the truck stops and they pull the two of us out. When we're outside, I see a train. I know the train. It's the same train they dragged me onto the night I left home. The same train that took me to the Cube. It all feels like ages ago. At least I'll be on the train with Theo this time. I won't be alone.

They bring us on, and we walk through a number of empty railcars, each of them identical to the one I stayed in. When we get to the end of the train, there is a car with no light, no chairs, and no windows. The Officials throw Theo and me inside. They tie us up to a pole, cover our mouths with tape, and shut the door.

It's just us now. I feel Theo on the other side of the pole. I know he's scared. I wish I could talk to him, but the tape stops me. I wish I could tell him I'm sorry for dragging him into this mess. I'm sure he would tell me the same.

The train ride is long and disorienting in the darkness. I have no idea which direction we're going, but eventually, we stop. Somebody comes to the railcar. When the door opens, the light shocks me.

"We've arrived." An Official walks toward the pole and cuts the rope with a knife. He yells, "Get up!"

I'm relieved to be off the train. At least we're not moving in an unknown direction. At least we're about to find out where we are. But the second we get off my feeling of relief disappears. I hear someone screaming from a car on the other end of the train. It's a young boy. He's being dragged off the train violently. He cries loudly and an Official hits the boy in the face. My heart sinks. I look away, knowing that focusing on the boy won't do me any good. When I look ahead, I see a large factory. I know there are prisoners inside of it, working diligently through unimaginable pain. Soon the young boy will join them, too. Is that where we're headed, Theo and me?

My fear is crippling. I think about Tearza and wish I could go back to the Cube. She was right. It wasn't easy at the Cube, but the Officials never hit us. They couldn't. They needed our skin to look fresh and unscathed for our Companions.

An Official grabs my wrist and drags me away from the train. We move along a path that leads to a factory. We pass a woman rubbing her arm in agony. I wonder how far into the Countdown the body she bears is. I think about the pain I felt in Mama's body during her last dance; I can't imagine working through that pain. The woman notices me staring at her and turns away, ashamed. I immediately regret looking her way. I wish I could tell her she has no reason to be ashamed.

We walk for what feels like hours, passing the massive factory and heading down a narrow path through trees. Finally, we stop in the middle of the forest. Trees have been cut down to create an open square. On all four sides, large wooden boards are facing each other. The boards have clasps in each corner and look to be the size of a large human, if not bigger. The Officials carry me to a board and stretch my arms and legs out, fastening them into the clasps. One of the Officials rips the tape off my mouth. I don't know why. I wonder if they expect me to thank them, but I just stare. I'm terrified. Is this how they're going to kill me? And Theo? I'm not ready to die. I think about the life I planned to lead; I think of Theo. They bring Theo to the board across from me. They're preparing us for our executions. Side by side. My stomach sinks. We will die together. But when they tighten the clasps around my wrists and ankles, I realize this isn't meant to kill me. It's meant to punish me. The clasps press into my bones and pull me in opposite directions. I'm being stretched like an elastic band. Before I can stop myself, I scream out in agony. As the sound comes out, I realize this must be why they took off the tape. They want to hear my screams.

Theo is placed on a matching board across from me. The pain was immediate once the clasps tightened around me, but I don't feel truly miserable until I catch Theo's eyes. We are experiencing the same pain simultaneously and it's torture. Knowing that everything hurting me is also hurting Theo is unbearable. I try not to show the pain on my face because I know this will only upset Theo more. I can tell Theo's doing the same for me. He's holding back. He is trying to be strong for me.

But I can see the creases between his eyes and the clenching of his teeth; his agony is the same as mine.

I think back to the night I spent with Theo under the tree, when he said *I would never hurt you, Lana.* This is the last thing Theo wants to see. I want to tell Theo everything is going to be okay, but I know I can't. I don't know if that's true. Instead, I shout, "I'm sorry." It's not enough, but it's all I can manage. I am sorry we are in this position, and I am sorry for Theo's pain. I don't care that the guards are listening. We're already in trouble. There's no point in hiding now.

Theo must feel the same way because, after a moment, he replies. "I love you."

And for a second his words are all that matter. The pain dissipates. I look Theo in the eyes, and he stares back at me. My heart is beating out of my chest, but as the words come out, I know that they are true. "I love you, too," I tell him. And despite the pain in our bodies, the breaking of our bones, the two of us smile.

The guards warn us to be quiet. We don't say anything else. But I keep repeating it in my head, letting it ease the pain. *I love you*, he said. *I love you.* And I love him back. I love him so much back.

I start to get accustomed to the agony as time passes. At certain moments, it feels like I am waking back up, and I realize I had passed out. I come in and out of consciousness. Theo does the same. The pain becomes so overwhelming. I just try to ride the waves and hope that it will end.

At some point—I have no idea how much time has passed—they finally release us. I collapse to the ground. The fall shocks my system and I cry out in disbelief. Someone hits me and I'm not sure why, and then I'm being pulled up. They drag me away from the square and onto the forested path. I find Theo's eyes. We're pulled in opposite directions. They are taking me away from him. I don't know where I'm going, but I get the sense that I'm saying goodbye. I try to speak, to tell Theo something, but I can't get any words out. My body is in so much pain. Theo and I keep eye contact as we're dragged further apart. I want to cry, worried I may never see him again, but I don't. He needs to know I'll be okay. I don't break our gaze until Theo becomes a dot in the distance. It's not until I'm pulled in another direction, until there is no trace of Theo, that I let myself go. I wail. The sound that comes out of me sounds weak and unrecognizable.

They pull me into a room and lock the door. It's pitch black and I'm alone. I try to scream but my voice is hoarse. I search the room for something to hold on to or somewhere to sit. I find a chair and sit down. As soon as I sit, I cry. I cry until there is nothing left inside me and then I drop down to the floor and curl into a ball.

I have no idea what they're going to do to me or Theo. I can't imagine them hurting us more than they already have.

CHAPTER 33

I'm stuck in this dark room with no windows. I have no concept of time. I imagine that days have gone by since the last time I've had human contact. The last time I saw the Officials. The last time I saw Theo. Every so often, and not often enough, someone delivers food and water through the slot in my door. It's nothing substantial. Usually a slice of bread and an apple, or a bowl of lukewarm broth. I'm always starving by the time it comes, but more than anything, I'm thirsty. My throat is bone dry from the lack of water and my body is weak. I've had a constant headache since the first time I woke up. I spend most of my time asleep.

I wonder, at my weakest moments, if this is how I'll die. Waiting in this room. Waiting for what? I have no idea. But I'm sure I'm waiting for something. If they wanted me to die, they wouldn't bring me food or water. They would just leave me here until nature took its course. Then I think that maybe this is just the way they have chosen to torture me. They want me to think I'm waiting for something. They will slowly bring less food and water until I get weaker and weaker, and my body eventually stops working.

Days pass and nothing changes. My body aches for some form of nourishment. I'm half asleep when I hear someone walk toward the door. I figure they are bringing food. Either that or I'm dreaming. It's hard to tell the difference between my waking hours and dreams. I hope that I'm awake and that it's food. I'm starving. Hopefully this time there'll be bread. But no food arrives. Instead, the door opens. Light comes in from a hallway and a man in an Official uniform stands outside. The light is blinding. I quickly shield my eyes.

I try to get up, relieved to finally be leaving, but I move very slowly. It hurts to move. The man grabs my wrist and pulls me out of the room. He drags me down a hallway and my body is limp. Maybe he thinks I'm not obeying him or maybe he just doesn't have the patience for this. Either way, I don't care. I'm too exhausted.

The Official drags me into another room. I'm not sure why I've been brought from one room to another, but at least this one has light. My eyes adjust and I'm happy to be out of the darkness. There is a table in the center of the room and two chairs on either side. The Official directs me to sit in one of the chairs and I obey. Moments later, Cordelia enters. She sits across from me.

As always, Cordelia waits for me to speak first. She looks at me, scanning my weak body and tired eyes. I can tell she thinks I look horrible. There's a satisfied smirk on her face. I think about not saying anything. I could wait for her to crack. But I know I don't have any power in this situation. If I want to get out of here alive, I need to comply.

"Hello, Cordelia." I don't recognize my voice. "It's nice to see you."

"I'm happy to see you're doing well," she says, in her special Cordelia tone. I know exactly what she means. She's happy to see I'm weak and dying. I give her my best smile, anyway, thanking her.

"You know, I really liked you at the Cube. I enjoyed your spunky nature."

My spunky nature? Is that supposed to be a compliment?

Cordelia takes a breath and then continues, "So I'm really hoping that you'll work with us here. We want to bring you back to the Cube, Eliana."

I'm shocked by this.

"You are beautiful and well-liked," Cordelia continues, "and we know our guests will continue to choose you as a Companion. We trust that this time alone has made you re-evaluate your actions."

"Of course it has," I tell her, desperate to go back. But I can't figure out why. Why would they ever let me back? "I'm so sorry for what I did. I'll never do anything like that again."

"That's wonderful. All we need from you is to tell us the truth. Just tell us everything you know and you'll get to go back. It's that simple."

"Okay," I say, preparing myself. "What do you want to know?"

Cordelia lets out her trademark laugh, then looks at me, dead serious. "I think you already know the answer to that."

"About Theo? You mean us leaving the Cube?"

Cordelia shakes her head. "No, no, you and Jacobson are hardly our concern."

This confuses me. I don't know what to say. How is me escaping with Theo *not* a concern? If that's not what she wants to talk about, what else could it be? What could be more important? "So, this isn't about what I did with Theo?"

"Please, dear." She says calmly. "Don't treat me like a fool."

"I'm sorry. I just don't know what you're referring to."

"Talk to me about your brother." My heart stops. "Loukas."

Why does she want me to talk about Loukas? What does he have to do with anything? "Loukas?" Cordelia doesn't say anything. She just waits for me to speak. "He was taken about a year ago... He was working on a coding project. It wasn't exactly legal."

"It was highly illegal."

"Right. And he got caught. He hadn't really done any damage, though."

"He was doing *illegal coding* work."

"Sure," I say, careful not to get too defensive. "But he never released it. Anyway, they took him just like they took me. So, I don't really know what happened after that. I believe he's at a Camp."

"What else do you know?"

"Nothing," I tell her, which is the truth. Cordelia doesn't seem satisfied. I think back to my time on the train. I remember Lilith bringing him up. Maybe that's what she's referring to? I explain this to Cordelia. I try to remember what Lilith told me exactly. She implied that Loukas was at a Work Camp and that he was getting what he deserved. When I give Cordelia this information, she still doesn't seem satisfied.

"I know that you know about him. Enough with the games."

"Know *what* about him?"

Cordelia stares at me for a while, waiting for me to say more. I don't know what else I can tell her. I am genuinely confused. Cordelia calls for backup. Two Officials enter the room. One woman and one man. Both of them are much stronger than I am. They stand on either side of me.

"I am going to ask you nicely one more time," Cordelia says. "Is there anything else you know about your brother? Tell me now."

"I know nothing," I look at Cordelia, desperate for her to believe me. "I have no idea what you're talking about."

"You're lying!" she yells in such a high-pitched voice it's like a shriek. I stare at her. I've never heard anything like it. Cordelia quickly composes herself. She motions to the Officials on either side of me. One of them grabs my head and slams it on the table. I lose consciousness for a moment but quickly come to. My head aches, the room spins, and Cordelia is staring at me. When I don't say anything, the male Official picks me up and throws me across the room. My body slams into the ground. I look down, in pain. My hands and knees are bleeding. I try to rub away the blood with my shirt but there's no use.

I look at Cordelia, pleading, "Please, I have no idea what you want me to tell you. I haven't seen or heard from Loukas since he left! Why would that have changed?"

Cordelia doesn't answer. She doesn't believe me. The Officials take me back into the dark room. Before I go, Cordelia says, "Whenever you're ready to work with us, ring this bell. But don't bother us until then. We can wait as long as you want," she slowly takes a sip from her glass. "But eventually, you're going to need more water."

Back in the room, my head spins. I wonder if it's the pain from hitting my head or the confusion that's making me feel this way. I lie down on the cold floor, weighing my options. I can't ring the bell because I have nothing more to tell them. But if I stay in here, I have no idea when they'll let me out. All I can do is hope that they'll need me for something. If not, I might end up dying here after all. I decide to wait it out. If I ring the bell and make something up, they will punish me even more when they realize I'm lying. I have to trust that they won't leave me to die. If I don't ring the bell and days go by, they will come back. I tell myself that must be true. I tell myself Cordelia was bluffing. I need to stay strong and believe this. It's the only thing keeping me alive.

Time passes and I begin to worry. I try to stay awake, but I spend most of my time sleeping. I'm weak. I'm weaker than I ever thought I could be. I try to keep myself alert by thinking about home—thinking about the ones I love. I distract myself with thoughts of Theo, too. I run through my favorite memories. Sometimes I try to go through old dance routines in my head, but that takes so much mental energy. I'm not able to recall things the way I typically do. I start forgetting simple things, like the names of Ethan's siblings or the sound of Mama's laugh. It becomes harder and harder to distract myself. Eventually, I lay awake for hours thinking about nothing. I'm amazed that the time passes, but it does. I have no sense of how long it's been, but I know I'm getting closer to the end. Whatever that means.

And then, just when I start feeling like I can't go on, someone comes to my door.

An Official brings me back to the room where Cordelia sits. This time, she doesn't wait for me to say something. She can tell I'm too weak and disoriented to tell her anything. Someone gives me food and water. They guide me to eat and drink slowly. I don't know how long Cordelia has been talking, but eventually, I make out the words she's saying. She wants me to drink from the copper vessel in front of me. I look at the mysterious blue substance skeptically but decide I may as well drink it. There's nothing left for me to lose. If they wanted me dead, they would have killed me already.

When I finish drinking, Cordelia lets out a satisfied chuckle.

"Good," she says. "Can you tell me your name?"

"Eliana Maria Sagona," I tell her.

"Where are you?"

"I don't know. Why don't you tell me?" I say, "Somewhere awful."
It all comes out before I can stop myself. It's like the words just fall out
of my mouth.

"Do you like it here?"

"No. It's horrible. You're torturing me." Once again, despite my
greatest efforts, I say the wrong thing.

"It sounds like you've got a lot of anger."

"Of course, I do. I hate you." I gasp. "Sorry! I don't know why I said
that."

"That's all right. I've given you a serum we've been experimenting
with. It's supposed to make you say what's on your mind. "Cordelia
whispers, "The secret ingredient is tequila." I can't tell if she's joking or
not. "Anyway, it seems to be working. It's like a truth serum, but more
intense. You can't lie, but you also can't hold back."

"Oh," I say, "shit."

Cordelia laughs. "Exactly. So, what are you so worried about us
finding out?"

"About Theo. That I love him. That we're in love. What have you
done to him? Is he hurt?"

"Please. Get over yourself. We don't care about your little
romance."

"Then what is it? I don't know what else there is to tell you. I don't
know what you want from me!"

"Of course, you do. You're going to tell me about Loukas."

"I told you everything I know."

Cordelia looks angry now. "You don't know where he is? You
haven't heard from the group of rebels?"

I shake my head.

"Rebels?"

Cordelia looks at me, surprised. "You actually don't know what I'm
talking about?"

"That's what I've been trying to say. I have no idea what's
happening."

Cordelia gets up and storms out of the room before I get an answer. I wait for someone else to enter, for someone to tell me what's going on. I finish the food on my plate and grab Cordelia's water glass, drinking every last sip.

I don't get the news for another few days. I spend the time eating as much as they'll offer and gaining back some strength. I'm moved from the dark room to a space with some windows and light. They bring me food three times a day, and it's a little overwhelming. I'm not sure what has caused this sudden change or why they are taking care of me, but I don't dispute it. I don't want anything to change.

Eventually, they tell me I'm going back to the Cube. They put me back on the train, but this time I'm in a standard railcar, like my first time. I'm alone. I have no idea where Theo is and I think of him the whole way back. I haven't seen him since the first day we arrived at the prison Camp. I have no idea where he is, and there's a good chance he won't be back at the Cube. Maybe he was taken somewhere else. Maybe he's in a cell. My heart drops for a moment. Could he possibly be dead? The thought makes me sick.

I need to tell myself that they brought Theo back. If they're sending me to the Cube, doesn't that make him more likely to be there? If only one of us was allowed to go back, wouldn't it be him? He's the Official, after all. On the other hand, they could be trying to keep us apart. No. I try to relax, telling myself he'll be there. I picture getting off the train—seeing him. *He's going to be there*, I repeat to myself. *He's already there, waiting for me.*

The train stops and someone comes to get me. Before we leave, the Official grabs my ear and pierces it with something. "An additional tracking device," he explains. Clearly, Cordelia doesn't trust me with just my Chip. "So, you can't escape again."

I touch my ear. It's uncomfortable. "How long is it in for?"

The Official laughs. "My guess is you'll die with it."

CHAPTER 34

When I'm back at the Cube, it feels like a different world. There's so much space. People are happy here. They're alive. I understand how Tearza must have felt now when she first arrived. I didn't truly understand how bad things could be for prisoners until I saw it for myself. The hunger we feel here is nothing like the hunger I felt in isolation.

An Official walks me back to the Cottage. He tells me Naomi will be expecting me for the Switch tomorrow morning. I'll have to gain weight and muscle quickly so I don't disappoint her. "We've warned Naomi about the state of your body," the Official says, "but you will still need to put in the effort to gain back mass. Your Chip has been adjusted for this regiment. We expect you to bounce back quickly."

"Sure," I say, but I can't help but feel angry. It's Cordelia's fault I look this way. She starved me for days on end. And now I have to rush and put on the weight?

"I hope Naomi won't be too upset," I tell the Official. I hope I can get some information out of him. "What has she been doing while I've been gone?"

The Official doesn't respond. I don't think he liked the question. We walk the rest of the way in silence. When we get to the Cottage, nobody is there. I'm a little disappointed, but I don't know what I was expecting. It's nighttime, so everyone must be exercising. The Official curtly says goodbye and leaves me alone in the Cottage. I go to my bed, which seems to be untouched since the last time I slept in it. I sit down and run my hands over the blanket. I never thought I'd be so happy to see this bed. I think about taking a nap but think better of it. I don't want to ruin my sleep schedule. I need to adjust back to my life at the Cube as seamlessly as possible.

I decide to go to the gym. As soon as I enter, I see Minji and Dylan. They notice me too and run over, relieved. Minji jumps on me and kisses me on the cheek. "Ellie! I thought I'd never see you again!"

"Me too." Her joy brings energy back to my body. Seeing them feels like coming home.

Dylan pats me on the back and asks me how I'm doing. I shrug. Neither of them mentions how weak I look, and I'm grateful for that. We just kind of pretend nothing happened.

The person I really want to see is Theo, but I haven't seen him yet. He's not in any of his normal spots. For a moment, I wonder if he didn't make it back. Maybe he's still at the other Camp, being tortured. But that's too painful to think about. I focus on the gym. I have to exercise. The Cube expects me to get my body back in shape as soon as possible so I have a lot of work to do.

I decide to start with some conditioning because I've lost so much weight and muscle. I begin with squats and lunges, using dumbbells like I usually do, but I drop them quickly. I'm not ready for the extra weight. When I'm done, I go for a *very* light jog around the track. I do some abdominal exercises, and then call it a night.

I tell Minji and Dylan that I'm heading to the cafeteria. They decide to come with me even though I warn them that I'm going to be eating a lot. The nice thing about needing to gain strength back is that the Cube actually wants me to eat. Naomi will be eating for me too, of course, but I won't have to work off the calories. At least for the time being. I load up my plate with food and eat every last bite, appreciating the freedom to eat whatever I want.

Minji watches me eat like she has never seen food before. She groans. "It's not fair."

"I'm sorry."

"It's okay," she says half-heartedly. "You deserve it."

The truth is my body needs this nourishment and we both know it. I feel bad eating this in front of them, but I warned them that this was my plan if they followed me to the cafeteria. Neither of them had any objections then. When I remind them of this, Dylan says, "I didn't think you could actually eat this much. I thought you were bluffing."

"There's no joking about my appetite. It's very real."

Dylan steals a fork of hash browns from my plate. He makes a sound, letting us all know how delicious it is. Minji helps herself to a bite too. They catch me up on what I've missed since leaving, but nothing really has happened. They tell me Theo arrived about a week before me. He hasn't said much to anyone. He's been really quiet and removed but seems to spend all his time with Samantha. I give them a vague recollection of what happened to me and catch them up on what's happened with Theo. I leave out the worst of it to spare them, but even the parts I include seem to upset them. "I'm so sorry," Minji says as she squeezes my arm. "You deserve all the delicious food and more. Can I get you a slice of cake?"

I shake my head, laughing.

But after I finish my first plate, I go for seconds. I'm standing in line for pizza when I see Theo. I stare at him, waiting for him to notice me. He's sitting at one of the tables with another Official and doesn't look my way. I recognize the Official. It's Samantha. I get out of the line, not feeling hungry anymore. I walk toward Theo tentatively. I know I can't approach him, because there are other people around, so I decide to walk by him. We've played this game before to get each other's attention in a public place. Usually, we both make eye contact, hold it for a moment, and then wait for the other at our tree. It's become a signal of sorts. This time, however, Theo barely looks at me. He barely makes eye contact, like he doesn't really care, and then keeps talking to Samantha. I'm hurt by this, but then I think it could be because he doesn't want to raise suspicion.

I tell Minji and Dylan I have to go and head to our spot by the tree. After I wait for an hour or so, Theo still hasn't shown up. I justify his absence for a while, thinking that he's just delayed. Sometimes it takes a while for one of us to get to the tree because we're with a friend, or the food line is longer than usual. But the delay isn't usually an hour. Eventually, it becomes clear Theo isn't coming. I'm confused by this, wondering why he isn't excited to see me in the same way that I am to see him. I try to shake off the feeling, hoping there's a sensible explanation. I walk back to the Cottage, tired and disappointed. I need to get some sleep.

My first switch with Naomi happens the next morning. I prepare for a typical switch, but before I leave, an Official comes to tell me that Naomi would like to speak with me before. I accept tentatively, knowing I don't have another option.

I meet with Naomi in the Switch-Pod room. Usually, I'm in this room alone, or with an Official, so it's strange to see my Companion here.

Naomi's face is brightened by her smile. "I'm so glad to see you're okay."

"Thanks," I say, unsure of what to say. Should I apologize for trying to escape? Is she mad at me for not trusting her? I decide to keep it safe. "I'm sorry Theo and I weren't able to join you on the second trip."

Naomi pauses before she speaks. She seems to be thinking. "I want you to trust me, Eliana."

"I do," I tell her because I'm not sure what else to say.

"I don't think you do, and I don't blame you, but I'm on your side. I really am. And even if you don't know that now, I think you will realize that very soon."

"Okay," But again, I don't know what she's talking about. What does *very soon* mean?

"You should be careful with your friend, Theo. He's from Group1 after all."

So are you, I think. But I don't say that.

"I know what you're thinking... that it's the same for me, but I'm different. I've lived an unusual life."

"Theo's different, too," I say before I can think better of it.

"Why? What's different about him?"

"He's..." I'm not sure what to tell her. I don't know what's safe.

Naomi senses my hesitation. "Why is Theo denying that he helped Hanna?"

"I'm not sure."

"Do you think he helped her?"

I think about what to say. "I'm not sure," I repeat. It feels like the safest bet.

"But he tried to escape with you? That's what happened, right?"

I'm afraid to admit this to Naomi. I don't know what she wants from us, or why she's asking all these questions about Theo. I decide to play Theo's actions down. I don't want her suspecting anything. "He came with me to the Ace Building, but he never planned to escape with me. I had to force him to help. And he regrets that now. He's ignoring me and focusing on his role as an Official." That's technically true, so hopefully Naomi believes me.

"Interesting..." Naomi says. "Well, like I said, you should be cautious. You need to take care of yourself, Eliana. You've got a bright future ahead of you. Don't let a boy get in the way."

"I won't," I say, but I don't know why Naomi's telling me this. I'm a prisoner. My future is ominous.

We finish the conversation and Naomi heads to her Switch-Pod. My mind is racing with questions. What is Naomi up to? What does she want from me? I take a seat in the Switch-Pod and moments later, I'm in Naomi's body. I wish I could be in her thoughts, too.

Over the next few nights, Theo continues to ignore me. I spot him in the cafeteria, in the gym, or at an Official's post around Oparius. Every time Theo seems to be beside Samantha. I've always been a little jealous of her, but Theo said he never really liked her. It doesn't seem that way now. He spends every minute with her. And he seems to be ignoring me.

Sometimes I wonder if something happened to Theo in isolation. I wonder if the government did something to him and he's not really himself anymore. But I know this can't be true. Minji and Dylan have talked to him, and he was completely himself: kind and normal. So, for some reason, Theo's deliberately acting differently with me.

Each time I see Theo, I become more distraught. The whole time we were apart, Theo was all I thought about. I kept replaying the way he screamed "I love you" to me, the way we looked each other in the eyes before we were dragged apart, and the way it felt to glimpse into his soul. I love Theo. I want to be with him and that hasn't changed for me. But clearly, something has changed for him. I always knew Theo was complicated, but I thought I had finally broken through that wall.

Tonight, I lie awake in bed until early morning, unable to fall asleep. Between Naomi and myself, my body has been consuming so much food lately, that I'm often crippled with horrible stomach pains. I feel them now, wondering what this drastic weight fluctuation is doing to my body. It can't be good for me. Even though I've gained weight, I still don't look like myself. I'm frail and weak, and when I catch my reflection at certain angles, I almost don't recognize myself. For a moment, I think that Theo might be ignoring me because he doesn't recognize me. But I know that's a desperate thought. Minji and Dylan recognized me instantly. Of course Theo knows who I am.

I want Theo to talk to me because I miss him, but I'm also desperate to talk about our escape plan. Obviously escaping on our trip with Naomi is no longer an option, so we have to figure something else out. Is it even possible now with this new earpiece? Does Theo have one too?

I keep thinking about Cordelia's questions. What did she want to know about Loukas? Why did she think I knew something? I worry about my brother and his safety. If Cordelia was asking questions about him, he must still be alive. But that doesn't really reassure me, because he also must be in trouble. I wonder if Cordelia's questions are about the work he did at home before being imprisoned. Maybe he was hiding things from me. That doesn't seem plausible though, because he did everything with Ethan. And Ethan would have told me. She must want to know about what Loukas is doing now, wherever he is.

I think about Ethan for a moment and how much I miss him. He's so different from Theo. He always lets me into his thoughts and his moods are consistent. I never doubt that Ethan wants me around. I never doubt that he loves me. I wish Ethan could be here to tell me what to do. I feel trapped at the Cube. I know I have to think of a way out. Maybe I can do it on my own, but I don't want to leave Theo behind—not after everything we've gone through together. I need to wait for him to come around. I'm not going to leave this place without him.

Despite the measly amount of sleep, I still wake up the next evening feeling recharged. After the Switch, I look for Theo. My goal for the night is to talk to him. He needs to explain himself. Even if what he says is unkind, I need to know what's going on.

I search for Theo all over Oparius, but I can't find him anywhere. After looking in the cafeteria, I decide to go for a run. Maybe I'll find him that way. I take a route by the ocean because it always looks beautiful at night all lit up.

In the middle of my run, I see Theo standing at an Official's post. Samantha is beside him and the two of them are talking. They're guarding a section of the pathway near the beach. It's an area I've never seen him guard before. He must have switched his shifts with someone when he came back. He's not in any of his usual places. It feels like he's trying to hide from me.

I watch the two of them laugh about something. Samantha makes eye contact with me and grins, satisfied, as if she knows something I don't know. I told myself I'd confront Theo tonight, but I start to think better of the idea. I'm afraid to hear what he has to say. Theo and Samantha look at each other, and it's not until I run right past them that Theo seems to notice me.

"Hey, Sagona," he calls out.

My heart stops. It's the first I've heard Theo's voice since coming back to the Cube. He sounds so cold.

"Come over here!" He tells me.

I stop running and walk toward them. I can tell immediately that this isn't going to go well. My heart beats fast in my chest. I try to look outwardly calm.

"What's up?"

"I just wanted to say that... me leaving with you, that was a mistake."

I'm not sure what he's implying.

"I think I lost myself a little. I got caught up in everything, and I made a lot of mistakes." His voice quivers when he says this. "But I'm seeing things more clearly again, and I've been thinking a lot. I don't think we should talk anymore."

"What do you mean?" I'm completely shocked. I can't believe he's doing this in front of Samantha.

"I'm sorry," Theo says, but he doesn't sound sorry.

"Can we talk about this alone?" I ask before I can think better of it. I'm desperate.

Theo shakes his head. "I'm sorry. There's not much else to really say. I've..." His voice shakes again. It's almost undetectable, I wonder if I'm imagining it. "I've got to stay focused."

I look at Theo for a while longer and I can see the sadness in his eyes. I want to cry, but I hold back tears. I won't give him that satisfaction. I don't say anything else to either of them, and I walk away.

On the way back to the Cottage, I let myself cry. I've been holding in so much sadness and anger from everything that happened to me in isolation. What happened to Theo at the prison Camp? Why is he spending all his time with Samantha? Does he really want nothing to do with me, or is he just scared? I don't know what to make of any of this. All I know is I'm exhausted. And I'm hurt.

It's the first time in a long time that I feel completely alone.

CHAPTER 35

The next week goes by with very few changes. Theo continues to ignore me, and I start to lose faith in him ever coming around. I gradually feel more like myself again, at least physically. My body feels stronger. I spend hours at the gym every night building strength. I'm determined to gain muscle and energy. I need it to feel some semblance of power.

I miss Theo every day, but I'm getting more used to his distance. There's nothing I can do about it. I can't let the sadness take over. If I do, I won't have the energy I need to move forward. I need to focus on myself, build strength, and try to get through my days with as few Theo sightings as possible. Every time I see him, it hurts me all over again. It's better for me to stay away.

I finish a long workout and go to bed early. I'm surprised by how quickly my eyes become heavy. I'm exhausted.

I'm in a deep sleep when someone shakes me. I jolt awake, startled. "Sorry," Minji whispers. "I tried tapping you gently, but you were fast asleep. Theo's got a message for you. He says he's waiting by the water."

I jump out of the bed. I surprise myself with how quickly I move. I'm shocked Theo wants to talk, and I can't help but feel excited. I try to calm down. I remind myself of how he's been acting. I remind myself that I'm mad at him.

I thank Minji and head out. I go over Minji's message again, trying to figure out where Theo is. *By the water*, somewhere I'd know. I remember one night when Theo and I went for a nighttime walk and stopped at a dock on the ocean. It was the night we almost had our first kiss. We sat on the dock, completely isolated. I figure that must be the place Theo's referring to. He must have picked it because of how remote it is. I head there as fast as I can.

When I arrive, Theo is sitting. His legs dangle off the dock. I sit beside him. "Lana," he says, relieved. "You came."

The way he says this happily, as if nothing has happened, makes me angry. I immediately wish I could have created a bigger distance between us. I hate that our shoulders are nearly touching.

I don't know what to say so I decide not to say anything. I wait.

"I'm sorry. You have every right to be mad at me. I haven't been able to explain myself."

"You've been too busy with Samantha."

"It's not like that. She was my chaperone."

"Your what?"

"Cordelia made Samantha stay with me. She shadowed me everywhere and it just ended tonight. I paused my Chip off so they can't track my location."

I'm silent, taking this in as Theo continues. "You have to believe me, Lana. Cordelia kept me from talking to you. But it's been killing me. I've wanted to look at you, talk to you, and be with you every moment."

"But I don't get it. Cordelia said she didn't care that we were together. She said she had much bigger things to worry about."

"Well, that's sure not what she told me."

"But why did you say all that to me? Why did you tell me not to talk to you again?"

"Cordelia said that I had to end things—that I had to make sure I never talked to you again. I knew it was the only way I could convince her to end the probation. It was the only way Samantha would ever stop following me."

"Wow," I say, shocked. "Cordelia made it seem like she didn't care at all."

"Maybe that was part of her punishment," Theo says. I realize the implication. Cordelia told Theo what to do so that his actions would hurt me. She wanted me to feel like he was breaking things off on his own accord. And it worked. Theo ignoring me like that was torturous.

"I'm lucky I'm even back here. I mean, we both are, really. Cordelia told me they were going to keep me in prison. The only reason I'm back at the Cube is because of my dad. Apparently, he begged Cordelia to allow me to come back to work here. So instead of keeping me away from you, she threatened to hurt you if I contacted you. And for a while, it was effective. I was scared."

"Wow. I can't believe your dad did that."

Theo looks conflicted. "I don't think he did it for me. He did it to maintain his reputation. If I became a prisoner..." I can fill in the blanks, imagining how that might look for a high-ranking Official like his dad.

I try not to take the comment personally. I know that's not how Theo feels.

"I'm still trying to figure out why they let you come back, though..." Theo says. "I'm happy about it, of course... but it doesn't make sense. What's the motivation? Who wants you here?"

The way he says this upsets me.

Theo notices my expression and corrects himself. "Of course, *I* want you here. And you're a valuable Working Guest. But G.O.s see prisoners as expendable."

"You're right. I've been thinking about that too."

"Just be extra careful right now, okay?" Theo sounds desperate.

"I will."

"I was so happy when I found out that you'd arrived. For me, I mean, the hardest part was knowing you were out there... knowing what they were doing to you. So, I don't really care why you're back. I'm just happy you are."

"Me too."

"I don't think you know how much I love you, Lana." Theo looks at me, and I can see the sincerity in his eyes.

"I love you too." And I know it's true, even after everything. Even when Theo told me it was over. I haven't been able to stop loving him. I don't know if I ever could.

"Come over here," Theo tells me. And I do. Theo holds me tight, squeezing my every inch.

"I've missed you so much," I tell him.

"You have no idea."

Theo kisses me softly. Everything feels right again. He wraps his arms around me, and I feel warm in his arms. We stay like this for a while, neither of us saying anything. After some time has passed, we start talking again. I fill him in on everything that has happened. Theo listens and I see the sadness on his face when I tell him everything that they did to me. He tells me he's sorry, and I know he means it. It's not his fault, and I remind him of that, but he still blames himself. He catches me up on everything that happened to him. Much of it sounds the same. He looked so thin when I first saw him back at the Cube, but he's looking better now. I'm happy to see the color back on his face.

"There's something I do need to tell you, though," Theo eventually says.

"What is it?" I ask, concerned.

"It's not about me. It's about Loukas."

"What about him?"

"When they were questioning me, I got some information out of Cordelia. I've known her for a while now and I know the way Officials work. I asked Cordelia if Loukas escaped and the way she responded... well my suspicion was confirmed. He's not at a Camp anymore. He's somewhere else. I don't know where, but I know he's gone. The Officials are really angry about it."

I remember Cordelia demanding information about him. I couldn't figure out why at the time, but now it makes sense, considering. "Where do you think he is?"

"I have no idea. But we'll figure something out. I promise."

I desperately want to believe that. We sit by the water for a while. When the sky begins to brighten, Theo asks me if I want to come back to his cabin. Officials get to sleep in their own cabins, so they have much more privacy than prisoners. I've never been to Theo's cabin before.

I follow Theo back to his place and he shuts the door behind us. It's just Theo and me in his room. We were alone together often before, but this feels different.

"How come you never brought me here before?"

"It seemed too risky. Before isolation, I used to have some friends around here. Now all the Officials hate me. There won't be anyone knocking on the door."

"That's good, at least for me."

Theo laughs. We look at each other for a moment. I can't help but feel a little nervous. There's something more intimate about being in his room and sitting on his bed. I don't know what to do with myself. I've been in Ethan's room a million times, but I've never been in any other boy's room. This feels different. Theo must sense my nervousness because he clasps his hands over mine and squeezes them.

"Are you tired?"

I shake my head. I was tired while walking over here, but suddenly I'm not at all. I take a deep breath and shift closer to Theo. I kiss him, slowly at first and then passionately. Theo puts a hand on my back and strokes my hair with the other. I wrap my arms around him. We keep kissing, unable to stop. Theo guides my body down to lie down beside him. We've never kissed like this before. We stop for a second, taking a moment to breathe. Theo looks at me, his brown eyes sparking, "You're so beautiful." I feel shy and respond with a kiss. We stay here for a while, but I don't have any sense of time passing. The moment is too perfect.

At some point, I look out the window and see the sun rising. Theo and I sit by the window, under a blanket, looking out at the sky. The colors are beautiful: the pinks and blues and oranges. It's such a peaceful moment, the two of us together like this. I close my eyes and let myself take it in.

Eventually, when the sun is up, and both of us are exhausted, I fall asleep in Theo's arms. I go to bed feeling the happiest I've ever felt. I tell myself I'll never forget this moment. I'll never forget how special everything feels.

CHAPTER 36

When I wake up, Theo's not in the bed. I look around, but the cabin is small and he's not here. I wait for a bit, thinking he might have quickly stepped out. When he doesn't come back, I look out the window to make sure nobody is around. I quickly leave, moving as inconspicuously as possible.

There's no one outside Theo's cabin. I walk by a few Official posts in the area and all of them are empty. It's dark out, but Naomi hasn't called for the Switch, so maybe it's early. Officials should still be on duty, though. I wonder if I slept through an alarm, or maybe someone got in trouble, and I should be in the main building right now? But then I remember how loud the alarms were for Tearza and find it hard to believe that I could have missed something like that.

I head down a path leading away from the Officials' cabins and toward the Cottage. I don't get far before I hear a sound coming from the other direction. It's a loud rattling sound, like heavy rain on a tin roof. I decide to follow it. Maybe it will help explain Theo's disappearance. I follow the path toward the border of Oparius and the rest of the Cube. The sound gets louder as I get closer. Eventually, I make out the noise—it's footsteps. It sounds almost like a herd. I back away instinctively, thinking that whatever's going on, it can't be good. But then I think about Theo. I realize he could be in trouble. I get closer to the sound until I see a large group of Officials walking in a line. I haven't been in this area before, so I don't know where the path they're on leads. But the Officials seem to be going somewhere. Keeping my distance, I move through the forest, parallel to the path. It seems so odd.

Cordelia is among the group, as well as many other Officials I recognize. But there seem to be others too—Officials I've never seen before. They seem to be heading somewhere in particular, but I have no idea where. The way they're all moving together makes it seem really urgent, like something important is happening. I move cautiously through the trees, parallel to the pack, keeping my eye out for Theo.

After a while, I spot him. He's ahead of me, towards the front, walking beside Officials I've never seen before. I can tell it's him from the breadth of his shoulders and the way he walks. I move faster, trying to catch up to him while also making sure I don't get caught. When I get closer, I make my way out of the trees and toward the path. I keep some distance, but I'm afraid that I'll be seen.

"Theo," I call out his name, but he doesn't look over. He must not have heard me. He keeps walking—following the others without even flinching. I head back into the forest and pick up a pebble. I toss it at him. It takes me a few tries before I hit him in the shin. None of the others notice, and neither does he. He keeps walking. He doesn't look over.

I realize he might be trying to be discreet. He's not going to simply look over at me and tell me what's going on—not in front of all these Officials. We promised each other we'd be more careful in front of others from now on. Deciding I'd better keep my distance, I head back into the trees.

Suddenly, one of the Officials makes eye contact with me. He's a muscular man with a long red beard. He stares at me, like he knows me from somewhere. It's a weird sensation. I'm sure I've never seen this Official before but something about him feels familiar.

"Eliana?" The Official says, almost in disbelief.

I stare back at him, unsure of what to say.

"How do you know my name?"

I don't know why I expect an answer from the Official, except that somehow I get the sense that he cares. He seems hesitant, trying to read my face. For a second, I think he might help me, but then he looks away, toward the Officials in front of us. I see that they're starting to enter a building, the main building that the Officials work in at the Cube. They're being ushered in by other Officials, many of whom I've never seen. I never realized there were so many Officials at the Cube.

The bearded Official becomes tense now. "You've got to get out of here," he calls to me. "It's not safe. Get out of here *now.*"

I run away from him, but I don't flee to safety. If it's not safe for me then it can't be safe for Theo. I have to talk to him, and I don't care if I'm in plain sight because I need to figure out what's happening. I think of the way Theo kept walking when I said his name. He's ignored me many times before. I've seen him dart his eyes, look anywhere but at me, and tense up any time he knows I've entered the room. But something about the way he reacted this time felt different. He didn't seem to be ignoring me. I got the feeling he didn't even know who I was.

I don't see Theo anywhere. The bearded Official runs over to me and tries to pull me back into the forest. I tell him I won't leave, and he starts shouting at me, insisting that I go. I refuse to leave without Theo. I tell him I won't leave until I find Theo Jacobson. I'm completely blowing my cover and I know I'm going to get us both in trouble, but I don't care. I'll do whatever I need to do to keep Theo safe.

We're close to the main building now. Almost all the Officials have entered. When we get to the door, the bearded Official tells the others that I'm not supposed to be here. He orders them to take me away. Before I can stop them, a group of Officials drags me from the building. I'm not strong enough to resist them, but I fight back. They release me when we're a fair distance from the building. One of the Officials glares at me and the other warns me to get out of here. It's strange. I should be getting reprimanded. When the Officials leave, I move toward the building slowly, but I don't go far. I may not be able to get in, but I'm not going to leave. I'm not leaving until Theo comes out. Or at least until I can figure out what the hell is happening.

When everyone is inside the building, the last Official closes the door. I start walking toward the building, thinking I might be able to slip inside now that nobody is watching. After just a couple of steps, the ground below me moves, at first just a little, but then violently. The force of it slams me to the ground. There's a deafening roar and I can barely move. It's not until I finally gather the strength to lift my head that I realize what's happened. There's fire everywhere. The building is gone. Smoke is swirling toward me at a formidable speed. I scramble up to my feet and run. Looking back over my shoulder, I see the entire building engulfed in thick black smoke. I can't see anything through the haze, but I know there's nothing left. The building is gone.

The smoke surrounds me, making me cough. I drop to my knees and cry. My first thought is Theo. Theo was in that building and there's no way he's coming out now. When I say this in my head, I don't believe it. I can't accept this as real. But I know it's true. I saw it with my own eyes. Theo is gone. I wail in agony, choking on my tears and coughing. The smoke is thickening by the second, and if I don't get out of here, I'm going to die.

I race away from the fire as fast as I can until my legs give out, but I'm still in a state of disbelief. My body aches from the fall and I need to sit. When the air is finally clear enough to breathe, I lean against a tree and close my eyes. I'm not sure how long I stay there. I don't know if I'm entirely awake. My head spins and my ears ring. Nothing feels real. I lie against the tree, moving in and out of consciousness. I don't know how long I stay here, but eventually, there's a sound like someone shouting my name. I know it can't be true, but then someone is shaking me. I try to see who it is, but I'm so dizzy, I can't tell. I blink my eyes and wipe the dirt and grit away.

It's Loukas. But it can't be. I close my eyes and look again. When I open them, my brother stares back at me. He's saying something, but I can't hear much because my ears are still ringing. I make out my name. My brother Loukas is in front of me. I don't know how he could be here, but it's him. He pulls me up and I try to steady myself. He asks me something, asks if I'm okay, but I can't talk.

Loukas tries to grab my arm for balance, but I jerk away from him and run toward the wreckage of the building. Toward Theo. I have to do it; I have to know. The smoke has begun to clear so I search through the debris. I look for Theo, but I know it's hopeless. He's gone. He's dead. *It's my fault,* I think. I let him go into the building. I let him out of my sight. I didn't save him. I couldn't save him, but I didn't even try. I begin coughing again and fall to the ground, crying. Loukas picks me up and carries me out of the rubble, into the woods, and down a forested path. I try to stop crying, but I can't keep it in. I don't understand what just happened. I don't understand how one moment I could be sleeping beside Theo, and then the next he could be gone. I look at my brother, Loukas, carrying me, but I can't make any words come. I don't know what to do.

Loukas puts me down in the middle of the forest, away from the smoke. I steady my feet and a second later Loukas is hugging me. I hold him tightly, taking in my brother's smell. I can't believe he's here, that he's alive.

When I pull away, Loukas looks at me with a grin that stretches all across his face. I'm shocked, but he doesn't seem shocked to see me. I'm overwhelmed with questions.

When I'm finally able to speak, I start with the first one.

"What the hell's going on?"

CHAPTER 37

Loukas doesn't have time to explain. He brings me to the beach, where someone is speaking to a crowd. I recognize the voice. It's Naomi. I look at Loukas for an explanation, but he gestures for me to listen.

"This has been a long time coming," she tells the crowd. I look around at the people listening. It's a crowd of Newbodies. I try to find Minji and Dylan. I spot them standing at the front. "I know some of you might recognize me as one of the Patrons here, but that was a disguise. I would never inhabit somebody else's body for my own pleasure. That's not why I came here. That's not what I believe in.

"I'm part of a resistance movement. We call ourselves EnEx, which comes from the Latin phrase *non-expectabo,* meaning 'done waiting.' EnEx is finished waiting for the government to give all of us the justice we deserve. We're finished with the Group system. We expect more from the government and we believe the time is *now.* Who's with me?"

The Newbodies roar with approval. I catch Minji's eyes; she looks feverish. Empowered. I can't believe this is happening. I remember seeing those words, *"non expectabo"* on one of Naomi's shirts, but I had no idea what they meant. I had no idea who she was. And this whole time she was working with Loukas?

It's hard for me to find Naomi completely sincere. I want to fight against the government, too. I believe that the time is now. But Naomi lived in my body. She used it every day for weeks on end. If she didn't believe in Camps, why did she participate in one?

Naomi keeps talking to the Newbodies. The crowd is loving her speech. She asks us to fight beside her. To join in the revolution. I look at Loukas and I can see the passion in his eyes. I wonder who planned the explosion. Who made it happen? I wonder if Naomi knew she'd be killing Theo with her plan.

Naomi has a crowd full of new followers. They're desperate to leave the Cube and to get the justice they deserve. That's when I notice Hanna. She's beside other members of EnEx. They are all wearing yellow and green. Yellow and green. I remember Hanna's clip. Jocelyn's dress. What is Hanna's role in all of this? She is more than Naomi's Keeper, I know that much. But who is she? Has she been with EnEx the entire time?

Naomi tells the crowd that changes are coming. EnEx is going to take down the government and create a new system. They will make things fair again, for the little people, the outsiders, the low-status Groups, and the ones who do all the work for none of the credit. I can see why her words are inspiring, but I don't know if I believe them. I don't know what I think right now.

I can't stop picturing the building in flames. The pile of debris. I can't stop going over the night before; if only I'd known it would be the last time I'd ever see Theo...

When Naomi's speech is over, I want answers. Loukas explains the details with enthusiasm. He doesn't start at the beginning; he just tells me about the end—the explosion. Loukas says they've been planning it for weeks. They had to figure out a way to get all the Officials from surrounding Camps to come to the Cube. It was difficult, but they found a way to access Cordelia's computer. They invited hundreds of Officials from various Camps to a party at the Cube.

The Officials from other Camps came to the Cube this morning, and EnEx was ready for them. They set up for a party and the Officials enjoyed themselves. Theo slept through all of this because he was off duty and unaware. It didn't matter, though, as long as Theo was somewhere in the Cube. EnEx was much more concerned about the Officials arriving from outside the Cube. They assumed Officials who worked here would be on the premises.

Apparently, Cordelia was shocked by the party. She ordered Officials to investigate who planned the event, but they couldn't figure out how it happened. Meanwhile, members of EnEx were hiding in various spots at the Cube. They locked themselves in secure locations and were guarded so that their bodies were unable to escape.

Once all the guest Officials were present and accounted for, a mass Hack was orchestrated. This was the hardest thing to plan. Loukas created a code that matched members of EnEx to Officials. When they activated the code, they were able to Hack each Official simultaneously. Every member of EnEx was now in an Official's body. And every Official was now in an EnEx body, locked up in secure locations. That's when all of EnEx, inhabiting Officials' bodies, walked to the main building and executed the Officials.

Loukas wants to show me the code, but I don't care about it. I ask him to show me where Theo's information is. Loukas seems confused and hesitant, but he listens. He opens his laptop from his backpack and pulls up a page with names on it. He tentatively points to one. I see Theo's name. Loukas confirms that Theo's body was Switched. Somebody else inhabited Theo's body and then walked it into a building, knowing that it would explode.

Loukas explains that he was the Official who tried to convince me to leave—the man with the long red beard. When he was heading toward the building, he noticed me and panicked, knowing he had to do whatever was necessary to make sure I was safe. He seems to think that this makes it all okay, as if the impact of Theo and everyone else dying could be softened by the idea that my brother protected *me*. Of course, Loukas has no idea who Theo is and why he matters to me, but I'm furious. I feel anger take over my whole body.

Loukas keeps explaining. When everyone was inside the building, EnEx set off the explosion. They killed hundreds of Officials and it's obvious Loukas is pleased by this. EnEx has been planning this rampage for weeks. There were many risks involved, but everything went according to plan. And now, Loukas tells me, everything will fall into place. The revolution we've been waiting for is starting. "It's finally happening," Loukas tells me. His eyes are wide with excitement.

I don't know what to say to my brother. I want to hug him, scream at him, and curl up into a ball and cry, all at the same time. I'm so relieved he's here. I've missed him for so long and now I need him more than ever. But I'm also not sure who he is anymore. I feel sick, realizing how many people he helped to kill. He doesn't seem to have any sense of what he's done. Real people died, people with lives to live, with hopes and dreams, with families. Not all of them were bad, not entirely. Theo wasn't.

I don't say any of this to my brother. When he finishes telling me everything, I don't ask questions. I don't know what to say.

Ever since he was taken, I've imagined what it would be like to see Loukas again. I thought nothing could make me happier. And now, here he is, and I don't know what to make of any of this. I'm happy to see him, of course. I'm relieved that he's alive. But I'm also furious with what he's done. I thought that us being together would make me feel whole again, but I've never felt less alone. It's all too hard for me to process.

I look up at my brother. It takes all my strength to keep from crying. "I'm so happy to see you," I say, and it's true. "I've missed you so much. There were so many days... so many times... I needed you, and now you're here." I take a deep breath and continue, "But right now, I think I need a moment alone. I need to take all this in."

Loukas seems confused, but he nods in acceptance. I walk away, not knowing where I'm headed. I walk down an empty path and it doesn't take long for me to decide where to go.

As I make my way through the Cube, I notice how eerily quiet it feels. All the Officials are gone. Dead. I think of Theo. I wish he was here beside me to talk this through. I have Loukas now. He's all I have. We always said that we would find each other, and he did exactly that. He came for me. But it wasn't supposed to be like this. Theo and I could have figured out a way to escape, too. We could've gotten out without hurting anyone. If they'd only waited.

But now it's too late. Theo is dead. Hundreds of people are dead.

I finally arrive at my destination and sit beneath our tree. I think about all of the times Theo and I sat here together. I close my eyes and feel him with me.

But Theo is not here. I'm completely alone. I don't know if I can trust Loukas anymore. Mama is gone. God knows where Ethan is.

It's just me now. I have to trust my gut.

I have to figure this out on my own.

END OF BOOK ONE.

Acknowledgments

If you've finished this book, you might suspect that love and family are major themes in my life. You'd be right. I feel lucky every day that I get to spend my life with the wonderful people who make my world complete. I am eternally grateful for the help and support I receive. I will spend the rest of my life thanking my family, friends, and the writing and reading communities I'm a part of for all that they do for me. If I ever stop thanking you, I'll then spend the rest of my life apologizing (because I'm Canadian.) Here are some people I would like to especially thank.

My husband and partner in life, Mike. This book wouldn't exist without you. You keep my wandering mind and excitable spirit steady enough to get the words down, you inspire me to go after the dreams that keep me up at night, and you encourage me to keep going on my most challenging days. You're also the first person who read *Newbodies* and I will always think of you diligently reading and editing my manuscript before bed, with your encouraging comments and many doodles. You worked carefully and lovingly—and on a time crunch!—while balancing work and our many commitments. You also listened to (and continue to listen to) my several late-night chats about my hopes and dreams for this book and all of the worries that come with it. I couldn't ask for a better partner. You know that. I love you.

Mom and Dad, thank you for being the type of parents who encouraged me to dream. Dad, you were the first person I told stories to before I could even put words together, babbling in my crib. You listened attentively then, just like you do now. When I got old enough, it was our nightly reading hour(s) that made me fall in love with the written word. Thank you for continuing to listen to and read all of my stories today. I'm especially excited to be writing our first book together and look forward to where that journey takes us. Mom, you are such a massive inspiration in my life. I don't think I've ever written a story that doesn't have a character who resembles you in some way. Thank you for always supporting me, for championing my writing, for teaching me to live life passionately, and to be headstrong toward my goals.

Savta, thank you for always being one of the very first to read every story I've ever written. Your constant support and loving encouragement is the reason I never stopped believing in myself. I'm so grateful to you. Grandma, I always told you I'd dedicate my first book to you. You're not here to physically hold *Newbodies* in your hands, but every step of the way I held you close to my heart.

To my brothers, sisters-in-law, and Peggy, thank you for prioritizing family, for knowing that people are what matter most, and for filling my life with purpose and love. Geoffrey, the sci-fi novel you wrote in that orange Duo-Tang will forever be my favorite piece of writing. Jordan, thank you for knowing your little sister well enough to convince me to follow in your footsteps, straight into the ArtSci program. I don't know if I'd be here without that.

This leads me to Anton. Thank you for being the best writing mentor out there, always providing encouragement and honest advice, being brilliant and wonderful, allowing me to learn from you, and giving me a real-life writer to look up to.

To my friends, who read this book amidst busy schedules. Thank you for putting in the time and for all of your supportive words. Thank you to my childhood friends (the HHA crew) who have been reading my attempts at novel writing since grade school, to my bookworm friends who make for the best pseudo-editors (especially to you, Ryan, for all the help and imagining this world with me so many years ago), and to my picante pals for listening to my many conversations about writing and continuously supporting me.

Mern, I'll always remember my early days of writing on our many trips (sometimes in inopportune places). Thanks for not leaving me behind at Buckingham Palace.

Moonshine Cove, thank you for believing in me. Thank you for making my lifelong dream of being a published author become a reality. Gene, thank you for your time and commitment to editing my manuscript.

To Alan Dino Hebel, thank you for giving me a cover that beautifully encapsulates *Newbodies*.

To everyone who grabs this book off a shelf, borrows it from a library, lends it to a friend, talks about it, or connects to the story in some way, I thank you. You've made my dream come true. To the readers who spill spaghetti on the cover, or who bring it to the beach, or who drop it in the bathtub, I forgive you. *Newbodies* isn't mine anymore. It's yours. It's ours. It's become a part of a community that I will always cherish–that I will always be grateful for. So thank you.

About the Author

Rachelle Zalter is a  passionate writer, teacher, and eater of bagels. Her work appears in the *Stockholm Review of Literature* and her plays and screenplays have been awarded by the Toronto Fringe Festival and Bluecat Screenplay Competition. She studied creative writing at Yale University. When Rachelle is not writing, you can find her rewatching *Gilmore Girls* or buying another mug for her tiny kitchen. She lives in Hamilton, Ontario with her husband and several plants. Look out for her upcoming novel, *Romi's Theorem,* a contemporary romance featuring math equations and a dreamy pottery instructor. This is Rachelle's debut novel.

rachellezalter.com

www.ingramcontent.com/pod-product-compliance
Lightning Source LLC
Chambersburg PA
CBHW020853020726
47497CB00005B/1383